Low And Slow

Low And Slow

A Novel of Navy Flight Training Behind Round Engines

D.E. "Butch" Bucciarelli

To all who sat behind a round engine
and heard the music.

CHAPTER ONE

PENSACOLA, FLORIDA
MARCH 1956

SERGEANT MAJOR Chester Henry Pflueger, United States Marine Corps, was disappointed when he found that his white glove was still pristine after he ran it along the top of every ledge, molding, and shelf in the room. He was a small man, with a small waist and chest. His head was large for his body, and because his hair was cut to a no more than a half-inch length on top and shaved at the sides, it looked perfectly square. He seldom smiled or showed any indication of pleasure. He had the reputation of being "meaner'n a snake." He liked his reputation and tried hard to maintain it.

The sergeant took a safety razor from a cabinet, unscrewed it, and removed the double-edged blade. He ran an index finger of his still virgin glove over the blade, and held up a fingertip with some dry shaving cream and hair residue on it.

"Who is the disgusting, filthy pig what shaves with this here razor?" The sergeant's voice was shrill, with a regional accent. His pale grey eyes scanned the room, stopping momentarily at each of the four cadets standing at attention before their bunks.

Dario D'Angelo, the razor's owner, was very familiar with loaded questions. His Italian mother had made him aware of them from an early age. If he admitted it was his razor, he was also admitting that he was a disgusting, filthy pig. Several answers popped into his quick mind, most of them impertinent. He doubted if he could persuade the sergeant to rephrase his question so he chose the most neutral response of his thoughts. "You have my razor in your hand, sergeant. I'm Cadet D'Angelo."

The marine looked at the razor, then at Dario, then at the razor again. Finally, his two beady eyes stared at Dario under a cold, mean frown. "D'Angelo, D'Angelo? You one of those thick-skinned Eye-tralians?" Dario recognized the sergeant's accent from many movies and radio shows which were set in Brooklyn.

"I don't know, sergeant. They tested and measured almost everything I have to get into this outfit, but I don't remember them measuring my skin." He knew he was being a wise-ass but the words came out before he could control them.

The sergeant shifted his weight from one highly-polished, Cordovan oxford to the other. "Oh, I see. We have here a dumb-ass Eye-tralian who doesn't know his skin size, do we? Well, thick or thin, you cut your skin with this here disgusting, filthy razor blade, mister, you gonna die of infection! You comprehend me?"

He knew he should just answer, "Yes, sergeant," but he couldn't. He was still a civilian at heart and felt free to counter his opponent. "Thank you for your concern, sergeant, but I use an antiseptic shaving lotion immediately after shaving. It will kill any minor bacteria that might have been transferred from the razor to me. I'd be happy to give you some, if you ever cut yourself." He spoke in a loud, precise voice.

The marine raised himself on the toes of his shoes in the attempt to increase his stature. He gritted his teeth, then opened his mouth as if to speak, but said nothing. Then he closed his mouth, and the tips of it turned up in the slightest wisp of a smile while he riveted his steely, grey eyes on Dario for a full thirty seconds.

The stare was successful. It caused a chill of fear to surge through the cadet's body. *He's etching me on his cold heart for future reference,* he told himself.

The sergeant put the razor on the table in the center of the small room, spun on his lustrous shoes, and walked slowly, stiffly and silently from the room. All four cadets gave a loud exhale and relaxed from their attention stance.

"I joined the navy, not the marine corps. Where in the hell are the sailors?" Dario cried out.

* * *

Dario and his roommates had been in the Indoctrination Battalion at Pensacola Naval Air Station for a week, and from the minute they logged in they'd been constantly harassed by enlisted marines who ordered them to do ten, fifteen, or twenty pushups at their slightest whim. As Aviation Officer Candidates (AOCs), the new program for men with college degrees, they would graduate from Pre-Flight with commissions as ensigns. Other classes of cadets were also in Pre-Flight: Naval Aviation Cadets (NAVCADs), made up of youths with at least two years of college and active duty sailors who had little or no college, but who passed a written two-year college equivalency test and were called "Fleet Types."

The marines, who conducted all military training, were not impressed with the new AOCs and their college degrees. On their second day at Pensacola several classes were "policing" the athletic field. The sky was overcast and the first hint of the coming summer high humidity was in the air. Before they started the police action, which was to clean the field of trash and debris, Sergeant Pflueger gave them their orders. "Now then, listen up. The AOCs with the certificates of completion from colleges, youze picks up the big rocks and the big pieces of paper. Youze NAVCADs with two years of college, but no certificates, youze picks up the little rocks and the little pieces of paper. And youze uneducated idiots with no college and no certificates, youze just stands there an' see how it's done."

Low and Slow

* * *

"He's the top sergeant of Pre-flight and you rattled his cage!" Bill Metz, one of his roommates told Dario when the sergeant left their room. Bill was a big, dark complected German from Milwaukee, with a very deep voice.

Besides the four bunks, their room contained a sink against the wall with a mirrored medicine cabinet above it, and one metal chest with a drawer for each cadet to store underwear and socks. The center of the room was occupied by an oak table and four chairs, for study and homework. There was also a closet where their uniforms and shirts hung. They wore officers' uniforms, with cadet insignia.

"I hate those loaded question games. Would you have told him it was my razor, if I'd kept quiet?" Dario asked Bill.

"Fuck no, my brother told me an officer never squeals on another officer. It's an unwritten law."

The cadets always listened attentively to what Bill said, because his brother had finished flight training several years before and was now flying with the Atlantic Fleet. It was Bill who gave them his brother's advice, which had them stand on chairs to clean the tops of cabinets, moldings and clothes racks before their room inspection, leaving only the scum on Dario's razor blade for the sergeant to condemn.

As Dario put his razor back in the wall cabinet, he looked at his reflection in the mirror. Gone were the flowing locks of light brown hair (the result, he always assumed, of his father's red hair and his mother's black), pushed into a slight pompadour and combed straight back along the sides into a duck's-ass at the back of his head. All that remained was a quarter-inch brush on the top and white skin on the sides, the traditional indoctrination white-sidewall-buzz-cut. His chiseled, cleft chin came from his father's side of the family, as did his blue eyes. How many times had he heard, "But you don't look Italian?" His father and mother came from the northern half of Italy, not the south or Sicily, from which so many escaped their extreme poverty. The men in his mother's family were all fishermen from Genoa.

His father, Babbo, came from a family who owned their own farm and could afford to educate him. He'd graduated from a technical school as a tractor mechanic.

Dario looked deeply into the blue eyes staring back at him, and saw in them a silent question: *What in the hell am I doing here?*

* * *

Within the next few days, Dario's class went through another complete physical examination, were issued uniforms that were measured for rudimentary tailoring, and filled out page after page of forms. One of the documents they completed was an emergency sheet, which each flight student would seal in an envelope, to be opened only in case of his death. On the form was listed the beneficiary of military insurance and other benefits. They were in a classroom, sitting at desks that were worn and rickety by the time World War II ended, when Bill Metz, who was sitting across from Dario, held up his emergency form for him to see. In large block letters he'd written across the top of the page: DEAR MOM, NO MATTER WHAT THEY SAY, IT WASN'T PILOT ERROR!

"My brother told me to do it," he whispered to Dario. "You get the last laugh on the navy."

Dario wrote across the top of his sheet, also in big, blocked letters: CARA MAMMA, NON CREDERE A QUELLO CHE DICONO LORO, NON É STATO UN ERRORE DEL PILOTA! (His mother, although a naturalized citizen who had lived in the USA since she was a child, had only recently begun to study English. Dario still spoke, and wrote to her, in Italian).

He relied on Bill's brother's advice, but he didn't even know what pilot error was. They hadn't studied anything about airplanes, and he hadn't even been near one since arriving in Pensacola. The only flight he'd ever taken in a navy aircraft was his indoctrination flight, which culminated his tests for acceptance into the AOC program.

CHAPTER TWO

SAN FRANCISCO DECEMBER 1955

IT WAS a beautiful, crystal-clear, San Francisco Bay area winter day. Dario had gone to bed right after finishing his music job the night before, and he hadn't eaten any breakfast. He didn't want to throw up in the airplane because of all the zooming and diving he supposed they were going to do. Although he was wearing Levis and a sweater, he was certain he'd be given a flight suit and a helmet. He was a movie buff, and he'd recently seen *The Bridges at Toko-Ri,* the movie made from James Michener's book about navy pilots in the Korean War. The flying and carrier scenes in the movie had inspired him. Dario was looking forward to his first navy flight.

Lieutenant Commander Randall E. Baird, USNR, was the name printed under the wings, embossed in gold on a leather patch sewn onto his leather flight jacket. Dario met him at a hangar on the Oakland Naval Air Station. Baird's face was clean shaven with sharp, handsome features. The pilot wore a khaki shirt and a black tie beneath his jacket, with green twill trousers below it. His fur-collared jacket had dozens of colorful patches on it, but Dario didn't have the foggiest idea what any of them meant. Baird shook his hand, and told him they'd be up for about an hour.

"They didn't tell me what to wear, sir."

"You're fine," Baird answered, disappointing the fledgling.

Dario followed him out of the hangar and into a small wooden building identified by the sign over the door as "Line Shack." Baird took down a clipboard from a nail on the wall, did some writing on it and handed it to Dario. "Fill your name in where I put the X, then sign this waiver." His voice was pleasant, but showed authority.

Dario read the waiver. It said, in so many words, that the government wasn't responsible should he be killed. *Who would be responsible,* he wondered? He signed it without asking.

They walked out to where the airplanes were parked, and Dario saw aircraft with their navy identification-types stenciled below their tails. AD-4, F9F-5, and F2H-2. He'd seen those types in *Toko Ri.* They walked past those formidable looking aircraft and stopped next to an airplane which was stenciled SNB-5. It wasn't what Dario was expecting. It looked like an airplane he'd seen in prewar movies, the kind the hero used to fly the serum through a violent storm over the Andes to stave-off an epidemic. Or, it could even have been the one that took Ilsa and Victor Lazlo to Lisbon and freedom in the movie, *Casablanca,* thanks to Rick and the purloined "letters of transit."

The plane had two round engines, two tails, and many windows down each side. They didn't enter it by climbing into the front like they did in the *Toko-Ri* fighters. They stepped through a door in the rear and walked up an aisle. Baird sat in the left seat and pointed to the one on his right. When he was seated, Dario couldn't see the ground over the instrument panel, he could only see out the side window.

"Look, D'Angelo, this isn't a flight lesson. We're just going up and fly around a bit to see if you're flight-oriented, which means to see if you puke. Here are two waxed barf-bags. If you have to throw up, do it in a bag, then seal it up. There are plenty more in the pocket behind my seat." He helped Dario fasten his seat and shoulder belts, and his parachute harness. "Here's the drill. I'm going to tell you a few things, and I'll answer any questions you have, but no dumb-shit questions, please. The last candidate I took up asked me what would happen if an engine fell off. How in the hell do I know what would happen if an engine fell off? We don't go around practicing engines falling off, for Christ's sake."

Dario really didn't understand what he was talking about, so he remained silent.

"If we have to bail out, I'll try to hold the airplane steady while you unbuckle your seat belt, walk back to the door, open it, and jump out. Count to five, if you can think of it, and pull that D ring straight out with both hands. Got that?" He pointed to a metal handle on the front of Dario's harness.

"Yes, sir. Then what do I do?"

"Well, if the thing opens, you just hang there until you land somewhere. Get a taxi back to the base and we'll refund the fare."

"Yes, sir."

How will I find a taxi if I landed in a field or even the bay? he wondered. He decided it was best not to ask. It was probably a dumb-shit question.

"I inspected the airplane before we got in it, and I've gone through the pre start checkoff list," Baird announced, as he put his hand on a handle. "This is called a wobble pump. I'm going to pump it to get up fuel pressure." He moved the handle back and forth and Dario saw a needle climb in a gauge. This procedure seemed very archaic to him. Even his 1948 MG-TC had an electric fuel pump, which gave fuel-pressure simply by turning on the ignition.

Baird put on a headset, gave one to Dario, and showed him how to push a button to talk over the intercom. Then he started the engines, one at a time. Next, he clicked some knobs on the ceiling and talked to somebody over his radio. He gave a signal with his thumbs to a sailor on the ground, and soon the airplane began to move. Dario still couldn't see anything but gauges and switches in front of him, but he decided that Baird was weaving the airplane, looking through the side windows to see where they were going. Baird taxied the airplane to the end of the taxiway, and stopped. Dario saw jack rabbits scurrying around in the field next to them. Then, Baird made each engine go up in RPMs, and pulled on various handles and turned various switches. They taxied out onto the runway, which had a big, white, number 27 painted on it. Dario looked out the side window at the rabbits. They were sitting on their hind legs, watching him, impervious to the noise of the engines

When Baird put on full-power, Dario was genuinely thrilled. He'd driven fast cars and had even raced his MG as a novice in three sports car races, but he'd never felt so much force from acceleration before. Any concern he had about his safety was immediately dispelled by the thrill. He liked it. When they were rolling fast, Baird pushed the control wheel forward. The nose dropped and Dario could see the San Francisco-Oakland Bay Bridge ahead. He felt no sensation as the airplane left the ground. He wouldn't even have known it was climbing if he hadn't noticed that the rabbits were getting smaller. Dario was excited. He congratulated himself because the first time he ever flew in an airplane, the first time he left the ground, he was sitting in a copilot's seat, not a passenger seat.

"Don't ask me to fly under the bridges, but is there anything you'd like to see from the air?"

"Yes, sir. My home. San Francisco. North Beach."

"No sweat."

Dario was given a tour that would have thrilled any tourist. But for him, a San Francisco native, it was even more thrilling because he saw parts of his city he could never see from the ground. The roofs of houses, rooftop patios, the tops of cars and buses, back yards; all had been hidden from his view before. The prospect of flying may not have been what had initially enticed him to try for pilot training, but he now knew he was going to like it. It was exciting, and the view was excellent.

They continued over the Golden Gate to Marin County. At Mount Talmalpais, they turned right to Vallejo, then over the Carquinez Bridge to Mount Diablo, and down the east side of the bay to San Jose, where they turned back toward Oakland. Dario knew exactly where they were as they proceeded, and continued to be thrilled by seeing familiar sights from the airborne dimension.

"You feeling all right, D'Angelo?"

"Yes, sir. Just fine."

"Good. Take the wheel and fly us home, I need a rest. Do you know where Oakland is?"

"Yes, sir. I can see it up ahead."

"Good. Take us back to the field. Turn the wheel the way you want to go, push it forward to go down, pull it back to go up."

"You really want me to take the controls, sir?"

"Sure. Go ahead, nothing to it." Baird pointed to the wheel as he spoke.

Dario's hands began sweating when he grabbed the wheel. He played roller coaster with the altitude for a while, but he finally relaxed and began to keep the airplane level. Pointing to Oakland was easy, and as they got closer, he even pointed the airplane toward the center of the airport. Baird didn't say a word; he just sat back and smoked a cigarette and acted as if he were bored. Dario certainly was not; he was becoming more thrilled with every second he had the controls. He thought of his dead father, who had taught him to love music, fast cars—and girls. *Babbo would be proud of me,* he thought. *He was never even in an airplane.*

His rapture was broken when Baird shook the wheel. "I got it," he announced. He talked to someone on the radio, mentioned "full stop landing," pulled back some handles and pushed one down. Dario heard some whining noises and saw some things move in one of the gauges. "Gear down and locked," Baird said aloud. He made several other open announcements about flaps and props, but Dario didn't understand them. He only knew they were pointing down at the painted 27 number, and they were going down fast. He held onto the sides of his seat tightly, ready for his first landing. He saw the rabbits sitting by the runway, still watching them. He felt a hard bump and was momentarily pushed down into his seat by an invisible force. Then the airplane bounced up into the air. Dario knew they were going up again because the rabbits got smaller.

"Damn Bug Smasher," Baird yelled. He wasn't talking into the radio, he was swearing aloud. They started down again and bounced again. "Damned piece of shit," Baird screamed. He put the power on and the airplane kept climbing. It made a circle of the field, and came back for another landing.

When they landed the next time, the bump was much more gentle and the airplane stayed on the ground. Baird wove his way back to where they'd started in silence. When they got to the area of the line shack, Baird stopped the airplane and turned off the engines. "You still all right, D'Angelo?"

"Yes, sir."

"You didn't get airsick?"

It suddenly dawned on Dario that Baird must have purposely made those bounces to test him. "No, sir. I feel just fine."

"No dizziness, no butterflies in the stomach, no nausea?"

"No. I'm fine sir, really."

"Good, good. Do you have any questions?"

He really wanted to ask him if many candidates got sick when he did those bounces, but he was afraid it might be a dumb-shit question. "Yes, sir, just one. I'm sure it's a dumb-shit question, but, what's a Bugsmasher?"

Baird laughed. "No, it's a good question, proves nothing's wrong with your hearing. It's what we call this airplane. It flies so slow the bugs smash on the windscreen. It's a ground-looping, bouncing son-of-a-bitch on the ground. We old fighter jocks never get used to them. When you get to make a choice, go for single engine. Then you won't have any training in these old bastards."

His statement made Dario feel very optimistic. Baird had said "when," not "if."

"You did just fine, D'Angelo," Baird told him when they got back to the hangar. "I'm giving you a four-O. That means perfect."

"Thank you, sir."

Baird shook Dario's hand. "Good luck, son." Baird hesitated, then said, "You know, I envy you. You're going to start flying just when some great new aircraft will be coming into the fleet. Even the T-28s you'll be flying in Pensacola have more power than many of the fighters I flew in the war. Give flying your best effort, D'Angelo. If you do it right it's fun, not work."

"Yes, sir. Thank you, sir. I'll do my very best." Baird turned and walked away. He was only a few yards away when Dario called out, "Oh, sir, Lieutenant Commander Baird."

He turned and faced him. "What is it?"

"Just one more dumb-shit question, sir. What does SNB five stand for?"

He laughed again, even louder than before. "That's not a dumb-shit question either, D'Angelo. SNB are the initials for Secret Navy Bomber, but that's a military secret. We scare the hell out of the Commies with that airplane. When I was in Pensacola, there was also an airplane called the SNJ, the Secret Navy Jet." He smiled. "You're lucky. They should be gone by the time you get there. The new T-34s and T-28s must have replaced them by now."

CHAPTER THREE

PENSACOLA

THERE WAS one Negro in Dario's AOC class. "The Token Nigger," as another roommate, who was from Mississippi, called him after Dario mentioned that it seemed strange that out of 80 cadets in their class, there was only one Negro. He was a handsome man. Light skinned, with pale brown eyes and straight black hair; his features were more Caucasian than Negroid.

One evening, during his third week in the navy, Dario found himself behind the Negro at the mess hall. They went down the cafeteria line and got to the entrees, one of which looked like fried chicken. "I would like a drumstick, please," the Negro cadet said to the white enlisted mess server standing behind the line.

"That chicken ain't got no drumsticks, nigger. That's a rabbit. It got legs." The server had a thick, southern accent.

The Negro accepted the piece of rabbit placed on his tray without comment and continued down the chow line.

Dario felt embarrassed. He'd played with many black musicians, and although he'd heard the derogatory name used regularly, he'd never heard a Negro called "nigger" to his face. He not only felt embarrassed, he felt anger at the server and a great sympathy for his classmate, who showed no rage or discomfort of any kind. "You should be reported for talking to a cadet like that, you asshole," Dario told the server, who scowled, but said nothing. "And I'll pass on that rabbit. Looks too much like fried cat. Give me the meat loaf." The server put the meat on his platter, and remained silent, with a scowl on his face. Dario followed the Negro and sat across the table from him. "Hi. I'm D'Angelo, Dario. I'm from San Francisco." They had gotten in the habit of using last name first, from all the forms they'd filled in. And, it was a customary part of any Pre-Flight introduction to ask or say hometowns, usually followed by college or university. He thrust his hand across the table

The Negro returned a firm handshake. "Thursted, Brandon. I'm from Philadelphia. I heard what you said to the server. Thank you. But how did you think of that bit about the cat? That was fast!"

"From my father. He told me never to eat rabbit in a Chinese restaurant. I just improvised from that." Dario began picking at his meal. He usually minded his own business, but he couldn't restrain his anger over the server's remark. "You should report that mess cook, Brandon. Don't let him get away with it."

"No, no," Brandon answered. He was calm, still showing none of the anger Dario felt. "It's better to ignore his kind. I've never been in the South before. I guess there will be many things I'll have to ignore. My family told me to go into the air force, but I didn't listen to them because I've always been fascinated by ships and the sea, and airplanes. But I'm sure we all are, or we wouldn't be here."

Dario sighed. "Well, I guess that makes me a fraud. I never gave airplanes a thought, nor ships. I was planning to be a Supply Corps officer in San Francisco, then I heard about this new program, and the flight pay, and the attraction wings have for girls, so I went for it. Frankly, I'm surprised I'm here. I didn't think I'd pass the tests, but somehow I did."

"Where did you go to school?"

"San Francisco State Teachers College. How about you?"

"Harvard."

"Harvard! Shit, I'm impressed. What'd you study?"

"Business. I'm going to law school when my navy commitment is over. What was your field?"

Dario was almost embarrassed to tell him his subject. He felt that, especially compared with business administration at Harvard, his education was inferior. He was already bothered by the impressive schools from which many of his fellow AOCs had graduated. They were Ivy League and Mid-Western universities he'd heard of in football newsreels. He was concerned about his ability to compete, scholastically, with graduates with such prestigious alma maters.

"Music," Dario said, sheepishly. "I majored in music education. I play a little piano."

Brandon's face lit up, exposing a mouthful of beautiful white teeth, perfectly symmetrical. "A classical pianist, an artist? How wonderful. I envy you. I love music. Who is your favorite composer?"

"Look, Brandon. I'm no classical pianist. I play a little of it, started with it, but I didn't have the dedication it takes to devote my life to practice. My real bag is modern jazz, bop. But to answer your question, it's Ravel, followed with a close second by Harold Arlen."

Brandon smiled, showing he was enthused. "Ravel is one of my favorites. He is so ethereal, but yet so vivid, so subtle, but yet so alive. It's as though he put the sounds of the sea and the wind into notes."

"Brandon, you're a poet."

"No, I'm afraid not." He sighed. "But I do appreciate the beautiful things of life. I wish I'd had the courage to study art, but I studied business to prepare myself for a career as a lawyer."

"I'll bet you'll be glad you studied a really academic subject, now that we've started our classes. I'm really concerned about my education. I still can't believe they let a music major into this program. I'm still surprised I got this far, but I don't think I have a prayer of making it all the way. I don't even know why airplanes fly."

"I flunked the mechanical aptitude test," Brandon volunteered. "Fortunately, my recruiting officer arranged for me to retake it. I just squeaked by, with a little help from him. How did you do on it?"

Low and Slow

"That's one test I cooled. My dad was a mechanic, had me working on cars from the time I blew out the family car's transmission."

Brandon held up and pointed his coffee mug at Dario. "Why not look at it this way. If they let a nigger into this program, surely it can also withstand the shock of a guinea jazz musician." He smiled, showing his beautiful teeth again.

"Guinea? What's a guinea?" Dario asked.

"Are you serious? You don't know that Italians are called guineas?"

"Not in California. We're called wops and dagos, but I've never heard of guinea before."

"We always called Italians guineas in Philadelphia, and in Boston." Brandon thought for a few seconds, then said, "I guess the coasts use different terms." He sipped his coffee while Dario ate his meat loaf and mashed potatoes. Finally, he asked, "What do they call us in California?"

Dario looked up at him, a forkful of string beans suspended halfway to his lips. "What do you mean, 'call us?' "

"Niggers. Are we just 'niggers' in California? Or are we also 'jigaboos,' 'spades,' 'coons' and 'jungle bunnies?' "

Dario didn't know what to say. He was surprised when Brandon first called himself a nigger, so he was silent as butter dripped from his string beans onto his platter.

Brandon sensed his hesitation. "Dario, when you chastised that southern bigot, I knew you were a sensitive person. I would be very pleased if you would be my friend." He held out his hand again. Dario put down his fork and took it. "Yo'all the class guinea, 'n ah'm the Token Nigger," Brandon said in a mock southern accent, flashing his superlative smile again.

Dario showed off his smile in return as he pumped Brandon's hand. "You left out 'spear chuckers,' " he told his new friend, finding himself completely at ease with his color.

D.E. " Butch" Bucciarelli

* * *

The class left the Indoctrination Battalion and settled into their training battalion barracks. After six weeks, they were finally given a weekend of liberty. Bill Metz had driven his car down from Milwaukee. It was a new, Ford Fairlane convertible. Dario was impressed because he didn't know anyone in San Francisco, his age, who owned a new car. Bill told him it was a college graduation gift from his father who owned a small manufacturing plant. He invited Dario to join him for liberty.

"What are you going to do, Bill?"

"What'n the hell do you think I'm going to do? I'm going to look for pussy and get drunk. I'm so horny, I'll fuck a goat if you'll hold it."

"Male or female goat?"

"Female, of course. I do have some morals, at least until I get drunk."

Dario knew he'd found a friend. "I like a guy with class. I'll hold it for you, if I get sloppy seconds."

"You'll have to work that out with the goat. I'm no pimp."

"A class-act, with scruples."

* * *

If Dario was surprised that Bill owned a new car, he was even further surprised when he saw it. It was two-tone; pink on the top of a chrome arrow that curved down the doors, then straight to the rear. Below the arrow it was cream-colored. The car looked like a double-dipped ice cream cone, strawberry and vanilla. It was not the type of paint decor that was popular in the San Francisco area, but he didn't say anything to Bill about his car. He was happy to have a friend and a ride, even if the upholstery was genuine Naugahyde, powder blue and white, and was protected by thick, clear, vinyl seat covers.

Although the car had been stored outside, it started immediately. They drove it to the automobile hobby shop and washed it. When they finished, Bill stood back, admiring his car. "What do you think, Dario? A real pussy wagon, ain't it? Wait'll these local hick-chicks see us in this with the top down. We'll have to fight 'em off. You got any rubbers?"

"I've got one in my wallet."

"I've got a box in the glove compartment, next to the church key, the half-pint of cherry brandy and the candy bars. There's a Scotch cooler, two blankets, two cushions and beach towels in the trunk. I came prepared for Pensacola. All we need is some beer, some ice, and we're ready for action. Pensacola Pussy, here we come!"

They bought local beer, Spears, whose motto was: "Why pay more when the brewery's next door?"

They changed in the dressing room at Pensacola Beach, and locked their uniforms and wallets in the Ford's trunk. Following the regulation against wearing civilian clothes during Pre-Flight, they wore their navy-issued bathing trunks. The late April sun was already intense, but they were wise enough to bring suntan oil, which they applied to each other's white backs. They recognized many students from their class at the beach, also in uniform bathing attire. They also identified about a hundred cadets from classes ahead of them, and dozens of other male bathers of mixed rates. Bill and Dario were getting good at recognition. After only six weeks in the navy, they could tell the difference between an enlisted man (called a white hat because they wore white sailor hats), and a Pre-Flight cadet, by their haircuts.

There were about twenty girls on the beach who weren't with men. Of those who were good looking, with nice bodies, they saw at least one hundred young men trying to set up their blankets next to them.

"It looks pretty hopeless," Bill said. "I don't think I could get laid here with a fistful of hundred-dollar-bills."

"There are two girls alone, over there." Dario pointed to two girls lying on towels, at the edge of the bathers. They seemed to be ignored by the other predators.

"Fuck, they're ugly, that's why," Bill grunted. Then he smiled. "But, ugly pussy is better than no pussy at all. At least they're prettier than goats. Do you want to make a pass at them Dario, or are you too particular?"

"I think they're both gorgeous. My father told me when it comes to sex, all women are wonderful, some are just better than wonderful."

"Which one do you want? The fat one or the one with the zits?" One of the girl's face was covered with bright red pimples. "I don't see any white puss heads on them, so she must groom herself. She popped them all before coming to the beach," Bill commented.

"Since you provided the car, I'll do you a favor and let you take the fat one. I'll take zit face." Dario didn't care about her craters; he was looking at a very nice pair of breasts, straining the halter of her two-piece bathing suit.

"Why is giving me the fat one a favor?"

"My father was an expert on women. He told me to never pass up sex with a fat girl." Dario held up his hand, making a small circle with his thumb and index finger, recalling when his father gave him that revelation, and made the same gesture.

CHAPTER FOUR

SAN FRANCISCO 1949

HIS FIRST professional job as a musician had been at the Veterans of Foreign Wars hall. The vets wanted to show the public that they did more than just get together and drink, so they put on weekly dances for the local kids to combat the postwar threat to the world even greater than godless communism—Juvenile Delinquency. The band consisted of a tenor saxophone, trumpet, clarinet, drummer, and Dario on the grand piano. They were each paid five dollars a night.

The hall had a large, hardwood dance floor, with a stage at one end. It handled banquets, basketball, and dancing. On his first night, a good-looking girl came up to the piano between songs and asked him if he could play "Bumble Boogie?"

"Can I play, 'Bumble Boogie?' You bet I can play it." he responded.

The number was a boogie improvisation of Rimsky-Korsakoff's violin piece, "The Flight of the Bumble-Bee." He played it for the girl, solo. Nobody danced while he played; the kids just stood around and listened. He played two choruses and finished with a big arpeggio. Everyone clapped and there were a lot of whistles. The girl who made the request came around the piano and gave him a big kiss, right on his lips. She lingered for what seemed to him like five minutes, transferring most of her lipstick onto his face.

"Thank you, thank you. That was just wonderful; I didn't expect to find Jack Fina playing here at the VFW."

"I'm not Jack Fina." His answer was banal. Of course he wasn't the boogie composer; he was just a sixteen-year-old boy who wanted to play like him.

The girl told him her name was Petal, and that she was almost eighteen. She had a big, round, pleasant face, brown eyes and light brown hair that hung to her shoulders. She was wearing a white silk blouse under an unbuttoned green sweater, and a skirt. Her breasts were huge, holding her sweater well away from her waist as it hung down loosely. To Dario, she looked mysterious, and beautiful.

She came back to the piano at the next break with a bottle of Coke and a wad of Kleenex. "You'd better wipe your mouth with these." She handed him the Kleenex. "I'm afraid I got a lot of lipstick on you."

He took the tissue and wiped at his lips, then looked at all the red deposited on it. "Thanks." He didn't know that to say, so he said, "I guess you really like Jack Fina."

Petal smiled. "Oh yes! I love his boogie. But honestly, you sound just as good. Where'd you learn to play like that?"

It was the first time he'd ever been asked the question. "I took lessons. I still take lessons. I taught myself to play 'Bumble Boogie.' "

During his break, they talked about Jack Fina, the dance, and their respective high schools. She asked for his telephone number. "We'll need a band for our senior prom. I'm on the committee." When she told him about the prom, she had a cocky look on her face, with a smile that had more meaning in it than Dario understood. She danced by him quite often during the rest of the evening, always with a different partner. When the dance ended she came up to him to say goodnight and to thank him again for his solo. "I'll call you about the prom," she added.

When he got home, Dario saw a light on in the parlor, a room his family only used when they had guests. The kitchen was the normal living area. He walked to the parlor and found his father, sitting in a chair, reading a newspaper. The room had dark wallpaper and heavy, wine-colored drapes that kept out all light. The stuffed furniture was covered with mohair, in various shades of brown. Crocheted doilies protected the arms of the furniture, and the patterned carpet had white cloth runners to defend it against footprints and wear. Dario guessed Babbo was there to hear about his first musician job, and not disturb Mama, who was asleep upstairs.

"How did it go?" Babbo asked. He was still looking at his paper, pretending to be nonchalant. "Did the other boys play as well as you? Did the kids like you?"

"It was great, Babbo. I'm going to like playing these jobs."

Babbo put down his newspaper and looked up at his son with his green eyes. He also had red hair, which made him often joke that one of his conquering ancestors must have been a Viking. His hair was thinning by the time he was fifty and there was some grey in it, but his mustache was still bright red. He was normal height, with broad shoulders and a thin waist, which he maintained without effort though he loved food and wine and indulged in them without restraint. He was always closely shaved and he trimmed his mustache daily with his straight razor. His hands were rough. They constantly revealed cuts, burns and scrapes, and there was always black grease under his finger nails and in the crevices of the skin. No matter how he scrubbed them, he could never completely remove the evidence that he worked as an automobile mechanic. He prized his mechanic's diploma, which was in heavy scrolls on parchment with a large gold seal at the bottom. It was framed, and hung on the dining room wall.

Besides being a very good mechanic, Babbo was also an accomplished mandolin player, and singer. He performed during dinner every Sunday at the Da Vinci Club, their Italian social center. After a year or so of piano lessons, Dario accompanied him.

"Mother of God, look at your face!" Babbo exclaimed. He stood up. "Your face, it's covered with lipstick." Then he began to do a dance, shuffling his feet to an imagined beat. "I told you Dario, I told you! Play the piano, play the piano. I told you, girls love musicians! You listen to your old Babbo and you're going to get even more girls than I did." Then he sat back in his chair, leaned forward, and took a deep breath. "Now, tell me everything. Tell me what happened."

"Nothing, Babbo. I played a solo of 'Bumble Boogie,' and some girl came up to the piano and gave me a big sloppy kiss, that's all."

Babbo's smile turned into a frown. "Didn't you take her out in the back and kiss her some more? Didn't you feel her tits?" He was almost begging his son to say, "yes."

"No, Babbo. We just talked. She gave me a kiss for playing for her. She may have a job for us, playing at a school dance."

Babbo leaned back in his chair and sighed. He raised an arm and pointed to the stuffed chair to his right. "Pull up the chair, Dario. It's time for us to have a little talk. It's time for me to tell you all the things my father told me, and some that I had to learn myself."

All Dario had ever been taught about sex at school was to wait until marriage because if you didn't wait, you'd probably get a venereal disease. He'd done a lot of "necking" with girls, at the movies, but the farthest he ever got was to feel a girls breast once through her sweater. He'd yet to get his hand, or any other part of his body, next to bare, feminine flesh. His father and he had always been close, but they'd never discussed intimate matters. Dario was embarrassed at first, but also fascinated by what Babbo told him that night.

"The greatest gift God gave man is ejaculation. There is no sensation that feels so good. God made it that way so man would reproduce and increase the species, so there will be more men to worship him. But, he also made a wonderful mistake. Unlike animals that must be in season to fornicate, we can do it all the time, and without reproducing." Babbo struck a match and put the flame to one of his Toscanelli cigarillos. He inhaled, then blew the blue smoke away from his son before facing him again. "Girls are put on earth for us to enjoy. I'm going to tell you how to enjoy them by making them enjoy you."

While he was speaking, Dario realized that his father was being deadly serious; there was no flippancy in his instructions. He began by telling Dario how to kiss. Then, Babbo told him, in intricate details, about a woman's erotic zones, and how to approach them, and how to stimulate each of them.

"Never, never to be bashful, never to give up because of light resistance, but never, never, force yourself on a girl. You will understand the difference between a 'no' that means a 'yes,' and a 'no' that means a 'no.' But remember, it usually means 'yes.' You must dominate, but never through physical force." He told his son how to copulate, and how to avoid pregnancy.

He told him always to tell a girl how wonderful and beautiful she is, even if it's a lie. Babbo lectured him for over an hour, and Dario didn't say a word; he just shook his head in acknowledgment. Just when he thought his father was finished, Babbo took a deep breath, and continued: "Now, Dario, the most important thing. There are two kinds of queers in this world. Those who go down on men and those who don't go down on women. You must give a girl complete pleasure, so she will give you complete pleasure in return." Babbo then gave him a thorough briefing on the art of cunnilingus, enjoining him to practice, "until you have a tongue like a hummingbird's wing."

* * *

He heard the telephone in the kitchen ring as he was practicing the piano. He knew that his mother would answer it.

"Dario, telephone for you, it's a girl," she said in Italian, using a mocking tone so popular in Italian opera. She was holding the receiver out to him as he entered the kitchen, rocking her head and shoulders, with a big smile on her face. He took it from her without comment.

"Hello." He looked away from his mother, who hadn't moved or changed the grin on her face. Babbo was sitting at the kitchen table, reading a newspaper and smoking a Toscanelli. He didn't look up.

"Hello Dario, this is Petal. Remember me?"

"Sure, sure I do. How are you?" His mother still hadn't moved. She stood there listening intently to everything he said, though she understood very little English. "Is anything happening with your school's prom?"

"No. Not yet. The reason I'm calling, you see, I'm baby-sitting tonight at a real nice place. They got a great big piano there and I was hoping you could come over and play it for me. We could talk about the prom, then."

"What time?"

"Come over at eight-thirty. The kids will be asleep by then. Their parents don't get home 'til midnight." She gave him the address, which was near the cable car line. "Don't be late. I'll be waiting for you."

"Sure. See you later." He put the phone back in its cradle and faced his mother, who hadn't moved. "It was a girl I met at the dance. She's the head of the committee for the senior prom at Woodrow Wilson High. I'm going to meet the committee tonight, our band might get the job. It's business, Mama."

It was the first time he'd ever lied to her. It was also the first time a girl had ever telephoned him.

* * *

It was a large, ground-floor apartment. The porch light was turned on, and as he looked for the doorbell button the door partially opened. Petal's face and hand appeared and gestured for him to enter. As he did, he saw that all the curtains in the living room were drawn and only a few lights were turned on. The walls, curtains and furniture were all in shades of off-white and looked very modern to Dario, very different from the heavy, dark interiors he was used to at home. Petal was wearing a white cashmere sweater with a pleated plaid skirt. Her big breasts were straining against the soft, goat hair. As he followed her into the living room, he watched her buttocks and received the transmission of female presence. A wave of warmth went through his body as his metabolism rose. "Where's the piano?" he asked, looking around the room.

Low and Slow

"Later," she whispered, with her forefinger held over her mouth. "The kids just got to sleep. Let's sit on the sofa and talk." She took his hand and led him to a large, overstuffed couch. Petal sat on it and pulled him down by his hand, next to her.

He was becoming very excited, but he was also frightened. Then, he thought of something Babbo had told him. "Don't be bashful. Girls don't like bashful boys. Remember, they want it as much as you do. They just don't want you to know how much they want it."

Petal was still holding his hand, sitting sideways on the couch, facing him. She leaned back, resting her side on the back of the couch, and looked into his eyes. "I'm sure glad you came over. I've been thinking about you ever since the dance."

"Thank you. I've been thinking about you, too. You're beautiful, Petal."

She pulled his hand and put it around her waist, leaned forward and kissed him. It wasn't like the smearing kiss she gave him at the dance; it was a soft, gentle kiss. He was enjoying it while his mind was busy thinking of the instructions Babbo had given him. He slid his tongue against her lips, and her mouth came open allowing it to enter. She moved her tongue into his mouth, but he wasn't expecting it. He instinctively started to push her tongue back with his. "Gently, Dario, always gently," he remembered his father saying. He sighed and relaxed, letting her tongue explore his mouth. Petal said nothing as he covered her breast with his hand and squeezed it gently. He liked the way it felt, and instincts began to control his actions even more than Babbo's instructions.

He wasn't even aware that he had a very hard erection, nor that he was pressing it against Petal's thigh in a pumping movement. He slid his left hand behind her back and tried to undo the clasp on her brassiere, but he couldn't get it undone. Petal leaned forward, put her hands behind her back and undid the fastener in a single movement. They resumed kissing and he put both hands under her sweater, feeling bare feminine flesh at last, kneading both breasts gently, while continuing to pump her thigh; he had a good rhythm going, without even being conscious of the cadence. Petal was also enjoying it; she was making low, moaning sounds and breathing deeply.

He was preparing to make the slide with his left hand down to her skirt bottom when something Babbo neglected to mention occurred; he began to ejaculate. When he felt it coming, he stopped pumping and tried with all his will power to hold it; but he couldn't. As he climaxed, he moaned, partly from the ecstasy of the sensation and partly because, as the victim of premature ejaculation, he was embarrassed.

Petal, evidently, was aware of what had happened. "Christ, Dario! Don't stop now. I'm so hot!"

She took his hand and was guiding it under her skirt, when he got a better idea. He got on his knees and pushed up her skirt. He knew what to do. Babbo had instructed him well.

While he was going at it intensely, Petal was moaning, and gasping loudly. Suddenly, she gave a loud gasp and shouted "Jesus!" and brought her legs together and squeezed them around his head so hard, his ears were ringing. He tried to raise his head, but he couldn't move it; Petal had him in a head lock. He was wondering how he would get out of it, when just as suddenly, she exhaled through clenched teeth and completely relaxed, releasing him. He raised his head, but, his chafed ears were still throbbing.

Petal was still breathing hard, and even in the soft light he could see that her face was still flushed. "Oh my God, Dario," she panted. "You crazy Italian. That was wonderful!"

Dario said nothing as she hugged him close to her. His embarrassment was cold and wet inside his undershorts and he wanted to go to the bathroom and clean up, but he kept kissing her neck per Babbo's advice to always linger-a-while, after.

Petal must have read his mind. "Use the bathroom in the hall," she instructed him.

When he finished, he went back to her. She was still sitting on the couch, and she had straightened out her sweater and skirt. He sat beside her, put his arm around her and kissed her.

Low and Slow

"That was absolutely fantastic. That was the first for me," she whispered in his ear.

"You were wonderful, too," was his banal response.

He kissed her on her neck, with one hand again working her breast. Her bra was still undone, so he pulled up her sweater and began kissing her nipples, softly. Babbo had been very precise about this procedure. Babbo told him that each woman's nipple/areola combination was unique. He called them, "The fingerprints of Venus." Petal's combination was big and soft, the nipple barely distinguishable, like an almost melted scoop of ice cream in the saucer of the areola. After working over both breasts, he put his hand between her legs and she began to make strange, soft noises again. Without being aware of it, he was again rubbing his erection against her leg. Petal suddenly pushed him back, leaned over and unbuttoned his fly. "Where's your rubber?" she asked.

His mind was spinning. Babbo hadn't told him about condoms. He couldn't tell her that this was his first experience with a girl, that he never owned a rubber in his life. "I'm sorry. I'm out of them," he said, thinking quickly, in desperation.

"Jesus Christ, Dario. You sure are different!"

He was resigning himself to the end of love making when Petal stood up. "I'll be right back." She returned in less than a minute with a towel, which she spread on the edge of the couch and sat on. Then she pulled him down, guiding him into her in one, natural motion.

"You be sure and pull it out in time," she instructed.

"I will, I, ah, oo, will, I will, I will."

He thrust slowly at first, and she responded with counter-thrusts in perfect timing. Petal was soon making the strange, soft noises again, which became louder as they progressed. When he fell on her he was exhausted, satiated, feeling mature, and already thinking about how soon they could do it again. He resumed the obligatory post coital petting, kissing her ears and softly blowing into them. "You were great. Was it good for you?" He wasn't being conciliatory. He really wanted to know.

"It was OK, but you'd better get some rubbers. I like it better when you don't have to pull it out," was Petal's love-kitten reply.

They went into the kitchen and split a bottle of 7-Up, pouring it in glasses over ice. Petal looked very good in the bright light of the kitchen. Her skin had a radiance he hadn't seen before. He took her face in his hands and kissed her nose and her lips. Babbo had warned him, "Don't just put it in, pull it out and roll off. If you want it again, you have to show them you like them, even when you want to leave and play Bocci Ball. Often, this is the most difficult part of making love, but it's the price you have to pay for future pleasure."

He did want it again. He looked at the clock in the stove; it wasn't quite 10:30. Petal must have read his mind again because she told him he should leave. "Sometimes, they come home early."

"But, what about playing the piano? I've been working on, 'Cow-Cow Boogie.' I want to play it for you."

"Jesus, Dario, get serious. There's no piano here." Her smile was thin. The sexual glow was gone. "Even if there was, you'd wake up the kids and half the neighborhood. You can play it for me at the dance next Saturday."

Dario's mouth opened, but he quickly shut it. The thought struck him that Babbo's lecture hadn't taught him everything there was to know about women.

* * *

As Dario entered through the back door, he saw the light on in the parlor. He hung his Levi jacket in the hall closet and walked to the lighted room. Babbo was sitting in the stuffed chair, reading a newspaper. The grappa decanter and an empty glass sat on the table next to him. He looked up at Dario. A soggy Toscanelli hung from his lip. He didn't even remove it as he spoke, "Well?"

"Well what, Babbo?"

Low and Slow

"You were with a girl tonight. If you don't want to tell me what happened, that's all right. But, if you need any help, or want to ask any questions, that's why I waited up for you."

Dario pulled the chair over close to his father and sat in it. He spoke very softly. "Everything went fine, Babbo. We did it, I liked it, she liked it. I, I did what you told me to do, with my tongue. She *really* liked that."

Babbo stood up and hopped up-and-down, waving his arms in front of him as if he were leading an orchestra. "I told you, Dario. I told you. They can't resist it!"

"But Babbo, she locked her legs around my head and squeezed. My ears are still ringing!"

Babbo stood still, sighed, raised both hands palms up and slightly shook them in the gesture of frustration. "I know, I know. It's one of the hazards of the game, Dario. You'll just have to suffer until your ears toughen up."

Dario unconsciously rubbed one ear, which was still throbbing. "And Babbo, I have to get some rubbers."

"Oh my God! I forgot all about those," he said as he slapped his head with his hand. "We never had such things when I was a boy. I'll ask your Uncle Lezio to get some for you, he has a friend who owns a pharmacy." Babbo let out another sigh, and sat back in his chair. He reached out and rested a hand on Dario's shoulder. "My son, you are now a man. You have begun the greatest adventure in life—the pursuit of women. You will never understand them, no matter how close you are to one, no matter how much your lives are intertwined. When you are madly in love and you think you are the master of the affair, be very careful, for it's then that you are most vulnerable. You can easily become the slave."

He took his hand from Dario's shoulder and put it on the arm of the chair for a few seconds, then raised it and pointed the index finger at Dario's face. "But none of my admonitions will restrain you. For tonight," he held his breath for a second, "tonight, you became a lover of women. Now, my son, you can't live without them."

D.E. " Butch" Bucciarelli

"You're right about that, Babbo. I can't wait to do it again! But I don't know when I'll see Petal."

Babbo lit a new Toscanelli with a big wooden match, striking it on the fingernail of his thumb. He took two long drags from it, exhaling the smoke as he spoke. "Dario, Maria-Rosa Borzillieri likes you. I see how she swoons when you play the piano, like you are Frank Sinatra. You should be nice to her, go over to her house, get to know her. I'm sure she's a virgin. It would be good experience for you." He had a lascivious grin on his face as he rolled the cigarillo around in his mouth.

Maria-Rosa was Dario's age. She took operatic singing lessons, and she had a good voice. Dario played the piano while she sang at the Da Vinci Club almost every Sunday. He was aware that she had a crush on him. She was always asking him to come to her house and play her piano, but he always made excuses to avoid it.

"Ugh, she's fat. I couldn't touch her. Did you see her hands? They're like sausages. Her big butt, it's like a sack of semolina flour."

Babbo took two long puffs from his cigarillo, inhaling the smoke deeply. When he'd blown it all out across the room, he looked at Dario. His grin was gone; he was serious. "Yes, she's fat. Some are fat. Some are skinny. Some are tall. Some are short. Some smell wonderful, and some stink. But Dario, they are all girls. Don't be too proud, or you may miss some of the best. Sometimes, the uglier they are the better they are in bed—they appreciate charity." He rocked his head from side-to-side, still sucking on his cigarillo. "And don't pass up the fat ones, Dario, especially not the fat ones." He held up his right hand and rolled his index finger alongside his extended thumb, making a little circle of about a half-inch diameter. "Tight, like a mouse's ear, son. The fat ones, like a mouse's ear."

CHAPTER FIVE

PENSACOLA

BILL AND DARIO carried the cooler and their blankets to the girls, who were both laying on their backs with their eyes closed, soaking in the subtropical rays. "Hello, ladies. I'm Bill and my friend here is Dario. Want to have a beer with us?"

Dario was a little surprised by Bill's direct approach. But he accepted it, as he had the automobile color scheme, reasoning that they must do things differently in Wisconsin.

The girl with pimples opened one eye and looked up at him. "What'n the hell kind a name is Dairy-o? Y'all some a those foreign kay-dets been down here of late?"

Her accent wasn't the southern dialect he'd heard Vivian Leigh use in *Gone With the Wind*. In fact, it wasn't like any accent Dario had ever heard in any movie. He understood most of what she said, but it was like understanding one of his North Beach neighbors speaking in the Sicilian dialect.

"What makes you think we're cadets?" Bill asked.

She sat up and leaned on an elbow, with her breasts pushing against her upper arm. Dario looked at them and sighed.

"Shee-it. I just look at you, that's how. I not only know y'all are kay-dets, I can tell by your haircut and white bodies that y'all ain't been to the beach before. I'll bet y'all are on your first liberty. Y'all are Pre-Flight kay-dets!" Both girls laughed. Dario looked at Bill, who wore an expression of incredulity that surpassed even his. They each realized what was happening. They were being put down by the two ugliest girls on the beach!

Bill quickly regained his "big man on the campus," demeanor. "You done found us out, Honey Child. I just love intelligent girls. Now, how about a beer?" He opened a can with the church key he'd brought from his glove compartment.

"What kind y' got?" the fat one asked.

"Spears," Dario answered.

"Shee-it," she squealed. "Now we knows you're nothin' but dumb-ass foreign kay-dets. Ain't nobody with any brains drinks that shit. But, makes no never mind. It's better than nothin', an' y'all kind-a cute. Sit your asses down here."

With great humility, Bill and Dario accepted her invitation in the full realization that neither of them had any control of the situation; they were being controlled by their lust. They soon learned that the fat one was Lucinda, and the girl with pimples was Mandy. After two beers each, which they seemed to guzzle down despite the improper selection, they loosened up enough to let Bill and Dario lie down next to them. In their discussion, Mandy told Dario that she'd never met an "Eye-talian" before.

He lay on his side and stared at her face. She had her eyes closed. He mentally played "Connect the Dots" between her pimples, always coming up with pornographic images. Finally, he connected them into the profile of a large breast, imagining one of the two real ones below. He could hardly wait to discover what her nipples were like. He conjured up their image in his mind. He imagined her areola to be a pinkish beige, with a big flat dark brown nipple. He dozed off staring at them.

After a nap, they all went into the water and the girls splashed around while Bill and Dario swam through the small breakers. Dario really enjoyed it. The warm temperature of the Gulf of Mexico, and the large, white kernel sand was a far cry from the frigid North Pacific and the dirty silt sand of the beaches near his home. He was telling Bill about the difference when they heard someone scream. They saw two of their classmates carry another classmate, who was writhing in agony, out of the water.

"Portagee man-of-war jellyfish," Lucinda told them. "They're here early this year."

They returned to their towels and sunbathed with the girls. "Y'all better put on some more of that coconut oil," Mandy told Dario. "You're gonna blister if'n y' don't. Pensacola sun just loves to burn white bodies like your'n. You're already red on your shoulders."

The girls told them that they were each eighteen, they lived north of Pensacola and worked at a paper mill. They'd gone to school together and both quit when they were sixteen to go to work. Bill told them that they were AOCs and they would be officers in a few months. The girls didn't know what AOCs were, and wouldn't believe that they would soon be ensigns.

"Shee-it," Lucinda said through her laughter. "Y'all think we just fell off'n the turnip truck? We been hustled by white hats an' kay-dets since we was twelve. We knows bullshit when we hears it. Y'all are Pre-Flight kay-dets. You won't be ensigns for eighteen months, if'n you makes it. Shee-it!" she laughed again.

Bill's face became flushed. He put it right in front of Lucinda's and shouted, "Then how come I've got a new Ford Fairlane convertible parked right out there in the lot, waiting to take us all for a ride? No Pre-Flight NAVCAD can have a car. If you're so damned smart, you must know that!"

They carried their gear back to the lot, with the girls following them, and stopped in front of the Ford. "There it is. It isn't bullshit, is it girls?" Bill wore a half-assed grin on his face. He was proud of his car. "Now let's all go for a ride."

Lucinda's voice lost some of its cockiness and became the nearest thing to sweetness they'd heard all day. "Not today, Bill. Y'all got a bee-oo-ti-ful car, but we got our own Chevy, an' we got to scoot on t'home now. Maybe we could go for a ride some other time?"

No matter how much they implored them with the promise of hamburgers and cold beer, they couldn't get the girls to come with them. The most they got was a tentative promise of a date for the following Saturday.

Dario tried to get a hug around Mandy, to at least squeeze her breasts against him and maybe get a kiss goodbye, but she dipped her shoulders around and avoided his attempt with expert agility. "Now don't y'all go gettin' all worked up, Dairy-o. We're damned well used to horny kay-dets gropin' at us, but none of that shit happens 'til we wants it t'happen, y'hear?"

"I hear, Mandy," he answered, frustrated.

They put their uniforms on and decided to return to the base before the mess closed. They were depressed. They'd been rejected by two ugly girls, even with the new convertible. It was dawning on them that in a very crowded, very competitive pond, they were very small fish—with white sidewall haircuts.

At the mess, they sat next to a senior NAVCAD who only had a few weeks to go before he received his wings and commission. Bill and Dario told him how they went to the beach hoping to find girls and found about five hundred other raptors with the same plan. They also told him how they were rebuffed by two girls, at whom they wouldn't have looked at twice on their home turf.

The senior cadet got a big laugh from their sad story. "I've learned, the hard way, that whatever I thought was cool with girls and worked at home had already been tried down here hundreds of times. These local girls get high-side runs made on them all the time, from a very early age. Have either of you ever gone deer hunting?"

Dario shook his head "no," but Bill answered, "Sure, every Thanksgiving."

"Well, then you know that every year a deer survives open season, he gets more and more wary and gets tougher to find and kill. These local girls are the same. The sailors start hitting on them when they're in junior high. Even if they lose their cherries they get tougher and tougher to score on. They get told so many lies, they get smart and start holding out until they can catch a husband. There's a saying about Pensacola girls that must go back to the first pilot classes in World War One. 'The white hats break 'em in, the cadets wear 'em out, and the officers marry 'em.' "

They all laughed. "It's a good story," Bill said, "but we sure as shit aren't going to wear out anything the way we made out today."

"What's the accent the local girls have?" Dario asked. "I could hardly understand the two beasties we met today. It's like no southern accent I ever heard before."

"It's not an accent, it's a twang. The locals are called 'Crackers,' and their speech is called the 'Cracker twang.' You'd better learn to translate if you want to make out on Pensacola Beach."

"What about you?" Dario asked.

"What about me?"

"You've been around for almost eighteen months. Do you make out?"

The senior cadet looked at Dario seriously for the first time. "Sure. I get laid a lot. The secret is to get out of town. At first I tried the pilot's hangout, Trader Jon's, downtown. The bar's always filled with girls, but I soon figured out that only the uglies let cadets hit on them. The cuties all make out with instructors. So, as soon as I finished Pre-Flight I bought an old Chevy and I never spent liberty in Pensacola again. I go to Mobile."

When the senior cadet left them, Bill and Dario got ice cream and coffee and returned to their table.

"Did you ever have any trouble getting laid in Milwaukee, Bill?" Dario asked.

"Hell no! Especially not after I got the convertible. Made out like a two-peckered billy goat. How about you?"

"I never had any problem. Lots of girls went for my piano playing, in high school, and especially in college." He took a bite of ice cream and continued, "Come to think of it, I guess I really I fucked up. I should have joined the Supply Corps and stayed in San Francisco, like I originally planned."

CHAPTER SIX

SAN FRANCISCO 1955

THE DRAFT had been hanging over Dario's head from the time he registered at age eighteen. He would have been drafted to fight in the Korean War, but he was granted a college deferment for four years, or until graduation, whichever came first. He planned his college courses carefully, so both events would occur at the same time. He figured that when his deferment ended, he'd let himself be drafted into the army. His plans changed when he met Mat Haven at a sports car race in 1954. Their mutual interest in cars initiated their friendship, but it was cemented when they realized they also shared a preoccupation for girls.

Mat graduated from the University of California, at Berkeley, a year before Dario was to get his degree from San Francisco State. After graduating, Mat went through the Naval Officer Candidate School in Newport, Rhode Island, then to Supply Corps School in Athens, Georgia. He was stationed in downtown San Francisco, at the Federal Building, working in the Navy Finance Office where he put in an eight-to-five-o'clock day. After office hours, Mat would go to the Yankee Doodle Lounge, across from Union Square. He was more than six feet tall, with the build of a football player. He had curly brown hair, and a handsome face, so in his uniform, there were very few women who didn't look at him and make a silent wish. Since joining the navy, Mat had become very successful, sexually, with women in their mid-thirties. Mat thought it had something to do with San Francisco being an embarkation and entry port during World War II. Although that war had been over for ten years, the Korean War for two years, and there was no fighting going on anywhere, women still slept with Mat like it was for the war effort, and the poor sailor should be satisfied before his life was cut short in valiant sea combat with the enemy. They had started this patriotic practice ten or twelve years before, when it was true, and they couldn't shake the habit.

Mat never bothered to tell them that he spent his days auditing navy contracts with civilian firms, and he'd probably spend his entire three-year commitment doing nothing else. The closest Mat got to saltwater was going halfway over the Bay Bridge to get to the officers' club at Treasure Island, and the only enemy he confronted was the occasional contractor who fudged on cost-plus contracts. "Why should I spoil their illusions with the truth?" he once confided to Dario.

Dario decided to emulate him and become a Supply Corps officer. This would mean serving a year more than the army, a further postponement of his intended career as a high school music teacher by day and jazz pianist by night, but by being stationed in San Francisco, he could still play a few gigs and jam enough to literally keep his hands in it. And, he would be near his mother. He didn't think he could survive more than a week without a plate of her homemade ravioli.

One day, during his last semester in college, Dario walked into the student lounge on campus and saw a naval officer in uniform standing before a card table. There were often military recruiters at the school, but he'd never paid any attention to them in the past. Because of his decision about the Supply Corps, he decided to speak to the officer, who was wearing a tropical-khaki uniform with two big gold stripes on his shoulder boards and gold wings on his chest over several rows of colorful ribbons. He was alone, standing up straight next to his table, with a cocky smile on his face.

Low and Slow

"Hi," Dario said, projecting a large, phony smile. "I'm graduating in February and I'd like to go to OCS and get into the Supply Corps. I'll do it, if you can guarantee I'll be stationed here in the city at the Federal Building." He was wearing a sport shirt, Levi's and loafer shoes. His hair was long compared to the lieutenant's and combed at the sides into a duck's ass at the back.

The naval officer was short and balding, with small dark eyes that slowly looked Dario up-and-down. He repeated the inspection several times until his smile turned into a frown as he stared into Dario's face. "Howryoreyes?" He spoke so fast that his words ran together. He reminded Dario of the fast talking movie star, James Cagney.

"My eyes? My eyes are fine, I guess." He almost stuttered with his answer. He was confused; he'd been caught off balance by the lieutenant's question. "What do my eyes have to do with anything?"

"Are they twenty-twenty? Have you ever worn glasses?"

"Look, I don't know what my vision is. I've never had my eyes tested. I've never had any problems and I've never worn anything but sun glasses in my life."

"Good. When can you get over to Oakland and take a physical?"

"Oakland? Why Oakland? I have an ensign friend who did all his processing for the Supply Corps right here in San Francisco."

"Supply Corps, who's talking about the Supply Corps? Why in the hell would you want to go into the Supply Corps when you probably have good eyes and can get into flight training? You might become a naval aviator, like me, and wear wings." The lieutenant sort of paused before he said "naval aviator," and his tone of voice became almost reverent, like he was saying God, or Jesus Christ, from the pulpit. It was the first statement he'd made at normal speed. "That is, if you've got the stuff to pass our stiff physical and mental exams. This ain't no OCS cakewalk I'm talking about. We take only the best, *la crème de la crème*. The competition is something fierce." A bit of saliva flew from his mouth as he said "fierce."

"Look, ah, sir, I've never even been up in an airplane. I don't know anything about airplanes. I'm a music education major. I doubt if I can pass your tests, but even if I did, why would you want me, a musician?"

The lieutenant gave him a small, genuine smile, insinuating that Dario had, at last, asked the correct type of question. "We don't care if you get a degree in Tibetan basket weaving. We want people who've demonstrated that they can complete a program. We want achievers." He handed Dario a colorful brochure that showed grey aircraft carriers and dark blue jets."

"Readiz," the officer said, smugly.

Dario browsed the brochure. He wasn't very excited about the prospect of training in beautiful Pensacola, Florida or Corpus Christi, Texas, but he did notice: "FLIGHT PAY $100 PER MONTH EXTRA.

He handed the brochure back to the lieutenant and told him, "Sorry. I'm really only interested in the Supply Corps."

"Can't help you. Bunchapenzilpushers. They're only worth a shit on payday."

* * *

Dario met Mat Haven at the Yankee Doodle Lounge that same evening. As he entered, he saw Mat, in his uniform, sitting at a booth at the end of the room. A petite girl with short blond hair had just gotten up from the booth and was walking toward him. Her hair fell loosely to the sides and she was wearing a white silk blouse and a short, tan, gaberdine skirt from which shapely nylon covered legs protruded, ending in brown and white wingtip high-heeled shoes. Her brassiere was working hard to stop her large breasts from pitching up-and-down as she walked; but it worked in vain. She seemed to be in her early twenties, which was young for one of Mat's girlfriends.

The blond looked right past him as she continued toward the front door. Dario continued to watch her breasts bounce up-and-down as she approached him. He stopped and turned when she was past him, and then admired the movement of her tight, round buttocks. He stared at them until she was through the door.

"Who was the doll with the beautiful ass?" he asked Mat as he sat down next to him. The waitress came, and he ordered a drink.

"She works near me in the Federal Building. I'm nuts about her, but I can't get anywhere with her. She just teases me. She's going with some zoomie lieutenant who's stationed over at Alameda. She only sees him on weekends, but she won't go out with me during the week. She saves it all for him."

Mat had more going for him than just his uniform and looks. He had a way with women that made them laugh, and Mat knew how to make that talent work for him. He usually got what he wanted, from the girls he wanted it from, so Dario was surprised to hear he couldn't score with the beautiful blond. He was just about to comment on it when Mat spoke again, "Those goddamn aviators get all the grade-A stuff."

Mat's statement made Dario gag on the first sip of his scotch, which had just arrived. "Funny you should mention that," he said, wiping his mouth with a cocktail napkin.

"Mention what? Not getting into her pants? I'm not proud of it."

"No, no. You said 'aviators. Those goddamn aviators,' to be exact. I talked to one today. He was recruiting at school. I wanted to find out about the Supply Corps, but all he'd talk about was my eyes. They've got a new program for college graduates and to get in, you have to have perfect eyes, no glasses allowed." As soon as he spoke, he was sorry he had. Mat always wore thick, heavy, horn-rimmed glasses.

Mat put his beer glass down and sighed. "Go for it Dario. I know about the new AOC program. The navy's building up its carrier fleet, needs pilots and has to compete with the air force to get college grads. It's a good deal. If you can pass the tests, go for it."

Dario was surprised; he and Mat had always talked about the Supply Corps. "But Mat, look at the good deal you've got here. Look at all the pussy you snag with that uniform. I don't know anything about flying. Why would I want to be a pilot?"

"Wings."

"Wings. What about wings?"

"Wings. You know, those gold things they wear here." He pointed just above a lone red and yellow ribbon on his chest. "You know what they are? They're not just wings, Dario. They're pussy magnets, they're leg spreaders. Girls go ga-ga for the jet jockeys who wear them. And those fly-boys jump into airplanes and go anywhere they want to go. They get away with murder. They wear custom uniforms, with vents and patch pockets, and Jodhpur boots with all kinds of belts and buckles. My commanding officer would put me in hack if I even had my initials engraved on my belt buckle. Those bastards are the prima donnas of the navy, Dario, and I'd give my left nut to be one. If you think I make out in this bus driver's suit, you should see how those swordsmen score with wings."

Dario was confused. Mat seemed to forget all the encouragement he'd given him about joining him at the Federal Building. "Why are they so special, Mat?"

Mat took a long pull from his beer and shook his head slightly. "I don't know. I guess it's tradition. The navy's up to its ass in tradition. Aviators are a different breed from black shoes, which is what they call us non-flying navy types. Their job is dangerous. The rest of the navy considers them expendable outcasts, and they are expendable. We have a saying in finance about their flight pay, 'We don't pay them more, we just pay them faster.' They have a lot of fatalities, Dario. That's the one thing you'd have to consider. Flying off those bird farms is not like sitting behind a desk in the Federal Building." Mat sighed and finished his beer. He sighed again and looked into Dario's eyes. "But the pussy's got to be worth the risk. I know a lieutenant commander who has a wife and kids here, but flies down to San Diego every other weekend and shacks up with a girlfriend. And sometimes he flies up to Whidbey Island because he's also got a bone buried in Seattle." Mat drank some beer. "Christ! All I get are World War Two leftovers within a mile radius of the Ferry Building."

The waitress came again, and they ordered another round. They talked about their cars, but Mat's mind seemed to be somewhere else. Finally, he told Dario, "Think about the AOC program, Dario. If you can pass the tests, go for it. I would, if I had the eyes. Just think. All that pussy, and extra pay to wine and dine it with!"

"I'm a piano player. What do I know about airplanes?" Dario shrugged his shoulders and drank his scotch.

CHAPTER SEVEN

A FEW weeks after his drink with Mat, Dario got a call from Brad Town, who was a hardware salesman by day and a band leader by night. He played clarinet and saxophone, but he didn't play any jazz. He was called "The Original Mayor of Squaresville," by local jazz musicians. The name he gave his band: "Brad Town and his Talk of the Towners," said it all.

Brad was a mediocre musician, but he was a very good businessman who got lots of bookings, so those who played with him worked a lot. The gigs were strictly Mickey Mouse; they used nothing but standard band arrangements, and his musicians had to wear dark suits and red bow ties—just like Mickey. The work was boring, because Brad permitted no jazz riffs, no improvisation, and his beats were as consistent and exciting as a snake's heartbeat on a cold night.

He called Dario because he needed a piano player for a job. Normally, Dario turned him down unless he really needed the money. When Brad called, Dario didn't need the money, but his ears perked up when he heard where the job was. "Alameda Naval Air Station Officers' Club, Friday, cocktail dance, twenty-five bucks guaranteed, and we get dinner and drinks."

"Who else you got for the job?"

"Jerry Dodger on tenor, Frank Shapiro on trumpet, Terry Good on bass and—I know you think he's square, Dario—the drummer is Herbie Ute."

Low and Slow

Brad had left Herbie for last, on purpose. He was a very bad drummer who had a hard time keeping a beat on his antique Dixieland drum set. Herbie banged on cow bells, wooden blocks, triangles, jinglebells and little saucer-size cymbals. His very large bass drum had a woodland scene with a stream cascading through it painted on the drum skin. There was a 40-watt light bulb inside the drum. The heat from the bulb turned a wheel that was covered with glass of several colors, which, when it turned, made the stream appear to be flowing.

Herbie always had his black hair cropped very close, which made his large, round head look like a basket ball with fuzz. He was five feet, nine inches in height, but his shoulder width made him seem shorter. He was a hod carrier by day, carrying one hundred pounds of plaster up a ladder, for 8 hours a day. When he wasn't carrying plaster or pounding his drums, he was lifting weights or punching bags at a gym. The muscles in his shoulders and arms were huge and when he sat over the drums, his arms and hands looking like Smithfield hams holding two little sticks. Although Herbie's sound was terrible, his worse fault was not keeping the beat for the musicians he was supposed to be supporting.

Dario made a pact with the bass fiddle player one night and, as he played his piano solo, he and the bass man played softer and softer, and finally stopped completely. Herbie just kept playing on, pounding the bass drum with his foot pedal, swishing his brushes across his snare drum, and hitting his tiny cymbals now and then, completely oblivious of what was going on—and not going on—around him. He was, indeed, following a different drummer—himself. It took him some time to finally realize that the band, and the dancing audience, were all still, and staring at him. Herbie got the point, but he never forgave Dario for making it.

"Oh no, not Herbie! No way, Brad. I don't think he's square, I know he's cubic. Somebody gave him a shirt with French cuffs for Christmas and he had his mother sew buttons on the cuffs. The last time I played with him, he lost the beat on every song. Why in hell are you using him?"

"Because he got the job," Brad sighed. "He knows some officer over there and he gave me the gig, on condition that I use Herbie. That club has a dance every weekend, Dario. It's steady work and they pay union scale. I need it. I've been trying to get something steady, so I jumped at this, Herbie's drums and all. You know the arrangements we use, you don't need any rehearsal. I need you Dario; please help me out."

He's being so nice I can't turn the sorry bastard down. Besides, I want to see what an officers' club full of naval aviators looks like. Maybe I'll even see that fast-talking lieutenant aviator recruiter, he thought.

"OK, Brad, I'll do it, if you promise you won't let Herbie do any ten-minute drum solos. When he starts banging on those cow bells and triangles, I want to get my foot wet by kicking it through his goddamn waterfall."

"Trust me, Dario, trust me."

* * *

The Talk of the Towners started their first set at five o'clock, although few people were dancing that early. The band was set-up in the far side of the club's dining room, but most of the action was still out in the bar where happy hour was in progress. They'd played some standard tunes for about an hour when Brad told them all to take a break. The club was serving them dinner.

Dario wanted a drink first. He felt he deserved it, after an hour of listening to Herbie's tiny cymbal and big bass drum. Herb had been on his best behavior though; he hadn't once dropped the beat and, best of all, he didn't have his drum light bulb plugged in. Brad must have got that concession from him. Overall, the job was going smoothly. The few couples who danced just talked to each other without paying much attention to the music, not hitting the band with requests. That would come later when the dancers had a lot more liquor in them.

Dario walked up to the horseshoe-shaped bar and ordered a Scotch from the bartender, after telling him he was with the band. His side of the bar was empty, but there were many people lined up on the other side of the horseshoe. A few of the men were in uniform, but most of the men wore civilian jackets and ties. The girls with them were all young, very, very attractive, and well-dressed. Not like the older crowds at the VFW, American Legion, Elks, Moose, Eagles, and Oddfellows Hall gigs that Brad usually booked. Dario could see the back of the head of a blond girl who was facing away from the bar, with four men standing before her. When the blond twisted her upper torso around to pick up her drink from the bar, Dario got a flicker of recognition from her breasts, the tops of which were exposed to the limit of accepted decency by the satin material of her cocktail dress, but the unexposed portions could be immediately imagined by any male with enough testosterone to disqualify him for a job in a chorus line. The blond turned just enough to give him a full profile shot, left side. He recognized her immediately. It was the blond from the Yankee Doodle, the one with the beautiful ass who scorned Mat Haven.

Of course, he thought. *She's with her naval aviator "zoomie" boyfriend! If that's the quality they get, that's for me. I want to be on that side of the bar, wearing wings.*

He took his drink and walked back into the dining room where the band members were sitting at a table near the bandstand, eating salads. "We've got steaks coming for everyone, medium rare. That OK with you, Dario?"

"Sure, Brad. Perfect. Did any of you see all the gorgeous chicks in the bar?"

"Yeah man, my little sister's out there. She'll be in later." It was Herbie who spoke.

Dario looked at him. Herbie was hunched up over his salad, with both elbows on the table, clearly revealing his double-cuffs with the buttons. He had a bread roll in one hand and a fork in the other. His hands, as always, were clenched into fists, as if his fingers were glued together by years of squeezing weights, hod handles and drumsticks. He used the roll to push the salad up onto his fork, then used it to guide the fork into his mouth. He was being very careful to eat over his plate so that the lettuce that didn't make it to his mouth fell on the china, not the tablecloth.

A sister of Herbie's couldn't have been in the bar, must have been in the ladies room. No woman who gave birth to that slob could have also borne any of the beauties I just saw, Dario told himself.

"My sis's a blond, a real cutie. She goes with a pilot dat's stationed here."

"She must be adopted!" Dario blurted it out without thinking.

"What the fuck you mean by that? I ain't got no adopted sister. She's my young sis an' I got two others older than me. What the fuck you talking about, D'Angelo?" Herbie had put his bread and his fork down on his plate and was staring at Dario.

One of the reasons his waterfall and bad playing were tolerated was because Herbie had split lips and broken noses of a lot of musicians who had complained about them. As Herbie took his elbows from the table and sat back in his chair, Dario watched him pound a fist into a cupped hand.

"Er, ah, I knew you had some older sisters, Herb. I just didn't know you had a young one, and all the girls I saw in the bar seemed very young. I just thought that maybe your folks adopted a young girl when they got older?"

His feeble excuse seemed to register favorably in the large head atop the twenty-inch shirt collar, because Herbie leaned forward, picked up his bread roll and started the lettuce conveyance to his mouth again. After a few mouthfuls, he said, "Yeah, she was a late baby. Surprised my folks, as well as all we other kids. She's the kid sis an' we all look out for her, understand?"

"Sure, man. I can't wait to meet her."

Later, Dario saw the blond and her escort approaching the band across the dance floor. He watched the way her hips swayed as she walked directly toward him, the reverse view of the one he'd seen in the Yankee Doodle Bar, but even better because the low cut cocktail dress showed a lot more of her than the business outfit she'd worn that day. He heard Herbie say, "Here comes my sis." He looked around the room but he didn't see any other girl approaching them. He looked hard at the blond's smiling face, staring at each feature. None were Herbie-like.

Maybe his folks did adopt her and kept it a secret? After all, Herbie said they were all surprised.

"Hi Sis, hi Bob." Herbie was still hunched over his snare drum although the music had ended. His head was hanging low and he spoke as if he were reciting a reading assignment before his fifth grade class. "Meet the guys in the band." He introduced them by their first names, starting with Brad and then the horn players. "And this is the piano player, Dario."

"How do you do, Herbie's sis. Is that what we call you or is there another name you prefer to be called by those of us not lucky enough to be your brother?" He was purposely being impertinent, but hoping it would go undetected by Herbie.

The blond gave a little laugh and threw back her head just enough to cause small dimples to form around her mouth. "Herbie's probably forgotten that it's Wanda. He's been calling me 'sis' all my life. I think it's easier for him to remember." Dario was delighted with her answer, which also showed a slight impertinence Herbie didn't understand.

Near the end of the break, Dario was standing by the baby grand piano going through the music Brad had laid out for the next set. He took every opportunity to look at Wanda, who was engrossed in a conversation with Herbie, Brad and Bob. She turned her head toward him once, catching him staring at her, and smiled.

He went to the bar again during the next break and spotted the fast-talking recruiting lieutenant he'd met in the school lobby. He went around to the James Cagney impersonator. "You probably don't remember me, but we talked a little when you were at San Francisco State a few weeks ago. I'm a student there, Dario D'Angelo."

The lieutenant looked up at him, his eyes slightly crossed. He was more than a little drunk. "We did? Wadwetalkabout?" Drink hadn't slowed his speech.

"Your program, I mean the navy's program. The AOC program."

The lieutenant squinted, trying to focus. "Whatchadoinhere if you're a student?"

"I'm also a musician. I'm playing in the band tonight. I hoped I'd run into you here."

"The music major! The Supply Corps! I remember you now. WhatcanIdoforyou?"

"Forget the Supply Corps. I've decided go for the AOC program, if I can pass the tests."

"Donworryboutathing. Get your butt over to my office on Monday morning and we'll get you processed."

The lieutenant gave him a business card that read, William F. Lawrence, Lieutenant, United States Naval Reserve, with an address at the Oakland Naval Air Station.

"Thanks, lieutenant. I'll be at your office on Monday morning."

As Dario walked away from him, Lawrence called out, "Hey! Howzyereyes?"

It took him a minute to decipher, but when he did, he yelled back to him, "They're getting better, lieutenant. They're beginning to open."

When the dance floor was full and people were dancing all around the bandstand, Dario suddenly became aware of Wanda standing next to the piano, watching his hands. When it came time for his solo he deviated from the written arrangement and played his own improvisation, using wild, jazz chords. Brad was giving him dirty looks, but Dario ignored him. Wanda was watching intently with a slight smile of approval on her face. When he ended his solo, Wanda gave him an even broader smile and made a silent clap with her hands. He looked at her hands. Her fingers were long and slim. They were delicate, beautiful hands, the antithesis of Herbie's catcher's mitts.

Someone switched babies in the maternity ward, flashed through his mind.

When the song ended, Wanda came around behind him and put a hand on his shoulder. "Where did you learn to play like that?" she whispered in his ear.

They always ask the same question, he noted, but remained silent.

Low and Slow

"You live in the city, don't you?" she asked.

"Yes."

"So do I."

"I know. I'm a friend of Mat Haven's. I saw you in the Yankee Doodle a few weeks ago, as you were leaving."

"Oh, really? Mat's an old friend. We work together."

"I know."

"Why don't you call me during the week? I'm in the book."

* * *

The Oakland Naval Air Station was tucked away on one side of the Oakland Municipal Airport. Dario walked into the front door of the administration building and asked the first sailor he saw where Lieutenant Lawrence's office was located. The sailor pointed to a door. "Go in there and ask the chief." He walked through the door and saw a sailor in a brown khaki uniform with stripes on his sleeve sitting in a wooden chair behind a large grey metal desk. The swivel chair was tipped back, sideways to the desk, and the man in it was smoking a cigarette and seemed to be staring at the pale-green wall of the room. Chief Petty Officer Casimir Kuwauski was the name etched into a thick brass plaque sitting on the front of the desk.

"Er, ah, excuse me, sir. I'm here to see Lieutenant Lawrence. I want to join the AOCs."

The chief slowly lowered his chair, turned it around and faced him. He looked like a storm had passed through his head, leaving a path of destruction. "Why does it always have to be early Monday morning?" the chief sighed.

"I saw Lieutenant Lawrence at the Alameda Officers' Club on Saturday night. He told me to come here Monday morning. Is he here?"

"No, he won't be here for hours. But I'm the one who starts the process. There are a lot of written tests and a physical examination. Takes all day. Can you stay all day?"

"I can stay all day."

"Yeah, I figured you could," the chief sighed again, even more deeply. "OK then, you can do the tests this morning and get your physical this afternoon. You start off with the questionnaire for your background check. You get a secret clearance if you get your commission, so the FBI checks you out before the navy spends a lot of money training you. If you're not sure about where your grandparents were born, just put in what you do know, like the country."

There were no questions that bothered him. His mother's family, Cresci, were all born in Genoa and his father came from Tuscany. He'd never been a member of the Communist Party or the Black Dragon Society, he'd never committed any homosexual acts and he could honestly state that he'd never used drugs, nor had he ever been arrested. He wasn't sure about using an alias, though, so he went to the chief. "This question about using an alias. I'm a professional musician. Sometimes I use the name Dan Angel when I play scab jobs, so I don't get in trouble with my union."

"Big deal. Angel isn't an alias, it's just a professional name. Put down 'none' and forget it. Save us all a lot of paper work."

* * *

Dario called Wanda that evening. "You blew me away when you asked me to call you."

"Why?"

"Well, you seem to be very close to Bob. I guessed you were going steady with him."

"I am, sort of. But Bob doesn't like music like I do, and he's busy all week and doesn't come over to the city. I was hoping you'd take me out to hear some modern jazz. Would you like to?"

"I've wanted to take you out since I saw the back of you leaving the Yankee Doodle Lounge."

"That's sweet. Where would we go?"

"Nothing much goes on at Bop City during the week. I'll take you

Low and Slow

to Jackson's Nook. It's where the real jazz nuts, who won't take a day job, play every night. How about Wednesday?"

"What time?"

"We should get there about ten. Do you want me to pick you up or do you want to meet me there?

"Pick me up, please. Then you'll have to bring me home."

Said the fly to the spider, he thought, in anticipation.

"I'll do that. I'll be at your place at nine-thirty."

* * *

There was a vibraphone set up with several George Shearing impersonators playing piano with the vibes, and a guitar, in synchronization. Later, a Negro girl sang some blues. Dario sat in and backed her up on three songs. They left a little after three a.m. and drove back to Wanda's apartment. She did most of the talking during the drive, lauding the jazz she'd heard, especially his piano. Dario was encouraged by her praise, and by the way the drinks she had seemed to affect her speech. Although he didn't count on liquor for seduction, he'd found it often helped by easing inhibitions, which usually led to a lowering of resistance and, finally, a reduction of clothes. He put his arm around her as they walked to her door. This was always the moment of truth on a first date. Would he be asked in for a night of love, or would it be option two: a kiss at the door and an exclamation about the wonderful time and "hope we can do it again sometime?"

At her door, he slid his arm around her waist and turned her face to his. He leaned to her to kiss her and she brought her lips to meet his. Their first kiss was a passionate kiss of one-minute duration, with a tongue exchange and lips moving in circular patterns. When they finally unlatched, he began kissing her right ear and, at the same time, moved his hand down to her buttocks, which he wanted to fondle even more than her breasts. Wanda pulled away from him.

"It's been a wonderful night, Dario. Thank you, but it has to end here."

D.E. " Butch" Bucciarelli

"But I though . . . "

"No. Let's not spoil it. There'll be other times, I hope?"

It was always difficult to argue with option two. He was very excited, but he never fought past that point.

"Will I see you at the O' Club Saturday?"

"Oh yes, I'll be there with Bob. But, you won't mention our little date, will you?"

"I won't, if you promise to go out with me again next week."

"We'll see."

* * *

Brad's music was boring, as usual, but, for Dario, seeing Wanda, ravishing in another skimpy cocktail dress, it was worth suffering the tedium. He and Wanda exchanged the usual niceties, Bob being none the wiser about their date, and they all met for a drink at the bar after the dance. The most Dario got away with was a wink at Wanda when Bob mentioned that he'd be out on a carrier during the week. Dario enjoyed the intrigue, but he would have enjoyed it even more if something really intriguing had happened.

He was getting into his MG, which was parked in the rear of the club's parking lot, when something grabbed him from behind. Dario wore a fourteen-and-one-half-inch shirt collar, and whatever was grabbing him had at least a sixteen-inch hand, because it closed around his neck like a cheap shirt that had shrunk. As Dario was spun around, he recognized the button on the French cuff.

"Not so fast, jerk-off. I want to talk to you."

It was going to be a one-way conversation, because the only sound he could emit was a gurgling noise.

"What's this shit I hear about you an' my little sis?"

"Gurgle."

Dario thought about trying to knee him in the balls. He was in a good position, Herbie was standing right in front of him with his knees apart, but he thought of another of Babbo's admonitions: "Be a lover, not a fighter. Get revenge with your brain."

"Somebody told me you was with my sis at Jackson's Nook, you shithead. You stay away from her, asshole. She's goin' with an officer an' I don't want her fuckin' around with no fuckin' piano player. You got that?"

"Gurgle, gurgle, gasp."

When he was free, Dario coughed a few times before he could speak, although in a squeaking voice. "Got it, Herbie." His throat hurt. He knew it would be sore for weeks.

He didn't call Wanda during the week, and he quit playing with the Talk of the Towners. He readily admitted the reason to himself— Herbie's fists. He wasn't a coward; he just didn't think losing teeth was worth the slim chance of seducing Wanda, as beautiful as she was. There were too many available girls, with anonymous brothers.

* * *

"D'Angelo, howzitgoin'?" Lieutenant Lawrence said, using his speed speech. He was standing next to his desk, in his office. On it was a wooden name plaque with a wood carving of a snow capped, cone mountain Dario assumed was Mount Fuji, because he didn't think the navy operated near Mount Kilimanjaro.

"Fine, lieutenant. Did I pass the tests?"

"Who is Dan Angel?" He spoke very slowly and clearly, which surprised Dario.

"Oh, it's just a professional name I use now and then when I play non-union musician jobs. Sometimes we can't get union scale for a job, so we use another name on the contract to stay out of trouble with the union. Everybody does it."

Lawrence stared at Dario and slightly turned his head from side-to-side. "It's an alias. You should have listed it for your background check. The FBI found out about it and they're holding up your clearance. Why didn't you put it down? It's a harmless thing, nothing to hide."

"I'm sorry. I asked the chief and he told me to leave it out."

Lawrence's face turned red and his usually flippant demeanor suddenly disappeared. "Goddamn it, D'Angelo, don't you ever lie because someone asks you to or tells you to. Leaving out something, like your alias, is the same as lying. There is no room in the navy for an officer who lies. It's the worst offense there is."

Dario was very surprised by the outburst, and very concerned. "Will this keep me out of the program?"

"It might. Those FBI spooks go ape-shit when they find something as simple as leaving out an alias." Just as quickly as he became agitated, Lawrence calmed down and his complexion returned to its normal color. "I know the agent in charge, I'll call him and try to smooth this over. Maybe I can get youbackonthetrack." Dario was relieved. Lawrence was back to normal; he was running his words together again.

Lawrence picked up some papers from his desk and looked at them. "You did very well on the written, especially on the mechanical aptitude. That surprised me. You're a music major and you did better than many mechanical engineering graduates I've put through. Howzcum?"

"My dad was a mechanic. He started me working on cars when I was very young."

"Your dad did you a favor."

"Thank you. He did me lots of favors." He didn't mean to be glib, so he added, "And Lieutenant, I'm sorry about not putting down the Angel name. If you can get me cleared, I promise I won't overlook anything like that again."

"Remember not to forget, D'Angelo. It's good you learn this now, and take it seriously, because, once you're in flight training, you'll find there are a hundred ways to get washed out of the program, and not flying well is only one of them." Lawrence spoke his words slowly, clearly—and separately.

Low and Slow

* * *

Chief Petty Officer Kuwauski phoned him at his home the week after his indoctrination flight with Lieutenant Commander Baird, and told him he had passed all the requirements and to come over to Oakland and get his orders. He went the following morning and after he read his orders, he called Wanda from a phone booth on the base. "I'm leaving for Pensacola next Saturday, going into navy flight training. Will you go out with me before I leave?"

"Dario," it was almost a scream, "you never told me. You're going to be an officer and a gentleman. I had no idea. Why didn't you tell me before?"

"I only recently got accepted, and I'm going to be an officer candidate for fourteen weeks, Wanda. I'm not an officer yet, and I don't know if they can make a gentleman out of me."

"Oh, but you will be, you'll be a wonderful officer. And you're going to be an aviator. How exciting for you."

He could detect that his status with Wanda was already upgraded. "Do you want to go out with me?"

"Yes, yes. Shall we make it Wednesday again?"

"How about Thursday?"

The less time Herbie had to find out about it, the better, he reasoned.

He took Wanda to a club on Market Street. They closed the place at two a.m., and took a cab to her apartment. On the cab ride to her apartment, Dario showed his hand. "Shall I tell the driver to wait while I walk you to your door, or are you going to let me come in?"

"Pay the cabby."

Option one! he rejoiced to himself.

Her apartment was small, one bedroom off a combined kitchen-living room. The walls were painted in the latest pastel shade of off-white, and the furniture was Swedish-modern, teak and course fabrics. She had some bourbon, which he mixed with Coke while Wanda disappeared into her bedroom. When she returned, she was wearing a bathrobe. Dario assumed, since she had partially undressed, she was going to let him make love to her. They sat on a couch and he began kissing her.

He got her bathrobe open and found that she was still wearing her bra and panties. They continued kissing and she didn't object while he fondled her breasts. He could feel the nipple between his fingers. It was so long and hard, she could dial a telephone with it. But, every attempt he made to move his hand between her legs was met with her hand pushing it away. He did, finally, get his hand behind her and kneaded the cheeks he'd admired. They were as firm as her breasts.

Dario's continued attempts to remove her panties were always met with her hand stopping him, so he slyly unzipped his fly and pushed what came out against her. He positioned himself so that only a few thousandths of an inch of man-made thread kept him from penetration; but the stuff wouldn't give; not a bit.

Wanda was excited, breathing hard, and even returning his frustrated thrusts. But every time he tried to pull down her panties, her hand stopped him. He was in a quandary, so after a few more minutes of battle against nylon, he backed off, zipped up his trousers and sat back on the couch. "It's getting late. I guess I'd better go," he said, hoping to get some sympathy from her.

He didn't. She led him to the door where he kissed her hard, in the slim hope she'd changed her mind, but she pulled away after a few seconds and said, "Thanks for a wonderful evening, Dario. Good luck in Pensacola. You be certain to call me when you finish! I want to see you, then."

Wings! I've got to have wings!

CHAPTER EIGHT

PENSACOLA

TWO CLASSMATES were killed in an automobile crash that first liberty weekend. Drunk, and driving his new Thunderbird much too fast, the cadet's car left the road and rolled, leaving a swath of cut palmettos and two dead college graduates inside a tangle of metal partially submerged in a swamp. The class also suffered three cases of second-degree sunburn, requiring hospitalization. Those three fell asleep on the beach after drinking too much beer, and they hadn't used suntan lotion. The jellyfish victim was also hospitalized.

His class was assembled in a large room on Monday afternoon where the marine captain in charge of their battalion lectured them about drinking and driving, using charts to show the loss of reaction time with each ounce of alcohol in the blood system. He ended the lecture with the warning that they could be court-martialed for sunburn, as it was "Willful destruction of government property," meaning their bodies.

Just before they were dismissed, a marine clerk made an announcement that brought Dario to attention. "If any of you can play a musical instrument, lay over to the band room today instead of going to military training. Chief Shaw needs musicians for the Cadet Band."

D.E. " Butch" Bucciarelli

Dario was delighted to get out of even one day of military training. He accepted, with some restraint, all the training he'd received so far, and he tolerated the pettiness of room and uniform inspections. He especially disliked military training, which was mainly marching, because it was conducted by marines. With an M1 Garand rifle on his shoulder, he followed the nasal commands of the drill sergeant with the rest of his class: "On, ta, threh, fo, on, ta, threh, fo," the marines droned as they marched in cadence. He couldn't understand why, since he was in Pensacola to learn how to fly airplanes, he had to tolerate robot marines giving brainless marching training.

He was the first to the band room after classes that day. When he entered the room he felt a warm glow of familiarity; it was like being back at the San Francisco State band room. There was a grand piano, music stands, all the musical equipment familiar to him. Nothing distinguished it as a navy band room, except the uniforms on the cadets who were filing in and taking instruments out of cases. Chief Shaw, the band director, was the antithesis of the trim navy and marine instructors he'd seen so far in Pre-Flight. He was fat, with a large beer belly that draped over his belt. He perspired constantly (even in the air-conditioned room), and continuously wiped his face with a large handkerchief. Eight prospective band members from Dario's class were there. The chief took them into a side room.

"The Cadet Band is a tradition that goes back to the start of the cadet program," he lectured. "It plays at every class graduation and at every local parade. We also travel, some weekends, to functions around the country. In the next few months we're going to Columbus, Ohio for a function at the Goodyear blimp factory, and to New Orleans. We practice every afternoon during the military training period. This *is* your military training. You march with the band, not with the rest of your class. You carry an instrument, not a rifle."

His last statement got a lot of "oohs" and "aahs" from the students. Like Dario, not many of them liked marching around with the old Garrand rifle, crunching gravel.

"Any questions?"

Low and Slow

Dario stuck up his hand, assuming the question he was about to ask would end his prospect of avoiding marching with marines. "Chief Shaw, I play mostly piano. I have a basic knowledge of most instruments, but I'm not really proficient at anything but the piano. Can you use me?"

"Can you read music?"

"Of course. I majored in music."

The chief gave a look of amazement, then smiled. "That's a first. A music major in flight training. Shows the navy's getting more democratic. Good, good. I need a cymbal player."

They filled out more paperwork and the chief had the others play so he could determine if they were good enough for the band. He gave Dario percussion music and a pair of brass cymbals. "Now, just count the beats and hit the cymbals where the percussion symbol indicates. Percussion music is different, because . . . "

"Chief Shaw, excuse me for interrupting you. I don't mean to sound like I know everything, but I do know how to read *all* band music. I studied orchestration, arranging and conducting."

The chief smiled, while wiping his forehead with his bandanna. "Forget the cymbals then. I need someone who can lead some cadets through the arrangements before I take them out on the field. Can you do it?"

"Sure. No sweat." Dario was beginning to inadvertently pick up marine vernacular.

"Good. You're my new band manager."

Dario was elated, but it sounded too good to be true. "What else do I do, chief?"

"Take the muster. Inventory the instruments and music when we go on trips."

"How about when the band's marching. Do I play cymbals then?"

"No. You stay in the band room out of sight. The manager doesn't march."

Dario almost fainted with joy. He was going to beat the marines. He decided to "go for broke," another marine phrase. "Can I practice on the piano, chief? I haven't touched one since I left home."

"Sure. Anytime the band room isn't being used, the piano is yours."

He almost pinched himself to see if he were dreaming. When he was certain he was awake he mentally thanked Babbo for making him start piano lessons when he was age seven. His father promised him that it would make him happy and impress girls, but even Babbo, in his broadest wisdom, could never have guessed it would someday get his son out of marching to the cadence of marines.

* * *

Dario wanted a car, but he was broke. He'd spent the money from the sale of his MG before he left San Francisco, paying bills and enjoying himself. He only received eighty-four dollars monthly as a cadet. "Just enough money to send home for money," as one cadet put it. His monthly pay barely covered the cost of a few days of liberty, and his laundry and other supplies, such as brass and shoe polish, wire collar stays, and buttons sewn onto metal points for emergency replacements. (The Navy Exchange Laundry was infamous for smashing buttons).

It was necessary to keep his uniform perfect to avoid being assigned demerits by the marines. The number of demerits given was determined by the severity of the infraction. They were only erased by marching on the grinder, a block-long gravel strip in front of the Cadet Club. Miscreants mounted their M1 rifles on their shoulders and marched during the free periods, while saintly cadets drank beer and watched.

He would have to finance a car. It would be easy to make payments after he received ensign's pay, and flight pay, but that was ten weeks away—if he made it.

On Saturday, Bill drove him to a car broker they'd heard about. It wasn't a dealership, or even a used car lot. The broker had an office in a white house trailer, set back from the paved road about twenty-feet and sitting on concrete blocks, rather than on wheels. The set back created a large parking area that was covered with crushed oyster shells, the ubiquitous gravel of the South Coast. There was a new, dark-blue Chevrolet convertible parked on it. It looked beautiful, contrasting with the stark-whiteness of the shells.

"Come on in boys, sit down. How about a Coke?" Les Harkil was the personification of a southern "good ol' boy," complete with a Cracker twang. He had on a diagonally striped tie and a vertically striped shirt that was pulled open at the collar, allowing the tie to fall obliquely across his chest. Wide horizontally striped suspenders held up trousers of a checkered pattern. It was hot in the trailer, and several electric fans tried to move the air around, without much success. Harkil had a perspiring, beet-red face below a bald head. He constantly wiped both with a towel. Dario and Bill accepted the drinks and sat down.

"That's a mighty pretty Fairlane y'all got out there, son. You want to get rid of it for somethin' else?" Harkil said to Bill.

"No, sir. It's my friend here, Dario, who needs a car. Guy in our class told us you had some good deals."

"You bet I do, son, I surely do."

"What kind of cars do you sell, Mr. Harkil?" Dario asked.

"Now then, y'all just call me Les, Dario. Well, son, I can get you any kind of car your little ol' heart desires. I'm a broker. I sell only new cars which I buy wholesale from dealers all around the country. What kind a car do you desire?"

"I'd love to have a new MG, the A model, but I can't afford it. I'm sorry, Mr. Harkil, Les. I didn't know you only sold new cars. I'm afraid I can only afford a used car."

"Lots of interest in them foreign cars. I can git you one down from New York. Probably take a week or so."

"I'm sorry, Les. I didn't mean to lead you astray. We're AOCs. I won't be able to buy a car until I'm commissioned, which won't be for several months. And, as I said, I don't see how I could buy a new car, even then."

Les Harkil put up a hand, as if to deflect Dario's words. "Now, don't you worry your little ol' head about that, Dario. I know all about the new AOC program and I've tailored a special plan, just for you boys. All I need is a two hundred dollar down payment, and I can deliver you a new car. You don't start payin' for it 'til you get your commission. And then all you pay is one hundred dollars a month. That's your extra flight pay, so you'll never miss it. Just make out an allotment to the bank and the navy makes your payment. It's just like gettin' a car for free."

It sounded too good to be true. So good, in fact, that Dario was wondering what tricks he could be hit with. He'd inherited much of the skepticism his mother had brought from "the old country," as Italy was referred to in his community. "Believe nothing you hear and half of what you see," was the philosophy he'd grown up with.

"But Les, what if I don't make it through Pre-Flight? What if I don't get my commission?"

This time Les Harkil held up two hands to ward off Dario's concern. "We won't worry about that. Odds are, you'll do just fine. You phone me next week an' I'll be able to tell you exactly what it'll cost, and when I can get you one of those lil' ol' cars. What accessories would you want? A radio?"

"No, sir, no radio. It's a sports car." Dario, the purist, said. "All I want extra, are wire wheels."

CHAPTER NINE

B ILL HAD arranged a meeting with Mandy and Lucinda at Pensacola beach. They changed clothes at the beach, but not into their uniform bathing trunks. Instead, they changed into colorful Hawaiian shirts, Bermuda shorts, and leather sandals. They'd purchased them at the Navy Exchange and hidden them in the Ford's trunk. They were out-of-uniform, and subject to many demerits if caught. They knew that they stood out in civilian clothes, with their short haircuts, so they'd decided to take the senior cadet's advice (and also mitigate their conspicuousness), by going east to Fort Walton Beach, which was beyond the bounds of their allowed liberty area. If caught there, and out-of-uniform, they would be in big trouble. But, he and Bill had decided to take that risk, rather than the certainty of sexual failure if they remained in fiercely competitive Pensacola.

When they told the girls they wanted to go to Fort Walton, they were surprised by their enthusiasm. "It's a bodacious beach," Lucinda told them, in what Dario now knew was her Cracker twang.

"And, it ain't crowded like 'tis here," Mandy added. "And they got dancin' on that beach." Her body looked even better to Dario than it had before, perhaps because he'd been fantasizing over it. But, he tried to avoid looking at her face. Not only did she have red bumps covering most of it, her features were also far from attractive. Her eyes, which were blue-grey, were set into her large head with too great a distance separating them. Her hair was difficult to describe; he couldn't even determine the color. It was apparent that she had made an attempt at becoming a blond, but it came out just a dingy light brown. It was thin, and cut short. She had a receding chin which went straight from her lips to her neck. Dario looked from her neck down to her feet.

From the neck down, grade AA choice. Skin clear and smooth, tight, and fully packed everywhere. But, the face!

Lucinda had an attractive face and beautiful, glossy-red hair, which hung down to her shoulders. But, she was overweight. Not the large firm type, kindly referred to as "big boned." Lucinda was just plain fat. The girls left their battered Chevy parked at Pensacola Beach and got into Bill's Ford. Bill gave Dario a wink as he lowered the convertible top. Dario returned his gesture by holding a thumb up, out of sight of the girls. Their nefarious intention was to stay overnight with them in a Fort Walton motel.

The day went even better than they'd hoped for. The girls really enjoyed themselves at the beach. They drank beer, swam and sunbathed. There was an outside pavilion at the beach where kids, teenagers and young adults were dancing in their bathing suits, most in bare feet. Mandy hauled Dario onto the dance floor and showed him how to dance to the music that was blaring out of the loudspeakers. He'd never heard the blues-country-rock-type genre before, but he liked it. While dancing, he finally got to press her against him and feel the firmness of her breasts. He also felt her waist and the small of her back. He liked what he felt. She was exciting him.

It was Bill who finally broached the motel subject. "Look ladies, why go all the way back to Pensacola? We don't have to be back to the base until tomorrow evening and you don't work again until Monday morning. Why don't we get two motel rooms and spend the night? We can clean up, go out and get some dinner, and then dance some more tonight. We can sleep late tomorrow and spend the day at the beach here. What do you say?"

The girls were positively receptive to the offer, so they got two

Low and Slow

rooms at an inexpensive motel two blocks from the beach. They changed clothes, then ate at an outdoor fish place and danced at a local bar. Dario and Bill wore their Hawaiian shirts and shorts, which was all they had. Being cocktail time, Lucinda and Mandy declined beer and drank Seagram-Seven whiskey mixed with 7-Up—7 & 7s, as they called them. Bill and Dario drank only beer and they were getting very excited with the progressive looseness the girls were exhibiting after three drinks. Bill had been making good progress with Lucinda, kissing her often while dancing. Dario hadn't been as successful, but he wasn't really putting his heart into it. The pimples were cramping his kissing technique. Besides, it wasn't Mandy's face he wanted to kiss; his objectives were lower, down in the AA choice section. The girls had one more drink when Lucinda announced she was tired and wanted to go to bed.

The usual moment of truth came when they got to the motel. Earlier, the girls had showered and changed in one room, and the boys in the other. No mention had been made of the sleeping arrangements. Bill again used his Wisconsin subtleness and made the proposal as they pulled into the motel parking lot. "How about staying with me tonight, Lucinda? We'll take the room you girls changed in, and Dario and Mandy can take the other room."

Dario grimaced, expecting to hear "shee-it no," and other expletives from Mandy, who seemed to be the dominant girl of the two. He was again surprised. Mandy, sitting next to him in the rear seat, turned to him and kissed him on his cheek. "Do you want that, Dairy-o?" She was almost purring.

He pulled her to him and kissed her softly on her lips. He put his mouth next to her ear and whispered, "Oh yes, Mandy, yes. You really turn me on."

"Shee-it," she purred.

He sat in a chair by the window with the lights off while she showered. When she finished, she came into the darkened room and got into bed. Dario quickly showered and got into bed with her. They faced each other, lying on their sides, naked. He put his hands on her face and gently pulled her to him. He kissed her eyes, her nose and her lips. She had changed from the tough-cookie, Cracker twanger to one showing tenderness and affection. This demeanor knocked him off his stride. He'd planned to enter her as soon as he could, less she change her mind and revert to her caustic manner. So, he returned her tenderness with slow, gentle foreplay. He began by kissing her neck, purposely avoiding the heavily pimpled area of her cheeks. He rolled her gently onto her back and continued kissing her, lower and lower. He was patient, although his desire was throbbing. Mandy was quiet, neither moaning nor purring. She did run one hand through his hair, but the other hand made no exploratory movement over his body.

When he arrived at her breasts he was pleased by the firmness of her erect nipples. He'd visualized them often, as they forced the thin material of her bathing suit halter, and they were even better than his fantasy. He continued kissing her body lower, toward her navel.

"You gonna fuck me or give me a cat bath, Dairy-o?" Her question brought him out of his sexual trance. He was momentarily confused. Nothing like this had ever happened to him before.

"But Mandy, I'm going to go down on you. You'll love it, I'm good."

Mandy pushed his head away from her belly and squirmed away from him. "Go down on me? What are you, some kind of Eye-talian pree-vert? Now you just get on top a me an' fuck me, y'hear? I told you before, none of this shit happens 'til I want it t'happen. Well, now I want it t'happen. What you waitin' for? Fuck me!"

"Yes, Mandy. I mean, I ain't waitin' for nothin', Mandy." They spent the rest of the night enjoying plain ol' sex, southern style.

* * *

When he was alone with Bill after breakfast, Bill told him that he and Lucinda had a great time. "Man, she was tight, Dario. If I didn't know better, I'd think she was a virgin." Dario just shook his head in complete understanding. He was curious about one thing, however, so he asked. "Bill, I've never been with a redhead. Was she red all over?"

"No way. Her hair's dyed. Pussy hair's black as your heart. Why'd you ask?"

"Oh, just curiosity. I've always wondered."

* * *

They dropped the girls off at their Chevy late in the afternoon. He gave Mandy a big hug and a deep kiss. He meant it as a sincere gift of thanks, not as etiquette required for parting. She'd been an unsophisticated lover, but she'd been responsive and satisfying, and she'd been fun to be with. He looked at her face. He didn't see the craters, the dingy hair, the flounder eyes or the receding chin. He saw a face that glowed from pleasure given, and accepted in return. He felt content. His life in the navy was improving. He had a piano, sex, and the prospect of a car. And, thanks to the band, he didn't have to march with marines.

"We'll be calling you again, soon."

"That's a ton a bullshit." Her voice was soft. "You got what you wanted, an' so did we, Dairy-o. Lucinda an' me, we knows what we are, an' what we look like. You ain't the first, nor the last, to fuck us an' forget us—which don't make no never mind to us. But, we ain't no push-overs. We decide who we fuck and when we fuck 'em." She gave Dario's hand a squeeze. "But you were real fun, Dairy-o. Thank you for being so nice to me. I liked it when you told me I was beautiful, even though I knew you was lyin' so you could get in my pants. I just looks stupid."

Dario put both hands around her head and kissed her on her cheek, impervious to the rocky texture.

* * *

When they got back to their barracks for Sunday night study, Dario wrote his first letter home. He hadn't written to his mother because she didn't like to receive mail, which she always equated with bad news. He wrote to his stepfather, Vito, who was the manager of the North Beach branch of the Bank of America. Vito was a very handsome man; tall, with thick black hair combed straight back on his head. He had been the most eligible bachelor in the Da Vinci Club, but he remained single and lived with his widowed mother, who had recently died. He had graduated from a local business school, and was notorious because he had his shirts laundered at a Chinese laundry, instead of by his mother. Vito always dressed immaculately.

Dario had been skeptical about him when his mother told him they were going to marry, shortly after Babbo's death. They waited a full year of mourning, then married and moved into a new, custom-built house. Once Dario was convinced that Vito wasn't after the money his mother received from Babbo's life insurance, he began to respect him because he made his mother happy. She bought a new car, took driving lessons, and was even going to an English class. She really wanted to speak English because she had a new television and wanted to understand the programs.

In Dario's letter, he told Vito he wanted to buy a car and asked him if he could get a loan from the Bank of America for the necessary two hundred dollar down payment. He sent it airmail to Vito at his bank address, so that his mother wouldn't be upset. Air mail letters were particularly alarming to her, as they usually came from a distant relative in Italy, begging for money.

He called Harkil the next day. He told Dario that he could deliver a new powder-blue MGA, with wire wheels, in two weeks. The total price was 2,800 dollars, including interest, taxes, shipping, license and insurance for one year. "After your down payment, you pay one-hundred dollars a month for twenty-six months. How does that sound, Dario?"

He wanted the car desperately. The new, streamlined MGA was a modern car, compared to the short, square MG-TC he'd owned before. "I want it, Les, but I don't know when I'll get the two hundred bucks for the down payment. I'd better wait until I graduate and order the car then."

"No need to do without the car, son. I'll order it. You'll get the money. I have faith in you. If you don't, we'll work out some other arrangement."

Dario was still wary. "But Les, I don't want to commit to something I can't handle. I wrote to my stepfather, but I don't know what his answer will be. He's a banker, and you see, Les, I'm afraid I don't have any collateral. I don't know why you should trust me either. I'm not a very good risk. I was a music major and I still don't know what I'm doing in this program. I don't know anything about airplanes. I'll probably wash out during my first week of flying and lose the flight pay that's supposed to pay for the car."

There was a short pause, then Les said, "Dario, let me tell you a fact. The navy does all my work for me. By the time I get boys like you for customers the navy has investigated your background, your character, your education and your reputation. If you was a no 'count cheat, gonna rob me of a car, you wouldn't be here in the program you're in. I have the most honorable customers in the world and I'll be proud to have you as one of them. And don't you go getting all negative about flying. I've been here all my life, son. I've seen cadets come through here with straw stickin' out of their ears, farm boys who'd never even driven a tractor, only mules. Some of them became the best damn fighter pilots the navy's ever had. You just apply yourself, Dario, and pay attention to your instructors. You'll do just fine."

Dario made his decision. "OK. Your's is a good deal, Les. Please order the car. Do you want me to come down and sign anything?"

Dario heard a sigh over the phone. When Harkil spoke again, his voice was more like a college professor than the southern good ol' boy. His English was perfect and his Cracker twang was gone, for a few sentences. "No, son. I told you, I trust you. You don't sign anything until we complete the transaction and you drive out with your new car. Call me in two weeks, Dario. And thank you for the order, y'all hear?"

"You're welcome, Les. And thank y'all."

Dario received a reply from Vito in ten days. In the letter was a money-order, payable to him, for two hundred dollars. There was also a letter. "Dear Dario, I am glad to hear that you are doing well. Your mother is well and very busy. She is doing very well in her English class. The enclosed loan is from me, pay me back when you can. I trust you, Dario. All the collateral I need is that you are a fine young man, but what else could Beatrice's son be? Good luck, have fun and be careful. Your mother worries about you flying airplanes. Someone told her that landing on aircraft carriers is dangerous. Sincerely, Vito."

"She should worry about jellyfish. So far, they're the most dangerous thing I've been near," he said aloud, to himself.

He felt very good about getting the money, and about Vito's letter. It went along with what Harkil had told him over the phone. He'd never given much thought to trust or honor. He'd learned from his father to always be respectful of other people's feelings, even if, as in the case of girls, it meant telling them lies to make them feel good. He would never cheat another person and he would never do harm to another, unless it was a matter of revenge. Babbo had been very emphatic about the necessity to get revenge, if he was wronged. Babbo told him that if the D'Angelos had been noblemen, the motto on their coat of arms would have been: "In defeat, malice. In victory, revenge!"

* * *

He saw the powder blue MGA sitting on the white oyster shells as Bill's Fairlane turned the corner and approached Harkil's office. He'd only seen photos of them in magazines, but the real car looked even better. The white top was up, as were the window side curtains. He had a premonition that he was going to enjoy this car and he was proud that he could buy it with only two hundred dollars and his reputation. It proved that his prospects were favorable. "Screw the Supply Corps," he yelled to Bill. "They don't get a hundred bucks a month extra to pay for a new car!"

Les had all the paperwork ready and all Dario had to do was sign some papers and give him Vito's money order.

Low and Slow

"That surely is a pretty little ol' doodle bug you got out there, Dario," Harkil said, wiping his head with a large blue handkerchief. "Only got twenty miles on it. It's the first one in town that I know of, but there's one little ol' problem. There ain't a dealer here in Pensacola, yet. You'll have to go to Mobile to get it serviced."

"Oh, that's no problem, Les. I'll do all the work myself at the base hobby shop garage. I'm going to make some modifications to it anyway, as soon as I get out of Pre-Flight."

Harkil stared at Dario in amazement. "Y'all know how t'work on these cars?"

"I surely do, Les, I surely do. My father was a foreign car mechanic. He gave me my first car, an earlier model MG. I did all the work on it myself, with his guidance."

Bill, with two other classmates, followed in the Fairlane as Dario drove his new car to Fort Walton Beach. He drove the MG slow, then fast, then slow again, breaking in the engine the way Babbo had taught him. As the two-car caravan of out-of-uniform, out-of-bounds AOCs headed east along the Gulf Coast, tops down, Dario admired the scenery. Scrub pine forests with palmettos and ferns were in the swamps to his left. To his right were low dunes sprouting sea oats and blending into the brilliant white, sugar sand beaches that made a picture frame border for the turquoise and blue sea of the Gulf of Mexico.

He pulled into a gas station on the outskirts of Fort Walton. The MG didn't need fuel, but he wanted to check the oil and inspect the engine for leaks or loose bolts. It was the first gasoline station he'd been to since leaving San Francisco. Bill had always filled up at the Navy Exchange station on the base. When he finished his inspection, he decided to use the toilet. As he walked around to the rear, he was shocked by what he saw. There were three doors. There were the familiar "Men" and "Women," but the third door was new to him. Its sign said "Colored." Before he returned to his car, he looked at the drinking water fountain. It was exactly the same as the one at the station where he worked in San Francisco. It produced a stream of cool water that made an arc from which a person drank without mouth contact. Hanging from the side of the cooler, by a chain, was a long-handled ladle, rusty where the blue porcelain covering was chipped away. It was marked, "Colored drink from this." He called Bill and the others. "Take a look at these," Dario pointed at the ladle and the toilet sign. "Can you believe this! I thought the South lost the Civil War and slavery was ended."

"Don't you know about Jim Crow?" one of the others said. "It's what the southerners call their segregation policy. Colored people can't go to white restaurants, or hotels, or schools. Even the movie theater downtown has a side entrance for Negroes. They have to sit in a separate balcony, way up high. Its called Nigger Heaven."

"Fucking red necks," Bill said aloud.

Dario had only heard the term recently. He was told that white southern farmers wore bib overalls without a shirt, so their necks were always sunburned.

Guineas and red necks. I'm learning lots of new words, he thought.

CHAPTER TEN

DARIO SIPPED his beer as he sat alone at the outside beach casino and watched a small girl dancing in leather sandals (unlike most of the other dancers, who were dancing in bare feet). She made such natural movements she wasn't aware that they were almost erotic. Lust rose in him as he followed the movement of her buttocks, which were small but stuck out almost level from her waist. He was pleased to notice that she didn't dance with the same boy each dance.

The beach music and the dancing were the same as the night he and Bill had spent there with Mandy and Lucinda. He hadn't seen or talked to Mandy since that weekend. She'd been right about the "fuck and forget." He no longer wanted her. She'd given him good sex and he was sure she would again if he took her out of town, but he didn't want to take advantage of her—and he did want someone more attractive.

Wearing his civilian out-of-uniform attire (Hawaiian sport shirt, shorts, and leather sandals), he went over to the small girl and asked her if she would dance with him.

"Yes, thank you," was her simple reply, which pleased him. After his experience with Mandy, he'd expected a more impudent answer. As they danced, she told him her name was Tammy Pointer and that her father was an air force sergeant stationed at nearby Eglin Air Force Base. She was nineteen, worked as a secretary on the base and was taking junior-college courses at night. She was born in Texas, where she'd spent most of her youth while her father moved from base-to-base within that state. She'd been in Florida for two years. Dario told her a little about himself. Since she was an air force brat, he laid it on thick about being a college graduate and that he would soon be an officer and flying airplanes, but she gave no indication that she was impressed.

Tammy's hair was medium length and curly. It was lustrously jet-black, with a silken-shine from the flood lights of the dance floor. Her dark eyes, almost almond in shape, were evenly placed beneath well-trimmed eyebrows. Her nose was small, but wide. Her lips were full and covered with bright red lipstick. Her breasts weren't large, but nicely proportioned to her size and looked firm within the halter she wore. Tight white shorts barely covered the buttocks which had excited Dario. Her skin was clear and dark, like she'd spent hours in the Florida sunshine. When he held her on the dance floor, he put his hand on her bare waist and felt the smoothness of her skin. She was tiny. The top of her head barely reached his chin. Her voice was soft, with a slight accent that was definitely not Cracker.

They danced for several hours, sitting and talking between dances. She didn't drink alcohol, only Dr. Pepper, while he drank a beer. He made his move at a few minutes past ten p.m. "I know it sounds corny, Tammy, but I've got a new car, just got it today. Would you like to go for a ride along the beach with me?"

Bill had told him that making out on the beach was the "in" thing in Florida. In his junior year, Bill and classmates from his college had driven to Fort Lauderdale over their spring break. "Man, the pussy liked it on the beach, in the open air," he'd bragged. "Just be careful. Don't get sand on your dick," he warned Dario in jest. Bill had loaned him one of his blankets and a beach towel.

"What kind of a car do you have, Dan?" He'd told her that his name was Dan Angel, so he wouldn't be accused of being a foreign cadet again.

"A convertible. The top is down, the moon is almost full. It'll be a beautiful drive down the beach road."

She hesitated, but he was optimistic because she hadn't said "no," immediately.

"Will you promise to bring me back when I ask you to?"

"Of course. We navy men are all gentlemen."

"That's not what some of my girlfriends have told me about sailors." She spoke with a laugh in her voice, not with malice. "And my father warned me about you navy men. You have a girl in every port."

Dario watched her mouth as she spoke. Her teeth were perfectly even and brilliantly white, a perfect contrast to her dark skin and red lips. "Well, this is the first port I've ever visited, so you can be my girl in this port. You're Miss Fort Walton Beach."

As they walked to his car he paused behind her and watched her tiny, erect buttocks bob up-and-down as she walked. When the got to the car Tammy exclaimed, "Oh, it's a sports car! I just love sports cars."

This made him feel good about his prospects. Babbo once told him that he could never be sure about what would attract a girl. "Sometimes it's a dozen little things that add up to make her want you, not just big things, like you are handsome and have lots of money. The more arrows you have in your quiver, Dario, the more chances you have to hit the bulls-eye."

"These seats are comfortable," she said as she sat in the passenger seat. "What kind of material is this?"

"It's real leather. All the finer English cars use it."

"Smells nice, too. I love the way new cars smell."

Dario couldn't pass up a straight line. He leaned across the transmission hump and kissed her on her cheek. "I like the way you smell, too."

"Thank you. I try to use just a little perfume, but not too much. I think too much perfume is overwhelming, don't you?"

"I sure do. You wear just the right amount, Tammy. And, I like your make up and the way you do your hair. In fact, you are a very, very pretty girl. Thanks for coming with me." She didn't reply. She just looked forward as he drove east.

The air was warm, and the moon was directly above them as he drove at 45 miles-per-hour. There was almost no other traffic on the road. He told Tammy about his old MG-TC, and how he'd raced it several times. He also told her about his father's skill as a race mechanic, and how he'd learned mechanics from him. "I'm going to modify this car as soon as I can, and race it, if there are any sports car races around here."

"Oh, they have a race at Hurlburt Field, every year. I've seen it twice, which is why I love sports cars. But I've never been in one before. It's real exciting, Dan. I like being so close to the ground and I'm just the right size for such a little car, don't you think so?"

It was another straight line he couldn't let pass. "I think you're the perfect size for everything, Tammy, and a perfect size, everywhere."

Again, she didn't reply. When he'd driven about ten miles out of town and saw no signs of habitation along the beach, he let the car slowly decelerate. "Shall we stop and take a walk on the beach? It's such a beautiful night."

"All right. If you can find a good place to park."

He pulled off at a flat spot in the sand next to the road, about three feet from the pavement.

"I can't find the door handle."

"It's a wire inside the door. Wait, I'll come around and get it for you."

He opened the door for her, and as she stood up, he put his arms around her and held her next to him. She didn't resist, but she kept her head down. He wanted to kiss her, but she only offered him the top of her head. He put his hand under her chin and tried to gently lift it, but she resisted.

"No," she said softly. "I just met you."

Dario released her and held her hand as they walked over the low dunes to the flat sand of the beach. Near the surf line they stopped and took off their sandals and walked barefoot, letting the warm sea waves end their journey to land around their ankles.

Low and Slow

"I hope there aren't any stinging jellyfish in this water. I saw a guy get stung by one at Pensacola Beach. He was in a lot of pain."

Tammy said nothing. She continued to let him hold her hand, but she remained silent. They walked for about five minutes before she finally spoke. "I think we'd better go back now, please. I go to church early on Sunday mornings."

Dario had already given up any hope of love on the beach in the moonlight. He guessed it would take at least two dates before he could get anywhere with Tammy, so he decided to give up for tonight and play Mr. Nice Guy. They turned and walked back toward the car in silence, still holding hands. She resisted again when he tried to kiss her as he helped her into her seat.

He started the car and when he released the clutch the MG didn't move forward. He gave the engine more power and tried again, but still the car didn't move. He looked at Tammy, and without asking she told him, "You're stuck in the sand, Dan. I thought you knew about pulling off the road along the beach. It's real easy to get stuck down here."

"What do I do now?"

"Try rocking the car from reverse to forward. Sometimes that gets it out."

He tried, but the rear wheels only dug deeper into the sand. When he got out and inspected them, he found that they were so deep the rear bumper was touching the sand. Tammy got out and helped him push the car, but they couldn't move it. "You're dug in real good, Dan. You'll need a shovel, and some boards, to get this one out. Or, someone to pull you out with a rope."

"I'm awfully sorry about this, Tammy. I'm just a jerk from California who's too stupid to know about parking in sand. I guess the best thing to do is try to flag down the next car and get some help. I'll get you home as soon as I can."

She came to him, stood in front of him and put her hands on his shoulders, her face turned up to his. "Everybody gets stuck in the sand here sooner or later, Dan. For you, I guess it was just sooner."

He hugged her gently, putting his cheek next to hers. He whispered softly into her ear, "Thanks for being so understanding. I do feel like a jerk, though. The big college graduate from California, with a brand new sports car, stuck in the sand his first time out in the real world."

While they waited for a car to come down the road, Dario tried digging out the sand in front of the wheels, with his hands. It was slow work, but at least it made him feel as though he was doing something positive.

"There's a car coming, Dan. From the Fort Walton direction."

At least he had the foresight to have the white beach towel out, ready to wave it as a flag when a car appeared. He grabbed the towel and went to the side of the road. The car was approaching slowly, and as it got nearer he could hear music from its radio playing at full volume. He stepped onto the pavement a few feet and waved the towel. The car stopped a few feet from him, blinding him with its bright headlights.

"Dario, what in the hell you doing out here? We've been looking all over for you, even checked back at the motel." It was Bill's voice, coming from his Ford Fairlane. Dario gave a great sigh of relief as he approached the car. With Bill were the two other cadets, and three girls. They were all laughing, talking loudly, and apparently quite drunk, including Bill.

"Shit, Dario. You sure beat us to the beach."

"I sure did! I'm the first to get stuck in the sand. Give me a hand, guys, I'm sure the four of us can push it out."

Tammy steered the MG as they pushed. After two attempts, it came out of its hole and rolled onto the pavement.

Bill pulled Dario aside and whispered, "We've got three enlisted WAFs from Eglin Field and we're going to score, big-time. We're going down the beach where there's a parking area the girls know about. Why don't you follow us and we'll make a party out of it. We've got beer, and rum and Cokes."

"Rum and Cokes, who drinks that?"

"The broads. And do they drink it! We're going to really score, Dario. How're you doing with that midget cutie?"

No luck. I picked a girl who has to get home early because she gets up at the crack of dawn to go to church. I'm playing it straight with her, though. I might get some action at a later date, who knows? I have to get her back to town now, I promised her. I'll see you guys back at the motel."

"That's pussy chasing. Win a few, lose a few," Bill commiserated.

Tammy was still in his car when he returned, after the Ford left in a squeal of rubber. He'd seen the look of surprise on her face when Bill first yelled to him. After he'd turned around and started back toward Fort Walton, he said, "My real name is Dario, Dario D'Angelo. I was born in San Francisco, but my parents came from Italy. When I use my name down here, people think I'm a foreign cadet from Italy, so I told you a more English-sounding name." He didn't look at her while he spoke.

She put her hand on his, which was on the gear shift knob between them. "I guessed it was something like that. Besides, I like Dario better. I've never been out with an Italian before. I loved the Italian actor, Rossano Brazzi in the movies about Italy, *Three Coins in the Fountain*, and in *Summertime*. Did you see them?"

"Sure did. I loved both of them. I used to go to the movies a lot. I love movies. Do you?"

"Oh, yes. I love them, too. I go all the time." She pulled her legs up and sat on them, turning in her seat and facing him. She put her arms around his right arm, hugging it. It was the first time she'd shown any affection. "Dario, do you speak Italian?"

"Yes."

"Would you speak Italian to me? I just love to hear it."

Babbo, you old rogue, you were right about the arrows. No more Dan for this Italian, ever again.

He looked in his rear-view mirror. There were no car lights. He stopped the MG in the middle of the road, put his arms around her and kissed her. *"Faccina mia, Lei è bellissima, molte dulce,"* he whispered in her ear. She was a beautiful little face, and nice, and sweet.

Back at the dance casino, he kissed her goodnight, standing by her car, and she let him hold her tightly. He didn't want to push his luck, so he only brushed his hand over the tiny cheeks which stood out like individual balloons below her waist. "I've got to go to New Orleans next weekend with the cadet band, but I'll have liberty the following weekend. It's my birthday. Would you like to go to the movies with me? I could pick you up on Saturday, we could have lunch in Pensacola, and go to the big theater there in the afternoon."

And hopefully, a little motel action after, he wished.

"I don't go to the movies in Pensacola. I only go on the base."

"Why not? It's a nice theater, it's air-conditioned."

She hesitated a second, then held her head up as she said, "Because I'm considered a Negro, Dario. My father is a Negro and my mother is a Filipina. Dad met her when he was stationed at Clark Airbase, in the Philippines. I don't go to the movies because they want me to sit in the segregated balcony. Do you want to sit with me up there?" She began crying, softly, pressing her face against his chest. He could feel her sobs as well as hear them.

"Don't cry, Tammy, please. You're a sweet, beautiful girl. I'll sit with you anywhere."

"No, it would be too embarrassing for me, and you'd get in trouble."

"What would they do, burn a cross in front of the barracks?" He was speaking too loudly, so he calmed himself down, he didn't want to upset her any further. He patted her back gentle as he told her, "Forget the red neck movie theater. How about driving down to Panama City? I've never been there before, have you?"

She pulled away from him slightly, and caught her sobs as she wiped her eyes and nose with a Kleenex she'd taken from her pocket. His question seemed to have cheered her up. "Oh yes, many times. It's big, compared to Fort Walton. There's a lot to do. They even have a marine show, with performing porpoises and seals."

"Would you go there with me, Tammy? We could have a nice, quiet weekend."

She didn't answer. She opened her car door and got in. Dario closed the door for her. Tammy rolled down her window. "Where would we stay?" she asked.

"We'd get a motel. I wish I could afford separate rooms, but I can't. But I'll get a room with two beds."

She remained quiet and looked perplexed.

"I know it sounds contrived, but believe me, it's not sex I'm after. It's companionship. I don't want to be alone on my birthday and you're the only girl I've met since I've been in Florida. Please go with me."

He had one hand on the sill of her window and she put hers on it. "For some reason, I trust you, Dario. I'll go with you. You call me and we'll decide where and when to meet." She took a piece of paper from her purse and wrote her phone number on it. "I go to school on Monday and Wednesday nights, so call me the Thursday before. Oh, and what do you want for your birthday?"

The answer flashed in his mind, but not to his lips. It was the one straight line he did resist. "Just having you with me will be the best present I've ever had." He reminded himself not to let her see his driver's license or ID card, because his birthday wasn't until the following month. He put his head through the open window and kissed her gently. "Goodbye, Tammy. I'll call you a week from Thursday."

"Dario, would you say goodnight to me in Italian, please."

He sighed. *"Ma certo. Buona notte, carissima. Non vedo l'ora accarezzare il suo meraviglioso culo."*

He had to admit to himself, "I can't wait to fondle your marvelous ass," did sound romantic in Italian.

CHAPTER ELEVEN

THE TRAINING intensified during the last weeks of Pre-Flight. Dario learned what made airplanes fly, why the weather changes, and when to salute. He was in the best physical shape of his life, the result of four hours of physical training every day. He'd run the obstacle course within the prescribed time, and swum one mile with his clothes on. He'd also gone through the terror of the Dilbert Dunker trainer, a mock cockpit that slid down a track into the swimming pool and turned over, simulating a ditched aircraft. Navy flight students had been called "Dilberts" by their instructors since before World War II.

He especially enjoyed, and excelled, at hand-to-hand combat training. His wrist and finger muscles, because of his piano training, were very strong, making his open-hand jabs lightning fast and solid. His instructor even commented favorably on his prowess.

One Friday morning, while the band marched and played for a Pre-Flight class graduation, Dario was in the band room playing the grand piano. He'd played "Three Coins in the Fountain," because he'd been thinking about Tammy constantly and counting the days until Thursday when he'd call her and confirm their date for the following weekend. He was playing with his eyes closed and head bent as he concentrated on the chord structure, and Tammy, when he heard a shrill voice with a Brooklyn accent shout, "D'Angelo! Just what in the hell are you doin'?"

Dario stood up, turned, and faced Sergeant Major Pflueger. He hesitated with his response for a few seconds, then said, "This big piece of furniture with the black and white things on the front is called a piano, sergeant. What I was doing was making noise come out of it. The noise is called music."

The sergeant stood with his left arm akimbo, while his right hand tapped his swagger stick against his knee. His wide brimmed, felt, campaign hat was tilted slight forward on his head. He glared at Dario with one eye closed, as if he were taking careful aim through the sights of his well-oiled rifle. "Well, it's good to hear some truth come out of that wise-ass mouth of yours, mister. It's noise, all right, but it sure don't sound like no music to me." Then the sergeant held out his left arm, tapped his wrist watch with his stick and said, "It's fifteen-hundred hours, mister. Do you know what that means?"

He hesitated with his answer for a split second, but he couldn't resist Pflueger's straight line. "Yes I do, sergeant. It means Mickey's little hand is on the three, and his big hand is on the twelve."

Pflueger clenched his teeth and spoke between them. "No, mister, it means you should be out there marchin' with the rest of them tootie-frooties, blowin' on their horns and beatin' on their tomtoms! You got some kind of a medical excuse?"

"No. I'm the band manager. I don't march."

Pflueger dropped his arms to his side and began to walk slowly, making a circle around Dario and the piano. As he walked, he continued to tap his knee with his stick. "You don't march? What do you mean, you don't march, mister? What do you do at fifteen-hundred hours, if you don't march?"

"I organize the music. I inventory everything for our trips. I . . . "

The sergeant interrupted him with, "Do you ever march, D'Angelo?"

"No."

Pflueger continued his circle, inspecting Dario up-and-down. He held his left-hand palm up, and tapped his swagger stick into it. "You look like a cadet, your haircut and your uniform's correct, I'll give you that. But if you can't march, you ain't no cadet, mister. A cadet is in training to be an officer. How do you expect to be a leader of men if you can't march them into combat?"

Dario bit softly on his tongue, trying to remain silent. He couldn't. He scraped his tongue with his teeth as words flowed out of his mouth. "I joined to be a naval aviator, sergeant, not a gravel cruncher. If I wanted to march, I would have let myself be drafted and I'd be a dog face soldier in the army by now."

He looked at the sergeant's face. Marines despise the army and hate the word "soldier," so he expected Pflueger's face to be swelling with rage, and red with anger; but, it wasn't. It looked calm and cool. Pflueger stopped, squeezed his swagger stick in his left hand, and gave Dario one last steely-eyed stare before he spun on his highly polished shoes and marched quickly out of the band room, leaving Dario standing in front of the big piece of furniture with the black and white things.

After the band had stored all their instruments, Dario told Chief Shaw about his encounter with Pflueger. The chief was wearing his white uniform, perspiration showing through the armpits of his jacket. "I was playing the piano and I don't know how long he was standing behind me. He seemed upset when I told him I didn't march."

The chief shook his head from side-to-side. "He had no right to come into the band room. But, if I call him on it, officially, it would just start trouble. Pflueger should know the band manager doesn't march, never has. It was that way when I got this job. He must have some special hard-on for you. Did you cross him, somehow?"

Dario shrugged his shoulders. "I don't know. In indoctrination, I didn't let him suck me into a loaded question. I guess I gave him a smart-ass answer and I saw a look on his face that I didn't like. I saw it again today."

The chief sat and wiped his face with a towel, still perspiring heavily. "You gotta watch out for marines. They've got heads like rocks, but once something penetrates, it never leaves. When something gets in their craw, they never forget it. There's nobody I'd rather have in front of me than a marine when a fight or a battle starts but the rest of the time, I stay away from them. You might remember that and do the same."

"But chief, they're all around us here in Pre-Flight. They run the show." His voice revealed his desperation. "I'll be glad when I finish Pre-Flight and get away from them."

"No such luck. They're out there as flight instructors, too. You won't get away from them until you get to a fleet squadron. Meanwhile, just try to keep out of their way and don't rattle their cages." Chief Shaw wiped the perspiration from the back of his neck. "I don't think Pflueger will make any stink about you not marching, but, if he does, I'll back you up. You were only following standing orders." The chief took off his jacket. The outline of his sleeveless undershirt was clearly visible through his sweat-soaked shirt. "You got everything ready for this weekend's trip?"

"Yes, chief. All ready for New Orleans."

* * *

He was told to report to the Officer-in-Charge of his battalion the following Monday afternoon. The cadets of Battalion Three had little contact with Captain Norman B. Speck, United States Marine Corps. He would appear at musters and at special lectures when he spoke to the whole battalion, but only those who'd made a serious infraction to the rules, and had to stand before him to be assigned punishment, ever saw him personally. And those that had said he was always pleasant and fair. Nevertheless, Dario was apprehensive about his summons. He knew he wasn't being called to the captain's office to be awarded extra liberty or free beer at the Cadet Club. Nothing good came from an order to report to a senior officer's office. He prepared himself by putting an extra special shine on his shoes, and carefully polishing his brass belt buckle, and then only handling it with a handkerchief, to avoid defiling it with fingerprints.

D.E. " Butch" Bucciarelli

Captain Speck was sitting behind his desk as Dario entered his office after knocking loudly on the door frame. The desk was standard military metal, painted grey and sitting on a grey carpet. It was facing the door, with a window behind it. Several framed pictures of fighter aircraft hung on high-gloss tan painted walls. Sergeant Major Pflueger was standing to the left of the desk. Dario advanced and saw Captain Speck's name plaque also had a carving of Mount Fuji behind his name. He came to attention before the desk and said, "Cadet D'Angelo reporting as ordered, sir."

Speck was tall and thin, with broad shoulders. His hair was cut shorter than required by regulation, as it was by most marines. He wore naval aviator wings on his tropical wool khaki shirt, above four rows of ribbons. There was a Silver Star, the Distinguished Flying Cross, and the Air Medal with clusters, as well as the blue and white ribbon for service in Korea.

"At ease, D'Angelo." Speck said it more as a matter of politeness than as a command. "The sergeant here is concerned about your military training, or lack of it, to be more precise. I talked to Chief Shaw. He told me you were following his orders, not shirking any duty by being in the band room playing the piano while the others marched. Sergeant Major Pflueger took the matter to Colonel Freeling, who wasn't aware of the situation. He's put out an order that you must demonstrate the Manual of Arms and field-strip the M1 rifle before graduation. I've had to cancel your Saturday liberty this weekend, and Sergeant Major Pflueger has volunteered to drill you, so you'll be able to graduate. Any questions?"

"No, sir. Thanks you, sir."

Dario looked at Pflueger, who was smiling. *I'll bet he hasn't been this happy since he last bayoneted a North Korean,* Dario told himself.

"Well, it's just one lost Saturday. You'll be an ensign in a few weeks. I've reviewed your record, D'Angelo. You're doing a fine job. Keep it up."

"Aye, aye, sir."

"Dismissed." Dario came to attention, spun into an about-face, and marched out of the room. He was just passing through the door when Speck called to him, "Oh, D'Angelo! Chief Shaw also said you're doing a fine job for him. He said the horn section has never sounded better."

Dario wondered if the captain's statement was for him, or for Pflueger? *Tootie-frooties they may be, but at least they're on key.*

* * *

"Goddamn marines!" Dario told Bill when he saw him at the beer bar of the Cadet Club that evening. "I've got a date this weekend with the midget cutie with the bubble-butt, and now I have to cancel it. Sergeant Major Pflueger is going to sacrifice his Saturday so I can learn to play with the M1 rifle and learn to lead troops up Mount Suribachi. My liberty's been canceled because of that prick."

"What're you going to do?"

"Do? What do you think I'm going to do? I'm going to watch Pflueger and learn the Manual of Arms, that's what I'm going to do. Shit, that lovely little thing will be all alone while I spend the weekend with Pflueger while he does his imitation of John Wayne in, *The Sands of Iwo Jima.*

* * *

Dario detected a hint of disappointment in Tammy's voice when he gave her the bad news over the phone, but she was very understanding. "But didn't you tell them it's your birthday?"

"It wouldn't do any good. Marines don't understand birthdays, because they don't have them. Nobody writes down the date when their birth rock is turned over."

"Will you call me again, soon?"

"Sure, *bellissima,* we'll go out the first weekend I get free." He said goodbye to her in lewd Italian.

CHAPTER TWELVE

ALTHOUGH HE thoroughly enjoyed his platonic time with Tammy and looked forward to another try at seducing her, his libido compelled him to put her in abeyance and accept Bill Metz's invitation to join him on his next liberty for Cuba Libras, and two sure-thing air force enlisted girls from Eglin Field. Bill had seen them for three weekends, while Dario had spent his playing big brother to Tammy, the band, and the M1 rifle.

"Dario, you won't believe these broads. All they want to do is screw and drink, drink and screw. I don't know what's wrong with those air force pukes, but they sure don't seem to satisfy their women. Your date, Julie, was with us the night we pushed you out of the sand. She remembers you, says you're cute and she wants to go out with you, which just shows how stupid and low class they are, and how perfect they are for us."

Everything went just as Bill had promised. They met the girls in Panama City on Friday night, went out of town to a beach and made out on the sand. They drank Cuba Libras, made love on—and un-der—their blankets (when the breeze dropped, the mosquitos came out), and swam in the dark waters, rum-brave against the dreaded, invisible jellyfish. His date was an experienced and aggressive lover who neither expected, nor dispensed, any obligation. She was a high school graduate from Iowa who used her air force enlistment to escape the boredom and restrictions of prairie life. Someday, she would return to that life, settle down, and be a respectable wife and mother. But first, she was sowing wild oats. Something that men had done for centuries was now possible for women, thanks to the modern military.

They dropped the girls off at the Eglin Air Force Base gate about one a.m. and drove to their motel in Panama City. They'd just turned a corner when they heard a siren behind them. Not a loud, long wail of a siren; just a "whee-uhh" short blast. The rear of the Fairlane was suddenly bathed in red light; deputy sheriff, red light.

"You boys been drinkin' tonight?" The deputy shined his flashlight through the open window onto their faces.

"Just a couple of beers, officer," Bill answered, with difficulty.

"Well, them is might-tee strong beers y'all bin drinkin', 'cause I can smell 'em way out here. Get out of the car, boys. I'm takin' you in for driving while intoxicated."

"But I'm not driving, officer. Why do I have to get out of the car?" Dario protested.

"Oh, don't you worry 'bout that little tech-no-cality. We got a charge that will fit you to a tee. It's called, 'plain drunk in public.' "

They spent the rest of the night in a cell with ten others who were in various stages of inebriation. They slept on a hard shelf in the peaceful sleep alcohol provides the condemned. They'd given their address to the booking officer, who then asked to see their military identification cards. They had no idea what was happening to them, but they discovered it at 7:30 the next morning. They were awakened by Chief Nederlander, who was in charge of the navy's Panama City Shore Patrol office. The chief was very businesslike, and not at all officious or critical. He took them in a grey navy Chevrolet to the Shore Patrol office, where Bill's Ford was parked.

"I don't know why the deputy stopped me," Bill told the chief. "I wasn't speeding. I didn't run any stop signs."

"When Deputy Sheriff Zephyr Jackson sees a pink and white convertible with Wisconsin plates and two young men in it at one-thirty in the morning, he plays the odds and bets you've been drinking. Zephyr does very well with his betting. He seldom loses."

"What do I do, chief?"

"The navy's guaranteed your bail, and you have to come back on Wednesday for a court appearance. You're in big trouble, Metz. If you can afford it, I suggest you see a lawyer named Martin. He has a way of handling these things."

"Can I see him today, Saturday?"

"Yeah, his office is at his home. Here's his card. You can use our phone."

Bill called and made an immediate appointment. The chief gave them directions to the lawyer's home. "Just listen to Martin," the chief told him. "He's local, knows the system, and he's as fair as any of 'em."

* * *

"Deputy Jackson isn't cheap and he doesn't give quantity discounts. I've been doing business with him long enough to know that," Martin told them. They were in his office, which was attached to his house. Martin was a very fat man, wearing a dark cotton bathrobe and carpet slippers. "It'll cost five hundred for the DWI and fifty for the drunk charge, including my fee. If you want to retain me, give me a dollar now and the balance before court on Wednesday."

Bill took out his wallet, pulled out a dollar bill and handed it to the lawyer who snapped it from Bill's hand. "I'll call my dad. He'll wire the money. We'll see you on Wednesday, Mr. Martin."

"OK boys, you got a deal. You just get the money and I'll take care of everything. Don't worry about a thing."

His appearance and manor did not breed confidence, but they did trust Chief Nederlander's advice.

Low and Slow

"Yeah, don't worry about a thing, except out-of-uniform and out-of-bounds. Too bad the mouthpiece can't fix the navy," Dario said to Bill as they drove away. "What'll we do now, we going back to the base?"

"Fuck no. We're still meeting the girls at noon. Look, if we're going to get kicked out of the program, it won't matter if we're here for one day or two days. Nobody in Pre-Flight's going to find out about it until Monday morning, anyway. We might as well have our fun, get some nooners. Condemned men get a last meal, don't they?"

They stopped at a phone booth and Bill called his father. "I got caught in a southern scam, Dad. The local yokels want to make an example of me, so I have to pay off everyone down to the dog catcher to get out of the mess." His father told him the money would be at the Pensacola telegraph office by Sunday evening.

Dario wondered what his mother would tell him if he called her. Every time he'd asked her for money while growing up, he had to argue with her to get it. He had a pretty good idea of what she'd say if he called. "Dario, it's cheaper to go to jail, and they have to feed you." Mama was always very practical with money. Her favorite saying was: "For buy, look. For free, take!"

* * *

They heard nothing from the Battalion Commander on Monday, but they were extremely worried, especially Dario. The fear of not getting his commission, and flight pay—which would also mean losing his car—was very real. A few weeks before, a cadet in another class was caught looking at someone else's paper during a test. He wasn't only immediately washed out, he was forced to wear a seaman recruit's sailor uniform and stay with his cadet class for two days, as an example for the others to see. It seemed to Dario that being drunk, out-of-bounds and out-of-uniform were much more serious than looking at someone's test paper. He was certain he and Bill would be washed out of the program.

D.E. " Butch" Bucciarelli

* * *

The courthouse building was an old red brick building in excellent repair, with glistening white columns and ornate gold leaf on its facade. It looked like the building of a prosperous business. Lawyer Martin was waiting in the entry. His once-white, wrinkled suit fit tightly on his body. Bill handed him a thick envelope containing five hundred and fifty dollars in cash which he took with a plump hand and placed inside his jacket.

"Thank you, kindly," he said. "Now, here's what you do, boys. When the judge asks you if you're guilty or not guilty, you just say 'not guilty, your honor.' Don't say another word, you understand? Just say 'not guilty' and everything will take care of itself."

The courtroom was as attractive as the outside of the building. Paneling, chairs, tables and benches were all varnished mahogany and modern air-conditioning made the room comfortably cool. When their case was called, the clerk read the charges against Bill, and then the judge asked him, "How do you plead? Guilty or not guilty?"

"Not guilty, your honor." Bill responded, standing at attention.

Dario answered the same after he was asked. He'd seen the scene in so many movies he felt as if what was happening wasn't real until he noticed the judge's hairpiece was slipping, which brought him back to reality. The reality was heightened when the judge called for the arresting officer to be sworn in. The deputy sheriff came forward and swore on a tattered Bible to tell the truth.

"Well, Zephyr, were they drunk?" the judge asked in a matter-of-fact manner when the deputy was settled in the witness seat.

"I'm not quite sure, judge. I thought they'd been drinkin', although they were drivin' OK. But it was late an' I thought I'd better take 'em into protective custody, just to be sure."

"I guess it's easy to be mistaken that late at night, eh Zephyr?"

"It surely is, Judge. It surely is."

"Charges dismissed," the judge said, hitting his gavel on a block of wood and causing his toupee to slip slightly farther to the side.

Low and Slow

Dario again felt as if the scene were from a movie. *I've escaped death row and the hot seat. I'm a free man,* he rejoiced to himself.

Outside the courthouse, they thanked Martin, who was very gracious. "No, I thank you, boys. You keep coming back to Panama City. We like the business you bring. It helps the entire community."

* * *

His joy of freedom was short-lived. When they returned to the base, they were ordered to report to the Commanding Officer of the entire Pre-Flight Corps, Lieutenant Colonel Freeling. The yeoman outside his office told them to put their hats back on, because they were getting a captain's mast, which the navy called "non-judicial punishment," which made it either another of the navy's many oxymorons or one of its more appropriately-named procedures. Dario wiped his shoes across the back of his trouser legs to remove any dust. They entered, stood at attention and saluted Freeling, who was also wearing his cap and standing behind a podium. Sergeant Major Pflueger was standing behind the colonel, wearing a broad smile, like he'd just won the hand grenade tossing event at the Marine Olympics. Dario noticed a ubiquitous Mount Fuji name plaque sitting on the front of the colonel's desk. In one corner of the room an American flag stood in a pedestal. There was a marine corps flag in the opposite corner.

Freeling looked exactly like a marine colonel should. He was handsome, with broad shoulders and a thin waist. His chest sprouted five rows of campaign ribbons under his wings of gold.

"You two were out-of-uniform and out-of-bounds, according to the Panama City Shore Patrol report. Is the report correct?" His voice was loud, clear, and stern.

"Yes, sir." They answered in unison.

"I see by your records that neither of you have received any demerits before. Also, your scholastic records are satisfactory."

Dario felt the first glimmer of hope.

"Because of your records, I'm going to give you two a break. I'm only going to give you seventy demerits each. Five more, and you'd be wearing white hats and swabbing destroyer decks before you knew what hit you. Do you understand how close you are to being washed out?"

"Yes, sir, thank you sir." They again responded as one.

"D'Angelo, it's a good thing the good sergeant here gave up his Saturday to teach you how to march. You two have only two weeks until graduation, if you make it, so I guess I don't have to warn you about wearing civilian clothes or going out-of-bounds again. Seventy demerits, that's fourteen hours on the grinder."

Dario looked at Pflueger and saw that his rare smile had turned to his usual frown.

"Yes, sir," they echoed each other.

"Dismissed!"

Bill and Dario saluted, did an about face, and marched from the room.

Dario was pleasantly shocked that he hadn't been washed out of the program, but he was also confused. He and Bill had gotten in trouble with the law, and broken all kinds of navy rules. But instead of being dressed up in a sailor suit like the test paper voyeur, they were only put on the edge of expulsion, with demerits they could erase. It would take him a long time to understand the unwritten workings of the navy, and that some infractions of the "boys will be boys" nature were tolerated; but cheating, definitely, was not.

* * *

They marched every evening and on Saturday. Dario's feet hurt, his shoulder ached, and his arms felt like they were going to fall off. There was a large gardenia bush growing near the end of the grinder that was exploding with lush, white blooms. Its pungent aroma was breathtaking. The only pleasure Dario got from the punitive marching was breathing in the sweet bouquet every time he came to a stop at that end and did an about-face. His journey to the opposite end, and the return, seemed to go quicker when he marched in anticipation of the perfumed reward. The gardenias, and the magnolia trees that flourished throughout the base, were new to him; they didn't grow in North Beach. They became symbols to him of his new life in the South, and in the navy.

With soreness, blisters, and boredom, he and Bill completed their 14 hours on the grinder the day before graduation. When Dario joyfully returned his M1 to the armory, he felt as relieved as a Spanish galley slave giving up his oar after being freed.

"I know another reason why I could never be a marine," he told Bill. "The assholes call their rifle, 'their best friend.' "

* * *

"That's the ultimate insult," Dario shouted over the shower spray. "You're telling me I have to hand that Neanderthal, Pflueger, a dollar bill when he salutes me?"

"That's right," Brandon Thursted told him. They were in the shower at the gym, after an hour of climbing a rope and other gymnastics. "It's another navy tradition. You have to hand a dollar to the first enlisted man who salutes you after you get your commission, and Pflueger has the concession. He'll be outside the door as we exit the graduation ceremony. He gets a buck from every one of us."

"My father would have wiped his ass with the bill first. He always did, when he had to pay a traffic fine."

* * *

"I, Dario Enrico D'Angelo, having been appointed an ensign in the United States Naval Reserve, do accept and do solemnly swear that I will support and defend the Constitution of the United States against all enemies, foreign and domestic, that I will bear true faith and allegiance to the same; that I take this obligation freely, without any reservation or purpose of evasion; and that I will well and faithfully discharge the duties of the office on which I am about to enter, so help me God." He swore the oath aloud with the rest of his classmates.

As he walked out the door with his commission under the arm of his white uniform, he put on his officer's cap. There was a line going out the door and Pflueger was at the end of it, snapping off salutes and collecting dollar bills. When Dario came to the end of the line, Pflueger said, "Good afternoon, Ensign D'Angelo, sir!" He snapped a salute, clicking his heels together as he held out his hand.

Pflueger hadn't used the names of the other new ensigns whom he saluted and Dario didn't like the affected smile on the sergeant's face. It was more than a one-dollar smile.

"Good afternoon, sergeant." Dario returned a slovenly salute and held out his left hand which was slightly clenched. "Catch," he said as he opened his hand and let nickels and dimes pour into Pflueger's palm. "I'm a little short, I owe you a nickel." He was pleased when the sergeant's phony smile turned into his standard frown.

The realization that he'd made it really hit him when he got his second salute from the gate guard at Whiting Field. He was no longer wearing cadet insignia. He now sported the shiny gold bars of an ensign. He'd completed the first important step of his training— he'd become an officer. Fourteen weeks of intense academic, military and physical training were behind him, and he was pleased with himself for completing the course with grades in the top ten-percent of his class. He *could* compete academically with Ivy Leaguers, in spite of his music degree from a teachers' college. But, despite his academic achievement, he'd come to the brink of failure because he broke the rules in the pursuit of girls and a good time. And, although now an officer, he could still be washed out and sent to destroyer duty, which would mean losing flight pay and subsequently his new MG. He vowed he would be careful, stay out of trouble, and work hard to get his wings. He would be celibate, if necessary, and wait to enjoy the spoils when he was a real naval aviator. Then he'd have another go at Wanda's synthetic fibers.

CHAPTER THIRTEEN

THE NEW flight students met in the Whiting Field auditorium for an introduction lecture. At the end, a mimeographed sheet was passed out which assigned them to flight groups and listed their flight schedules. Dario couldn't find his name anywhere on the list. He almost panicked. His anxiety must have been showing on his face as Ensign Brandon Thursted walked up to him. He'd often seen Brandon during their weeks together in Pre-Flight, but they'd never socialized together. Dario always greeted him with "Hello, Toke," which they both understood was short for Token, as in Token Nigger. "Hi, Jazz Guinea," or some derivation, was always Brandon's reply.

"Looking for your name, Jazzman?"

"Hi, Toke. Yeh, I can't find it."

"You're on a different sheet. So am I. We're in the same flight group. We're with the outcasts. We're assigned to SNJs."

Dario couldn't believe what he was hearing. He didn't believe it until Brandon handed him another mimeographed sheet and he found his name on it. He didn't even know that there were still some SNJs around. They were the Secret Navy Jets Lieutenant Commander Baird had joked about back in Oakland. The S signified scout, the N was for trainer, and the J, somehow in another of the navy's mysterious ways, was the designation for the North American Aircraft Corporation. Far from being a jet, the SNJ first flew in the 1930s. Like the Secret Navy Bomber he'd flown in with Baird, it had a tail wheel, not a modern nose wheel. It had been the advanced trainer of the air force and the navy during World War II, and had seen duty with almost every allied country in that war, including combat. All Dario had ever been told about it was how lucky he was that it was being replaced by new aircraft; the T-34 primary trainer and the T-28 advanced trainer. He'd also heard that the SNJ was a student killer—hard to fly, and even harder to land—and that they were so old, and so tired, they were referred to as: "Twenty-thousand parts flying in close formation."

"This is bullshit. I'm not going to take it!"

Dario went to the Squadron Duty Officer and asked permission to talk to the Commanding Officer of his training squadron. "What do you want to see him about?" the lieutenant (junior grade) SDO asked.

"I got assigned to SNJs. I want to fly T-34s."

"You're wasting your time. Mainside Pensacola makes the assign-ments before you get here, probably some white hat picks names out of a hat or throws darts at a roster. I don't know how they do it, but once they're cast in the concrete of lower rank Mainside bureaucracy, we can't change them—even if we wanted to." The SDO's indifferent manner indicated that they didn't want to.

"But why did I get stuck with them? I was near the top of my class, academically. Why me?"

"I told you, they probably drew your name out of a hat. We thought we'd have enough T-34s by now, but we don't. We fill gaps with the few SNJs we've got that are still flyable."

There was an instructor standing in the room as Dario and the SDO were talking, reading a list on a clipboard, which was hanging on the wall with dozens of other clipboards. He followed Dario out of the office and called to him as he walked down the hall. "Hey, mister." Dario heard him, but kept walking, not thinking he meant him. "Hey you, the SNJ ensign, hold up!"

Dario spun around and saw the officer he'd seen in the duty office. He wore a dirty khaki flight suit, with boondockers (World War

Low and Slow

II GI combat boots the navy issued as flight boots). There was a leather name tag on his flight suit, LT P. D. Tyler, USNR. He was a little overweight and his light brown hair was very thin. "Yes, sir," Dario answered.

"Let's go to the ready room and have a Coke and a little talk." Dario walked alongside him and told him his name. The ready room was a lounge area, filled with chrome-tube furniture with dark-green vinyl covering on the seats and backrests. There were metal tables covered with ragged aviation magazines—most with the covers missing—and the walls were either blackboards or notice boards, with schedules, lists, and instruction sheets held against them with thumbtacks. Five hundred pound bomb casings, cut in half and filled with sand, were sitting on their fins at each corner of the room, reeking of stale tobacco. A large fan, on a pedestal, stood at the far end of the room and slowly rotated its attempt to cool the room. The magazines and the papers on the wall rattled when the air stream passed over them.

Lieutenant Tyler went right to a tall Coke machine and put two nickels in the slot. He grabbed two bottles as they came down the chute, dripping condensation as they hit the humid air of the room. He opened the first one and handed it to Dario. When his was opened, he unzipped a small pocket on the arm of his flight suit and took out a package of cigarettes. He offered one to Dario. "Smoke?"

"No thanks."

"Watching your health, eh? That's being very optimistic for a new SNJ Dilbert." He laughed, blowing out smoke from his cigarette as he lit it. "I wanted to talk to you because I heard you tell the SDO you didn't want to fly SNJs. We don't usually get students who question their orders. You must be one of the new AOCs."

"Yes, sir. I am. I got my commission last Friday."

Tyler laughed. "I guess we'd better get used to a new breed. Guys who've been in the navy such a short time, they still aren't afraid to ask the reason why!"

"I thought I was joining a jet navy, but what do I get? My first flight, my indoctrination flight, was in an airplane that looked like it was the Lisbon Express from Casablanca. Now I find that I'm to train in an airplane designed before World War Two. What else is down the line?"

"Don't worry. There really are jet trainers in Advance." Tyler inhaled his cigarette, and took a drink of his Coke. "I don't blame you for complaining about the SNJ," he continued. "They are a piece-of-shit compared to the new trainers. But you're stuck with them and there's nothing you can do about it. But don't take it out on us here at Whiting. Some anonymous white hat over at Mainside picked you."

"Lieutenant Tyler . . . "

"Call me Pete," the lieutenant interjected.

"Thanks, Pete. If someone had it in for me, like a marine drill sergeant, could he get me put in SNJs?"

Tyler drank from his Coke bottle, then took a long drag from his cigarette. "Hell yes! Those marines have the kumshaw and buddy systems working everywhere. If the sergeant didn't know some yeoman who worked in the assignment office, he'd know someone who did. They trade favors, duties, and material all the time. You know who the sergeant is, I take it."

"Yes. The Sergeant Major of Pre-Flight cadets. He got pissed off at me because I was the band manager, marched me around with an M1, and made me learn to field-strip it, blindfolded. He's a real prick. I sure wish I could get even with him."

"Well, forget it. There's nothing you can do about it. Marines are different, just stay away from them."

"You're the second person who's told me the same thing."

"Well, that proves it's good advice." Tyler took another long drag from his cigarette. He looked Dario over as he exhaled. "Look, I know you're disappointed about getting Jay Birds, but you should consider yourself lucky."

"Jay Birds, I haven't heard them called that. I heard they were Secret Navy Jets, though. But no matter what they're called, why am I lucky to fly those old rickety airplanes? You said yourself, they're pieces-of-shit." Dario was almost shouting at Tyler.

"I know, I know. But, you're getting the last opportunity to master that ground-looping son-of-a-bitch. If you can hack it in them, you'll be a good stick and rudder man the rest of your life. Take it as a challenge. If you can fly the Jay, you can fly anything."

"But I don't know if I can fly it, Pete. I've never flown anything in my life. I'm sure the T-34 would be plenty of a challenge for me. I'm sure that prick Pflueger got me assigned to SNJs because he knows I'll wash out in them."

"Then prove him wrong. Learn to conquer it."

"How?"

"You have to rehearse. That's how I learned to fly them. I made it through in them, five years ago."

"Rehearse? Funny that you use that term. I'm a musician. I know how to rehearse an orchestra, but how in the hell do I rehearse an airplane?"

"What do you play?"

"Piano."

"Classical piano?"

"Yes, some. But mostly modern jazz, bop."

"Bop! You like Thelonius Monk?"

"Hell yes! His 'Round Midnight' is great. He plays some way-out chords, but somehow he makes them sound tasty. How do you know about him? Are you a bop musician?"

Pete laughed. "Me? Nope. I just love to listen to it." Tyler took a last drag from his cigarette and then stubbed it out in a nearby ashtray. "OK, listen up, Dario. Here's how you rehearse an airplane. Before every flight, you study the training guide and know just what maneuvers are expected of you. Then, fly the airplane through them in your mind. Pretend you have the stick in one hand and the throttle in the other. There's even an SNJ cockpit in the hangar you can sit in and hold the real things. Let me ask you this, when you play, do you know ahead of time where you're going with your notes?"

"Of course. That's what it's all about. When I play jazz, I'm always working toward the idea I want. I have to anticipate where I'm going."

"You have hit upon the secret of being a good pilot. If you can stay ahead of the airplane, anticipate what it's going to do and what you're going to do, you'll never have any problems because you'll be in control. If you get behind the airplane, it flies you."

Dario appreciated the advice he was getting. He liked Tyler.

"Here's something else I want you to remember. More SNJ students get an unsatisfactory flight from ground loops than for any other reason. If a wing comes up, the other has to go down, and if it touches the ground—and just scratches the paint—it's an automatic down. The way to avoid ground loops, is to keep the tail down. You do that by keeping the nose up. When you land the airplane, imagine that you have a big hook in your lap, right in the middle of your seat belt. You put the control stick in that hook and you hold it there with your right hand, like your sister's virtue depends on it. If you let that stick come out of the hook the tail will come up and you're likely to lose control. Just remember the hook."

"Do you instruct Basics, Pete?"

"No. I'm over at Tactics. I teach formation flying in T-28s and Jay Birds. Maybe I'll get you as a student when you get over there?"

"I'd like that. Do you know any marines who can pull strings?" Dario laughed as he spoke.

"I know a lot of marines. Tactics is loaded with the assholes."

CHAPTER FOURTEEN

WHEN DARIO called Tammy, she seemed very enthusiastic about going to Panama City. When he saw her, he was happily surprised because she looked even better than he remembered. The makeup she wore gave her cheeks a rosy hue, which, with the contrast of her dark skin, gave her a very exotic look. He picked her up in Fort Walton and they drove to Panama City, where he got a room at the same motel he'd had with Mandy.

After a day at the beach, they returned to the room and changed in the bathroom, one-at-a-time. After dinner they danced, and Tammy let him kiss her and hold her tightly. When they returned to the motel he waited outside the room, while Tammy changed and got into her bed. After she called to him, softly, through the open, screened window, he undressed in the bathroom and then came into the room in the dark, but he didn't get into his bed. He got into bed with Tammy, naked. She didn't protest. She had her back to him so he put one arm around her waist. He kissed her neck and her shoulders, while fondling her breast with one hand and her buttocks with the other. Things were progressing nicely. She wasn't fighting him or making any negative movement to avoid his advances. He gently rolled her onto her back and kissed her, putting his tongue slightly into her mouth. He could tell that she was getting aroused because she was moving her hips ever so slightly. He pulled down the sheet and began kissing her nipples. They were tiny, like the Ju-Jube candies he used to buy at the movies. He moved his hand between her legs and began to rub her gently.

"Oh, no," she moaned.

He felt it wasn't a "no" that meant "no." It was a "no" that meant surprise. He continued for several minutes and then spread her legs apart.

"Dario. I'm a virgin."

It was a condition he hadn't even considered. "Do you want me to stop?"

"I, I don't know. I've never gone this far before. I don't want to disappoint you. I guess I'll just leave it up to fate, and to you."

He was the male of the species, he was in control, he had the strong desire to perform the most human of human acts. But, he didn't. He laid next to her and held her hand. "I'm not the one, Tammy. You're too sweet a girl. You deserve better than me."

"You're disappointed," she sighed. "I wanted to please you."

"You do please me, Tammy. I'm not disappointed. You're fun to be with, you're kind and thoughtful. I'm the one who's sorry. I should have known you're a virgin."

"Oh, it's all right. It felt good, Dario. I didn't know how to react, but it felt good."

He kissed her gently on her lips. *"Bona sera, cara mia.* Go to sleep. We'll get up early, have a nice breakfast and then spend the day at the beach."

He squeezed her hand, left her bed and got into his.

Babbo would be pissed, he thought. *He just wouldn't understand.*

* * *

The students in his SNJ ground school weren't all from his AOC class. It included Naval Aviation Cadets and officers who'd come to flight training already commissioned from the many college Reserve

Low and Slow

Officer Training Corps, from the Officer Candidate School at Newport, Rhode Island and from the Naval Academy at Annapolis.

One of the things he liked most about being an officer—besides the pay—was the ability to wear short-sleeved, open-collar shirts. They were much cooler than the long-sleeved shirt and tie cadets were required to wear in Pre-Flight. He wore no undershirt, which he felt constraining and hot, so he bought a dozen shirts and changed them daily. The other commissioned benefit he enjoyed was his freedom. As an officer, he was no longer regulated from reveille to taps. He had classes and flights, but the rest of the time was his own.

The other privilege he appreciated was the officers' club. Friday afternoon happy hour at the club (which was really two hours, 4 to 6 p.m.), was one navy tradition Dario had no problem accepting, because drinks cost only twenty-five cents. He'd been told that anything goes at happy hour. It was common ground where rank was observed, but not flaunted. It was the time to vent petty gripes and frustrations, because almost anything done or said at happy hour was supposed to be sacrosanct. A junior officer could be outspoken in drink and he wouldn't be reprimanded when sober. This laxness was supposedly allowed so senior officers could spot any morale problems without the burden of chain-of-command and other navy management requirements. It was a "let your hair down" drinking session for men who worked together all week under strict and formal rules. In many fleet squadrons, attendance was mandatory.

Dario went to happy hour on his first Friday at Whiting Field. It was a white, one story building with a lobby before a long bar that led to the dining room. The rooms were built around a large outdoor swimming pool. He found Bill Metz sitting at the crowded bar. "Have a Cuba Libra," he told Dario.

"That all you drink now? No more beer?"

"Those air force broads got me hooked on them. Drinking them reminds me of fucking them in the sand." Four months in Florida and a commission hadn't robbed Bill of any of his Wisconsin charm.

An hour later, a marine major came up to Dario while he was standing near the bar with Bill and several other students. The major appeared to be in his mid-thirties, was an average height and medium build. He had small, dark, eyes, but his most striking feature was his completely bald, shaved head, which shone from the sunlight reflected from the bar mirror. Unlike most of the other officers who were wearing short-sleeved shirts, the major wore a tailored tropical wool, long-sleeved uniform shirt and tie. As with most Korean War pilots, he had four rows of ribbons below his wings.

"They tell me you're the ensign who owns that new MGA," the bald, major said. His voice was a surprise. It wasn't the gruff, deep marine-speak Dario expected. It was high, thin and nasal. Dario also detected a slight southern flavor in it.

"Yes, sir."

"I'm Major Hildripp. I'd like to have a look at it, sometime. I own a British sports car, myself."

Dario waited for him to say what kind he owned, but the major remained silent, sipping at his glass of beer. "What mark of British sports car do you have, major?" He asked the question, knowing he was playing straight man.

"Oh, it's an XK-140 Jaguar. It's the M model, if you know what that means." The major seemed to be reveling in the fact that his Jaguar cost almost three times as much as the MGA.

"Sure do. M for modified. Two-inch SU carbs, nine point five-to-one compression ratio, wire wheels, and beaded rear fenders instead of skirts." Dario spit out the information, as if he were reading it from a sales brochure.

"Well, you seem to know your sports cars. I've also got a competition leather belt across my bonnet—we call them hoods here, you know. Drive your MG over to the Tactics hangar someday, so I can look it over, and I'll show you my Jag. What is your name, mister?"

"It's D'Angelo, sir, Dario D'Angelo."

"You one of the new AOC ensigns, D'Angelo?"

"Yes, sir, I have that distinction."

"I know they had to teach you four-month-wonders a lot in a short time, but evidently nobody told you you're supposed to wear a skivvy shirt under your open-collar shirt. We don't want all that Italian body hair on your chest showing, do we?" The major then did an imitation of Sergeant Pflueger by spinning on the heels of his highly-polished Cordovan shoes and walking away.

"Fuck, Dario. What the hell was that all about?"

"What am I, Bill, some kind of goddamn marine hate magnet? Why won't those bastards leave me alone?"

He walked over to Pete Tyler, whom he'd seen at the far end of the bar area. Pete was the antithesis of Hildripp. His uniform was rumpled and wrinkled, and his shirt showed the salt of dried perspiration rings under his arm pits. Like Dario, he wore no skivvy shirt. His belly hung slightly over his belt and his hair length was several weeks beyond regulation. Dario approached him and was pleased to be immediately recognized and welcomed. "Hey there! The jazz piano man. Come on over here, D'Angelo. How you doing in your ancient history class? Has ground school taught you how to wind up the Jay Bird, yet?"

"I'm doing fine, Pete, just fine. And I'm getting a better attitude about the old relic, thanks to you."

"One of these days you've got to play a little piano for me. There's a piano in the dining room, you know."

"Do you think I could use it?"

"Sure, sure. The club manager's a nice guy. I'll introduce you."

"Pete, do you know a Major Hildripp? He's over in Tactics, where you are. He just gave me some shit about not wearing a skivvy shirt."

Tyler lowered his head and looked at Dario with his eyes rolled back in his head, as if he were looking over granny-type reading glasses. "You been here only a week and you've already run into Major Nugent Jefferson Hildripp, the Third. He's called 'The Madman,' and also, 'Super Marine.' "

"No, he ran into me. I've got a new MGA and he wants to see it, told me he has a Jaguar."

"Not just a Jaguar. It's the shiniest, best tuned Jaguar there is. We think he's transferred his marine rifle fetish to his car. He spends all his spare time polishing it, even gets under and cleans the frame. Hildripp is single. He's the proper marine, who believes that if the marine corps wanted him to have a wife, they'd issue him one. But he's married to that car. He'd take it to bed with him, if there was room."

"Is he a formation instructor?" Dario asked the question with a slight tremor of trepidation in his voice.

Pete shook his head from side-to-side. "Not anymore, thank God. He's just not suited to instruct. He's too highly strung. He used to be, but he constantly yelled at students over the radio, that's where he got the reputation as a madman. He's the operations officer. He still schedules himself as a check pilot now and then, when he's short of one, but you won't get him as an instructor."

"Why'd you call him 'Super Marine,' Pete?"

"Because he sleeps and eats the Corps. He's a first class aviator, almost an ace in Korea with four airborne victories, and I respect him for that. But he's also a first class bastard, and even some other marines in our outfit realize it. He has few friends, doesn't even have a dog. He hates everyone who isn't a white, southern, Anglo-Saxon. He is the epitome of prejudice, Dario. He loves cars, flying, eating barbecue, country music, and his authority over subordinates."

"Jesus, Pete. You seemed to have made a study of him."

"You can't be around Nug Hildripp for two years without studying him. He wants to be studied. He purposely makes himself noticed. It's the only leadership skill he has."

CHAPTER

FIFTEEN

DARIO MET his instructor, Ensign Hamminis, in the ready room. He was a "Plowback," a former NAVCAD who got ordered back to the training command when he got his wings and his commission. He was lanky, and still looked like a teenager. Dario was certain Hamminis was younger than he was, which did not instill a lot of confidence, especially as his voice broke occasionally when he spoke. "Were you an AOC D'Angelo?"

"Yes, sir." Though they were the same rank, Dario addressed him as "sir," as a student-to-instructor courtesy.

"I'll be up front with you. I'm pissed off! I have a degree, but I had to go through the whole program as a cadet to get my wings. But, I won't take it out on you. I'll treat you just like every other Dilbert I have."

"I had no doubt about that, sir. I didn't invent the program. I just joined it. If it had been available, I'm sure you would have, too."

"Yeah. You're right. I guess I'm just jealous. Right qualifications, wrong timing."

Hamminis explained to Dario that his first flight in the SNJ was only an introduction to the airplane. Dario would be sitting in the front seat and observing while Hamminis flew it from the rear seat. After they reviewed all the emergency procedures, Hamminis explained his personal bail out technique. "If we have to exit the aircraft in flight, I'll yell 'bail out' twice, but you'll only hear me once because I'll be out of the airplane the second time I yell it. You got your barf bags?"

"Yes, sir." Dario slapped his hand on a flight suit pocket in front of his calf, which held several wax-lined vomit bags.

"If you run out of bags, use your hard hat."

After they'd inspected their assigned SNJ, Dario climbed onto the wing, stood by the front cockpit and waited for Hamminis to get into the rear cockpit, another student-to-instructor civility. As Dario was being strapped into the airplane by one of the ground crew, he became aware of the odor inside the airplane. It was a combination of hot radio tubes, burned oil and aviation gasoline. The high octane, aromatic AVGAS smelled very different from the gas he was used to pumping at gas stations. It had an almost sweet odor.

He was again thrilled by the acceleration of takeoff. When the nose came down, as the tail wheel lifted, and he could see the runway in front of him, he heard his instructor's voice in the headset, which was built into his helmet. "Put your right hand gently on the stick and feel the way I move it. Notice that I don't pull back hard, I just let the airplane fly itself off the runway."

It did. The airplane left the ground without any abrupt maneuver.

"Pull up the landing gear, D'Angelo."

Dario had anticipated the order because the gear could only be raised from the front cockpit. The only revenge possible against Pflueger was to do well, so he'd studied hard during the two weeks of SNJ ground school. He'd spent hours of his free time reading about the mechanics and sitting in the mock cockpit, touching every switch and control until he could touch them blindfolded. He'd asked Tyler lots of questions and gotten good answers, many that weren't in the book. When he got into the cockpit with Hamminis, he already felt at home in the venerable airplane.

He knew how to work the gear handle, and also that doing so was futile unless he first pushed down the power push, which energized the hydraulic system. He did both and heard the whine of the gear coming up.

"Congratulations! You remembered the power push. You're already way ahead of most students I've had on their first flight."

"Thank you, sir," he said aloud, although Hamminis couldn't hear him. To be heard, he had to take the microphone out of its clip on the side console, hold it to his mouth, push the button built into it, and speak. In modern T-34s and T-28s, the mikes were mounted on the pilot's helmet and the button was in the throttle so the pilot didn't have to remove his hand to transmit. The hand-held mike was yet another indication of the obsolescence of the ancient beast he was flying. But, following Tyler' advice, he was determined to tame it.

"You got your goggles on tight, D'Angelo?"

Dario took the mike from the clip and answered, "Yes, sir."

"Open your canopy. I'm going to do a slow roll. When we get inverted, all kind of crap is going to fall out of the bilges. Dirt and gravel from shoes, cigarette butts, candy and gum wrappers, pencils. Maybe even a few beer bottle caps. Hold your breath while we're going over so you don't breathe in any of it. Put your hand on the stick and follow me through the roll."

The aircraft rolled smoothly around its longitudinal axis. As Hamminis had promised, dirt and a few unidentifiable objects did fall past his eyes, as they were inverted.

"See what I mean!" Hamminis said. "I always do a roll right away to clean out the bilges."

There *was* a bilge in the SNJ. The pilots' feet were placed on two rails, and below the rails were the guts of the airplane. There was a right and left fuel gauge down there, which were mechanical floats covered with a glass, similar to the gauges in Model A Fords, which were discontinued in 1932.

"Hold on tight. I'm going to do a split-S and show you what five-Gs feels like."

Before Dario could answer, the aircraft rolled inverted and the nose was pulled down. He heard the air increase in velocity past his open canopy and saw the ground when he looked up; they were in an upside-down dive. He looked at the altimeter. They'd been at 6000 feet and it was spinning down, rapidly. As the ground neared, he felt pressure on his shoulders, his buttocks and his neck. It was a sensation he'd never felt before. He was watching the altimeter unwind and listening to the screaming engine, and the howling air, when, suddenly, everything got quiet and the sunlight got dim as he blacked out from the loss of blood to his brain.

The sound and the light returned slowly. Dario first became aware of consciousness by seeing the microphone floating weightlessly over the instrument panel as they passed through zero Gs. Its curled chord was beneath it like a slack kite tail. Suddenly his body was straining at his shoulder straps, because the airplane was now trying to throw him out with negative Gs.

"How you feeling, D'Angelo?"

He grabbed the mike as it started to fall. The airplane was flying straight and level again.

"Fine, sir. That was really something."

"A five-G split-S, into a two-and-a-half negative G pushover. You try that in a T-34 and you'll be flying without wings. These Jay Birds might be old, but they're tough old bastards. No nausea, D'Angelo? You don't feel sick to your stomach?"

"No, sir. Let's do it again."

Hamminis laughed into the mike. "No time. Takes too long to climb back to altitude. We've got to get back to the field."

As they approached the north field at Whiting, Hamminis told Dario to pull back the throttle. As he did, a loud horn honked in the cockpit.

"You know what that noise is?"

"Yes, sir. It's the warning horn. Tells me that the power is back for landing, but the landing gear isn't down."

"Right. And if for some reason the horn doesn't work, the tower will yell to you over the radio if you try to land with the gear up. The old story is that a Dilbert landed gear up. When he was asked why he didn't hear the tower yelling at him, he said he couldn't hear the radio because there was a loud horn noise in the cockpit."

Dario waited until Hamminis was out of the airplane before he climbed out; more etiquette. They walked to the hangar together. "That was your first and your last joy ride, D'Angelo. Since it's Saturday, you get the rest of the day off, but we're scheduled for a flight early Monday morning and *you* are going to fly the airplane. Know what's expected of you, study the syllabus, especially emergency landings that we'll be practicing. Any questions?"

"You mentioned your bail out procedure. Do we ever get any bail out practice?"

Hamminis laughed. "Nope. We practice almost everything else, but bailing out is the one thing we don't practice. It's something you have to do right the first time."

"Yes, sir."

As he entered the ready room, he saw Brandon Thursted with his instructor. Brandon was ashen. He was sitting on a high stool, his head was hanging down and he was speechless as his instructor lectured him. Dario watched until the instructor left, then went over to Brandon, who hadn't moved. "Hey there, Toke. You look like you could pass for white. What happened?"

Brandon looked up at him. There were red rims around his dark eyes. "I threw up, Jazz Guinea. I vomited my guts out."

Dario laughed so loudly everyone in the ready room looked at him. He slapped Brandon on the shoulder. "Is that all? Shit, Brandon, I heard that half the students who go through here puke on their first hop. Bill told me his brother puked his first four flights. You just have to keep going up until you get over it. That's why they give us lots of barf bags."

"I forgot my barf bag. I didn't even have time to take off my hard hat. I threw up my breakfast all over the airplane."

Dario laughed again. "Toke, you've got to stop filling up with hog belly and grits before you go flying, that's all. You probably ate too much and you were nervous, so you threw up. You'll be fine next flight." He tried to reassure his friend. He was honestly sorry for him, but he was secretly happy that it didn't happen to him, because he'd also eaten a big breakfast. He was learning the schadenfreud feeling of, "It happened to him, but it can't happen to me," was an important part of military flying mental attitude.

"It wasn't the breakfast, Dario. I didn't eat very much." Brandon lowered his voice, "I, I . . . I was afraid, Dario. The airplane movements had nothing to do with it. I was just plain scared."

Dario realized that levity wasn't going to bring Brandon out of his funk, so he became serious and told him, "I"m sorry for you, Brandon. But worrying about it here isn't going to help. Come on, let's go get some lunch. You've got to be hungry, your stomach's on empty."

They met at the mess after they'd showered and changed into civilian clothes. Brandon had cheered up considerably and Dario continued to make his vomiting sound as trivial as he could. As they were drinking coffee at the end of their lunch, he asked, "Brandon, all joking aside. I have a serious question to ask you."

"You, serious! What do you want to ask me, if I really covet white girls?" Brandon smiled, showing off his perfect teeth. "That seems to be what every white man thinks."

"Shit. White girls covet *you*. We know you guys have dicks so long you can't wear Bermuda shorts. No, I do have a serious, sensitive question. It came about because of a girl I met a few weeks ago. Brandon, how do you go to the movies in Pensacola?"

Brandon stared at him for several seconds before answering. "I don't go anywhere in Pensacola if I can help it, Dario. I stay on the base. I thought you knew that. I don't even have a car. There's Jim Crow out there, and to Jimmy, my ensign bars mean nothing."

"No, I didn't know you stayed on the base. I'm sorry Brandon. I never thought about it before. I heard about Nigger Heaven at the movie theater and I just wondered how you handled it."

"I handle it by not giving them a chance at me, that's how. I'm here to learn how to fly and I don't have to leave the base to do that."

Dario stood up. "I've got a great idea, Brandon. Let's get our coats and ties and go for a nice ride. This area may be full of red necks, but it's still got a beautiful countryside. We'll end up at Mainside and have a luxurious sit down dinner at the Mustin Beach O' Club instead of coming back here for the buffet line. The smile Brandon returned would have made the advertising executives for his toothpaste manufacturer rejoice. "And Toke, bring a barf bag. That overcooked hamburger you just ate won't match my upholstery."

As they were driving out the gate, top down, in the glorious sunshine of northwest Florida in July, they passed a gleaming black XK-140M Jaguar coming from the opposite direction, also top down. Dario waved to its driver (whose sweaty bald head reflected the sun's blaze), as was the custom between sports cars. Major Hildripp did not wave back; he glared at Dario and spit over his door onto the pavement.

* * *

The officers' club at Pensacola was the most prestigious in the area because it was the club used by the admirals who were stationed there. It was gleaming white, with columns at the entrance that made it look like a former plantation mansion. Coat and tie were de rigueur, as were manners and comportment. There was no ID check to enter, but Dario did think that the maitre de gave Brandon the once over; but Brandon didn't seem to notice. When they asked for a table for two, they were led to a small table in a corner that was covered with white linen and set with silver and wine glasses. When they sat, Brandon took his linen napkin and placed it on his lap. The maitre de took Dario's from the table and placed it over his. He then handed each of them a large, parchment menu. "The soup de jour is lobster bisque, gentlemen," he told them. "Would you like to see the wine list?"

"Yes, please," Brandon answered.

"Very good sir." He handed him a hard cover folder. "Your waiter will be here directly to take your order. Bon appetit, gentlemen."

Brandon opened the folder and read from it. "They have a good wine list. I'm going to have a steak, so one of these Bordeaux should go well with it. Is that all right with you, Dario?"

"Yeah, sure, sounds good." He hesitated before asking, "What's a Bordeaux, Toke?"

Brandon stared at his friend. "You're putting me on."

"No I'm not. I know nothing about wine, except Dago Red that comes from a barrel. From as far back as I can remember as a child, I was given wine with water at dinner. But, it was always red, always homemade and always served in a stemless glass. And Toke, we drank it with fish. I told you when I met you. I'm a fraud. I'm a gentleman by act of congress, only. Teach me, will you Toke, please."

Brandon laughed.

"What's so funny?"

"You. You're the white man. You all suppose to teach us uncivilized, ignorant, no account colored folk to be civilized."

Brandon suggested they order the soup, to be followed by a steak with a baked potato and asparagus hollandaise. Dario readily agreed after Brandon explained what bisque and hollandaise were. The waiter came, and Brandon ordered the wine. When it came, he sampled it. "Very good. Nice on the palate, "he told the waiter.

When the bisque arrived, Dario grabbed the large spoon that was placed across the top of the plate and began dipping it into the soup and slurping it up. "This is good. Even better than the fish soup my Mama makes."

"Dario. Let's start here. You're eating your soup with the dessert spoon." Brandon pointed to a spoon on the right of Dario's plate. "That's the spoon to use. It's called a bouillon spoon. Use it when the soup comes in a small bowl, like this one."

"Oh, shit." Dario turned his head around and searched the room. "Did the waiter see me? I'll probably be thrown out if he did."

"He didn't see you, but he probably heard you. Don't slurp, Dario. Place your spoon in the soup and fill it by moving it forward. Then, place it to your lips and drain it slowly and quietly into your mouth. Watch me." Brandon did it correctly.

"Where'd you learn all this Emily Post stuff, Toke? They give you a course at Harvard."

"No. I learned it at home. Our dinner table was always set formally. We had servants."

"Servants! Your family must be rich!"

"Well, they are well off. My father was a successful lawyer. He's a judge now. He inherited his practice from his father. In fact, my father's family goes back to England, by way of the West Indies, and they were all lawyers. That's why I'm expected to follow the Thursted tradition and become one myself."

"Somehow you don't seem enthused about it."

"Oh, I'm resigned to it. Of course, my secret desire is to become an artist. To paint. I dabble, but nothing will ever come of it."

The steak came and Dario watched Brandon before he picked up his own fork and steak knife. "Anything special I'm supposed to do with the steak?"

"Don't put catsup on it."

"I'm safe there. Catsup is like bisque and hollandaise. Not Italian cuisine."

"Good. Well, bon appetit," Brandon said, cutting his steak.

"Buon' appetito," Dario answered.

* * *

Flying was coming more easily to Dario than he'd even hoped for. So much so, he was actually enjoying it and looking forward to each hop. He studied and rehearsed each maneuver, over-and-over, as Tyler had recommended. But he'd even taken that advice one step further; he gave them musical beats, making the number of beats fit the particular maneuver. And, he was careful with the joystick. He didn't jerk or yank it around, he treated it as if he were playing music with it. *Forte,* when needed, as in a stall to a spin; and *pianissimo,* when delicacy was required, especially in landings.

Before a student completed a segment of training, he had to fly with a different instructor and prove to him that he could do the proscribed maneuvers correctly and safely. This checked the teaching ability of the student's regular instructor, as well as the student's learning ability. At the end of Dario's introduction phase, his check instructor had him fly the required maneuvers and then told him to fly to Pace Field and make a touch-and-go landing. Dario flew to the large, square, grass field and made a perfect three-point touch down, then immediately took off again.

"This time, make a full-stop landing and taxi back to the end of the field," his check instructor told him over the intercom.

He complied, remembering to hold the stick in the imaginary hook on his belt on landing. He gently applied the toe brakes evenly so he wouldn't skid the tires on the slippery grass. The airplane rolled out straight. He taxied back to the end of the field and stopped. He sat there, with the engine at idle, waiting for further instructions to come through his headset, when his instructor tapped him on his left shoulder. Dario jerked his head to the side and found him standing on the wing next to his cockpit.

"Take off, do one touch-and-go, and then a full-stop. Don't forget to come back and get me," he yelled in his ear through the blast of the idling propeller.

No "Good luck." No "Be careful." No "Remember your procedures." Just an unsaid, "Do it!"

Dario saluted. His legs were shaking slightly, but he taxied forward and took off exactly as he would have if the check instructor was still in the rear seat. When he got airborne and raised the landing gear, he yelled at the top of his lungs. "Yes, I can do it. I'm alone!" It was sophomoric, but he just felt like yelling out loud. He had to do something to release the immense pride he felt in himself.

He circled in the pattern, made the touch-and-go, and took off again. The airplane felt different to him without an instructor in the rear. He felt closer to the airplane. It was his. He didn't have to share it. The feeling was intimate, almost like being alone with a woman. He circled again, made a full-stop landing, and taxied back. When the instructor got in the airplane and had his intercom hooked up, all he said was, "Take us home, D'Angelo."

"Yes SIR!," he yelled.

The SNJ was initially an advanced trainer when Biplanes were still used for Basic Training. The Jay was tough to fly, and there were many accidents when it became the first airplane for a cadet to fly. The new T-34 wasn't only to replace the SNJ's aging airframe that held the aging engine, it was also to provide a more docile, less powerful (flat opposed six cylinder of 285-horsepower), and more forgiving airplane for the initial phase of flying. Dario was proud that he had soloed the ancient, unforgiving Jay Bird on his 13th flight after only 14 hours of flying. He'd loved every minute he'd spent behind the round, nine cylinder, 850-horsepower engine.

His next flight was solo, from takeoff to landing. After he completed the required acrobatic maneuvers, he practiced an emergency landing, pretending that his engine quit and he had to glide to a wheels-up landing in a field. He picked the spot where he would land and maneuvered his airplane over it at exactly 1500 feet. This imagined spot was the "high point." He then made a descending circle to set up for a landing into the wind, and took the plane down to 500 feet before adding power and climbing back to altitude. He was confident that he could have made the landing if the engine failure had been real.

"The most important thing is not to change your mind," Hamminis had told him. "Once you pick your landing spot, never, never deviate. If you think you see a better field on the way down, you probably won't have enough altitude to make it. Stick with your initial decision. It's usually the best."

When he'd landed and taxied to the parking ramp, a navy photographer took his picture standing next to the SNJ. He was told that his "solo picture" would be sent to his hometown newspapers. He was given copies several days later, and he sent one to Vito, along with a money order for two hundred dollars, and a letter of thanks. He sent another to Mat Haven.

CHAPTER
SIXTEEN

WHEN THE competition sway bar for his MG's suspension arrived, Dario took his car to the base hobby shop garage and put it up on blocks. He made other modifications to the suspension that Babbo had emphasized, and he installed scoops in the front of his brakes for cold air to enter, and drilled holes in the rear for hot air to escape. Being able to brake later than the competition, especially at the end of the fast straightaway, was almost as important as having more power. To that end, he pulled the engine, installed a racing camshaft, increased the compression ratio, had the flywheel lightened, and had the engine balanced.

* * *

Brandon Thursted had overcome his nausea, but he still wasn't doing well in the air. He required several more flights than Dario before he was declared "safe for solo." When he finally did solo, Dario waited for him in the ready room. "Congratulations, Toke," he said as he pumped his friend's hand. "I'm supposed to cut your necktie in half, but that's one navy tradition that's falling by the wayside because we ensigns get to wear short sleeved shirts, with no tie."

"Thanks. I think I'm over the hump at last, Jazz Guinea. I felt good up there, although I was a little nervous. I just did things by the numbers. At least I found my way back to the field. I'm more confident now. I know I'll never be a fighter pilot, but I think I can do a good job in multi-engine patrol planes. All I have to do is get through primary training in these Jays, and I'll be off to training in Hutchinson, Kansas. And, there's no Jim Crow there."

They'd become close friends, finding camaraderie from accomplishing a common, difficult task. They usually ate dinner together, then went to the base movie. One night there was a cartoon featuring a new character, The Road Runner. It received such applause and shouts of "more" from the audience, it was run again after the main feature. Dario's musical ear heard something in the bird's "beep, beep," and the whooshing sound of rushing air that followed as the bird sped down the desert highway.

He and Brandon were each scheduled for a solo flight the following morning. In the line shack, checking out their airplanes, Dario said, "Brandon, come up on button five right at ten o'clock, stick your mike out of your cockpit into the slipstream, and hold down the transmit button for five seconds. Do it several times and then go back to the squadron's frequency."

"What you up to, Jazzman?"

"If it works, even you'll understand, boy. It's time to have some fun in this chickenshit program. We've been taking it too goddamn seriously."

At exactly 10:00, Dario heard a whooshing sound in his headset that lasted for five seconds. He heard it again, twice. Then, he switched to the squadron's frequency. Every student and instructor from his training unit who was airborne would be on that frequency. He pulled the throttle back to 1300 RPMs, pushed the transmit button on the microphone and held it next to the warning horn. He then pulled the throttle below 1200 RPM and back, twice. Then, he stuck the mike into the slipstream. He hoped that he'd imitated, The Road Runner.

Within a minute he heard "beep, beep, whoosh," in his own headset. "Boy" Brandon *had* figured out what he'd done.

There were no deductive problems with the rest of the SNJ students either, because by week's end, the air was filled with Road Runners. The following week, the Commanding Officer had an order posted forbidding the practice, quoting some military law that forbade unauthorized radio transmissions. Dario felt a perverse sense of pleasure, knowing he'd violated some standing regulation that brought a bit of levity into the lives of the students without harming anyone, or anything.

* * *

"My MG goes a lot faster now, Brandon. I'll take you for a ride after I'm secured from flying today. Meet me here in the ready room."

Dario wanted to cheer him up, because several weeks after his solo, Brandon was having difficulty with his flying again. He received a "down" (unsatisfactory), on a check flight. He and Dario often discussed the rumor that, while token Negro flight students were allowed into the program, very few ever got their wings. The fact that they hadn't seen any Negro flight or ground school instructors tended to prove the rumor's truth. Brandon, however, claimed that he felt no discrimination from his instructors, even the one who gave him the down.

"The check instructor did everything he could to get me through, but when I made a mistake and he told me to try it again, I was even worse. Once I get nervous, my nervousness compounds, geometrically. I get up tight and I jerk the stick all over the cockpit and over control the airplane. He had to give me a down, Dario. I deserved it. I know I'll do better on my recheck, though. I'm going to concentrate on relaxing and not making that first mistake."

Unlike Brandon, Dario didn't have any difficulty passing his checks. When he got into the cockpit of the ancient SNJ, was strapped in and looked at his instruments, he felt the same as he did when he sat before a piano. He felt at home and he was ready to make music. From engine start to shutdown, he thoroughly enjoyed every minute he spent in the airplane. He loved flying. It was the love of machinery that Babbo had instilled in him, combined with the rhythm of the maneuvers he performed. He made the airplane do what he wanted it to do, just as he did with a piano—with his brains and his eyes working through his hands and his feet.

His life was so full of his flying and his car, he no longer had the gnawing concern that life was passing him by if he didn't get laid regularly, even though Babbo often told him he couldn't make up the loss of a sexual encounter. "Every time you let one get away, it's gone forever. Sex is the opposite of wine. You can't store it. It doesn't get better with age."

CHAPTER SEVENTEEN

MAT HAVEN, now Lieutenant (junior grade), sent Dario a letter, congratulating him for soloing. Dario was surprised to read that Mat had extended two more years to get sea duty. He was going to the Far East on the *USS Midway*, an aircraft carrier, assigned to the ship's Supply Department. "I got weary of the rat race here. Same old job, day-after-day, and the same old retreaded broads. After hearing real sailors talk about the girls in Japan, Hong Kong, and the Philippines, I decided to find out for myself. I want to see if the ass is really keener on the other side of the Pacific, ha ha."

One Friday night, returning from a date he'd had with a cocktail waitress from Woody's, a bar just outside the gate of Mainside Pensacola, he was driving fast on his way back to Whiting Field and he was stopped by a deputy sheriff. "I clocked you at over seventy miles-an-hour, mister. That's reckless driving in Escambia County. Our speed limit is forty-five."

He wasn't sure of how fast he was driving, but 70 seemed reasonable. He was probably going over 80, so he shrugged his shoulders and accepted the citation without comment. He would just pay the twenty-five-dollar fine and forget it.

But, he had to suffer double jeopardy for this traffic infraction. Because of the high number of cadet deaths on the highways, the navy had a point system for traffic violations. Ten demerits, and the culprit lost his auto's base sticker. Two weeks after receiving the ticket, he received an order to go before the base Commanding Officer, Captain Nord, for a captain's mast. He had his hair cut the day before, and shined his shoes and brass belt buckle that morning. When he entered the CO's office, he came to attention and saluted, his uniform cap placed squarely on his head. He had carefully wiped any fingerprints from its black plastic bill as he was waiting to be called. "Ensign D'Angelo reporting, sir."

The captain was a tall man, with broad shoulders. He was standing behind a polished wood podium placed in the center of his office, wearing his gold-braided cap. He returned Dario's salute.

"D'Angelo, my chief tells me the scuttlebutt around the base is that you're the one who started the Road Runner mania. Is the rumor true?"

Dario was surprised. He thought the captain's mast was for his traffic violation. A wave of fear passed through him as he answered, "Err, ah, yes sir."

The captain smiled and said, "I'm curious. How'd you think of it? And stand at ease."

Dario put his hands behind him and stood in the military position that is only slightly more relaxed than the attention stance. "I don't know, captain. I'm a musician. I guess when I saw the cartoon, I just heard the sounds and knew how to improvise on them."

"You know you violated a regulation against unauthorized transmissions, don't you?"

"Yes, sir, I know it now. I haven't done it since I read your notice, sir."

"Good. Sometimes I think the navy's getting too goddamned many regulations, taking all the fun out of it, but Mainside got wind of the gag, so I had to cover my ass and issue that notice. Anyway, you're not here because of the Road Runner, you're here because of a reckless driving offense. What's your story?"

"Well, captain. I was driving over the speed limit, but I wasn't driving recklessly. It's just a technicality they have in this county. Over sixty, and it's considered reckless driving." He looked at the captain's desk. There was a name plaque with a mountain on it, but it wasn't Mount Fuji, it was Mount Vesuvius. He'd grown up with a painting of it that hung in the Da Vinci Club in North Beach. He looked into Captain Nord's tan face, and at his blue eyes and blond hair. He knew there was no way Captain Nord came from Naples.

"You're right about one thing, D'Angelo, it's the technicalities that get you in the end, whether they make sense or not. Reckless driving usually gets ten demerits and the loss of your base sticker. I'm going to be lenient with you, though, because this is your first traffic violation, and I got a kick out of the Road Runner—at least the first time I heard it. I'm only going to assign you nine demerits. That puts you right on the edge, so you'd better be careful."

"Yes, sir. Thank you, sir."

"But, if your musical ear hears anything else that you think would be funny, please save it for your next base."

"Yes, sir. Dario hesitated for a few seconds. "Captain Nord, sir, may I ask a question?"

"Sure. What is it?"

"I think I recognize that mountain on your name plaque as Vesuvius. Are you a Neopolitan?"

Captain Nord laughed. "No, I'm a certified Swede from Minnesota. I was stationed in Naples. Our air station there is called Capodicchino. Had a great time, best pizza in the world. Do you speak Italian, D'Angelo?"

"Yes sir, but I have trouble with the Neapolitan dialect."

"I know what you mean. I took Italian lessons before my transfer, but when I got there, I couldn't understand a thing the locals said. OK, carry on D'Angelo." Captain Nord put his hand to his cap and held a salute.

"Aye aye, sir." Dario returned the captain's salute, did an excellent about-face by spinning on one toe and one heel, and marched out of the office.

CHAPTER EIGHTEEN

D ARIO ENTERED the sports car race held at Hurlburt Field, (one of Eglin's satellite fields), as a novice, citing the other three Sports Car Club of America novice races he'd run. After this race, he'd race in the normal category in any SCCA-sanctioned race. He asked Bill and Brandon to be on his pit crew and he also invited Tammy, who lived on Eglin. He hadn't seen her for weeks, but he'd talked to her on the phone several times. They got to the track at seven a.m. on the Saturday of the two-day race. Bill drove his Ford with Brandon, folding chairs, and a table they'd checked out from the Special Services camping locker. Tammy was expected later in the day.

There was also someone there whom Dario hadn't expected. Major Hildripp was in the pits with his Jaguar under an erected pipe structure with a canvas cover. Hildripp was sitting in a folding lounge chair next to the Jaguar, wearing driver's coveralls and a pith helmet. There was a man polishing the Jaguar. The man wore brightly-colored Bermuda shorts, a tee shirt and a baseball cap, but his shoes were highly-polished Cordovan uniform dress shoes, with olive-drab socks.

When the polisher turned, Dario recognized the square head and whistled. "Pete was wrong about one thing," Bill and Brandon had looked up at his whistle, "Major Hildripp does have one friend. It's Sergeant Major Chester Pflueger. Wouldn't you know that those two pricks would know each other? Come on. Let's go over and talk to them. I want to find out what Hildripp knows about racing."

"Not me. I don't want anything to do with those guys," Brandon protested. "I'll wait for you here."

"Bullshit, Toke. This isn't their territory. I'm racing and you're one of my pit crew. Let's go."

"Dario, that red neck major doesn't like coloreds. You know that."

"Sure I do. That's why I want you to come with me. Let's go rattle his cage. Just call me 'massa' a few times in front of them and everything will be just fine. Have an oily rag hanging out of your back pocket, stay behind me and shuffle a little bit as we walk over." That finally got a laugh from Brandon.

Hildripp recognized Dario as he approached. He looked at him and smiled; then he looked at Brandon and turned his head away from him, as if he didn't exist.

"Good morning, major. What a surprise to find you here. Hello, Sergeant Major Pflueger. You probably don't remember me, you have so many cadets going through Pre-Flight. I'm D'Angelo, the former non-marching band manager. Here's the nickel I owe you." Dario held out his hand with the coin, but the sergeant ignored it.

"I remember you, sir," Pflueger said, accenting the "sir" so it sounded like a slur. He turned to Hildripp. "I taught this officer how to march and carry a weapon. It's a good thing I did, because he barely finished Pre-Flight, marching off seventy demerits. He's a marching expert now." Both marines laughed.

"We have something in common, D'Angelo. Sergeant Major Pflueger also taught me how to march. He was one of my ROTC instructors at Ol' Miss."

"This is my crew, Bill Metz and Brandon Thursted. We were all in the same AOC class."

"I remember Ensign Metz. He also got good at marching." Pflueger laughed again. Hildripp didn't even acknowledge the introduction.

"Have you raced before, D'Angelo?"

"Yes. Three novice races in California. This will be my last novice race. How about you, major?"

"This is my first sports car race, so I'll be in the novice class with you." He sighed. "It's a shame they don't have a larger novice turn out so there could be two races. Too bad we all have to race together. It's not fair, fielding your little MG against my Jaguar. And, there are two air force pilots driving Porsches, and three Austin Healys. About the only thing in your performance range is the Jowett Jupiter, and the older MGs. You all can have a good race together—in the back of the field." Hildripp and Pflueger laughed together, softly.

Dario bit his tongue, but it didn't restrain it. "I don't expect to be in the back of the field, major. I only race to win." Dario surprised even himself with his statement, and it produced a very loud laugh from Hildripp and Pflueger.

"Well, we like our flight students to have confidence, but we don't like them to be stupid and cocky. Do you think that just because you've raced three times, you have an edge? I've been driving fast cars most of my life. Just because I haven't raced with the SCCA before doesn't mean that I don't have experience. I've raced midgets and stock cars. This fancy racing will be a Sunday drive." Hildripp got up from his chair and pointed his finger at Dario's chest. "You be careful out there, D'Angelo. Don't push that little car of yours too far. Accept the fact that it's no match for more powerful cars, like my Jaguar."

Dario had come close to beating Jaguars with his old MG, and his new one was faster. It didn't have the power of the Jaguar, but he knew his brakes were better.

"What do you fighter pilots say? 'Watch your six o'clock position.' Well, watch yours, major. You're going to see your mirror full of blue MG. I'm going to stay right on your ass. I'm going to stay there and hang on like a bulldog. I can make a lot of mistakes when I'm behind you, but if you make just one, I'll pass you."

The major and the sergeant were laughing again as Dario and his crew walked away.

Low and Slow

* * *

The airfield track was laid out with hay bails delineating the course. The straightaway was about one-half mile in length, and ended with a very sharp turn to the right. Dario went cautiously during the morning practice session. He came into his pit twice and adjusted the tire pressure until he had just the adhesion he wanted.

Tammy arrived just before noon, wearing the same halter and short-shorts combination she'd wore at the beach when Dario first saw her. But in bright daylight, she looked even better. She brought sandwiches, potato salad and soft drinks. Dario hadn't thought about food or drinks, and he was grateful for Tammy's thoughtfulness. He could see she was surprised when he introduced her to Brandon. He hadn't told her he would have a Negro in his pit crew; it simply hadn't occurred to him. When he saw the amazed look on her face, it was like the light bulb going on in his head that cartoon artists use to show the genesis of an idea. His friend, Brandon, was lonely, restricted to military bases as a prisoner of Jim Crow. He was also educated, handsome, and had a brilliant career ahead of him. Tammy was attractive, intelligent, and she was getting an education—which at least proved she understood its importance. Best of all, she was sweet, thoughtful and completely sincere. Brandon could give her a secure life, without the burden of trying to pass for white, and Tammy would make him a wonderful wife.

So, then and there, Dario decided to play Cupid. "Brandon, would you show Tammy around? Why don't you take her out to the turns during my second practice? Would you like that, Tammy?"

"Yes. If it's no trouble for Brandon."

Brandon seemed shy at first, but the toothpaste-dream-smile soon exploded across his face. "No trouble, no trouble at all. A pleasure . . . it will be a pleasure," he mumbled.

Dario's fastest lap during the afternoon practice would determine his position for the main race on Sunday. He would be racing against the clock, not the other cars. Dario knew how to get his best lap time.

He purposely went to the pre practice line-up late, and was the last car on the track. When the practice began, he went very slowly for several laps, as if he had engine trouble. This ploy let the other cars get well ahead of him, so when he made his fast run his engine and his tires were at operating temperature, and he had a clear track— the slower cars were well ahead of him. He made four fast laps before he caught up with the Jowett Jupiter and several MGs. He passed them and then he slowed, knowing there was no way he could get a faster lap in traffic. He left the track and came into his pit.

"What's wrong?" Bill called to him. Dario backed into the pit and shut down the engine.

"Wrong, wrong? Nothing's wrong, you twit." He affected an English accent. "Everything's simply wizard. The car's going faster than stink, as we chaps say. Why wear it out in practice?" He looked around the pit. He spoke normally. "Where are Brandon and Tammy?"

"They're at the timer's shack waiting for the times to get posted. You'd better watch it, Dario, I think Brandon might just steal your midget from you. I've never seen him so happy. It's a good thing I'm wearing dark glasses, he's flashing his choppers so much, I'd be snow-blinded without them."

Dario said nothing, just smiled a weak imitation of Brandon.

* * *

"One minute, forty-seven point zero seconds. The fourth fastest lap of the novice group," Brandon announced.

"What was Hildripp's time?" Bill asked.

"One minute, forty-five point five. He had the third fastest time. The two air force Porsches were the fastest, one minute, forty-five seconds flat for each of them."

"That means the major and I will be side-by-side in the second row when the green flag drops for the start. It'll be a drag race to the first turn at the end of the straightaway. He'll out drag me, but I'll give him trouble in the turns. It's gonna be a fun race tomorrow, I promise."

Low and Slow

* * *

The three ensigns were staying at the Eglin Bachelor Officer Quarters. Dario invited Tammy to join them for dinner at the officers' club. He saw her when she entered the lobby and hurried to her. He'd only seen her in shorts and halter, and a bathing suit before, and although she was attractive in that casual attire, she was now stunning in a white dress with a flowered pattern, cut like a sarong. She wore a magnolia in her hair. Her dress and the flower made her look as if she'd just come down to the beach to dance a seductive hula at the luau for the captain of the Yankee clipper ship anchored off shore.

"Dorothy Lamour! We've been waiting for you." Dario greeted her, taking her hand. "I take it back. You look better than Dorothy Lamour, or Maria Montez, or Yvonne De Carlo. In fact, you look better than any movie star!" He led her to the bar where Bill and Brandon were sitting. Like Dario, they wore sports jackets with ties. "Gentlemen, if Tammy's beauty doesn't bring me luck tomorrow, it'll be because I don't deserve it." Tammy was blushing, though it wasn't apparent in the dim light of the club lounge.

After dinner, Dario asked the band leader to play "Three Coins in the Fountain." When it began, he asked Tammy to dance with him.

"Do you like Brandon?" He asked her when they were in the middle of the dance floor, surrounded by other dancers.

"Yes, very much. He's interesting and he's been very nice to me. He hasn't looked down his nose at me at all. I've dated colored air force officers and most of them gave me the impression that the daughter of a sergeant should feel grateful they'd even talk to her."

"Brandon's not like that. He's down to earth, got things pretty well figured out. We have a lot of fun together. We're good friends."

"He's asked me to go out with him. Since it was obvious to me that you were matchmaking today, I assume you don't mind if I do?"

"Tammy, nothing would make me happier. Brandon is a real gentleman, even knows what spoons to use. You are a very sweet girl, I think you two could be good for each other."

"But not you and me? Good for each other, I mean."

Dario hesitated, then held her out and looked into her eyes before saying, "Tammy, you're too good for me, and I mean that as a compliment."

She bent her head low, avoiding his eyes."Is that why you didn't make love to me in Panama City?"

"Yes . . . no. Ah, there were several reasons. I wanted to, oh, how I wanted to, but I guess I had to prove something to myself. I had to prove to myself me that I wasn't totally selfish." Even talking about it was exciting him. For a split second, the thought passed through his mind of telling her not to date Brandon, of taking her out and making love to her, after all. He was sure that she would let him, with enough lies. "There's more to a relationship between a man and a woman than making love. I had a wonderful weekend with you, Tammy, enjoyed every minute of it."

She looked at him, and emitted a slight sigh. "So did I, Dario. It was wonderful."

He pulled her to him, held her tightly, and whispered in her ear, *"Avremo sempre la Città di Panama!"* He thought 'We'll always have Panama City,' the paraphrased line from *Casablanca*, fit the situation nicely, especially in Italian.

* * *

Dario excused himself from the group early in the evening, saying he needed a lot of rest to be fresh for the race in the morning. He was reading in bed when Bill came into the room they shared, several hours later. Bill was loaded.

"How are things going, Billy-boy?"

Bill looked at him, trying to focus, with much difficulty. "What are you up to, my fine Italian friend? You playin' Cupid or something, going to bed early with that 'need the rest' bullshit. I've seen you close the bar and still make an O-dawn-thirty takeoff." Bill sat on his bed and began taking off his shoes. "Tammy's father gave her a ride to the club so I gave Brandon the keys to my pussy wagon. He's gonna take her home when the club closes. Meanwhile, those two are still playing Fred and Ginger out on the dance floor. I told you to look out, ol' buddy. You gonna lose your midget cutie."

"Good. She's too nice for me." He turned off his reading light. "*Bona sera,* Bill."

"Any girl's too nice for you. You're a rat-fucker, like me, D'Angelo. Good night to you too, you tricky dago."

* * *

The race cars made a slow warm-up lap around the track. As they came down onto the straightaway, the starter dropped the green flag and every driver floored his accelerator. It was a drag race to the first turn. The two Porsches were leading and Hildripp's Jag was very close behind them when they reached the first turn. Hildripp had out accelerated Dario to the turn, but he caught up with him because Hildripp hit his brakes sooner than he did. This was exactly what Dario hoped would happen. He stayed right behind Hildripp through the winding parts of the back course, but the Jaguar distanced itself from him again when they got to the straightaway. After several laps, one Porsches pulled out with mechanical problems and Hildripp was pushing hard on the tail of the remaining Porsche. During the tenth lap, the Porsche spun out on a sharp turn and struck a hay bale. There were five laps remaining.

Dario and Hildripp stayed in the same positions for the next four laps. With one lap to go, Dario gritted his teeth and held his foot on his accelerator when he saw the brake lights of the Jaguar glow as Hildripp slowed for a turn. Dario passed the Jag and pushed his brake pedal hard. The MG wanted to slide to the left, but Dario caught it with the wheel turned in the opposite direction. Then he instantly moved his foot from the brake pedal to the accelerator and held it while his engine screamed.

His mouth was so dry his tongue was glued to its roof; he was running on pure adrenaline. He looked in his mirror while in the S turns of the back course and saw the black Jaguar filling it; Hildripp had stayed right on his ass. The checkered flag was at the middle of the straightaway and the Jag would out accelerate him to it. Then he noticed the Jag wasn't where it should be. Hildripp wasn't set up properly for the last turn.

His brakes have faded, Dario rejoiced.

Dario raced through the turn on the outer edge of his tires' adhesion. When he entered the straightaway and looked in his mirror again, he didn't see the Jaguar. He came down the straightaway and saw the checkered flag waving at him. He'd won the novice race.

He did a victory lap and waved to the flag workers at each turn, who gave him the "thumbs up" sign. As he came to the last turn, he saw Hildripp standing next to his Jaguar. It had slid into the hay bales; the front end was crumpled. He waved as he went past him, but Hildripp didn't give him a thumbs up, only a cold, mean stare. It was the same snakelike stare he'd seen on Pflueger during his first room inspection in the Indoctrination Battalion.

"Semper Fi, you asshole. Road racing ain't the Halls of Montezuma. You can't win all the time." He said it aloud, knowing Hildripp couldn't hear him.

There was jubilation at his pit. Bill shook his hand and slapped him on the back. "Congratulations, Dario, you did a great job. I can't wait to go over and look at Hildripp's car. They announced that he put it in a hay bale. Did you see it?"

"Yeah. Looks like the front end is totaled. I'll bet his brakes faded. I was riding on his tail, made him try to go deeper in the turns, forcing him to brake harder. The Jag's brakes just can't take it. They fade when they get hot."

Tammy put her small arms around him, while he was still in the car, and gave him a congratulatory kiss. Brandon was standing on the other side of the car talking to a diminutive, attractive Filipina lady, and a handsome Negro of medium build. They came over, and Brandon introduced him to Sergeant and Mrs. Pointer. The sergeant was a light-skinned Negro who spoke very softly and slowly. Dario could tell it was he who gave Tammy her gentle demeanor.

He got out of the MG and said, "Let's all go over and see Major Hildripp's Jag get towed in. And try not to laugh, Brandon. Just because I beat him, I don't want to rub it in—not much!" They both laughed.

The Jaguar's grill was demolished, and the hood and both front fenders were smashed. Hay straws stuck out of the front tires, trapped between the wheel and the rubber. His once immaculate black car was a wreck.

Dario's entourage stood some distance behind the pit as he walked up to Hildripp. Pflueger was pulling the Jag's fenders away from its tires with a crow bar.

"All it needs is a new grill and the fenders pounded out," Dario called out. "Good thing you had your bumpers removed, major, at least they weren't damaged." Hildripp glowered at Dario, not answering. "I'll bet your brakes got hot and faded. Jags are notorious for that." He used his phoney English accent again and said, "You did have air scoops installed on your brakes when you had the leather bonnet strap fitted, didn't you, old chap?"

"D'Angelo," the major finally said, his head turned away from Dario and looking in the direction of Brandon, Tammy and her parents, "I don't know how you got your MG past me. I still can't believe it!" Then he turned his head, faced Dario and spoke more softly, "Maybe I can. Maybe you put a voodoo curse on me, you nigger lover."

CHAPTER NINETEEN

DURING THE next week, Brandon asked Dario to drive him into Pensacola so he could order a car from Les Harkil. It began to rain on the drive, so Dario stopped and put the MG's top up. This made it cozy in the closed car, and Brandon was in a happy, talkative mood.

"I've never owned a car before. I drove my father's and my brothers', but I never had my own, didn't need one."

"The Plymouth you want is a great car, Toke. You'll love its big, wide seat. You can get a lot of action on that seat. You'd better talk to Bill about how to stock the glove compartment and the trunk. He's an expert."

"Dario, I have a confession to make to you."

Dario feigned stopping his car by momentarily hitting the brakes. "I knew it. I knew it all along. I watched you dance, Toke, you ain't got no rhythm! Youze really white, trying to pass for black so's you can get on welfare."

Brandon laughed at Dario's racist joke, as he always did. "No, white boy, it's even worse than that. Much worse. I'm a virgin."

"What? I don't believe it. You guys all got broke in screwing your sisters as soon as they could walk, everybody knows that."

"I don't have any sisters."

"Your cousins?"

"No, Dario. I mean it, be serious. I'm a virgin. And what's worse, I've never even had a girlfriend, never dated much. I like Tammy. I'm going to take her out. That's why I'm getting a car."

Dario softened his tone of voice. "I had that figured out, Toke, and I'm very happy, for both of you."

"Tell me how to treat her. Tell me how to act around her."

"Don't eat your soup with your dessert spoon and don't drink red wine with fish."

"Come on, Jazz Guinea. It's your turn to teach me!"

Dario laughed. "I can't teach you a thing, Brandon, at least nothing you need. Just be yourself with Tammy, and Jesus Christ, I was only kidding about Metz! Don't take any advice from that pervert. He'll have you stocking your glove box with candy bars and comic books."

* * *

Brandon got his new car, dated Tammy, and still managed to pass his flight checks. Rather than diminish his flying ability, Brandon seemed to do better since he was mobilized and had an off-base diversion. He was more relaxed and much happier. Dario, and the rest of the students in their flight group, could see the change in his life. He was friendlier to everyone and took everything with a relaxed stride they hadn't seen in him before.

In early November, Dario and Brandon finished Fundamentals and moved their flight gear to lockers at the Tactics Department hangar at South Whiting Field, where they would begin the formation flying segment of the syllabus. They checked out the new ready room and saw the CO's and Hildripp's—the Operations Officer—photographs on the wall.

"The major awaits us, Toke. Wait 'til that red neck marine gets you up in the air. He's gonna turn you whiter than a Rinso wash."

"Fuck him."

"Fuck him? Where yo' gettin' that kinda talk, boy? You been hangin' 'round with dem no 'count white-trash boys again?" Dario enjoyed taunting Brandon with the southern slave dialect, so common in many movies he'd seen. It was a proof of their friendship that he could do it, knowing that it amused him.

"He hates guineas too, especially nigger lovin' wops."

"There just might be more truth than jest in that comment, Brandon. I think we both better steer clear of Major Meanness, just as far as we can."

Despite what Dario said, he was certain he'd encounter Hildripp often, so he cut up a T-shirt and made a dickey. He'd seen one of his college girlfriends wear them under her sweaters. His dickey covered the chest hairs above the V in his open-collar shirt front, without retaining the heat an extra layer of clothing would create. Wearing it would prevent Hildripp from accusing him of being "out-of-uniform," by showing his hairy Italian chest.

Brandon was amused by Dario's dickey chicanery. "I wonder why Major Hildripp is so concerned about your chest hair?"

"Because he's jealous, that's why. He's a goddamned hairless eunuch."

CHAPTER TWENTY

"**F**ORMATION IS where you start flying like a military pilot," the ground instructor told the class. Dario was sitting next to Brandon in a classroom in the Tactics hangar. "This is where we separate the men from the boys. And not with a crow bar, like they do in Greece." His old joke got the anticipated laugh from the students. "In the carrier navy, you never fly alone. You either are, or you have, a wingman. We're going to teach you to fly so close to each other you won't need the radio, you'll be able to read lips. You'll learn to fly combat formations so you can protect each other from enemy fighters. We'll teach you how to keep tight around the ship, so time between landings will be at a minimum. A close recovery sequence means less time the carrier has to steam off course, into the wind, which makes the ship's captain happy. One of the most important lessons you'll learn about carrier flying is, whatever makes the captain happy will make you happy." This statement was also rewarded with the expected laughter.

"On a more serious subject, gentlemen, you all know what's going on in Hungary right now. Tanks in the streets, executions and imprisonments, refugees fleeing across the border. The Soviet Union is showing their hand, men. They can't tolerate democracy, but the enslaved people in their satellites are willing to die for it. One day, you may be flying combat to support those willing to die for freedom. One day, you may need your wingman to save your ass, and you must save his. If that day comes, you'll understand how everything you learned in formation flying will make you a more effective weapon. And the most effective weapon is the one that returns to the ship, and can be used again."

Brandon and Dario looked into each others face. They had been watching the news on the TV in the BOQ lobby for the last few evenings. They'd seen the massacre scenes in film smuggled out of Hungary. But the action they watched on the screen was halfway around the world and, except for the compassion it evoked, they didn't feel affected by it. Dario had always envisioned his future in the navy as one of flying on and off a carrier in a bright, tropical sunshine, between debauched visits to exotic ports. Now it dawned on him that he was going to be trained to be a weapon. He could be killing Russians between those takeoffs and landings—and they would be trying to kill him!

After two weeks of ground school, they were assigned to flights of four students. Brandon was in Dario's flight, along with Ensign Joe Schade and a coast guard officer, Ensign Jim Ryan. Brandon and Dario were ecstatic when they learned their instructor was Pete Tyler. He told them they'd be doing a lot of flying before Christmas, when all flight training closed down. It was the only time flight students were granted leave.

As Tyler predicted, the training was intense, both in its pace of two flights almost every day and the strain of flying formation for over an hour on each flight. The students would takeoff individually and meet over a predetermined point on the ground where the first student to arrive would orbit the point, flying in a shallow turn. The other three students would join up on him as they arrived and fly in a line from the leader, like one leg of an inverted V with the leader at the point of the V. Once settled in this formation, the leader would dip the wing away from the line, which signaled the second aircraft to move to the opposite side. The number three and four aircraft would remain in their original positions. This was called a cruise formation. It was much easier to fly than the rigid, four-in-a-line formation, called an echelon formation; left or right echelon, depending on which side of the leader the line was on.

Once the students had joined up and were in cruise formation, they would orbit until the instructor arrived to put them through various maneuvers, usually preplanned on a sequence card. Only the lead pilot could relax, a little. The others had to use stick, rudders and throttle constantly to maintain position on the airplane he was following. The fourth airplane had the toughest job. By the time the adjustments of numbers two and three reached him, they were amplified. Consequently, the lead was changed often, so the burden was shared. The leader would signal the number two aircraft to slide back into the echelon formation. He would then move out and slightly lower his speed to move back until he was at the end of the formation. He would then match his speed with the others, and slide into the number four position.

The flight always returned to the field in a right echelon formation. They flew over the active runway, and at the center of the field the leader banked sharply to the left. The second aircraft would continue down the field and would bank when the first aircraft was thirty-degrees behind his wing. The third, and the fourth, would do the same. This procedure was called "the break." It was the method used on aircraft carriers to give a 60-second separation between arrested landings, or "traps," as they were called on the ship.

Formation flying was fun for Dario, but Brandon was having trouble again. He constantly over controlled his aircraft, making it difficult for those flying on his wing. Tyler gave him special instruction on the ground, trying to get him to overcome his tendency to move the stick and throttle in jerks, rather than as a coordinated movement. Brandon wasn't as upset about his poor flying as he had been in Fundamentals, though. "It'll come to me. I'm just a little slow at learning new things in an airplane. Hell, just a few months ago, I got sick just sitting in one on the ground. Look how much I've progressed!"

Brandon had come a long way, but he had a much longer way to go. There was still formation flying to finish and, after that, they'd transfer to Barin Field for the hard grind of air-to-air gunnery, and, finally, carrier qualification. Bloody Barin, as the base was called, had the worst accident rate in the Training Command, proving what Dario's mother heard was true; carrier landings, especially by students, were dangerous.

Brandon was spending almost every weekend at Eglin Field with Tammy, staying at the BOQ. He told Dario that they never left that base because of the Jim Crow restrictions, but Eglin had almost every amusement they could want. They swam at the officers' pool, played tennis, bowled, went to movies and danced at the club. He also told him Tammy was going to Philadelphia over the Christmas holidays to meet his parents.

"Looks like you'll have to borrow one of those Annapolis graduates' swords next June, Toke, to cut the wedding cake."

Although his complexion didn't change, Dario knew his friend was blushing. "June's a long time off, Jazz Guinea."

CHAPTER TWENTY-ONE

DARIO WAS anxious to get back to the city of his birth and his youth over Christmas leave. He was sorry he wouldn't see Mat Haven, who was on the *Midway*, cruising around the Western Pacific. Mat wrote him often, telling him about the wild liberties he was having with his aviator buddies. "The ass runs the gamut from excellent, on up," he'd written. But, Dario was looking forward to seeing his family, his musician friends, and perhaps make another attack against Wanda's formidable fibers. He didn't have wings, but at least he was a pilot.

One week before leave, Dario's formation group was scheduled for a flight with a check pilot. Tyler had prepared them for the test, putting them through every maneuver the check pilot could throw at them, and being super critical when they didn't do everything perfectly. Even Brandon had sharpened up and was flying much smoother. On the morning of the check hop, instead of finding Lieutenant Sexton, the scheduled check pilot waiting for them in the ready room for briefing, they found Major Nug Hildripp.

'I'm replacing Lieutenant Sexton on this flight," the major said without any further explanation. He then gave them a standard brief in his high, nasal voice. "I'm going to be looking for smooth, coordinated flying. When you pass the lead, I want you to come down the line like you were on a wire. No jerking up-and-down, no swaying side-to-side. Like on a wire, got that!" His eyes roamed the room, stopping for a few seconds at each student. "Any questions?"

Dario had watched Brandon as Hildripp spoke. He was tensing up because, not only did he have the shock of finding Sexton replaced by the head red neck of the Tactics Department, Hildripp ends his briefing by telling them he would be looking for exactly what Brandon didn't do well; fly smoothly.

"You will rendezvous over Point Charlie at 1030 hours, altitude 6000 feet." Hildripp looked at his watch. "It is now 0940."

Each student looked at his own watch, then stood at attention as Hildripp left the room. "He forgot to have us coordinate our watches, like they do in the movies," Dario said, trying to inject some levity into the situation.

"He's after me!" Brandon shouted. "That bastard knows I've had some trouble. He's going on the flight to give me a down."

Brandon was probably correct, and there wasn't a thing they could do about it. Dario reached out his hand and put it on Brandon's shoulder. "Bullshit, Toke. He's after me, because I beat him in the road race and made him smash his beautiful Jaguar. You just take it easy, be cool. He's not after uppity niggers. He's after cocky dagos who befriend them."

Dario split from Brandon on the flight line and caught up with Schade and Ryan as they were inspecting their airplanes. "Look guys, Brandon's really uptight. Let him get to the rendezvous point first, so he can start out leading the flight. It'll give him a few minutes to settle down. Let's meet five miles south of Point Charlie, say 6000 feet at 1020. Then we can fly up to Brandon in loose formation and join up on him."

Low and Slow

* * *

"Where have you been?" Brandon asked over the radio as the three SNJs joined on him and flew in a good, tight cruise formation, circling and waiting for Hildripp. No one answered.

There was complete silence until 1043, when they heard Hildripp's voice over the radio for the first time. It came over the airwaves in an even higher pitch and with a more nasal sound than it did on the ground. "Cowboy 2-1, this is 5-9er. Is what I see supposed to be a formation? It looks more like a bunch. Get your formation tightened up, 2-1. That's the sloppiest goddamned flight I've ever seen."

Brandon's SNJ had the number 21 painted on the nose and under the wings. Dario was flying in the number two position. His number was 27. Ryan was in 14 and Schade had 54. Hildripp was flying 59. In the air, side numbers where always used to communicate, pronouncing each number individually. The Tactics squadron's call sign for SNJs was "Cowboy," which everyone assumed had something to do with the aircraft's factory name, "Texan."

"Move it up, 2-7. He's your buddy, don't you want to get close enough to kiss him?" Hildripp transmitted to Dario.

Brandon's flying became erratic. He wasn't holding an exact altitude; he was climbing and diving about 50 feet above and below 6000 feet, which sent a ripple down the entire formation.

"Goddamn it, 2-1, can't you hold an altitude? Level the flight out, you're making it tough on your good buddy." Hildripp's voice had even increased in pitch. "OK, 2-1, begin your sequence. Roll out on a heading of 2-2-0 and hold your altitude. Do you think you can follow my simple request, 2-1?"

Brandon didn't answer.

"Did you hear me, 2-1? Roll out on a heading of 2-2-0, over," Hildripp shouted.

Ending his transmission with "over," demanded an acknowledgment. Brandon was afraid to take his left hand off the throttle to lift his hand mike and answer the instructor, so Dario answered for him. "Roger, 5-9er. My heading 2-2-0. 2-1, out."

"Something wrong with your voice, 2-1? It sure didn't sound like you. I'd better get closer so I can see your lips move." Hildripp flew his aircraft very close to Brandon's, just ahead and above Dario.

Brandon overshot the 220-degree heading by 5-degrees, so he turned back to the left to get on the correct heading. "Jesus Christ almighty," Hildripp yelled. "Didn't you learn to lead your compass in a turn, 2-1? You overshot the goddamn heading. You'd better settle down, 2-1. If I don't see some better flying soon, I'm going to take this flight back and give you a down." His voice had raised in volume and pitch as he castigated Brandon.

When Brandon finally got the flight on 220 degrees at 6000 feet, Hildripp told him to pass the lead. Brandon did nothing. "Is there something wrong with your radio, 2-1? I told you to pass the lead. Acknowledge my transmission." Hildripp's spoke more slowly, as if he were speaking between clenched teeth.

Dario would have made the transmission for Brandon again, but Hildripp was looking right into Brandon's cockpit. When Brandon finally reached for his mike, he pitched up the nose of his aircraft when he moved his hand. "Roger, 5-9er," he mumbled. "Passing lead. 2-1, out." Brandon then dipped his right wing. This signaled Dario to move to that side to make a straight echelon line. Brandon would then move to the left and back, easing his aircraft to the rear of the flight, and Dario would then be the new leader.

When Brandon dipped his wing to signal, he did it with too much movement. It changed the heading of his airplane and made the entire flight jerk to the right, then struggle to get back into the correct formation.

"A dip, goddamn it 2-1. You're only supposed to do a dip, not a turn!" Hildripp yelled. "Now pass the lead and do it fast. I'm getting goddamn tired of your shitty flying!"

When Dario slid over into echelon, Brandon hit the top of his helmet with his right hand and then pointed to him, signaling that he was passing him the lead. Brandon then moved out to his left and started to ease down the line. Hildripp was still flying very close to him, watching every move he made. "You're out way too far. Close it up, 2-1." Then Hildripp laughed, "Or are you leaving the formation, 2-1? Sorry, it ain't that easy. You gotta perform."

Brandon *was* too far out, but he *was* moving down the line. He was well clear of Dario and passing the third SNJ in the line.

"Goddamn it, 2-1, why don't you listen to me? You're flying so far away, I asked you if you are leaving the formation. Answer me, 2-1, goddamn it!" Hildripp knew it was very difficult for Brandon to make the lead change and take his hand off the throttle to pick up the hand mike. Unless his power was at just the right setting, the plane would go back too fast or not at all. Dario was straining his neck looking down and behind, watching Brandon.

"Roger, 5-9er," Brandon finally transmitted, "moving in closer." Brandon's SNJ suddenly dropped back too fast. He added power to stop it, but jerked up his nose and turned at the same time, pulling it up too fast and too far to the right. His prop cut into Schade's airplane, the last in the formation, cutting off part of its tail. It went into an immediate, spinning dive.

"Oh shit," Hildripp yelled, "now you've done it, Thursted. Bail out, 5-4, bail out, bail out, bail out! You're in a spin. Thursted, you bail out too. You have a fire in your engine compartment." Hildripp was screaming at the top of his lungs. "2-7, orbit here with 1-4," he radioed to Dario.

"Roger, 5-9er. 2-7 orbiting, out," Dario responded.

"2-1, this is 5-9er. I ordered you to bail out!" Hildripp yelled. He then transmitted on a guard channel, the emergency frequency monitored by all aircraft and ground stations. He used a cool, calm, "this is your captain speaking," manner of voice. "Mayday, mayday, mayday. This is Cowboy 5-9er. I have a midair, ten miles southwest of Point Charlie. One student has bailed out, but no joy on a chute. The other is going down. I am on his wing. His prop is bent and his engine has stopped, and there is a fire in his engine compartment. I have ordered him to bail out, but he is not responding. He is not injured, but he seems to be frozen on the controls. Repeat, midair ten miles southwest of Point Baker, one student out of his aircraft, the other aircraft going down, with pilot still aboard."

Dario made a turn to his left to see what was happening.

"Thursted, bail out, goddamn it." Hildripp was screaming again. "Do you read me? Bail out, you're on fire, bail out!" Hildripp's voice had reached such a peak, it was almost inaudible. As Dario turned, he saw Brandon's SNJ circling down, trailing smoke from the engine. Schade's aircraft had crashed in the trees and was burning. Hildripp's airplane was next to Brandon's, following him down as he continued to shout over the radio, "Get out, you stupid nigger! There's still 4000 feet, plenty of altitude to bail out. You're a Harvard graduate, you should be smart enough to bail out when you're on fire!"

Dario tapped the top of his helmet and pointed to Ryan who answered him with a thumbs up. He then pulled off all his power, dropped his landing gear for more drag, and put the nose straight down, quickly losing 2000 feet. He was disobeying his last order, but all he could think of was helping his friend. He came alongside Brandon's airplane, on the opposite side from Hildripp. He raised the gear and dropped half flaps, to slow to Brandon's speed.

"D'Angelo," Hildripp screamed. "What in the hell are you doing here? I ordered you to orbit. Get back up there! That's an order."

Dario ignored him and got closer to Brandon's SNJ. He could see the stopped propeller was bent back, the cowl was badly damaged and the engine was bent at an angle. The force of the prop hitting the other aircraft had bent or broken, the engine mounts. There were flames coming out of the engine cowl, obviously from a broken fuel line. He didn't see any damage to the cockpit, but Brandon was staring forward, frozen in his seat.

"Toke, it's the Jazz Guinea. You've got to get out of there, Toke, you're burning. Don't try to crash land it. Jump, Toke, jump." He transmitted his words slowly and softly. His friend was frozen with fear and he hoped he could bring him out of his panic with the soft, friendly words of a familiar voice. "Toke, push back the canopy, climb out, and let go. Then count to three and pull the rip cord. Come on Toke, you can do it."

"D'Angelo, you little dago bastard," Hildripp shouted, "this is a direct order. Get away from here. Orbit with 1-4. Do . . . you . . . read . . . me?"

"Thursted's frozen at the stick, you asshole! Your screaming at him is making it worse. You go up and orbit. I'm not leaving Brandon." Dario's transmission was spontaneous but as the words left his mouth, he realized how serious the consequences could be.

The flames were creeping farther back on the fuselage of Brandon's SNJ as it continued to lose altitude in a spiral. "Brandon, Brandon, it's Dario, Toke, the Jazz Guinea. Get out of the airplane, Toke. Do it for me, do it for Tammy."

When he said Tammy, Brandon raised his head for the first time. He looked up at Dario's cockpit and Dario saw his grey, expressionless face as he turned his head from side-to-side slowly, in a negative gesture. Using Tammy's name had evoked the first response from Brandon, which gave Dario an idea. He had to do something fast because they were down to 1,000 feet. He spoke in his mike, trying to sound as calm as possible, even though he was starting to panic. His hands were sweating through his gloves.

"Toke, you can't die without getting laid, Toke. You can't die a virgin." In desperation, seeing the altitude needle near 800 feet, he yelled, "Brandon, get out of there, get out for Tammy!"

As if he'd pushed a magic button, Brandon's canopy flew back and he rolled out of the cockpit in one motion; his chute opened almost immediately. His damaged SNJ tightened into a graveyard spiral and flew into the tops of the scrub pine woods that cover lower Alabama. The wings broke off as they hit the trees and a split-second later there was a huge ball of fire as the fuel, spilling from the broken tanks in the wings, reached the fire in the engine which had dug into the pine-needle-covered earth. Dario added climb power and began his return to 6000 feet, belatedly following Hildripp's order.

"Mayday, mayday, mayday, this is Cowboy 5-9er. I have two students down, approximately eleven miles southwest of Point Baker. One parachute is open, situation of the other is unknown." Hildripp's speech was slow, calm and at an almost normal pitch. Then he added, in an even slower and clearer voice, "I'm going to have your gold bars, D'Angelo."

* * *

The crash crew found Brandon hanging from a tree limb, about twenty feet off the ground, and rushed him to the hospital at Mainside. He was badly bruised and scratched, and had a dislocated collar bone. Schade's body was found two miles away. He'd jumped, but his head had struck what remained of his stabilizer as it spun, crushing his forehead within his crash helmet and killing him instantly.

Pete Tyler was at the hospital when Dario went to see Brandon the day after the accident.

"I thought for sure Brandon was going to ride his Jay Bird in and die, Pete. And poor Joe. He never had a chance. He was a good pilot, he didn't do anything wrong, but he got killed. It makes me wonder if it could happen to me?"

"Get used to it, Dario. You lose many friends in this game, especially when you get aboard ship. Some of the best get killed because something goes wrong that's no fault of their own. When that happens, when someone you know busts his ass, don't get depressed. Don't let Schade's death work on your head. Get back in your airplane and fly the son-of-a-bitch, fly it better than you ever have before."

Dario looked directly into Tyler's face and said, softly, "I can't get back in it, Pete. I'm grounded. Major Hildripp put me on report. He wants me court-martialed for disobeying his order."

Low and Slow

* * *

Lieutenant Renauld Kern Fox, III, was etched in the plastic name plaque on the legal officer's desk. There was no mountain. His office was very small. It was in the Administration Building at Whiting Field, down the hall from the larger CO's office Dario was familiar with.

"Call me Foxy," the tall, thin officer said to him. He wore no ribbons or wings on the breast of his uniform shirt. "Now, tell me what happened."

Dario told him his story. He liked the way the legal officer listened, without comment, while writing notes on a yellow legal pad with a pencil as he told him about the flight and the accident.

"Let me be sure of one thing, D'Angelo. Did you fully understand Major Hildripp when he told you to orbit with the other airplane?"

"Yes. But I knew Brandon was panicked by his shouting. I hoped that when Brandon saw me, he'd come out of it. Thank God I was right. Another hundred feet and his chute wouldn't have had time to open."

"And he jumped out when you told him he had to get laid before dying?" Fox laughed after he asked the question.

"Yes."

"And you think that Major Hildripp was tough on Thursted, because he's a Negro?"

"Hell, yes. He intimidated him, and not just because he's a Negro. He's a Harvard graduate, uppity nigger."

"I'm a Harvard graduate," Fox said, still laughing. "Thursted must be exceptional."

"He is. He wants to make it through the program, even though flying is tough for him. He worked hard at it, even got over being airsick."

The legal officer leaned back in his swivel chair, chewing on his pencil. "Major Hildripp has petitioned for a court-martial. He says you not only disobeyed him, you were also insubordinate, called him an asshole."

"He is."

"He may be, but ensigns are supposed to keep it a secret." He laughed again. "Now, the secret's out. You broadcast it over the squadron's frequency." He laughed louder.

"Hey Foxy, this is serious. My neck's sticking out and you're laughing while I'm peeing in my pants with fear. What will happen to me if I'm court-martialed?"

"Oh, not much. Loss of commission, loss of pay, a year in Portsmouth Naval Prison, maybe two. But I'm kidding you, D'Angelo. There isn't going to be a court-martial. I got Ensign Ryan's statement, and he confirmed yours. Major Hildripp used racial slurs against Thursted. It'd be bad publicity for the navy. Captain Nord's got orders to be the CO of a deep draft ship, so he's on track for admiral, if he doesn't run it aground. He's not going to want any waves made in his command before he leaves. I'll explain it to him so he'll understand how high the waves could get."

"Jesus, that's a relief to hear."

Fox put the pencil on his desk and laughed. "Too bad though. It would be an interesting case. I'd love to get, 'you can't die without getting laid' in the record." He laughed again."

"So you think I'm in the clear?" Dario asked.

"Yes, as far as a court-martial goes." Fox did not laugh this time. His voice became almost serious. "You will go before the Student Pilot Disposition Board though, and they'll undoubtably wash you out of flight training. You didn't have any aspirations for a career in naval aviation, did you?"

"I, I really haven't given much thought to a career, but flying's become important to me. I want to finish and fly with a squadron out of Alameda. I want to fly from a carrier, see the world, do the whole bit. What will happen to me if they wash me out?"

"You'll probably spend the next two years as a black shoe on a radar destroyer escort in the North Atlantic. But you won't lose your commission, or be fined."

"Losing my flight pay will be worse than a fine. I'll lose my car. Isn't there anything I can do?"

"Yeah. Plead insanity." He laughed. "You have to be crazy to fly those old SNJs, anyway."

* * *

The five officer board sat behind a long table covered with green felt in a conference room. Dario had on freshly-starched khakis, with a full undershirt, just to be sure. He'd spent the previous hour polishing his shoes and his belt buckle, and his hair had been cut the previous afternoon. Sartorial perfection, he'd discovered, was an important part of military justice.

"Do you admit you knowingly left your formation?" the head of the board, a commander, asked him.

"Yes, sir. I know I should have made a request to Major Hildripp, but when I looked down at Ensign Thursted's aircraft and saw it was on fire, I felt there was no time to waste making radio transmissions. Ensign Thursted and I are very good friends. I knew he'd listen to me, he'd come out of his panic. Thank God I was right."

"Did you use profanity toward Major Hildripp over the air?"

"Yes, sir. I did, after he used it against me. I wasn't thinking. I was scared. Brandon was going down, fast."

When the questioning was over, Dario was excused. Jim Ryan appeared next, then Pete Tyler, who was the flight's regular instructor.

After an hour, Dario was called back before the board. He had resigned himself for the worst, for expulsion. A captain who hadn't asked him any questions before, spoke; his voice was level and without emotion. "Ensign D'Angelo, the board has found your performance on the formation check flight was unsatisfactory. Since this was your first down, you will be allowed to fly the check flight again. That is all, you are dismissed."

Dario could not believe what he was hearing as the captain spoke, but when he finished, he realized that he had not been washed out. He had another chance. Blood rushed to his head and he almost fainted with relief. He felt like one of the characters from a movie who had been found innocent by a jury. He said, "Thank you, sir. Thank you, gentlemen," and spun on his heels and marched quickly from the room. He wanted to get out before they changed their minds. Pete was waiting for him outside.

"Pete. They didn't wash me out. I get to refly the hop. I can't believe it Pete. I get another chance. I'm sure you had a lot to do with it, Pete. Thank you, Pete."

"I did what I could, Dario, told them you were a good student with lots of potential. I think what saved you was your honesty. They intimated to me that you were forthright, didn't try to bullshit them."

"What a relief, Pete. I thought I was getting an ulcer, my stomach's been churning since Hildripp tried to get me court-martialed. I still can't believe it's almost over, Pete. When can I fly the hop? I want to get this whole goddamn mess behind me, Pete. When can I go up again?"

"Calm down, Dario, calm down. I'm very happy for you, but it's not quite over. You won't be able to fly the check until after Christmas leave. And Dario, don't get too complacent. I'm certain Hildripp will be your check pilot, again."

"Shit, Hildripp, again! How can that happen?"

"He's the Ops Officer, Dario. He controls the scheduling and the instructor assignments. That's the breaks of naval air."

* * *

Brandon made the wise choice of dropping from flight training. He and Tammy became engaged, and he received orders to a destroyer escort radar ship stationed at Goat Island, in Naragansett Bay. The vessel provided an early warning defense line between Greenland and Iceland where the ships were purported to roll in an arc up to 100-degrees in winter seas. Brandon said that, after Hildripp and SNJs, it would be relaxing.

There was a short memorial service for Joe Schade at the base chapel which Dario attended. The students all sang a few hymns, and listened to a standard prayer from a chaplain who never met Joe.

CHAPTER
TWENTY-TWO

"JESUS CHRIST, it's Admiral D'Angelo," his Uncle Lezio said as he met him at San Francisco International Airport. The youngest of his mother's four brothers and still a bachelor, Lezio was Dario's favorite. He let Dario drive his custom Chevrolet long before he was old enough to do it legally, and he got Dario condoms by the dozens when he became sexually active. A fisherman, Lezio was short, with fair skin and black hair which he wore long. Wire-rimmed glasses, bushy eyebrows, a thick, black moustache and an ever present cigar always made Dario think of Groucho Marx when he saw his uncle.

Dario was wearing his dress blue uniform, with one lonely gold stripe on each sleeve, and above the stripe, the gold star insignia of a line officer. Wearing it on the flight earned him a military fare discount. Lezio gave him the traditional Latin embrace, then pushed him out and looked at him. "You're skinny. Don't they feed you down there?"

"No ravioli. Just meat and potatoes."

"Well, your mother and your aunts will soon take care of that. They've been cooking for a week."

As soon as he was alone in his stepfather's den he dialed Wanda's phone number. It was Saturday night, and he really didn't expect her to be home, so he was pleasantly surprised when she answered. "Hello

Wanda, it's Dario D'Angelo. I'm back from Pensacola for Christmas leave. How are you?"

"Oh, hello Dario. I've wondered how you were doing down there. Did you finish? What kind of jets are you flying?"

"Not yet. I got my commission and I'm flying . . . er, ah, SN Jets."

"Oh, I don't think they have those at Alameda. Are you still playing the piano?"

"Not very often. I haven't had time for music. The training is really intense. I'm sure anxious to get my hands on a keyboard, though. If you're not busy tonight, how about going to a jam session with me?"

"Sorry. I don't go out with navy men anymore, especially naval aviators."

"What? Why not? What happened?"

"You remember my former boyfriend, Bob? Well, when I thought he was out on a carrier during the week, he was often with another girl in San Diego. She found my phone number on something he left there and she called me. We compared notes. He'd been lying to both of us. He told me he was out on a ship during the week, and he told her he trained reserves on weekends. He's a lying bastard."

It was the first time he'd ever heard Wanda use profanity. "But, Wanda, you can't blame me for what Bob did."

"Yes I can. I think deceit is the first thing they teach you in Pensacola. As soon as I broke up with Bob, I got calls from friends of his, guys I knew were going steady with other girls. One was even married."

"No! I don't believe it!" He feigned incredulity.

"It's true. You're all a bunch of oversexed egomaniacs, with no morals."

You're wrong. I passed on Tammy!, he wanted to counter, but didn't.

"Please change your mind. I've been thinking about nothing but being with you again. I haven't been out with a girl since our last date."

"All the more reason to say 'no more navy.' Why, even your friend Mat Haven made a pass at me before he left on a ship. I went out with him, only because he was leaving, and I ended up fighting him off. I almost called my brother, Herb."

"How is good old Herbert?"

"When I broke up with that cheat, Bob, the Alameda O' Club manager suddenly fired the band. Herb's playing every weekend with a Dixieland group at the It Club, over in El Cerrito."

"Come on Wanda, I just want someone to talk to, to be with. I don't want sex. I'm lonely, I just want companionship. Honest, that's the truth."

"That girl Bob was seeing in San Diego really opened my eyes, Dario. She's been in San Diego, around navy men all her life, and she really understands them. She told me how a girl can tell if a naval aviator is going to lie to her. Do you know how we tell, Dario?"

"Yeah, yeah. I've heard it before. 'If his lips are moving, he's lying.' "

"No, you're wrong. If he's breathing, he's going to lie." With that revelation, Wanda hung up her phone. Dario listened to the dial tone for a few seconds before hanging up his.

He said goodnight to his family and went to bed with the excuse that he was tired from the long overnight flight from Pensacola. He thought about wearing his uniform to the Yankee Doodle the next afternoon, but he felt naked without wings on his chest. He decided to wait until he had his best bait before he went trolling in uniform.

I guess it's going to be a wholesome family Christmas, he told himself as he fell asleep.

* * *

Several days later, he walked around North Beach. He walked past his high school and finally walked to the only house he'd ever lived in, which his mother had sold after his father died. It was now owned by a Chinese family, but it looked the same. He ended his walk at Uncle Lezio's house a few blocks nearer the Embarcadero. It was a small, wood-framed, two story house on a very narrow lot. Lezio was out fishing, so Dario got the key out of the ceramic toad which sat in his garden, climbed the stairs and opened the door. He went immediately to his piano, which Lezio kept for him in his dining room, pulled out the bench he'd sat on for thousands of hours and played for two hours, ignoring it being out of tune. He thought of when he'd first learned the jazz chord structure and couldn't get his fill of it. He was on top-of-the-world then, playing modern jazz while in his teens. It all seemed so long ago. He still loved music, would always play jazz and classical, but somehow it seemed petty compared to flying. If he was remiss in music, the audience heard a few bad notes, which were quickly overlooked. If he was careless with flying he could lose his life, or cause another to die. He'd never been concerned about his piano playing ability before a job, but he was constantly thinking, with apprehension, about the flight check he had waiting for him when he returned to Whiting Field. The gnawing in his stomach was still there. Not being court-martialed, and not being washed out of flight training had not removed it. He knew Hildripp was waiting for him.

* * *

Friday night, he drove his mother's car across the Bay Bridge, heading for El Cerrito, and the It Club, where Wanda said Herbie Ute was playing. It was a little before one a.m. as he sat at the end of the bar, unseen by Herbie, and watched the cascading stream in his bass drum. The group was awful. The cornet player was tinny, even for Dixieland, and the trombone was much too loud. Herbie exacerbated their faults with his uneven tempo. Dario drank two Cuba Libras and suffered through the noise.

The group finished shortly before two a.m. They all unclipped their bow ties and unbuttoned their shirts before covering their instruments, leaving them in place for the next night's performance. When Herbie left, Dario got up from the bar and followed him to his car. He'd played this moment over in his mind since he thought of it during the hand-to-hand combat instruction he had in Pre-Flight. Herbie was opening his car door when Dario called to him, "Hey, you

Neolithic cretin! Wanda *was* adopted. She couldn't be related by birth to an ugly ape like you."

Herbie spun around with his hands up in a prize fighters position, the ever ready street fighter. "Who's that?"

"It's Dario D'Angelo, you dickhead. Take a good look. Surely you remember me? I'm the big, bad piano player who tried to fuck your little sis." He approached Herbie, holding his face up so it could be seen in the dim light of a street lamp.

"What the fuck do you . . . arrgh." With his open hand, fingers held tightly together and supported by his thumb, Dario had jammed the end of his fingers into Herbie's throat just above his collar bone. He'd gone between Herbie's fists with such a flashing movement, his hand was almost invisible. He only jabbed Herbie's windpipe though; he didn't try to grab it and pull it out, like he'd been taught. He didn't want to kill Herbie, he only wanted revenge for the night he'd almost strangled him because he'd taken out Wanda.

Herbie was gasping for breath, with both of his large hands at his throat. Dario cupped his hands and popped them over Herbie's ears. The concussion from the trapped air forced into his eardrums stunned him. He fell to his knees, dazed. Dario waited for several minutes, until he was certain Herbie was breathing fairly regularly and was semiconscious. Then he leaned over and spoke into one of Herbie's inflated eardrums. "You'll have a sore throat and a headache to remember me by, asshole, just like I did after you attacked me. We're even now, Herbie; but if you ever mess with me again, I'll come back and break off your arm and beat your stupid waterfall drum with the bloody stump."

CHAPTER
TWENTY-THREE

H E MET Pete Tyler in the ready room on his first morning back at
Whiting Field. "Did you have a good leave, Dario?" his instructor asked.

"It was OK, Pete. Nice to see my family, but sort of boring. I did go
to a few jam sessions, saw a lot of friends."

"Well, I hope you're well rested, because you *are* going to get
Hildripp for your check ride. He scheduled himself, just as I knew he
would. You're just going to have to fly a perfect hop, so he can't find
any fault."

"Who are the other guys I'm flying with?"

"Good students. None of you should foul up. Hildripp can fake
being human until somebody makes a mistake, then he starts screaming and goes ballistic."

"You know, Pete, I've been thinking about that. Last week at Bop City,
I was sitting-in and there was a guy with a new wire recorder contraption,
recording us. He played it back later, and it sounded pretty good, very
clear. I thought about our flight when Joe Schade got killed. If I'd had a
wire recorder and got some of Hildripp's transmissions! Well, maybe
Hildripp would have been threatened with a court-martial, not me. If I
could only have a wire recorder going in my plane for my check, I'd
purposely mess up a maneuver to get him screaming. Then we could

play it back in front of him when there's a lot of people around. It might be enough to show him up as the airborne madman he is. My father once told me that sometimes the only way you can get revenge on a strong man, a man with power, is to humiliate him."

"Forget it. You don't have a recorder, for starters, and if you get another down on your repeat check ride, you will definitely be shit-canned from the program. And that's a positive, not a maybe. It's not worth it. Besides, he knows how you fly. He'd know immediately if you faked something wrong and he'd send you back to the base alone, with an automatic down. You just come out with me today and tomorrow, and fly two good warm-up hops. Forget about everything, except how smoothly you're going to control your Jay Bird on your check ride."

"Aye, aye, sir." Dario threw his friend a mock salute.

* * *

On the morning of his third day back from leave, he went to the ready room to be briefed for his check flight. He didn't know the other three students in his flight, they'd all been behind him in the program. Hildripp gave the same briefing he'd given on the flight with Brandon, until the end.

"I've only flown with one of you before and that person knows what I expect of him. We'll be on channel six today, and when I transmit an order, it's execution better be starting as I'm releasing the pressure on my mike button." He looked directly at Dario's eyes while smiling his beady-eyed smile. "I'll rendezvous with the flight over Point Able at 1435, at 4000 feet. Be in left echelon. As I approach you, I want to see four airplanes that look like they're wired together, each airplane exactly the same distance from the other. If you start the flight out in a good formation, everything should go like clockwork for the rest of the flight." Hildripp then cruised the room with his eyes, as if inspecting each student for a uniform violation. "Any questions?" The room was silent. "Flight, dismissed." The four students stood at attention as Hildripp left the ready room.

"Wow, 'The Madman' really sends you out with a relaxed mental attitude," one of the students said aloud.

Dario felt that he had to say something. "Since you know he's called 'The Madman,' do you also know that I was with Hildripp when there was a midair?"

The three students nodded their heads in acknowledgment.

"Don't let him shake you up, and believe me, he tries to do just that. He shrieks, he screams, he calls us names, and the worse you fly the louder he yells. He's going to be after me, but I'm going to ignore him and just fly the airplane the best I can. Do the same. Don't let his screaming get to you. I'm sorry I brought this on you guys. Hildripp seldom does check rides. He's just doing it to get me."

"Don't worry, D'Angelo," one of the students said. "We got this far in the Jay Bird, we're not going to let 'Hil-shit' get to us. We'll all back you up and fly a great hop. First one over Point Able is leader, right?"

"Right," the remaining students echoed.

Dario welcomed the camaraderie they'd shown him, camaraderie born of sharing adversity. He was glowing inwardly with confidence as he walked down the line of parked SNJs, looking for 68, his assigned aircraft. Suddenly Tyler reached out from behind a parked line truck and pulled him behind it with him. Tyler was wearing his flight suit, with his leather flight jacket over it, and his flight helmet slung over his arm by its strap. "Dario, we've got a plan. Two other instructor buddies and I are substituting for the other three students. We'll pull them out just before they get in their planes and tell them to go to the BOQ, and stay there. You take off normally, get to Point Able first, and take the lead. Then just do what Hildripp tells you to do and leave the rest to us. We'll all have our dark goggles on so Hildripp won't recognize us, no matter how close he gets to us in the air. We've got a wire recorder going in the tower and we're going to put on a flying circus that should give Major Asshole a heart attack."

"Jesus, Pete!" was all Dario could think of to say.

"You forget what I just told you. No matter what happens, you knew nothing about it. You just follow all of Hildripp's orders and you won't be implicated." Tyler hesitated before speaking again. He looked down at his flight boot and kicked an imaginary rock. "I want to see you get your wings, Dario. You're the kind of wild horse rider we need in this man's flying navy. I'd feel secure with you on my wing, anytime."

They shook hands, and Dario was almost overcome with emotion from the great compliment. Tyler was sloppy in his attention to his uniform, was lackadaisical about rules and regulations, and wasn't career-oriented. But Dario felt more pride hearing what he'd told him than he would have if the compliment had come from the leader of the Blue Angels.

Dario orbited Point Able at 4000 feet and the other three SNJs joined up on him, one-by-one. The flight flew a very tight formation in a left echelon, and waited for Hildripp's instructions. Dario looked down the line of the formation. Each aircraft was exactly equidistant from each other. It was the best echelon formation he'd ever seen. The other aircraft in his flight were 22, 16 and 13, but he didn't know which aircraft Tyler was flying. They all wore dark lenses in their goggles and the fur collars of their leather flight jackets were all turned up, which was usual in the chilly January skies.

When Hildripp arrived, he radioed, "OK, 6-8. Begin your sequence." The sound of his voice over the radio was almost nauseating to Dario, as it brought back memories of the fatal flight.

After putting the flight into a cruise formation, Dario began the first maneuver on the sequence card, a level 30-degree banked turn for 360 degrees. After the turn, Dario was to pass the lead. He did the turn at the correct angle of bank and maintained altitude, perfectly. When he rolled out on the original heading, he put the flight back in echelon, and passed the lead. The formation remained tight and perfect, and Hildripp remained silent as Dario smoothly moved down to fourth in the echelon. Then 2-2, the new leader, began a turn. The bank passed through 30-degrees and increased to 60-degrees. At this, the screaming began.

"No, no, 2-2. Roll out, 2-2. Roll out. You've got your flight in 60-degrees of bank. Roll out, roll out, roll out!" Hildripp shrieked at the top of his lungs until his voice broke, and it became a screech.

For the next twenty minutes the flight was complete chaos, with Hildripp continually shouting into his mike. Each order he gave was executed incorrectly. Aircraft were turning in the wrong direction, were climbing when they should descend, and were changing the lead front-to-back. When the flight finally got back to straight-and-level, it was down to 2000 feet and 2-2 was in the lead again. Hildripp regained a little composure and spoke as if he were talking to mental patients. "2-2, return to home plate. Do you read me, 2-2? I said return to home plate. Let's go home before there's an accident. Nod your head if you read me, 2-2, please."

2-2 nodded his head, but at the same time he raised and lowered the nose of his aircraft. The entire flight gyrated up-and-down like a ribbon blowing in a breeze. Then 2-2 started to change the lead, but instead of going beneath and behind Dario to replace him in the number four spot, he moved in front of him and took the number three spot. Dario eased power to let him in, as the yelling returned, louder and clearer. "What kind of shit was that, 2-2? I've never seen a flight so dicked up in my life." Then Hildripp lowered his voice and tried to show some calmness again. "Just stay in fourth position, 6-8. I think 2-2 might have carbon monoxide poisoning. 1-6, you are the leader by default. You take this flight home. Go back to South Whiting. Do you read me, 1-6?" The flight continued straight ahead. "I said return to home plate. Do you read me 1-6? Take this flight back to the fucking field. Go home!"

1-6 turned toward the field, but he turned *into* the echelon—the biggest no-no in formation flying because keeping position is impossible. Dario pulled off his power completely and dropped back, but the instructor impostors knew what was coming, and they kept a semblance of a formation.

"Jesus Christ, 1-6, you turned into the echelon! You can't turn into an echelon, 1-6. Nobody turns into an echelon, 1-6," his voice was pleading. "Do you want to have a midair? I don't want any more midairs, do you hear me! Take this flight home, 1-6!" Hildripp's voice was breaking again, at the top of his audible range. "Do you read me, 1-6? I'm on channel six, acknowledge my transmission."

A feeble, garbled voice came over the air. Dario thought it was Tyler's, but he wasn't certain. "Roger, channel six," the voice mumbled.

"Yes, channel six is our frequency, but I want you to take the flight home, goddamn it. Now, let's settle down. I've had enough of this shit!"

Suddenly, 2-2, in number three position, rolled his airplane and flew upside down.

"No, no, 2-2! You're inverted, 2-2! You . . . are . . . upside . . . down . . . 2-2. Roll your aircraft level, 2-2, and stay away from the other aircraft. Don't hit the other aircraft, 2-2!"

As 2-2 rolled level, 1-6 rolled inverted and 1-3 kept his position on his wing, rolling inverted in formation with him.

Hildripp's voice went ballistic. "Don't do that, 1-6. Don't do that, 1-3." His voice lowered as he transmitted, "D'Angelo, return to Whiting independently. You seem to be the only one up here who hasn't gone completely nuts. I don't know if they all have carbon monoxide poisoning, or if they all ate something that's making them crazy, but I've got to get them home in one piece. Do you read me, 6-8?"

"Five by five, sir. 6-8 returning to home plate, independently. Out," Dario answered.

"Thank God. My radio does work," Hildripp said. "They must have eaten something bad for breakfast."

Dario monitored channel six while he flew back to the field. The major was yelling his lungs out as the airplanes changed leads upside down and did some other bizarre maneuvers. He landed, taxied in and parked his SNJ. A crewman jumped up on the wing to unstrap his parachute and harness. "Wow, you all right, sir? You're soakin' wet!

They piped the radio sound down to the line shack. You students all get exhaust poisoned up there? We think Major Hildripp is gonna blow a gut, for sure. You OK, sir, you want me to get the flight surgeon?"

"I'm just fine, thanks. In fact, I'm feeling wonderful."

When he got to the line shack, Hildripp's voice *was* amplified through a loudspeaker. There were plane captains, mechanics and students standing around listening, laughing every time Hildripp gave forth another stream of shouted commands and expletives.

"Goddamn it, put your flight in right echelon, 1-3. You are going to fly down runway 9 and break. You are landing on runway 9, do you understand? Put your flight in right echelon."

The flight flew in the opposite direction, down runway 27. They were still in left echelon and when over the center of the field, the leader broke *into* the echelon.

"No, no, 1-3. I told you before, you can't break into the echelon 1-3, nobody ever breaks into a fucking echelon. Never, never, never. And 1-3, you are landing on the wrong runway. Do you read me, 1-3? You . . . are . . . landing . . . the . . . wrong . . . way! Runway 9 is your runway, runway 9, runway 9, runway 9!"

The three miscreants finally got their airplanes on the ground, one landing on runway nine and two on runway two-seven, while Hildripp orbited the field screaming at them.

Dario waited for Tyler and the other two instructors in the line shack.

"You did a good job," Tyler told him. "Now just play dumb. We'll handle everything."

He followed Tyler and the others to the ready room.

By the time they got there, the wire recorder had been carried down from the tower and rewound, ready to replay the radio communications it had recorded during the entire flight.

"How'd it come out?" Tyler spoke to the technician who was standing next to it.

"Loud and clear, sir. We got it all, five-by-five."

Hildripp came storming into the room. His face and his bald head were bright red, and dripping with perspiration. His flight suit was soaked under his arms and around his chest. "I've got the flight surgeon coming over to check you students for carbon-monox . . . " He recognized Tyler and the other flight instructors standing next to Dario. "What's going on, Tyler?"

"Play the recording," Tyler said to the technician. As soon as Hildripp's voice came out of the speaker, everyone in the room—except him—began to laugh. There was a large crowd just outside the door that slowly filtered into the room and joined in the laughter. Hildripp stood quietly and listened. His face turned from red to white, as he shook his head from side-to-side in disbelief. His shouts from the recording sounded even more outrageous than they had in the air; not even human, at times.

Hildripp looked directly at Dario and shouted over the recorder, "Were you in on this, D'Angelo?"

Dario stood silently for thirty seconds. He was ready to deny complicity, but he couldn't. Almost as if he were hearing some dialog in a bad film, he heard his own voice speaking clearly, "Yes, sir, major, every bit of it, sir. In fact, I was the one who first thought of recording your airborne screaming, sir."

Hildripp glowered at him for a few seconds, then silently turned and left the room.

Pete shook his head in disbelief. "You shouldn't have done that, Dario. I like your balls, but you didn't have to do that."

Dario, who'd been standing as if in a trance, turned to Tyler and spoke, haltingly. "Yes, I did, Pete. Yes, I did. I couldn't help it, because, because. Shit! It's just the way I was brought up. Anonymous revenge is worthless. Now he knows I got even with him, for Brandon and for Joe."

Low and Slow

* * *

Dario jumped the gun and went to see Lieutenant Fox, the legal officer. "Now what have you done? I'm seeing you as much as I see some sailors with creditors on their asses."

He told Fox about the flight and how he admitted to Hildripp that he was involved.

"Did you follow all of Major Hildripp's orders during the flight?"

"Yeah. I played dumb in the air. I just couldn't keep my mouth shut when he confronted me on the ground."

"I think you'll be all right. You didn't do anything wrong, except technically, perhaps, not radioing Hildripp that the others were impostors when they started their shenanigans. But that would have meant informing on fellow officers, something that's just not accepted among officers. But, of course, it all depends on how much of a stink Hildripp makes and how Captain Nord reacts. I can usually influence Nord if it affects his career, but I don't see any downside for him if he busts you and the barnstormers. Especially, since he leaves for his ship next week. You'll just have to wait and see."

Much to Dario's surprise, no repercussions arose from "The Madman Flight," as it became known. Hildripp was so humiliated, he requested an immediate transfer, and it was immediately granted by Captain Nord.

"The skipper was glad to get rid of that asshole," Tyler told him. "We tied the can to Hildripp, Dario. Wherever he goes, he'll be known as 'The Madman.' I think we did the navy, and even the marine corps, a lot of good by humbling him." They were sitting at the officers' club bar, talking over drinks. "But, you've got a can tied to you, too, kid. You'll have the reputation of a wise-ass who was one of 'The Madman Flight,' and there may be some hard-ass marine instructor down the line who won't take kindly to it. You should have kept your mouth shut, like I told you to."

"I know, I know." He took a sip from his drink. "But it was worth it." Dario smiled, because he also knew that copies of the recording were in demand, and were being widely distributed.

CHAPTER TWENTY-FOUR

ALABAMA

NAVY AUXILIARY Air Station Barin Field was in Alabama, near the Gulf of Mexico, about twenty miles west of Pensacola. To get to the infamous "Bloody Barin," where he'd be taught air-to-air gunnery, and then learn to land on an aircraft carrier, Dario drove his MG through an agricultural district. Some fields were green with potato plants, and some were plowed, with the black soil lying fallow. The culmination of this training—if he made it—would be six actual carrier landings. It was a cold, and drizzling March morning when he pulled into the base for the first time.

The BOQ at Whiting Field was an old, run down World War II relic; but, the one at Barin Field looked like it had been captured from the Confederate Army. The two-man rooms were so small they required bunk beds. Dario's room had one small window, which afforded no cross ventilation when the door was closed. There was no desk or table for study.

He met his new roommate that afternoon. Ralph Kramer was tall, well built and looked like he should be chewing on a wheat stalk. His light-brown hair was completely unruly, sticking up in shocks on top and growing in a cowlick pattern in the back. He was a farm boy from Kansas, and as they walked to the officers' club together, Ralph walked like he was stepping between furrows. He spoke slowly and deliberately, as if he were coaxing a temperamental mule.

"I've written my uncle. He's a member of Congress. I know the AOC program came as a sudden shock to the navy, but that's no reason to ignore the rules. Those rooms were originally built as barracks for enlisted men and they're not big enough for two officers. I may sound undemocratic, but the navy was never supposed to be a democracy. They're always telling us, 'rank has its privileges.' Well, goddamn it, my rank might only be ensign, but I want the privileges it's supposed to get. I want a bigger room!"

"Did you study law, Ralph?"

"Naw. I'm a geologist."

Dario liked him.

* * *

There was one thirty-caliber machine gun mounted in the cowl of the SNJ. Its firing mechanism, which Fokker invented in World War I, was synchronized to fire only when the propeller was clear of the bullet's path. The breech of the gun came into the cockpit and was armed manually by the pilot, who pulled back the breech handle and then rammed a cartridge into the firing chamber. From then on, the gun was fired electrically by a trigger in the control stick. Unfortunately, the gun constantly jammed, and although it was contrary to operating procedures, it was necessary to manually eject stuck shells and rearm the gun, unless the student wanted to spend his naval career in SNJ gunnery. Technically, it was a flight violation if there was more than one unfired cartridge in the ejection box. But, the armoring crew knew the futility of following the regulations, and ignored the violators.

The gunsight was mounted on top of the instrument panel. The students shot at a large, cloth sleeve which was towed well behind another SNJ flown by an instructor. Each student in a flight of four had bullet tips that were painted a different color. When a bullet passed through the cloth sleeve, it left some paint, which identified the accurate student pilot.

One of the first things Dario noticed when he and Ralph visited the flight line of the gunnery squadron was some SNJs making a whistling noise as they taxied. He asked an instructor about the phenomenon and he could hardly believe the answer he got. "Sometimes the firing synchronizer gets a little out of whack and a slug goes through the prop blade. The mechanics at the prop shop just file the hole smooth and take a little bit off the opposite blade to balance it. They work just fine, but they whistle." They inspected the SNJs on the line and found five with holes.

"And we were told only boatswains mates and queers whistle in the navy," Dario told Ralph. "I can't believe they don't throw those old props away and put on new ones."

"There probably aren't any new ones. They navy's starting to scrap the Jays, melting them down. My uncle tells me that even the Mexican Air Force won't take them anymore, even for free."

"How is unc' doing with getting us luxury accommodations?"

"Now don't you laugh, Dario. My uncle tells me that something's going to happen very soon. We may move slowly in Kansas, but we move deliberately."

Several days later, Ralph came into their room while Dario was lying on his bunk studying the gunnery manual. "It's happened, Dario. Good old Uncle Melvin came through. They can't give us single rooms because there aren't enough to go around, so they have to pay us a housing allowance if we want to move off the base. It's called, Basic Allowance, Quarters, in navy lingo."

Dario dropped his manual and sat up in his bunk. "How much?"

"Eighty-five smackers a month for ensigns, and we don't have to pay the forty-seven to the mess if we want to eat somewhere else."

Low and Slow

Dario laid back down on his bunk. "A lot of good it does us here in East Jesus, Alabama. What's to rent in Foley? Share a barn with a mule?"

"No, you stupid West Coast clod. Just five miles from here is one of the most beautiful, white-sand beaches in the world, Gulf Shores. There are dozens of summer rentals there, empty all winter and crying for tenants. We can get one for peanuts. Get your ass off the bed and let's go find one before the ensign land rush begins."

They found a cottage with three bedrooms. It was raised on pilings, about eight feet above the sandy ground, as where all the structures in the beach area. A screened porch across the front faced the beach. The off-season monthly rent was only sixty dollars.

"Our own little snake ranch," Ralph said as they moved their few belongings into the sparsely furnished house.

"What's a snake ranch?"

"It's a house occupied by a group of bachelor naval aviators. The yeoman at finance told me, when I applied for my quarters allowance. Said, 'you going to move into a snake ranch, sir?' I played dumb with the yeoman, but I asked an instructor later. He told me that out in the fleet most single aviators live off the base. Nobody with any balls lives in the BOQ."

When they were sitting on the screened-in porch, drinking beer from their own refrigerator while watching the waves hitting the beach, Dario felt at home for the first time since joining the navy. He'd lived in five different rooms, with many different roommates—selected by the navy, not by him. None of them had been any trouble, but living in BOQ rooms was a constant reminder that his life was transitory. Now, he had his own room, and Ralph had his. The third bedroom was ready for Bill Metz, who was expected in a few weeks.

"I'm going to like this snake ranch living," Dario said. "I have a private room where I can bring a girl, if I should find one cast up on the beach from a shipwreck, or find a farmer's daughter sitting on a fence."

"You always have girls on your mind, don't you?"

"That's not true, Ralph. I also think about cars, music and flying. But girls have priority. We could have some good parties here, if we could find some girls."

* * *

That night he and Ralph walked along the beach in the starlight, admiring the phosphorescence in the waves that rolled against the shore. The white-sugar sand wasn't the soft, dry sand that had trapped his MG the night he went to the beach beyond Fort Walton with Tammy. This beach was hard; packed solid from the winter storms.

"You ever see the movie *Pandora and the Flying Dutchman,* Ralph?"

"Naw."

"James Mason and Ava Gardner, came out a few years back. Anyway, there's this guy with a race car in the movie. He tries to break some speed record, racing down a flat beach in Spain. This beach reminds me of it. I'm going to try something in the morning."

The next day, Dario drove his MG onto the beach and had almost ten unobstructed miles of flat, hard-packed sand before him. He accelerated the MG and pushed it to 100 miles-per-hour. The only obstacle on the beach was Pixton's Pier, a fishing pier built on pilings, which ran from the road to two hundred feet out in the Gulf. Dario stopped and counted eight pilings toward the road from the bait shack on the pier, where he could go under it with minimum clearance. On his next run down the beach, he counted the pilings, gritted his teeth and went under with only a foot or less (there was always some bouncing), between the top of the windshield and the base timbers of the pier. He went back to the cottage and persuaded Ralph to go with him for another run.

Ralph screamed something unintelligible as they approached the pier going over 80 miles-per-hour. He put his hands over his eyes and crouched down in his seat as they sped under it. When they did, there was a loud schussing sound for an instant. "Are we clear," Ralph yelled, his hands still over his face.

Low and Slow

"No sweat, Ralph. It's easy. I count the pilings from the bait shack. I'll get some white paint and mark the spot to go under, on each side. If you got excited, think what it will do to a girl. It's better than a roller coaster ride! I'll have to get plastic seat covers, like Bill Metz, because they'll be peeing in their panties."

"Dario, you are a devious bastard. There you go again, always thinking of girls."

Dario let the MG coast to a stop, letting the engine idle. He looked at Ralph and said, "You hicks may be slow, but you're sure observant. You're absolutely right, Ralph. I don't spend every moment thinking about it, but chasing pussy is a big part of my life. It's why I joined the navy, it's why my father got me to play a musical instrument, and it's probably, subconsciously, why I love to drive sports cars. I want to attract girls who like excitement like I do. Unfortunately, all I've been doing lately is thinking about it. We've got the beach, but where are the girls?"

CHAPTER TWENTY-FIVE

IN MID-APRIL the clouds left and southeast Alabama suddenly became bathed in bright, warm sunshine. The Gulf's water color turned from dull grey to the blue and turquoise Dario remembered from Panama City and Fort Walton Beach the summer before. The sea's temperature climbed several degrees every day, making swimming and body surfing a pleasure again. The third week of April was the week before Easter, and the sun came out every morning with a promise of clear skies and balmy breezes for the day. With the sun, and the Easter vacation, came the girls. They came from Mobile, they came from college campuses like Ol' Miss and Auburn. They came from as far away as Birmingham to enjoy the sunshine and the beach. Every rental cottage on the island was suddenly full.

"Oh, yes. The week before and after Easter are always busy, if the weather's good," Mrs. Brandywine, their rental lady, told Dario and Bill Metz. "Then it will quiet down again until June, when our season really begins. It gets blistering hot here in July and August, but even then it's cool compared to the heat they get inland."

The beach was only occupied near the center of Gulf Shores, where the road from Foley met the beach road perpendicularly. There was paved parking there, with no sand dunes separating it from the water. Now that this part of the beach was finally occupied by bathers,

Dario drove his MG slowly past them before accelerating to Pixton's Pier, where he would speed under it between the pilings. On one of his cruises past the bathers, he spotted two girls lying on a blanket. He drove to his cottage, just across the road, and called to Bill, who stuck his head out the screen door.

"What's up?"

"Pussy alert. There are two girls alone on the beach, and they aren't fat and they don't have pimples. Put some beers and ice in your cooler and let's go hunting."

"Should I bring the cherry brandy?"

"Uh-uh. These girls look the college-type. Maybe bring some Cokes and the rum."

One young person was a redhead and the other was a blond. Both had equally attractive bodies, although their breasts weren't visible because they were lying on their stomachs, seemingly asleep. Dario and Bill walked up to them, carrying the cooler full of drinks.

"How are we going to approach them, Bill? I don't think these are Pensacola Cracker, smart-ass broads. We've got to be subtle."

"Dario! What am I ever, if not subtle, I ask you? Trust me. I'll be the model of tact and decorum."

Dario kept his mouth shut, for once. *From a guy with a pink and cream car, who can know when he's serious?* he rationalized.

They stopped behind the girls, looking down on them.

"Hi, girls. It's hot out here, you must be thirsty? How about a rum and Coke?" Bill spoke in a voice slightly louder than normal.

The seemingly sleeping girls raised their heads first, then raised their sunglasses as they surveyed the interlopers. Dario was immediately attracted to the redhead. It was the deep blue of her eyes he saw when she raised her glasses and her half-mocking smile that enthralled him. The orthodontist, who'd guided her teeth to their perfection, deserved every penny of his fee. They glistened within a slightly wide mouth, with full lips that had to be the envy of every thin-lipped harpy whoever saw them. The whiteness of her teeth was highlighted by the contrast of her freckles, which were almost the same color as her dark red hair.

Neither girl spoke, but the redhead raised, turned and sat up. Dario almost drooled when he looked down at her breasts. They were a perfect size and her nipples were clearly outlined through her Bikini halter. He sighed. He fantasized that, without any doubt in the world, her nipples were dark, dark brown with perfectly spaced little bumps circling the outer edge of her areolas, like decorations on a fine china plate.

Hot house tits. Definitely, hot house tits, he thought. He remained standing still, his mouth slightly open, with just the hint of a drool escaping at one edge. The redhead turned her upper torso to the left to talk to the girl lying beside her. As she did, her legs moved just enough to allow several pubic hairs to pop out of her bikini bottom, along her inner thigh. The curly hair was bright auburn. Dario gasped.

"We're doing just fine all by our little ol' lonesome selves, aren't we Aud," the redhead said to her companion.

Dario almost swooned. It wasn't a Cracker twang, it wasn't a southern drawl, it was the voice of Scarlett O'Hara from *Gone With the Wind*. It was genteel, naughty, sweet and haughty, all in one.

"But we're not!" Dario blurted out. "We're not doing fine all by our lonesome selves. We live over there and train as pilots at Barin Field all week. We never get to meet any girls, you're the first girls on this beach since we moved in. We're harmless. We just want to share a drink with you and talk. Surely you'll be kind to a couple of poor, lonely servicemen."

The redhead lowered her sunglasses and stared through them at him. "Does that line of corny bullshit ever, actually, work?"

"I don't know. I just made it up. I've got other corny lines. I'll go through them all, but I'm not going away."

She turned again to her friend. "What do you think, Aud. Should we tease these lonesome service boys? Or should we send them back to their poor, boring endeavors? Like driving a sports car up-and-down the beach?"

Hope sprung in Dario's heart. "I'll take you for a ride in it. Down the beach, fast."

"Mmm, maybe. I do like fast cars."

Bill put the cooler down and sat on it next to the blond. "Hi, Aud. Our two friends here seem to be having their own conversation, so how about you and me having ours? Is it Aud, for Audrey?"

"Wish it were, more's the pity." She'd raised herself to her elbows, which exposed cleavage that was above average. In contrast to the redhead's freckles, Aud had clear, pink skin, heavily oiled with suntan lotion. She had an attractive face, with light-brown eyes and a small, almost button nose which complimented her bright, blond hair. "It's Aud for Audley. My parents love old family names. But just call me Aud. Are you going to feed me a line of bullshit like your friend fed Michelle?"

"Me? No way. I don't use bullshit lines, don't believe in 'em. What you see is what you get. Plain ol' Bill Metz, from Wisconsin. Graduate of the University of Wisconsin, ensign in the US Navy, flight student at the base over there, and madly in love with you since the minute I saw you. Will you marry me, Aud? Aud, oh, what's your family name?"

"It's Sibold," she said with difficulty, through her laughter.

* * *

Michelle Duquesne went for a ride down the beach in Dario's MG later that afternoon. She loved cars and she was excited by speed. When he approached Pixton's Pier, which now had white spots painted on the pilings he drove between, Michelle screamed from fifty yards before and continued until they were well past it. It was a scream of excitement, not of fear. After the pier, he slowed to a stop and looked at her. She was exhilarated. There were small beads of perspiration over her lips and her face was flushed, making the contrast of her freckles even greater. Dario thought she was even more gorgeous when she was excited.

"That was wonderful! I couldn't believe it when you didn't slow for the pier. I was frightened, but I didn't want you to stop. You drive your car so fast, almost like a racer."

"It *is* a race car. It's tuned for sports car racing."

"Do you drive it in races?"

"Of course. I was lucky enough to win the last time out, over at Eglin Air Force Base." He said the words, nonchalantly.

"Do you always win?"

"No, I'm afraid not." He decided to be humble—and truthful. "It was my first win in four races, and it was only a novice race."

"What else do you do, besides racing cars and flying airplanes?"

"Not much. I play some piano. Music was my major in college."

Dario stood by for the inevitable question he always got whenever he told someone he played the piano: "Do you play classical?"

"Do you play any modern jazz?" she asked, completely surprising him.

"Michelle! Stop it. You're being too perfect. Most girls don't even know what modern jazz is. Don't tell me you like it?"

She turned in her seat toward him, rested her head on her shoulder and looked up at his face over her lowered sunglasses. "I have all the George Shearing, Stan Getz, Ella Fitzgerald, and Oscar Peterson LPs. I drive my mother crazy playing them. She's stuffy because she only likes classical and opera. You see, my family is a patron of the arts. They're on committees that support our symphony and our opera. But I hate it. I went to a jazz concert a few years ago and I've been a fan of modern jazz ever since."

Dario took her hand. It was the first time he'd touched her. "I'd like to show you how some classical music is cool, it's not all bad. I'd love to play for you sometime."

She pulled her hand from his, gently, and sat back in her seat. "Perhaps you can." She spoke so softly, he hardly heard her add, "Tonight."

Low and Slow

* * *

Michelle was from Montgomery, two hundred miles to the north. Her family had been there for generations. Her ancestors were French settlers from New Orleans. She was staying at her family's summer home at Point Clear, on Mobile Bay, about twenty miles west of Gulf Shores. From the way she spoke, with perfect grammar and elocution, Dario knew she was a far cry from the paper mill girls, WAFs, and cocktail waitresses he'd been with so far in the South.

Bill and Dario followed Aud's car in Bill's Ford, going to Michelle's home in Point Clear. The sun was setting over Mobile Bay as they entered a driveway through two large stone pillars, with a stone arch between them. "Jubilee 1911" was carved into the arch. The entrance had been the only break in a stone wall which went on for blocks. They drove down a long drive with closely-cut lawn on each side. The drive made a turn, and they saw a large stone mansion situated on the shore of the bay. When he saw the arched entrance, Dario expected to find "Tara," Scarlett's plantation home in *Gone With the Wind*. Instead, the building he saw looked more like a French chateau. Jubilee was surrounded by spreading oak trees, with gardenias, azaleas, and magnolias also growing near to it. All the landscaping was well groomed and vibrant.

"Either your redhead is the gardener's daughter or you have hit upon some very rich, red pussy," Bill commented in his usual suave manner.

"And I was surprised when she told me she had a piano. There's probably a music room big enough for a full orchestra."

They were met at the front door by a maid. Dario had never been in a house with a maid before; it *really* made him feel like he was in a movie. He was the tramp, brought home by the rich, flighty, spoiled daughter—much to the chagrin of her overly-tolerant parents. Only there weren't any parents at the house. Michelle explained that she was there alone; her parents remained in Montgomery until June, when her mother moved down for the summer and her father came down whenever he could get away from his business.

"My grandfather built this house to celebrate the fiftieth anniversary of the start of the Civil War. He never admitted it ever ended." The entrance way and salon were floored in marble, with expensive rugs at strategic places. Michelle started up a long, winding, staircase, also marble. "Make yourselves at home while I clean up, and don't be bashful. Sarah will get you anything you want. I'm going to have her bring me up a vodka tonic while I dress. She'll show you where the music room is."

Sarah, the colored maid, showed them to the room and took their requests for rum and Cokes, as if she made them regularly.

"Jesus," Dario muttered, looking over the room. Elegant, stuffed chairs and couches were placed around the room, with small tables between them. Dario didn't know the period, but he knew they were French, old, and expensive.

"If this is the music room, what's the living room like?" he asked Bill. "It's not big enough for a full orchestra, but big enough for a string quartet and a good sized audience." He opened the lid of the grand piano and played a few chords. "Steinway, the best, and in perfect tune. Did I crash and burn last week, Bill? I think I'm in heaven, only you wouldn't be there, so this *must* be real."

"It's real, asshole. You just fell into some tall cotton. I wonder if you can handle this one, Dario? She's out of my league."

"My father once told me that you can't tell the difference between a contessa and a milk maid, when they moan and scream in ecstacy. My father was very democratic." He sat down and played a warm-up exercise. "But you're right, Bill. If I'm going to get anywhere with this one, I'll have to play her gently. I don't think she's been hit on by white hats and cadets. More likely polo playing fraternity boys, and I'm not in that league. I don't have any sheet music for the likes of Michelle. I'll have to play her by ear."

When she entered the room, Dario broke into strong, full jazz chords. Michelle wore her hair up, fastened on top of her head with a jeweled clasp. She had on a sleeveless, white silk blouse, which hid little more of her breasts than the bikini had. She'd put on deep red lipstick and a hint of rose rouge on her cheeks. A strand of perfect pearls accentuated the fine lines of her thin neck, contrasting the freckles. She smiled broadly, showing approval of what she heard.

Aud returned from her nearby home while Dario was still playing. She already seemed to be very fond of Bill and, after listening to Dario play a few songs, they left by the French doors and went out into the garden which ran down to the shore of the bay. Dario looked over the piano, beyond the doors. The moon was coming up behind them, and it was already bright. He could see a wharf and boat house made of the same stone as Jubilee. Michelle came to the piano and took the position so many girls had before; standing at the edge, looking at the keyboard, at his hands.

"I'm going to play some Ravel for you. I want to show you how some of his chords and ideas are almost jazz." He talked as he played. "Hear the chords, Michelle. They're cool. I get many ideas from Ravel—and Debussy. I'll bet they'd be playing cool jazz if they were alive today, like this. He then played his jazz interpretation of the Ravel music."

"You do play very well, Dario. I'm very pleasantly surprised. Most pianists I meet play songs just as they're written. I've never met anyone who can improvise like you."

"How long did you study?"

She laughed. "You're guessing."

"No, I'm not. You're too knowledgeable. I'll bet you play classical piano and you play it well. I played for you, now you play for me." He slid to the end of the piano bench and stood up.

"I'm awful, really, I make mistakes."

"You couldn't be awful, Michelle. Play for me, please." He took his Cuba Libra and sat in a stuffed chair at the side of the room.

Michelle shrugged her shoulders, sat on the bench and adjusted it forward. "You asked for it." She played a Chopin piece, brilliantly. Dario was very surprised. Michelle was almost concert quality, much more than just a competent amateur. He got up and stood behind her. When she finished, he leaned over and kissed the back of her bare neck, just above the pearls. The aroma of her perfume filled his nostrils. It was gardenia, the flower he'd come to associate with the South. She wore just a hint; it was pleasant and tantalizing, promising things exotic.

She shook a little as he kissed her, as if he'd tickled her. "Please don't." She spoke without turning to face him.

"It was only meant as a compliment for your playing, nothing more. Trying to seduce a girl with a kiss on the back of the neck isn't my style." He moved to the side of the piano, taking the same position she had when he played. "Why did you tell me you hate classical music? You play like a professional."

"My mother is a concert pianist, although she seldom plays professionally anymore. I grew up with music being forced on me. I had to practice every day, take lessons, play for recitals. I just got tired of it. I turned to listening to jazz to rebel, and ended up loving it." She slid to the far edge of the bench and gestured to the center of it. "Play more, Dario, please."

The "please" came out "pu-leaz." He would do anything she wanted when she said, "pu-leaz."

* * *

Sarah served them a cold supper later, and Dario used the correct silverware, thanks to Brandon's training. When they were leaving, Dario asked Michelle when he could see her again.

"Gulf Shores is the closest and best ocean beach we have. I'll probably be over every day, if the weather stays pleasant," she told him. "Maybe we'll run into each other again, there?"

"I don't want to just run into you, Michelle. I want to see you again, soon."

"I'm sorry, but I don't like to make plans. If we meet again, it'll have to be serendipitously, like today."

Bill and Aud were locked in an embrace by his car, as Dario and

Michelle stood in her doorway. He tried to hold her, to kiss her, but she protested by holding out her arms to ward him off. She said nothing.

"Goodnight, Michelle. Thanks for a beautiful evening. You have a beautiful home and a beautiful piano, and you play it well. How about just one more corny line. I think we could make some beautiful music together."

"Goodnight, Dario. Thanks for the exciting ride, and for the jazz."

She turned and disappeared into the unlighted salon. He got a gnawing feeling of loss in his stomach.

* * *

Dario flew a gunnery hop every day the following week. When his formation crossed Gulf Shores Beach on its way to the gunnery range ten miles offshore, he looked down at the ant-like figures lying on the beach and wondered if one of them was Michelle. He'd been thinking about her, constantly.

His flight wasn't shooting live ammunition yet, but when he dove on the sleeve in a dry run, he made a machine gun noise with his mouth while holding down the inoperative trigger. He felt like the pilots in a hundred war movies he'd seen, where the camera gets a close-up of the gloved finger on the trigger button and then pans to the guns firing from the wings.

He called Michelle from a phone booth Tuesday night, but Sarah told him she wasn't home. On Wednesday, he rushed to change from his flight gear to his uniform, after he was secured from flying, and raced to the beach. There, he looked for Aud's car first and, not finding it, changed into shorts in his cottage and drove up and down the sand, looking for Michelle. He knew it was always too late in the day by the time he got there, but he tried anyway. He phoned again Thursday night and got the same negative answer from the maid.

On Friday, he got away from the hangar at two p.m. He rushed to his locker and changed to his uniform, then ran to his MG. He drove fast, hoping to get to the beach before Michelle left, if she'd been there that day. He was going down the Foley to Gulf Shores road at over 80, careful that there were no other cars on the road near him, and especially not behind him. He was always looking in his rear-view mirror for police. He'd been sloppy the night the Escambia County Sheriff's posse got him, so he'd been very vigilant since. As he neared the bridge over the inland waterway, he slowed. When he hit the crest of the bridge, he saw a policeman standing in the road ahead of him. He was wearing a light-blue uniform with dark-blue piping on the collar and sleeves, and on his cap. He was waving his arms and pointing to the side of the road. Dario followed his point and parked on the shoulder.

"Howdy," the policeman said, walking toward the MG. He had the local accent and a red complexion.

Dario saw the Baldwin County Sheriff's emblem on his shirt sleeve. "Hello, what's the problem, deputy?"

"No problem, sir. Please let me see your license so I can write you a speeding ticket."

"Speeding? I was only going 40 when you saw me coming over the bridge. I wasn't speeding." He handed the deputy his California driver's license.

"Oh, I'm not talking about over the bridge, sir. I'm talking about two miles t'other side of it. My partner's there with a new fangled electronic eye beam doohickey the county paid a lot of money for." He looked at Dario's license, and at the gold bars on his shirt. "You hold the record, so far, Ensign D'Angelo. My partner radioed me that y'all pushed his little needle up to eighty-five miles 'n hour. My, my. I don't see how these little ol' doodle bugs stay on the ground goin' that fast. Anyways, at that speed I'm supposed to take you into town 'n lock you up 'til the judge can see you. But my partner, Beauford 'n me, we don't want to get you young navy flyers in big trouble with your COs, so I'm only ticketin' you for sixty in a forty-five. We like what you are doin' here for the local economy. You all are real nice boys." He handed Dario a duplicate of the ticket he'd written while he was talking. "Yo'all just go'n see Judge Hamrick Saturday mornin'. He does traffic violations then, at his house. You'll just have to pay a little fine. Nothin' to it. But, I don't know how long Beauford 'n me can rightly keep cheating the county, Ensign D'Angelo, so I suggest that you slow down, just a little. I'm not sayin' to stay under forty-five, y'hear. Beauford 'n me's got to get the county some income from their new fangled gadget, but we surely don't want to take you to jail. That would take all the fun out of it."

"Thank you, officer. You're a real gentlemen."

"Why, I thank *you*, sir. Those are mighty kind words. You'll like the judge, too. He's a genuine, Julep sippin' southern gentlemen."

Judge Hamrick's court was on the porch of his ancient wood house in Foley. Dario parked the MG in the street and walked up the azalea lined walk leading to it. He got there early, so he could spend the day on the beach looking for Michelle. He'd given up phoning her, in the realization that the only way he would see her again was by meeting her "serendipitously," as she put it, and he knew it would have to be on the beach.

The judge had a flowing white moustache that matched his full head of flowing white hair. He looked just like Frederick March playing the older Mark Twain in a movie. He had on a plain-white shirt but normal necktie—not a black-string tie, which somewhat disappointed Dario. The judge poured him a glass of lemonade, and got right to business. "Guilty or not guilty of speedin', son?"

"Guilty, your honor."

"Ten dollars fine, plus five dollars court costs."

He paid, and the judge wrote him a receipt, which seemed to take forever. Dario was anxious to get to the beach and every minute seemed to drag on at half-speed. Finally, the judge finished writing and carefully tore the receipt from his book. He handed it to him, and looked across the lawn at Dario's car.

"That car of yours looks like its mighty fast. How fast will it go, son?"

Dario knew he should 'soft pedal' its speed, but he couldn't help bragging about his MG's performance. "Over a hundred, judge. It's tuned for racing. I won the novice race over at Eglin last year."

"My, my. Isn't that somethin', a little car like that," the judge said, slightly shaking his head. "Would you care for a slice of watermelon, Ensign D'Angelo? I just got one that promises to be bodaciously sweet. It's the first of the season."

Dario hated to say "no," to the kind old gentleman, but he was anxious to get to the beach. "Thank you, sir, but I have to hurry back to Gulf Shores."

"Too bad, too bad. But the watermelon'll be in season for several months, and if you keep hurryin', that pair of deputies with those magic beams will be givin' you a return ticket. Why, in just the two weeks since they got it, I've had more business than I have since the war ended. I think I'd better double-up on my lemonade supply."

"Goodbye, judge."

"Good day to you, son. And, thank you kindly."

Several blocks from the Judge's house, Dario stopped the MG in the middle of the street. *I'm breaking one of Babbo's cardinal rules,* he told himself. *I'm letting Michelle control my actions. I'm her slave, and she doesn't even know it! If she's there, she's there. If she isn't, to hell with her.*

He spun a U-turn and returned to the judge's house. The old gentleman was still seated on his porch. Dario parked the MG and walked up to him. "My mouth keeps watering, thinking about that sweet watermelon, judge. I *would* like a piece of it. Can I change my plea?"

The judge, who wore a look of surprise as Dario was approaching him, smiled broadly as he stood up and gestured to a seat at a table near the porch's edge. "You surely can, son. You surely can. Sit over there and I'll have Jehmima bring us each a generous slice. I just hate to eat alone, but I have to, since I lost my dear wife. Why, even the best of dishes always tastes better with a dash of company."

* * *

On Monday, Dario's flight made its first live firing runs. He armed his gun, rolled his SNJ and dove for the sleeve. As he got within range and saw it in his sight, he squeezed the trigger. He fired the pre-scribed short bursts until he was almost into the towed sleeve, then passed under it and climbed to rejoin his flight. They continued to make runs until their ammunition was expended, then they flew back over Gulf Shores.

Again, he looked down at the ant people on the beach and thought about Michelle, although he was trying to get her out of his mind. He'd searched for her Saturday and Sunday; he was through search-ing for her.

CHAPTER TWENTY-SIX

F LIGHT OPERATIONS were suspended for two days, as a storm came up from the Gulf and lashed the coast with heavy surf and inches of rain. Dario walked on the beach with Bill and Ralph and watched the unusual large, grey waves break over the end of Pixton's Pier and roll over the beach and over the road at some low spots. They each wore tennis shoes, which left deep footprints in the wet sand.

When the storm passed, the hot, late April sun shone down and dried the beach in one day. On the second day, Dario took Bill with him in the MG for a high-speed run. They were wearing only their bathing suits and sandals. He drove two miles away from the pier at moderate speed, then turned around and accelerated through the gears. He looked at the speedometer as he neared the pier; it was beyond the 100-mile-per-hour mark and bouncing even higher. He aimed between the painted spots on the pilings and held his foot to the firewall.

For a split second, his already experienced depth perception warned him that something had changed when he heard a "thump" and felt something go through his hair. They were well clear of the pier by the time he realized what had happened. The windshield was resting across his arms and Bill's lap. He let the MG coast to a stop. The windshield was shattered, but the hundreds of small broken sections were held together by the flexible safety plastic in the center. He had cuts on his forehead and on his arms from small pieces of glass that had flown loose, but they were only superficial. He looked at Bill. He also had some small cuts.

"You OK?"

"No. I need a Cuba Libra. In fact, I need lots of Cubies."

"Don't move. My side of the glass will sit on the steering wheel. I'll get a towel to lift the windshield off you."

When he'd removed the glass, he inspected the MG. The pier had struck the windshield posts about two inches below the top of the windshield, and what Dario felt go through his hair was compressed air from the less than one-inch it passed under the overhead timbers. Bill hadn't felt the air because he was crouched down.

"You were safe, Bill. You were hiding down in your seat."

"Big fucking deal. I was a inch or so farther from death than you were."

Dario felt foolish. He'd endangered his best friend's life, as well as his own. They put the smashed windshield in the trunk and drove back to the pier. Dario drove up to the space between the marked pilings and parked beneath it. He and Bill got out and looked at the marks in the timber where the windshield posts had struck.

"I don't understand. This is the right spot. There are my white spots."

"The storm, you jerk! The storm washed more sand up on the beach." Bill came near Dario, putting his face just a few inches away. "You asshole. Here I fly my ass off and get paid extra because it's dangerous, and I ride with you for free. I'm going to add a sentence to my survivor's sheet. 'Dear Mom, if the top of my head is missing, blame that crazy wop, Dario D'Angelo!' "

Dario thought for a second that Bill was serious until he saw the scowl on his face turn into a laugh. Dario began to laugh with him. Bill returned the laughter even louder, then began to roar. Dario roared even louder. They hugged each other and rolled in the sand, laughing hysterically. The adrenaline was filtering out of their systems and they were both euphoric, because they'd cheated death. A dozen or so bathers and fishermen who'd seen the MG go under the pier came up to them. They made a wide circle around the young men, who were now sitting in the sand, slapping each other on their backs and laughing.

"You'll have to move your spots," Bill said between laughs.

"No I won't. I made a plexiglass racing screen at the hobby shop. I was getting ready to put it on anyway. It's less drag, more top speed. It's only seven inches high. It'll clear the pier."

More laughter came from each of them.

"But do one thing, please. Always make a slow pass first and check the sand height. I don't think even a lucky wop like you is going to get a second chance with a fuck-up like that."

They deposited the windshield in a trash can near the beach, after Dario had broken off the lower corner which held his base sticker. He kept the corner in his door compartment. When he entered the base the next morning, he held it up for the guard, who hesitatingly saluted it and waved him through.

* * *

Dario saw Bill at the officers' club one afternoon during the following week. They often had a drink there, before leaving the base for Gulf Shores.

"I just talked to Aud on the phone," Bill told him. "She told me to tell you that Michelle is back at Jubilee and they're coming to the beach tomorrow, if the weather's good. I thought you just might be a little interested." Bill had a grin on his face that looked like a cat-that-ate-the-canary.

"Shit. I have a gunnery hop at two o'clock."

"Too bad. Aud said they usually leave about four."

"No way I can make it by four. It'll be five o'clock at the earliest, even if I disregard deputy Beauford and his magic ray gun."

"As they say, that's the breaks of naval air." Bill sucked his rum and Coke through the ice cubes in his glass.

"It's probably a good thing. Who needs a broad who won't take phone calls, wants to meet only 'serendipitously.' I'd forgotten all about Michelle. Too bad, though, she's got a beautiful piano."

"And beautiful knockers, ass and everything else. Audley told me she's been in Montgomery."

"You're getting pretty thick with Audley, aren't you? What's a nice girl like her doing with a person of ill repute like you?"

"Can I help it if the old Metz charm's overwhelmed her? Too bad you can't make it tomorrow."

Dario thought about faking a cold at sick call in the morning, but he didn't want to miss his flight and get behind with the syllabus.

CHAPTER
TWENTY-SEVEN

THE WEATHER was bright and hot the next afternoon; perfect beach weather. As Dario's gunnery flight flew over Gulf Shores Beach, he looked down and knew that one of the ant-like figures he saw on it was Michelle.

He'd made two good firing runs and his machine gun functioned perfectly. He hadn't had to pull back the breech and eject even one bad round. On his third pass, he approached the sleeve at the right speed and position, and he could see the tracers penetrating the cloth sleeve as he fired. On his fourth and last firing run, he got a little behind so he added a little extra power. He fired one, then a second burst, when he saw a flash in front of the gun and felt a vibration from his engine which caused the entire airplane to shake violently. He instinctively reduced the power to idle and pulled out of the firing pattern, turning toward land. His engine continued to vibrate, though much less since he'd reduced the power. He was confused and frightened. Then he remembered his emergency procedures and pulled back on the stick hard, zooming up until his airspeed dissipated to 85 knots. "If you lose power suddenly, immediately convert your excess airspeed into altitude," he remembered an instructor telling him. When he leveled off, he'd gained 500 feet, which earned him an extra mile of horizontal gliding distance. He trimmed the elevator so the SNJ was gliding at a constant 85 knots, the most efficient gliding speed to cover the most distance over the ground. He pulled the circuit breaker for the landing gear warning horn, which had been honking since he pulled back the power. (He was glad that his frivolity with the Road Runner prank made him so expert in the workings of the horn). He was still worried, but he knew he was reacting correctly and he thought he knew what was wrong. The airplane was at fault; he wasn't.

"Hardtack 4-3, this is Hardtack 6-3. What are you doing?" his instructor, who was perched above the flight watching their gunnery runs, radioed.

"I have an emergency, 6-3. I think a bullet went through my prop. I saw a flash and the engine started vibrating. I pulled off the power and I'm heading for shore at best-glide speed."

"What speed is that, 4-3?"

"Eighty-five knots."

"Good head work. I'll join up on you. Break, Hardtack flight, return to home plate. 4-3, I'm going to tower frequency."

Dario did the same, and heard, "Barin Tower, this is Hardtack 6-3. I have an emergency. Hardtack 4-3 has an engine vibration. We are fifteen miles south of Gulf Shores. Student is gliding toward Canal Field. Alert rescue boat and helo."

"This is Barin Tower. Roger, Hardtack 6-3. Rescue being alerted. We'll monitor your tactical frequency. Good luck, out."

Dario watched his altimeter slowly winding down from the 6500 feet he had when he started his glide.

"I'm back on tactical, do you read me, 4-3?"

"Roger, five-by-five," Dario responded.

"There's little or no wind, so you should make it to land. Have you tried putting back a little power? Just a little will help your glide ratio, guarantee you'll make it to feet-dry."

"I'll try." Dario slowly advanced his throttle and the engine vibration became more intense until, suddenly, it raced wildly and black oil covered his windscreen. He jerked the throttle back, pulled the gas mixture to cut off and turned off his magnetos. He was certain that his propeller had broken off and was falling into the tranquil blue and turquoise waters of the Gulf of Mexico.

"Now what happened, 4-3?" the instructor asked.

"Now I've got no prop, no power, no nothin'."

He saw his instructor flying on his left wing. "I can't see any damage, except there's oil coming out of the hole where the shaft used to be. Looks like it broke off clean."

When the vibration began, Dario became an automaton, doing everything he'd been taught to do without thinking about it. Now, he had time to assess his situation. Even though he had an instructor with him, he was still the pilot-in-command of his aircraft. He would make the decision to bail out or ditch the aircraft in the sea—if he couldn't make it to land. Since the propeller had separated and the engine was shut down, his flight was silent except for the sound of air rushing past his cockpit.

He checked his gauges and noticed his rate of descent had diminished. He thought about it for a few seconds and reasoned that, since the propeller was no longer turning the engine, its compression was no longer creating cylinder drag.

"6-3, this is 4-3. I just figured it out. I've got a better than normal glide ratio. My Jay Bird is now like an airplane with a fully-feathered prop."

"You're right. That'll give you a better chance to make land, might even make Canal Field."

Dario was feeling good. The adrenaline was easing off and he was relaxing. "My Jay Bird is now a Gee Bird, sir."

"What do you mean, D'Angelo?"

"It's a Sierra November Golf, a Secret Navy Glider."

The instructor did not answer.

When he was two miles from the beach, he was sure he could make it. He'd purposely pointed toward the parking lot at Gulf Shores, although it was slightly left of a direct line to Canal Field, the navy practice landing field which was two miles inland from the shore. He did it because he hoped Michelle was on the beach, near the parking lot. He was at 1500 feet when he crossed the beach.

"Hardtack 4-3 is feet-dry," he transmitted.

"Roger, 4-3. You can turn right a little and make a straight-in to Canal Field."

Dario knew he could, and he should, but for a dead-stick landing he'd been taught to pick a spot, fly over it at 1500 feet and circle to a landing. He opened his canopy. Oil sprayed on him, coming over the windscreen. He wiped his eyes with his sleeve and pulled down his goggles. He was pumping pure adrenaline through his system again. He was frightened, but this didn't detract him from doing what he'd practiced dozens of times during his early training. He was a student of rote, doing everything in proper sequence, "By the numbers," as the navy called it. He began his turn back toward the beach.

"What're you doing, D'Angelo? Turn toward Canal Field. You can make a straight-in to runway 3-0," his instructor radioed to him.

"No sir. I picked the beach to land on and I've committed myself to land there. I'm not supposed to change my mind once I've picked a spot."

The instructor was astonished. "But . . . but, you can land wheels down at Canal Field."

Landing on unimproved terrain was supposed to be with the wheels up because the SNJ was prone to flip over on its back if the wheels encountered any obstruction during roll out. Even in a soft field, such a flip could be fatal to the pilot, either by crushing him or by fire which could erupt from burst fuel tanks. He turned off his battery switch to avoid an electrical short which could ignite the fuel in a crash landing. Doing so also cut radio communication with his instructor, who was screaming an order to him to land at Canal Field. But, Dario couldn't hear him.

When his turn took him back over the beach at low altitude, he saw about fifty people on the sand to the west of Pixton's Pier, near the parking lot. Most were standing up, looking at him. He continued, and lined up with the unoccupied section of the beach east of the pier. He lowered his landing gear handle. There was no hydraulic pressure without the engine-driven pump, of course, but the SNJ was designed so that gravity pulled the wheels down. He rocked his wings vigorously from side-to-side, locking the gear in place. He put the flap handle down and pulled up the handle on the emergency hydraulic pump and pumped the flaps full down. When he was near the sand, he held the SNJ a foot off the surface until it dissipated all its speed and lowered itself gently. It felt as solid as any landing he'd ever made on concrete or asphalt. He let the aircraft roll and decelerate without using the brakes, but just before it stopped he hit the left brake and spun the airplane around 180 degrees. He was pointed west, along the beach. He stuck his head out of the cockpit and saw people running toward him. He also saw, and heard, his instructor's SNJ fly low over him.

Dario turned the battery switch on and waited thirty seconds for the radio tubes to warm up before he called him. "Hardtack 6-3, this is 4-3. I'm on the deck with boots down and laced."

"D'Angelo, goddamn it. I ordered you to land at Canal Field." The voice was loud, and shrill. "Didn't you read me?"

"No, sir. I turned off my battery. Didn't want to catch on fire if I flipped over."

"I thought you were crazy, dropping your gear, but it seems to have worked out." The voice was calmer.

"I knew the sand was hard, sir. I drove my car on it recently."

"OK, OK. Stand by your aircraft, D'Angelo. Somebody from the base will be here to pick you up."

"It's not necessary, sir. I live within walking distance."

There was a ten-second pause before the instructor replied, his words precise, and in a slow meter. "Shut down your radio and turn off your battery, D'Angelo, I'm going home. I can't take any more of your bullshit."

He remained in the cockpit for a minute longer while blood replaced adrenaline, just as it had a few days before in almost the same spot after he'd hit the pier with his MG. He began to get the post-excitement-euphoric feeling again, and he started to laugh. He removed his oily helmet, released his parachute and shoulder straps, and climbed out of the cockpit onto the wing. He stood on it and looked down. There were about twenty people, most of them in bathing suits, standing around the wing. One of them was Michelle, with Aud and Bill standing beside her. They all began to clap. Dario blushed, but no one in the crowd knew it because his face was covered with engine oil. He didn't know what to do, but he instinctively put his two hands together and held them over his head, prize fighter style. When he jumped off the wing onto the sand, Michelle came to him, put her arms around him and kissed him. He could feel her Bikini-covered breasts pushing against his oily flight suit. He could also taste the engine oil as she moved her lips and her tongue over his.

When Michelle finished the kiss, she stood back. Grimy engine oil was smeared over her face and body, staining her white Bikini. He'd been fantasizing about her since he last saw her at Jubilee, though he tried to forget her. But even in his most wishful fantasies she'd never looked as beautiful as she did there, covered with black oil contrasting with her white Bikini and the white-sugar sand of Gulf Shores Beach.

"You're going to have a tough time outdoing that serendipitous arrival, my hero," she said, softly. To Dario, her sweet, southern-accented voice was music. He pulled an oily glove off his hand and inspected the cleanliness of his fingernails. Then he looked at Michelle and, in his best, nonchalant David Niven impersonations, said, "A piece of cake, actually, my dear Michelle." He'd been waiting for the right moment to use that RAF movie phrase since he began flying. He couldn't imagine a situation that would ever be more appropriate. He was the king of the mountain—and he was in love with Michelle Duquesne.

CHAPTER
TWENTY-EIGHT

WHEN LIEUTENANT Commander Chibowski, the training squadron's maintenance officer, arrived in a navy pickup thirty minutes later, he didn't call Dario a hero. "Goddamn it, D'Angelo. You did a good job, but you could have made it to Canal Field and saved me the trouble of having a crew come out here and remove the wings and lift everything onto a flatbed truck." He was gruff and looked mean. His uniform was crumpled, with grease spots on the knees and on his shirt. He carried a clip board.

Dario was listening to him with his arm around Michelle, smearing even more engine oil over her. "I'm sorry, sir, but I committed myself to landing on the beach and I knew better than to change my mind."

"But your instructor ordered you to land at Canal. I followed the emergency on my radio."

"I'd turned my radio off, and I'd made the decision to land on the beach. I'm not supposed to change my mind once I commit myself."

Chibowski held up both hands for an instant, then let them drop to his side. "Well, you did save the belly by lowering the gear, even though you shouldn't have. You're supposed to land wheels up on an unimproved surface."

"I knew the sand was packed hard, sir. I drive my MG on it all the time."

Low and Slow

Chibowski was in his early fifties. He was a mustang, a former enlisted man who'd come up through the ranks. Mustangs knew every trick, every excuse in the long list of tricks, and excuses used by sailors for centuries. They knew them because they'd used them. He looked at Dario, looked at Michelle and looked at Bill standing next to them, holding Aud's hand.

"If the prop wasn't missing, D'Angelo, I'd think you just dropped in to join a party."

"I live here in Gulf Shores, sir. My friends just happened to be on the beach."

Chibowski sighed. "Well, it's not for me to decide if you did it right or wrong. You brought the airplane back in one piece, and yourself too. That's the main thing. If you can end your flying career with an equal number of takeoffs and landings, you've been a success." Then he lowered his thick eyebrows and gave Dario a stern, fatherly look. "But take this advice from an old salt, son. Sometimes there's just a fine line between courage and stupidity. Remember that."

"Yes, sir."

* * *

An hour later, Bill, Audley and Dario were drinking Cuba Libras, sitting in the screened porch of the snake ranch. They'd showered and changed and were waiting for Michelle, who, according to Aud, took a long time dressing. They were all going out for dinner.

"We saw the two Jay Birds coming in from sea," Bill said. "I knew something was wrong because they didn't sound right, even for those old clunkers. When they got closer, I knew one of them was silent. Then I saw its prop was gone and there was oil all over the cowl, but I didn't even think about it being you until you hit the high point over the pier. Then, when you circled down to final and flew right over your white spots, I just knew it was you. I told the girls and we started running down the beach."

"The funny thing is, Bill had just told Michelle and me how you lost your MG's windshield. It upset us, to hear how close you came to disaster. Then, when we got to your airplane and saw you standing there on the wing, I thought Michelle was going to faint."

Just then Michelle entered the room and it was Dario who almost fainted. Her still damp, dark red hair was combed back on the sides of her head. Orange-red lipstick was her only makeup, and she again wore silk culottes of white and red. Dario stood up and met her as she came through the door. He kissed her softly on the lips, then put his head next to hers with his lips at her ear. He detected the faint fragrance of gardenia. "We're going to the Pink Pony to celebrate my cheating death, but I'm really celebrating finding you again. It was fate who shot off my propeller. He's the king of serendipity."

* * *

After dinner, Bill drove Aud in her car, returning them to Point Clear while Dario and Michelle followed in his MG. The top was down, and the air was warm and balmy, with just a hint of the humidity that would inundate the coast in a month's time. It was a clear night with no moon, but the stars were set on high-intensity and were much closer to the earth than usual. Michelle had drunk several vodka tonics over the course of the evening, but she seemed sober when Dario agreed to let her drive the MG home. She took a back route, driving on the country roads which were laid out straight on the section lines. She was going 60 miles-per-hour as she approached a 90-degree turn to the left. By the time Dario realized she wasn't slowing down for the turn, he also knew that it was too late for her to make it. His instincts took over. He reached up and turned off the ignition, then he held the steering wheel firm. He kept the car pointed straight, preferring to run off into the field to rolling over if she tried to make the turn. The MG bounced up over the edge of the road, which was elevated, and then continued down a dirt road which continued along the section line from the paved road they'd left. The car bounced high on the rough road and came to a stop as he pulled on the emergency brake. Suddenly, there was complete silence as they sat there, surrounded by young cotton plants on each side of the narrow road. Dario switched off the headlights.

"I'm out of breath. I've never been through anything so exciting!" Michelle said, panting.

He leaned across the transmission tunnel, put his arms around her, turned her toward him and kissed her. She responded, turning her excitement into unbridled passion. She kissed him on his neck, on his face, his ears. He was inside her blouse, kneading the breasts he first saw on the beach weeks before. He got out of the car, took a folded blanket from the trunk and laid it, still folded, on the sloping hood of the MG. He helped her out of the car and held her, kissing her neck, and chest and nipples. The alcohol and the excitement of the drive and his foreplay had her aroused to a high pitch. He led her to the front of the car and lowered her onto the hood. He removed her culottes and panties, and made love to her under the stars. Michelle responded, meeting his thrusts with ardor, with her feet on the front bumper and her knees pointing up to the sky.

Afterwards, they lay on the blanket in a patch of cool grass, looking up at the starlit sky. They saw a star fall across it, from west to east, leaving a long trail which lasted for several seconds. It was instantly followed by another, shooting from north to south. "I seem to have a proclivity for corny phrases when I'm with you. Stars fell on Alabama, just like in the song," he said.

She squeezed his hand. "Dario, since I met you, I haven't been able to get you off of my mind. I though I would when I went back to Montgomery, but I didn't. When I saw Bill today, and he told us about your pier crash, it frightened me. Then, as if by magic, you land on the beach. You have such an adventurous, exciting life, while mine is so boring. Will you share some excitement with me?"

He leaned over her and kissed her, putting one hand on her breast. He hadn't fully explored them yet, or the rest of her body. But he would, soon, and the anticipation was almost as great as he knew the satisfaction would be.

"Yes, and you ain't seen nothing, yet."

He left her at Jubilee with the promise to return the next evening, then picked Bill up at Aud's, which was several houses up the shore.

"I think I'm in love" he told Bill, after they'd driven several miles in silence.

"You'll get over it. I do, at least three or four times a month."

* * *

Dario spent the next day writing an accident report about the prop loss. The Public Information Officer interviewed him and had photographs taken of him standing next to the disassembled SNJ which was stacked on a flatbed trailer.

It was raining when he left Gulf Shores for Jubilee in the late afternoon. This posed a problem in his MG, because not only was there no windshield to attach the top to, the windshield wipers wouldn't work on the low, racing windscreen. He wore his flight goggles to stop the rain drops from hitting his eyes and blinding him, and a khaki raincoat over his Hawaiian shirt and Bermuda shorts. He was hurrying. He'd thought about nothing but Michelle since he left her the night before.

The deputy was standing in the road and Dario knew he'd been caught going too fast between the light beams, again. He parked the MG and got out of it because he couldn't get his wallet out of his shorts with the rain coat over them. The deputy saw his bare legs protruding beneath his raincoat and yelled, "Jesus H. Christ! Ain't you got no pants on, mister?"

Dario held the raincoat open, showing him his Bermuda shorts and Hawaiian shirt. "I'm decent, deputy. I'm not a flasher."

He got another ticket for going 60 in a 45.

I wondered if the judge will have more of that sweet watermelon? Dario thought as he drove to Point Clear.

Low and Slow

* * *

He spent the night with Michelle, in her bed at Jubilee. He explored her body. Her nipples were exactly like he'd guessed they would be, and her passion when he performed cunnilingus was very demonstrative, although her scream was softer than the one she gave when he drove her under the pier. "Oh, Dario. I can't get enough of you. I wish we could just stay in bed and make love forever."

"And I can't get enough of you, Michelle. I thought about you all day. I don't know how I'm going to tear myself away in the morning. I'm already dreading it."

She turned away from him, lying on her side with her back toward him. "There's something I have to tell you, Dario, and it's very difficult." She hesitated, then continued. "You're not the first man I've made love with. You're the second."

He didn't laugh aloud, only to himself. He knew she wasn't a virgin when he made love to her on the MG hood, although tonight he'd discovered she was very inexperienced. "It doesn't matter, Michelle. We're together now, that's all that counts. What you did before has nothing to do with me, or with us."

He would never tell her what sexual experiences he'd had before he met her. Babbo was very emphatic about that. "If you don't tell them enough, they think you are an amateur. If you tell them too much, they think you are a male whore. Tell them nothing. Silence confuses them. It's a mystery women cannot comprehend."

"Yes it does matter. You see, the first was my fiancé. Is my fiancé. Dario, I . . . I'm engaged."

He kissed her on her back. Then he turned her over and held her head in his hands, looking into her deep blue eyes. He held up her left hand. "You were engaged, you're not anymore. I just broke the engagement. Besides, I haven't seen a ring on this hand since I met you. Whoever he is, you couldn't love him and be like this with me, I already know enough about you to know that."

She turned her head away from him again, looking at the far wall of her bedroom. "You're right. It's all happened so fast. I don't love him. I know that now." She turned and faced him. "My fiancé is the son of my mother's classmate from college. We've known each other since we were children. When we got engaged, I knew I was doing what my family, and his, expected of me." She turned, and lay on her stomach, still looking at him. "My fiancé is Donald Sculthorpe Eighton, Junior. He's every girl's dream. He's rich, he's six feet tall, and he looks like a Greek god. He was educated at Auburn and he's in the service, like you."

Panic engulfed him. "Is he a marine?"

"A marine? No, he's in the air force. Why would you think he's a marine?"

"It's nothing. It's just . . . I'm being paranoid. I have trouble with marines."

"Well, don't worry about Donald. He's a navigator on cargo planes. He's stationed at Brookley Field, over in Mobile, but his unit's flying in Europe right now. I only wear my engagement ring when I'm with him, or with my family. That's how unenthusiastic I've been about our betrothal. We've postponed our wedding until he gets out of the service. After that, Donald will go to law school, and eventually enter politics. My life, my future, is all laid out for me. I'll be holding up babies for Donald to kiss." She leaned over and kissed him. "Then, along you come. An Italian from San Francisco, with a MG sports car . . ."

"And nothing else, and making payments on the car."

" . . . who plays beautiful jazz piano, races his sports car and flies airplanes, and makes love to me in a way I didn't even know existed. Oh, lover. How can I ever go back to Donald? He's so definitely, insufferably, excruciatingly boring."

"Fuck Donald." He put his arms around her.

"No, fuck me," she replied.

Low and Slow

* * *

Judge Hamrick's lemonade and his verdict was the same as before. "Ten dollars fine plus five dollars court costs. I have some delicious strawberries, just picked, and some fresh cream Ensign D'Angelo. Jehmima's gone today, but she left everything ready for us. Please join me in the kitchen. I want to hear all about your landing on Gulf Shores beach. I read about it in the paper, 'No prop, no power, no nothin'."

The judge lead him through his living room, which had a high ceiling and was paneled in dark wood. Dario saw the framed photograph of a naval officer in blue uniform, with an ensign stripe and gold wings, sitting on a sideboard. Next to it was a framed citation above a Silver Star medal. He stopped and glanced over the citation. It had been awarded, posthumously, to Lieutenant Joseph Sterling Hamrick, USNR.

"My son, Joey." The judge had stopped at the kitchen door and was facing Dario. "He came through Barin Field, back in forty-four. He made it through all kinds of combat in the Pacific war, then got called back for Korea while he was in law school. His luck ran out there, he was hit by flak after he bombed a bridge. He destroyed the bridge, though, got that medal." Dario saw that the judge's eyes were beginning to water. "Joey liked fast cars too, Ensign D'Angelo. He had an old Ford hot rod he tinkered with all the time. He was always gettin' tickets."

* * *

He'd been spending every night with Michelle at Jubilee for over two weeks. He would arrive around six p.m. and leave early in the morning. After a few nights, he began bringing his uniform and driving directly to Barin Field for eight o'clock muster. He'd completed gunnery and was in Carrier Qualification ground school. He would start flying Field Carrier Landing Practices (FCLPs), the following week.

One day, he was pulled out of class and told to go to the Commanding Officer's office. When he got there, the chief at the front desk told him the CO wanted to see him about a traffic ticket. He entered the CO's office and stood at attention, wishing he'd had time to put on a freshly starched uniform and get a haircut. All he had time to do was comb his hair and run his shoes over the back of his trouser legs.

Captain Levin was a very large man with a full head of grey hair. There were five rows of ribbons beneath the gold wings on his shirt. His desk plaque had a cone mountain on it, but it didn't look like Mount Fuji or Mount Vesuvius. Dario was pleased to see that the captain was sitting behind his desk, not standing at a podium—and he wasn't wearing his hat.

"At ease, D'Angelo. Sit down. I don't make a formal thing about traffic tickets." He motioned to a chair beside his desk. "First, I want to congratulate you for bringing back the SNJ. You seem to have pissed off your instructor by not landing at Canal Field, but nobody can fault you for getting the aircraft, and yourself, safely on the ground. Well done."

"Thank you, sir."

"The shore patrol says you've received two traffic tickets here in Baldwin County. They go through the traffic reports, you know. It's the Chief of Naval Air Training's order. More students are killed in traffic accidents than in airplanes, so he's hot on traffic violators. I often wonder if he'd ease off if our aircraft fatalities finally passed those in automobiles, but I'm not privy to the admiral's policymaking. I'm just stuck with disciplining those who get the tickets. Are you familiar with the rules?"

"Yes, sir. Ten traffic violation points and I lose my sticker and base driving privileges."

"That's right. But, I'm only going to give you nine points. That'll put you right on the edge, so you'd better be careful." Dario watched as the captain opened his file. He saw the captain read the entry from Whiting Field, where he'd also been given the break of only nine demerits. "Ooophs." He looked up at Dario and shrugged his shoulders. "Sorry, D'Angelo. The admiral won't let me give half demerits."

Low and Slow

"I understand, sir. But it won't be too bad, sir. I'm starting CQ now and I should be off to Corpus in a few weeks. I can park outside the gate and catch the bus for Magnolia Field, there. And sir, nobody seems to know, but perhaps you can tell me. Do my points follow me to the Advance Training Command?"

"They're supposed to, but I think the chief might mislay your file, if 'No Prop' doesn't get in any more trouble with the local constabulary."

"He won't, sir. He promises."

"Good. Tell me, how did you think of saying 'No prop, no power, no nothin'?"

"I don't know, captain. I was scared, but I kept thinking of the funny side of the situation. It helped keep me calm."

"Let me tell you something. If you ever get in combat, remember, it's the first thing you transmit when you complete a mission that gets you a medal. If the message is good, the press will pick it up, and suddenly you're a hero. 'Sighted sub, sank same,' 'Scratch one Jap carrier,' for instance. They got medals. I thought about it when I heard about you saying 'No prop.' I liked it. I told my Public Information Officer to send your story out for publication. The local press picked it up, and he'll get it into *Naval Aviation News*. Have you met him?"

"Yes sir. He had some publicity pictures taken of me."

"He's a real bullshit artist, but he's good. Don't be surprised if the story he gets published is nothing like what happened. It's hype that greases the wheels and gets the money to keep the navy going. We need those PIOs to compete with the enemy because they're experts, way ahead of us."

"You mean the Russians, sir?"

"Hell no! I mean the air force! They're getting all the appropriations."

Captain Levin wrote something in Dario's file, then closed it. "That's all, D'Angelo, unless you have any questions."

"Yes sir, just one, captain. What is the mountain on your name plaque? I've seen Mount Fuji, and knew the owners served in the

Western Pacific. I've seen Mount Vesuvius, but I've never seen that one."

"It's Mount Etna. I flew PB4Ys out of Sigonella, in Sicily. It was great duty. I loved Sicily. Are your folks from there?"

"No sir. My father came from south of Florence and my mother came from Genoa."

"I should've known. No Sicilian I ever saw had anything but black hair and dark-brown eyes. Carry on, D'Angelo, and good luck."

"Aye, aye, sir. And, thank you, Captain Levin."

CHAPTER TWENTY-NINE

CARRIER LANDING practice was a completely new flying experience for the students in Dario's group. They were bussed to Magnolia Field, another navy practice field about ten miles northwest of Barin, before sunrise. The flights took place at first light, when the air was as still as it would be all day. He had to leave Michelle's bed at three a.m. to get to Barin on time to catch the bus outside the gate.

The FCLP flight pattern was flown at 150 feet of altitude, at 65 knots airspeed. Stall speed at their operating weight, with flaps and landing gear extended, was about 57 knots, so maintaining airspeed accuracy was very important. By flying their practice passes early—before the sun began to heat the land—it was possible to fly the pattern and maintain airspeed without lots of power and control changes. Later in the day, the planes would climb from hot air rising from a black, plowed field and settle when flown over a field planted with corn or cotton, as the plants absorbed the sun's heat instead of reflecting it. The land around Magnolia Field was a checkerboard of planted and plowed fields.

The Landing Signal Officer stood at the edge of the runway. Although he had radio contact with the students for emergencies, his landing signals were all made manually, with paddles, to simulate the worse-case situation; radio failure, or silence to avoid detection by the enemy. He held one paddle (slightly larger than ping pong paddles), in each hand. They were made of a tube frame, with horizontal tubes to which strips of brightly-colored cloth were attached, which fluttered in the wind. He wore a flight suit which was striped with the same chartreuse and bright orange, satin cloth. The LSO used the paddles to signal the pilot to raise or lower his nose, to increase or decrease his speed, or to turn. When the approaching pilot first saw him, the LSO would be holding his paddles straight out, at arms-length, making himself look like a fluttering cross. As long as his arms and the paddles remained in this position, the student was flying the correct speed and pattern. A complete pass to a landing without any correction by the LSO was called a "Roger" pass, a perfect pass.

At 65 knots, the SNJ's nose was cocked up very high, too high to see over the cowl. The student had to stick his head out the left side of the cockpit, into the slipstream, to see forward. His right hand was on the control stick, his left hand was on the power throttle and his feet were on the rudders. He flew by the LSO's signals. There was almost no opportunity to look at the airplane's instruments. When the LSO decided that the aircraft was at the correct speed and at the right position, he would suddenly lower one paddle along his leg and place the other against his chest. This was the "cut." It was a mandatory signal, and the instant it was given the pilot cut his power completely, let his nose drop and then pulled the stick back into his lap, which brought the nose up and stalled the airplane. Hopefully, it would slam down in a three-point attitude in the space where the arresting wires would be strung across the carrier's deck. The tailhook would catch one of the wires and bring the aircraft to a sudden stop. There were no wires on the runway at Magnolia, however.

If the LSO put both paddles over his head and waved them furiously, it was the other mandatory signal: "Wave-off." The pilot then added full power and climbed. On the carrier, the LSO had a net below him, over the water, into which he would dive, if the climb wasn't fast enough. A wave-off was given if the approach was very bad, or if the deck was fouled with another airplane or some other obstruction.

Low and Slow

The instructors often referred to the carrier as "the boat." This was against the naval traditions Dario had been taught, which said that a boat was something that was put on a ship, like a lifeboat. It was another aviation insolence against the traditions of the black shoe navy. Dario and his fellow students were already beginning to feel the special, conceited demeanor of carrier aviators. It was a special task; they were a special breed. They knew there wasn't anything else in military flying that required the training, the skill and the fortitude, like flying an airplane on-and-off a boat. They flew two 45-minute hops each morning, making about eight landings per period. Each landing, except the last, was a touch-and-go. There were usually four SNJs in the FCLP pattern. Each student would make about 100 landings on the field before going out to the boat to do the real thing.

There was no ready room at Magnolia Field. Dario usually slept in the tall grass near the end of the runway, between flights, trying to make up for the sleep he'd lost dallying with Michelle during the night and getting up at three a.m. The only amenities at the field were a crude toilet and a Coke machine that dispensed ice-cold bottles. For many, including Dario, a Coke was breakfast.

Ralph Kramer, his fellow snake ranch occupant, showed up one morning with a very bad hangover, which he told Dario felt like five days of bad weather. He was sucking on cigarettes and drinking Coke after Coke to put out the fire. He felt better just before it was his turn to fly, because he vomited. "A real naval aviator's breakfast," he told Dario. "A cigarette, a Coke and a puke."

Dario then watched him takeoff, join the bounce pattern, and fly eight almost "Roger" passes.

* * *

Dario didn't know what being in love meant. It had been the theme of at least half of the many movies he'd seen and it was the subject of most of the songs he'd played, but none of the lines and none of the lyrics fit how he felt about Michelle. When he left her in the morning, he missed her before he was a mile away from Jubilee. He wanted to spin his car around and go back to climb into bed, between the cool, crumpled sheets and put his body next to hers. But there was more than sex that attracted him, which was what was so strange to him. He enjoyed being with her, doing things with her, going places with her. He finished flying early, so they had the afternoons and evenings together. They didn't always go to the beach. They went to Mobile and all around its bay. She showed him a part of the South he didn't know existed; the food, the history, the architecture and the gardens. He was discovering a new world, and everywhere they went—especially at night—there was the perfumed fragrance of tropical flowers mingled with the gardenia scent she so tastefully wore.

Their sex was always exciting for both of them. Her desires were almost insatiable and he was happy to exhaust himself for her. They made love in his room at the snake ranch, under the stars on the beach, and in her bed at Jubilee. They never spoke about what they would do after he carrier-qualified and transferred to Corpus Christi, or when First Lieutenant Eighton returned to Brookley Field in Mobile, or when Mrs. Duquesne came down from Montgomery to Jubilee for the summer. Dario never discussed it with her, but each occurrence was inevitable, and any one of them would demand a decision.

CHAPTER THIRTY

IN THE THIRD week of their affair, the Cadillac sedan in Jubilee's driveway alerted him that decision time had arrived. He parked his MG, went to the front door and rang the bell instead of just entering and yelling, "Michelle, baby, I'm home." Sarah answered the door and gave him a nod over her shoulder, which indicated something was going on behind her, in the living room.

"Good afternoon, Sarah. Is Miss Duquesne in?" He winked and waited as Sarah told him she would find out. He waited at the door.

He had a great rapport with Sarah. He never gave her an order and he always cleaned up after himself. Michelle told him to leave his laundry for her, but he took it to the base, giving the excuse that his wash-khaki shirts and trousers needed the heavy starch which only navy laundries had perfected. He didn't bother telling her they had also perfected the art of smashing every fifth button and soaking indelible laundry marks through the material.

Sarah returned to the door and opened it wide. "Come in, please, Mr. Dario. Miss Michelle is with her mother." She led him to the living room. Michelle was there with an older woman who walked to meet him with her right hand extended. He took it in his and shook it gently. As his fingers wrapped around her hand, he could feel the large diamond in the ring that he'd seen flash as she put her hand forward.

"Buon giorno, Signore D'Angelo. Posso chiamarLa Dario? Sí, La prego di chiamarmi Isabella."

Dario's mouth dropped and hung open. She'd spoken perfect Italian. "Yes, Isabelle, you may call me Dario. How is it you speak Italian? I'm amazed. Are there Italians in your family?"

She laughed, tilting her head back. It was apparent to Dario that she'd been at least as beautiful when she was young as Michelle was now. She didn't have Michelle's auburn hair though, hers was a sandy light-brown. Her sun dress looked very expensive, as did the plain gold bracelet she wore on one wrist. She wore more makeup than Michelle, but not an excessive amount. She was smoking a cigarette in a long holder. He'd never seen anyone actually use such a holder, only actresses in old movies. Isabelle Duquesne was slightly shorter than her daughter, and her body was just a little heavier. Her breasts were larger than Michelle's and looked just as firm. She was still a very attractive woman.

"No," she answered, bringing his mind back to their conversation. "I'm of English and French heritage. I studied your beautiful language in school. It is, after all, the language of music, which was my subject." Her southern accent was soft like Michelle's, but slightly more pronounced. He looked at her eyes. They were blue, like her daughter's, but not as warm. He thought that if he ever saw her angry, he'd see it first in her eyes.

"Michelle's told me a lot about you, Dario. Some of which sounds like a press release for a teenager's idol."

"Mother," Michelle said, with a touch of despair in her voice. "Don't believe me. Wait and judge him for yourself."

"That seems a fair request. I would love to hear you play the piano, Dario. Would you play for me, please."

"Of course. It's always a joy to play on your beautiful Steinway." He suddenly realized he hadn't even greeted Michelle, nor had she said anything to him. She was sitting in a chair beside an open French door. He walked to her, took her hand and kissed her on her lips. "You didn't tell me your mother would be here. What a wonderful surprise. Is she going to join us for dinner at Pic-a-Rib?" They'd made no plans to go to their favorite restaurant in Daphne, a small town a few miles up the shore, but he said it to give a reason for his arrival.

"Mother knows everything, Dario. I told her you've been staying here with me, I didn't want her interrogating poor Sarah. I told her I love you and I'm breaking off my engagement with Donald."

"We'll talk about that later." Isabelle's tone was condescending. "Come, Dario, let's go into the conservatory, I'm anxious to hear you play. I don't understand this music my daughter fancies so much, but perhaps you can make me a believer."

He followed her to the music room, still holding Michelle's hand. He released it as they entered the room, walked to the Steinway, propped up the lid and opened the key cover. He adjusted the bench to the distance from the piano he preferred, sat on it and played several arpeggios to limber his fingers. He'd been thinking about what to play when he started for the room, the perennial problem when asked to audition; and this was an audition. He played a Ravel pavane, and tried to be classically perfect. When he finished the piece, he slid into a jazz rendition of a popular song based on the same refrain, then ended back in the classical version. While he played, Michelle and her mother sat to his right side. He never looked at either of them, but he could see and smell cigarette smoke. When he finished, he sat still, looking forward, his head slightly bent. He was always his own worst critic, but he felt he'd done a good job.

"I am impressed. You play very well, Dario." He turned on the bench to face Isabelle. Her cigarette had burned down, almost to the tip of its holder. "You did the Ravel admirably. Then, I think I understand a little of what you did with your variations. Did you transcribe them yourself?"

"No, Isabelle. There are no transcriptions. Nothing was ever written down." He looked directly into her face. She seemed excited. Her face was flushed and she sat up straight in the upholstered chair, not touching its back. Michelle remained silent, but was smiling. Dario hoped that he'd lived up to the degree of piano virtuosity she'd touted to her mother.

"But, if it wasn't transcribed, how did you practice it enough to memorize it?"

"I didn't memorize it. I never play any jazz variation the same way twice. I only memorize the basic chords to a song and the melody line. I improvise on those chords and the melody, and it's different every time I play it. In jazz, the music matches the musician's temperament at the time, the audience's feelings, or even the time of day. It's what improvisation is all about. It's what makes jazz exciting."

"Yes, I see. Well, I don't, really, but I see what you mean about exciting. That seems to be what my daughter has found in you. Excitement. Michelle is still very young. She has yet to realize that excitement is not enough to sustain a long-term relationship."

"Isn't it better than a relationship based on boredom?" he asked.

"It may be. But so often what begins exciting turns into boredom from being over done. Don't you agree?"

"I don't know, Isabelle. I haven't gotten to that stage with anything exciting I do, yet. I hope I never do."

"But you miss my point entirely, Dario. I mean, it's the excitement between a man and a woman which is so fleeting. It's nothing to do with what men do alone, or as a team, for excitement. You understand what I'm saying, don't you?"

He decided to drop the repartee. He could feel himself getting sucked into one of the 'no possible way to come out ahead' arguments women do so well. Isabelle was using Mama's method of arguing by asking questions and forcing her opponent to make *her* point. He turned to Michelle. She was sitting back in her chair. He walked over to her and sat on the upholstered edge, bent over and kissed her on her lips.

"Hi. You're being very quiet. When you told your mother that you loved me, did you mention that it's requited?"

Michelle took his hand. She didn't seem upset, but he didn't know her true relationship with her mother. Michelle had seldom spoken of her parents, except to complain about the classical music they forced on her, and the boredom of their society.

"Yes I did. But I think she thinks you're after my money, which is silly. Michelle stood up. "If we're going out for dinner. I'm going up to change. I'll be down in a few minutes, sweetheart."

Isabelle sat back in her chair when Michelle left the room. She lit another cigarette and inhaled it deeply. "I'm glad you're taking Michelle out for dinner. I'm sure you have a lot to talk about."

"Somehow, I think I'm going to be mostly listening."

"I must admit, you do make a lovely couple. I can see why Michelle finds you so exciting, Dario. But Michelle is spoiled. She's had every-thing she's ever wanted, sometimes before she even knew she wanted it. If it gets down to a decision, I don't think my daughter will sacrifice her creature comforts and a future which promises great wealth and position, for a physical attraction she thinks is love. Love that over-comes all obstacles and endures all sacrifices only happens in the movies."

Dario laughed to himself at her use of one of his favorite descrip-tive phrases. "And in the movies, the aristocratic parents threaten their wayward daughter with penury and ostracism if she runs off with the destitute musician—or was he an unpublished poet?" he said.

Isabelle exhaled smoke as she laughed at his statement. "You may be genuinely in love with my daughter, but I don't think you know her very well. Michelle is very impulsive, but she's also very pragmatic. At the risk of sounding trite, Dario, let me say that, in the long run, Michelle will do what's best for Michelle. And, although it may not seem so at the time, it will probably be what's best for you. At least, I sincerely hope it is."

He heard Michelle 's footsteps coming down the stairs. He took Isabelle's hand and kissed it. *"Buona sera, Signora Duquesnè."*

"Buona sera, Signore D'Angelo. Lei è molte gentile. Non é un musicista indigente."

* * *

"What did my mother say to you in Italian?" Michelle asked as soon as they got into the MG.

"She said I wasn't a poor musician."

"Of course you're not! You're a wonderful musician."

Dario laughed. "She used the word for indigent, like poor from having no money. Which is what I am."

"What did she mean by that?"

"It was just a joke. I used a character from an old movie."

After they'd driven a few miles, Michelle spoke again, "What are we going to do?"

"Do about what?"

"Us. I'm not going to give up sleeping with you just because my mother came to Jubilee." She leaned over the transmission and put her hand around the back of his neck. She kissed him near his ear and whispered, "Darling, do you think I could ever go back to that boring life? You've spoiled me, lover, spoiled me for any other man. Dario D'Angelo has to take care of me from now on, because he saved my life, saved it from dullness. It's an old Chinese custom, slightly modified."

* * *

"You'll just have to marry me and take me with you to Texas." Michelle tore the meat from a rib with her teeth as she spoke. Her lips and chin were covered with barbeque sauce. Her announcement came as no surprise to Dario. The thought of marriage had been in the back of his mind, although repressed. He wanted to be with her, wanted her to come with him to Texas, but he knew they couldn't live together unmarried. If they "shacked up," his Commanding Officer—wherever he was stationed—was sure to find out, and cohabitation without the benefit of wedlock was not an acceptable standard for a naval officer. Overnight and weekends were overlooked, but Michelle would have to have her own place, and he, his, and he could barely afford one, let alone two, apartments.

"Have you thought about what you'd be giving up if you married me? I have no money, Michelle. I *am* an almost indigent flight student. I live from payday to payday on my ensign's pay. My flight pay all goes to make the payment on my car and I put more money into it to keep it going. I'm a poor candidate for a husband, especially for you. I'm afraid you're spoiled, baby. You've always had everything you've wanted."

"Yes. It's true. I'm spoiled. I always get what I want. Well, so what? That applies to you. I want you, so since I'm spoiled, I'm going to have you." She chewed more meat from a bone while Dario drank his beer and reflected on her logic. "Besides, I have some money."

She ate the ribs with her hands, with sauce all over her fingers and hands. He loved to watch her eat ribs. She turned the meal into a southern ritual.

"My grandfather left me a trust fund. I get it in four years, when I'm twenty-five. I don't know how much it is now, but it was several hundred thousand dollars when he died, which was years and years ago."

Dario whistled. "Beauty, wit, talent, sex, a two-hundred-grand inheritance and she wants me to marry her. I must be dreaming. This doesn't *even* happen in the movies."

"I'm sure my father will advance me some money from my trust. How much should I ask for, how much will we need to get to Texas?"

He didn't know what to answer. He'd tried to avoid thinking about what he would do after he carrier-qualified, but now he had to make a decision and, once made, it would be the same as picking an emergency landing spot. Selection meant commitment.

"Dario. I asked you how much money we need to get started? You do want to marry me, don't you?"

Did he? He knew he either had to take the cut, or wave-off.

What the hell. There aren't many Michelles in the world. Why stop when you're having fun? he told himself.

"Of course I want to marry you, Michelle. But I hope you understand, if you marry me you won't be able to live the way you've been living, not for a long, long time. Maybe even never. My father died several years ago. On his deathbed he bequeathed me his luck, but all he left me materially was an upright piano. I don't have a trust fund and I won't use a penny of yours. Not now, and not ever. You've got to understand, I've got too many Italian hang-ups built into me, it's to do with my manhood. I could never take money from a woman."

"Don't be so principled, Dario. It's my money. I'll just get enough so we can set up housekeeping in Corpus Christi. You can pay me back when you make admiral."

"Michelle, we've never talked about the future. I don't think I'm going to stay in the navy. I love flying, but I don't think I'm cut out for a career, there's too much bullshit involved, and nobody makes admiral unless he went to the Naval Academy. And I don't know what I'm going to do when I get out of the navy. I planned to be a school teacher and a weekend musician."

Michelle put her ribs down and stared at him. "Dario D'Angelo, I declare. I think I already know you better than you know yourself. I have confidence in you, you'll never be content to be a school teacher. Whatever you do will be unusual and it will be exciting, and I will be with you, sharing it."

* * *

Isabelle was in the living room, smoking, when they returned to Jubilee. Dario followed Michelle as she entered and stood in front of her mother. "Dario and I are going to be married, mother, and soon. I'm sorry to disappoint you about Donald, but Dario and I are in love and we want to be together. I'm going with him to Texas, as soon as he's transferred."

Isabelle responded with no more emotion than if Michelle had told her that it had begun to rain. She continued to suck cigarette smoke from her long holder, which she continuously turned in her mouth. "I understand, dear. I telephoned your father an hour ago and told him I thought you might elope. He sends his love. You also have my love. I hope you will both be very, very happy. Sarah should be finished packing your things by now. We'll send your other things from Montgomery when you settle. Just tell us where you're staying."

Dario couldn't see Michelle's face, so he stepped around to her side and looked at her. It was white, as he suspected, which made her freckles look like chocolate flakes on vanilla ice cream. He'd guessed what Isabelle was up to before she even finished her statement.

"But mother, we're not eloping tonight! Dario has to finish his carrier training and make his carrier landings before we go to Texas. I'm not leaving yet."

Isabelle smiled, exposing small wrinkles around her mouth and eyes. Dario thought they were sexy, showing the promise of experience. "Oh yes you are, my darling daughter. You've made your decision, and your father and I respect it. You want independence from us and you have it. Our decision is for you to leave our household, immediately."

"But, I have to talk to Daddy. I need some money from my trust fund."

"Excuse me," Dario interjected. "Michelle, I told you. I won't let you take any money from your trust. We'll make out. I'll get a pay advance when I get my orders to Corpus."

"But Dario," Michelle turned, facing him, "it's my money."

"My, my. Not even married and already fighting about money," Isabelle said. "Well, my dear, you needn't. The argument is academic. Your father told me to tell you there could be no advances from your trust. Although we give you our love and good wishes, we're giving you nothing else. We're against this marriage and to support it in any way would be hypocritical."

Michelle began to say something, but stopped before any words left her mouth. She inhaled deeply and then softly exhaled her resolve. "Very well, mother. If that's the way you and father want it. I'll be the disgraced daughter, cast off by her snobbish parents for marrying beneath her station in life."

"Oh, no you don't, Michelle. Don't accuse us of class snobbery.

I told your father that Dario seems to be a gentleman and we would be proud to have him as a son-in-law. We oppose a marriage because you're being impetuous and we don't believe it will last. Our concern is as much for Dario as it is for you. And when it ends, don't blame your father and me for its demise."

Dario saw the coldness in Isabelle's eyes and wondered if her prescience was as real as her seriousness.

CHAPTER THIRTY-ONE

RALPH KRAMER sat next to him on the bus and fell immediately asleep, his head facing Dario and exhausting the odor of rum and cigarettes as he snored loudly. *He'll be heading for the Coke machine when the bus stops,* Dario thought. *A naval aviator's breakfast will fix him right up.* Dario wasn't feeling so well, himself. He'd spent the night with Michelle in his room at the snake ranch, where they'd made love and talked about their future all night. He still had misgivings, but he was happy with the prospect of having Michelle with him.

After his third FCLP touch-and-go, he was climbing to enter the pattern for his fourth when he heard his LSO's voice in his headset. It was somber and businesslike. "Aircraft in Magnolia pattern, this is Paddles. Join up on 2-3 and return to Barin Field, over."

"1-7, roger," Dario transmitted. He added power and started to climb. He saw 2-3 ahead and to his left, doing the same. As he turned to start his interception, he saw the reason for the interruption of their landing practice. At the 45-degree position from the end of the runway, there was an SNJ sticking tail up in the field. It had gone in nose first, the wings were bent forward from the impact and the fuselage was crumpled. He read the big black numbers on the underside of one wing: 19. It was Ralph's aircraft.

"No!" Dario yelled aloud in his cockpit. "Oh shit, Ralph, no! Not you, Ralph. Oh shit, oh shit!"

He wanted to land, run over to Ralph and find him alive, but he knew better, knew he couldn't have survived that crash. He couldn't do anything for Ralph now but mourn him. He concentrated on his intercept with 2-3.

* * *

There was a memorial service for Ralph in the base chapel on Saturday. Dario and Michelle rode to the base with Bill in his Ford. No official cause for the accident had been assigned, but it was apparent that Ralph had let his nose come up just before he was controlled by the LSO. With the nose up, it took only a split second for the SNJ to lose the precious few knots they flew above stalling speed. The aircraft stalled, and the left wing dropped, starting a spin, and there wasn't enough altitude in the 150-feet altitude pattern to recover from a spin. It dove, nose first, into the foot-high cotton plants which had absorbed the sun's rays and caused Ralph's aircraft to settle, and for Ralph to react instinctively—and erroneously—by raising the nose, instead of by adding power. Death for Ralph was instantaneous. Sudden stoppage broke his neck.

In a strange way, Ralph's death made Dario feel less concerned about marrying Michelle. He thought he was infallible in an airplane, he couldn't make a mistake. But Ralph's death proved that nobody was infallible. Joe Schade's death from Brandon's midair proved that something could get him that was not even his doing. And, what if there was war with the Russians, or the Chinese—or both? He though about the judge's hero son, hit by flak when his luck ran out.

"Why worry about the future?" he told Bill, whom he asked to be his best man. "We may not have any. I'm going to marry Michelle and enjoy life, while I have it."

The marriage was performed at noon the next day in Pascagula, Mississippi, where there was no waiting period. Michelle wore a white dress with a white hat and veil. If Dario had any apprehensions about marrying her, they were dispelled when he saw her in her wedding dress as she stepped out of Audley's car. He felt adrenaline rush through his body and thought it must be love, because he didn't even think about sex; he just wanted to be with her, to take care of her.

Audley had bought corsages and boutonnieres, something Dario had forgotten. They looked the proper wedding party as they stood in the bright sunlight halfway up the courthouse steps, with a preacher looking down on them. Then Dario heard the words he'd heard in dozens of movies. When the preacher reached, "Speak now, or forever hold your peace," there was loud noise from the top of the court house. Prisoners in the county jail, which was the top floor, had their heads pressed against their open bars and were yelling advice. "Don't do it!" "You'll be sorry!" "When's the baby due?" The preacher stopped reading, lowered his Bible and looked at the wedding party over the top of his reading glasses. "I'm sorry. They always seem to wait for that phrase. Just pay them no heed."

He continued, and the prisoners remained silent until Dario kissed his wife for the first time. This produced loud whistles and yells from the topside gallery. When the kiss ended, he and Michelle waved to them and Michelle threw up a kiss from her hand. Dario saw both black and white faces pushed against the bars; evidence of the democracy of the jailhouse.

They drove to Biloxi and spent their wedding night at the White House Hotel, in a room overlooking the Gulf of Mexico, the sea which had brought them together. Their immediate future was several weeks in a motel until Dario "hit the boat." Then, a long drive to Texas in the open MG followed by another several weeks in another motel until they could find an inexpensive, furnished apartment. Dario was into his last fifty dollars for their one night honeymoon, but he wasn't concerned about money. He'd signed the register, "Ens. and Mrs. Dario D'Angelo." He was her husband and her protector. Somehow, he had to also be her provider. There were many married ensigns, many without flight pay and some, even, with children. They seemed to survive on an ensign's base pay and married living allowances. He'd decided to sell his MG and buy a cheaper, used car so they could use his flight pay for living expenses. He'd sell it when they got to Texas.

They made love, slept, awoke and made love again. They held each other very tightly throughout the night.

* * *

The newly married couple rented a motel room near Gulf Shores. After a few days, Dario suggested they find a housekeeping unit with a small kitchen so they could prepare their own meals and save money.

"Oh, Dario, I'm such a ninny. I can't boil an egg. We always had Sarah at Jubilee and Mildred in Montgomery to do all the cooking." Michelle was wearing a bikini, her only attire during the day. She slept during the morning and arose just before Dario got home, usually around one p.m. They usually went to the beach, then. "But I promise, when we get to Texas, I'll enroll in a cooking school so I can learn to make you wonderful meals." She put her arms around his neck, holding her hands together behind his head. She kissed him, putting her tongue as far down his throat as she could force it. At the same time, she slid a hand down and inside his bathing trunks. "I don't even care about eating." She pulled him toward the bed.

In just several days Dario admitted to himself that he'd made a mistake. Michelle didn't have the foggiest idea about money and he realized that there was no way he could ever materially satisfy her. He saw his future as just another naval officer with a spendthrift wife, living in military housing with cheap furniture bought on credit. It wasn't what he wanted and it wasn't what Michelle deserved. Her mother had been right, of course. They had been impetuous. He loved her with all his heart and he would always love her—or at least the memory of her. But, every time he tried to start a serious discussion with her, about money, about their future, she would change the subject by exciting him, and he would end up with his head between her legs with her moaning a chorus of orgasms. Afterward, each satiated, the cares that seemed so important to him before were forgotten. He was aware of what she was doing, but he didn't care. Deep in his heart he knew it couldn't last, but he wanted to get all of her that he could, while it did.

They'd been married for two weeks when Bill dropped him off in front of his motel. Dario was anxious to see Michelle. He had something important to tell her. The MG was gone and he thought she'd just gone into Foley, until he found the note on the bed. "Darling, I had to go to Mobile to do something important. I'll explain later. I love you madly." It was signed with her "M."

Waves of hot flashes rippled up-and-down his face and torso. They'd gone to Mobile many times together, to sightsee and for dinner. Michelle never mentioned any friends or relatives living there, but her former fiancé lived there when his squadron was at its Brookley Field home base. He spent the rest of the afternoon alone, staying in their room. He tried to read, first the textbook of one of the many navy correspondence courses he had to complete before promotion, and then a week-old news magazine. He couldn't concentrate on either. At seven, he went for a walk along the beach. He tried to take his mind off Michelle, but found it impossible. Everything reminded him of her. He walked to Pixton's Pier and saw the white marks he'd made on the pilings, the ones he'd driven through with her in his MG the day he met her. He turned suddenly and walked the other way.

Calm down, Dario. What you are experiencing is jealousy, the green-eyed monster. You're being irrational and jumping to stupid conclusions. You've no right to suspect your wife of anything.

A whiff of a gardenia bush in front of their motel caused him a great anxiety with its reminder of her fragrance. It gave him a knot in his stomach.

He was laying in bed in the dark, unable to sleep, when he heard the unmistakable throaty exhaust of his MG, as its driver changed gears and pulled into the parking lot. He was on his stomach, feigning sleep, when Michelle opened the door quietly and entered. She came over to him, leaned over and kissed him on his cheek. He could smell alcohol.

"Dario, sweetheart, are you asleep?"

"I was. I'm awake now."

"I'm sorry I'm so late. There was an accident in the Bankhead Tunnel. I was stuck in traffic for over an hour."

"You're lucky it didn't rain. I've been hearing thunder, out over the Gulf."

"I know. I could see the lightning as I came through Foley."

She began to undress in the dark. Dario said nothing; he'd decided to wait for her to tell him where she'd been. Naked, she got into bed next to him. He put an arm around her waist and pulled her to him. He put his head in the crook of her neck and breathed in deeply. There was still the faint aroma of her gardenia perfume. He crawled on top of her and she spread her legs and guided him into her. They made slow, quiet love. He fell asleep when they finished. He was exhausted from his early morning flying and the anguish he'd gone through waiting for her.

When he awoke, he looked at the phosphorescent hands of his watch. He had to get up in an hour and drive to Barin to catch the bus for Magnolia Field. Michelle was sleeping in his arms. He shook her gently. "Michelle, wake up. I've got something to tell you."

She awoke slowly, moving her head from side-to-side as if to shake out the sleepiness. "Whaaa . . . what is it?"

"I make my carrier landings next Friday. I should have my orders to Corpus by the following Tuesday, assuming I make six good landings."

"I do declare, Dario D'Angelo," she yawned. "Sometimes, you can be so silly. Of course you'll do six good landings. You're a wonderful pilot."

"I just hope I'm in a good frame of mind to fly Friday."

"You're wondering where I was today, aren't you."

"It was yesterday, but you're right. I assume you were with Donald. Who else do you know in Mobile?" He spoke with more anger than he wanted to show.

"I had to see him and tell him about us. I owed him that. I knew you'd understand."

"All I understand is that I come home all excited to tell you we'll soon be on our way to Texas and I find you gone and only a note saying that you're in Mobile. Then you come home late with booze on your breath. Now you tell me you were with your former fiancé. Why am I supposed to understand? I don't understand it one damned bit. Why didn't you wait for me and ask me about going before you went?" He'd raised his voice higher than Michelle had ever heard it before. It wasn't a shout, but in the early morning darkness it was loud.

"Donald called Aud. He was only at Brookley for one day. His airplane flew off to San Antonio last night. It was the only opportunity I had to see him."

She began to cry. He put his hand on her face and felt the tears running down her cheeks. He was sorry he'd yelled at her. "It's OK, Michelle. I'm sorry. I was just being a jealous fool. You've seen Donald, you've told him you're sorry but you love me, and you told him goodbye. He's out of your life."

Her sobs grew louder and deeper. "No he isn't. That's why I'm so upset. Donald's been going crazy since he found out about us. I called Aud to see how my mother was reacting to our marriage, and she told me Donald's been on the phone to her and my mother every day. He told Aud he would be at Brookley today and he wanted to see me, desperately. I met him at the officers' club to tell him goodbye, and that I was sorry."

"Well, isn't that what you did?"

"He was so hurt, Dario. I never realized how much he loves me. He wants me back, even though I've been with you. He said he would pay for an annulment and marry me as soon as it's final." She put her head on his chest and sobbed. He ran his fingers through her hair and patted her head. It took several minutes for her crying to subside. "Oh, I'm so confused. I love you so much, but I know I'm no good for you. I can't cook, I can't do anything. I'm spoiled rotten and I'm already a burden to you." She sobbed twice, almost losing her breath.

She coughed and cleared her throat. "And, I'm so sorry, Dario. I just can't live in a motel any longer, no matter how much I love you."

He wasn't shocked. He wasn't upset. He was only a little sad, but he was also relieved to hear of a way to get out of the marriage without hurting Michelle. That was what he was most afraid of. He'd hurt his college girlfriend, badly, and she'd accused him of being just like his father. Babbo had hurt his mother, and probably many, many other women. Dario did not want to be like him, in that respect.

"You've decided to leave me and go back to Donald, haven't you Michelle?" He said it to the ceiling, hiding his relief by feigning martyrdom.

"No, I haven't. He wants me to, but I haven't decided. You decide for me, sweetheart. Tell me money doesn't matter. Tell me I love you so much I won't care about living in a motel or a small apartment, living without even a piano in the house. Tell me you won't get tired of always being broke, because I spend all your money on clothes and silly things. Tell me you won't miss your MG. Tell me I don't miss my mother and father, and my friends." Her head was still resting on his chest.

"I know. We've created an impossible situation. Find out what I have to do to get the annulment."

"All you have to do is sign a paper. Donald's already talked to a lawyer about it."

"Well, that's that, then. The end of a love affair . . . that's the title of a song."

"Oh no, it may be the end of our marriage, but not the end of our love. I'll always love you, Dario."

She kissed his stomach, working lower and lower until she took him in her mouth. He moaned in ecstasy.

This is what love is really all about. The rest is all bullshit, he told the ceiling.

Low and Slow

* * *

When he spotted the *USS Antietam* on the horizon, he was stunned by the magnificence of the scene. The large grey ship was creating a virginal white ribbon in the azure water. He almost pinched himself to make sure he wasn't dreaming or watching a Cinemascope movie. He knew it wasn't a movie when he pushed back the canopy in his descent for landing; he could smell the sea. The carrier was going fast and turning, leaving the arc of the wake a mile behind it. It was turning into the wind to make their relative landing speed slower.

Dario was the leader of the flight of four SNJs that flew out to the ship. In their briefing before the flight, they all agreed that they would fly the closest and most precise formation possible, to look good around the ship. When he approached for his first landing and stuck his head out into the slipstream, he spotted the LSO on the platform with his arms outstretched like a crucifix, the satin streamers on his paddles were straight out in the thirty knots of wind blowing over the deck. He got the warm feeling the LSO could reach out with those paddles and pull him safely aboard to land on the big white 36 painted on the deck. Dario's actions were by the numbers, following the paddle instructions with careful, slight corrections. As he got closer, his adrenaline pump worked at top pressure as he approached the cut. It came, and he reacted, ending with the stick in the imaginary hook on his belt. When the tailhook caught, he was thrown forward with a force new to him. His torso was held firmly in his seat by the tightly adjusted seat and shoulder harness, but his head bobbed forward. His aircraft was trapped by the arresting wire. He was aboard. He was thrilled.

But there was no time for him to revel in his accomplishment, there was another SNJ landing just seconds behind him. He saw the launching officer standing in front of him with his arms in the air. He taxied forward and stopped, and the launching officer put his forefinger in the air and spun it around. Dario complied with this signal by pushing the throttle forward so his engine raced enough for the launching officer to hear it running smoothly. When he was satisfied, the officer went down on one knee and pointed down the deck. Dario released the brakes, added full power and headed down the pointed path. Because of the speed of the ship, his SNJ was going 30 knots-per-hour, standing still! It leapt into the air after accelerating another 30 knots.

After his last trap, he climbed to 1500 feet and orbited one-half mile in front of the ship. When the other three SNJs had joined up on him, they received a transmission from the ship. "This is the captain speaking. Congratulations, gentlemen. You have completed the training which makes you unique among aviators. You are now carrier-qualified. Well done!"

Another voice came over the air and gave them their route back to Barin Field. "Trapper 1-1, this is Eskimo Pri-Fly. Your pigeons to home plate, 340-degrees, forty-five miles. Contact Barin Tower at feet-dry. Out."

Dario tipped his left wing down momentarily, and the second SNJ moved into cruise formation. He looked down into its cockpit and saw a mouthful of teeth and a thumb being held up. He thought back to when he began formation flying. It had been demanding. It had taken Joe Schade's life and Brandon's dream of flying. He thought of all the mornings at Magnolia Field, with bittersweet memories of Michelle. He thought of Ralph's crash. He looked ahead over the blue and turquoise Gulf of Mexico and saw the bright, white strip of the sugar sand beach in the distance: Gulf Shores. He looked down the row of the other SNJs, their yellow color a bright contrast against the sea, their propellers making an almost invisible silver circle before them. He'd never felt more pleased with himself in his life. Not when he played jazz for the first time, not when he made love to Petal, not when he beat Hildripp in the sports car race, and, not even when Michelle first kissed him and covered herself with oil that day on the beach.

"To hell with everything but this!" he yelled aloud in the cockpit.

When his flight entered the ready room they were each handed printed cards with their names typed in. "Know ye by these presents that the great painted deck has absorbed the shock of qualification landings by Ensign Dario E. D'Angelo, USNR, on 22 June 1957 aboard the *USS Antietam* in the Gulf of Mexico." The printing was superimposed over a drawing of an aircraft carrier, with puffy clouds in the background.

* * *

Sarah, the maid, answered the phone at Jubilee. "Hello, Sarah. This is Dario. I got a message through a friend that Mrs. Duquesne wants to talk to me. Is she there?"

"Yes, sir. I'll get her. It's nice to hear from you again, Mr. Dario."

"Thank you Sarah. It's nice to hear your voice, too."

Isabelle came to the phone in less than a minute. "Hello, Dario, and congratulations. Audley Sibold told me you have completed your training here, that you landed on the aircraft carrier. You'll be leaving for Texas soon, I understand."

"Yes. And it was Aud who told my friend Bill you wanted me to call you."

"Yes, yes, I asked her to get a message to you, if she could. Dario, could you possibly stop by this evening? I'm here alone and I'd like to talk to you before you leave."

"I can be there around seven."

"That would be lovely. Until seven, then."

"*Sí. A fino stasera,*" he answered her in the language of music.

* * *

"Tell her you've changed your mind and you're not going to agree to the annulment after all," Bill told him as they drank rum and Cokes on the screened porch at the snake ranch that afternoon. "Tell her it'll cost them five thousand bucks to get rid of you. And cash, no checks. If they knew you like I know you, they'd know it's a bargain."

"Christ, Bill, I thought I was the only one who used bad movie plots in real life. I wonder what the Uniform Code of Military Justice says about extortion?"

"Only kidding, Dario. What do you think the old broad wants?"

"How in the hell do I know? Maybe she wants me to play some more jazz? Maybe Michelle told her what a great lay I am and she wants me to go down on her? I just don't know, but I'll find out at seven."

He didn't get to Jubilee until eight, because he'd stayed with Bill and drank more Cuba Libras. He wasn't drunk when he rang the bell that would summon Sarah, but neither was he sober. "Good evening, sir. Mrs. Duquesne is expecting you." She opened the door wide and stood beside it. As he passed her, she whispered, "I'm sorry about you and Miss Michelle, Mr. Dario. We all liked you around here. You're a real gentleman."

"Thank you, Sarah. That means a lot to me." He meant it.

Isabelle stood up as he entered the living room. "Good evening, Dario. Thank you for coming. Won't you please sit down? Would you like something, a drink perhaps?"

"No, thank you. I've been celebrating too much as it is." He sat in a high-backed stuffed chair.

"I see. Well, I wanted to talk to you to tell you how sorry I am."

"You knew it would happen, Isabelle. You predicted it."

"Yes. Of course I knew. I know my daughter. I told you she was spoiled. Michelle wants everything, but she couldn't have both you and a life of luxury, so she opted for Donald. I warned you, but you were deafened by love." She walked to a table and picked up her cigarette holder, inserted a cigarette and lighted it with a silver lighter from the same table. She took several long drags before continuing. "But I didn't ask you to come here so I could rake you over the dying embers of your affair. I'm not gloating. If I thought your marriage could have worked, I would have helped as much as I could. I know it sounds cruel, but my husband and I ostracized Michelle for her welfare, and for yours. We hastened the inevitable, hoping it would be less painful the sooner it ended."

Low and Slow

She looked very beautiful, wearing a low-cut cotton summer dress which showed off her breasts to perfection. Her looks, probably because of the rum, were exciting Dario.

"What I want to tell you is something very personal. It might help you to understand, and perhaps also lessen the hurt and anger I know you must feel." She sat on the edge of a chair across from him, leaning toward him as she spoke very softly. "Neither Michelle nor my husband know it, but there was once a Dario in my youth. He was a Czech, a violinist and a communist. I met him while I was studying at The Juilliard School in New York. My God, he was beautiful, and exciting, and I was ripe for all that political nonsense. It was so radically different from my upbringing, I reveled in my rebellion. But unlike you and Michelle, Lazlo Slovak and I didn't give our union the sanctity of a wedding before we ran off together.

"I loved him with such passion and fervor, it took me six months to realized that love wasn't enough to keep me content with slivovitz, potatoes and dogma. You and Michelle were wiser. It only took you a few weeks to realize passion and excitement can't overcome your roots, your family, and the traditions and comfort they bestow."

"So you left Lazlo with no regrets and lived happily ever after, just like Michelle will with Donald."

"No. It wasn't that easy and it won't be that easy for you, or her, either. I've never been able to love with such abandon since Lazlo, nor do I expect to, ever again. But, I know I did what was right for me, and for him. I left while I still loved him. Had I stayed, my love would have turned to contempt and, eventually, the cruelest act one human being can inflict on another—ridicule."

She inhaled deeply from the cigarette in her holder, holding it to her side while she exhaled the smoke. "Since I'm telling you a secret, Dario, I'll tell you another. I keep a bottle of slivovitz in our home. My husband can't imagine why I take a drink from it now and then. It brings me back to my time with Laz, and I'm happy and content with the memory. I'm reminded of how fortunate I was to have loved him, and how lucky

I was to know when it was time to leave. Eventually, you'll have the same realization. But, you'll always have your memories."

Dario had heard enough. He stood up, walked to her and took her free hand in his. "Goodbye, Isabelle. You are one beautiful, lady. If I were twenty years older—well, I'm not, so it's easy to say—but if I were, I'd bring a bottle of grappa and try to make you forget all about Lazlo Slivovitz."

She laughed, tilting her head back and showing off her small wrinkles, again. "I find the taste of grappa even more despicable than slivovitz. But, perhaps I might have gotten used to it."

He bent over and kissed her on her cheek. She let him linger there for a few seconds, then she pulled back, slightly trembling. "Donald doesn't know what he owes you, Dario. I doubt there will ever be another man who could tempt my daughter away from him. After you, I'm sure all men will seem insignificant in comparison. *Adio, Signore D'Angelo.* I hope you find your slivovitz so you will always remember my daughter."

* * *

On his way to Texas Dario stopped in Mobile to sign the annulment papers at Donald's lawyer's office. The firm's name was the names of six individuals and the office took up the whole fifth floor of a large downtown bank building. When he identified himself to the receptionist, he was asked to wait. Finally, a law clerk took him into a small room where he was introduced to a notary. He swore before the notary that the marriage was never consummated and that he agreed to the annulment. He noticed the law clerk staring at him, and Dario guessed he was wondering if he was homosexual. He wanted to assure him that he wasn't, that there were very few places on Miss Duquesne's person where the marriage hadn't been consummated. But he remained silent, signed, and left.

He drove out of town with everything he owned—except his piano at Uncle Lezio's—in the trunk and passenger seat of his MG.

Low and Slow

Pensacola, Gulf Shores, Basic Training, Jubilee—and Michelle, were all behind him.

Goddamn it. I made it through Pre-Flight and Basic, but I got in a lot of trouble. I'm going to turn over a new leaf in Advance. I'm going to stay out of trouble, he promised himself as he crossed into Louisiana.

CHAPTER THIRTY-TWO

TEXAS

WHEN HE got to Corpus Christi, he found it even hotter and muggier than Alabama. The Advance Training Command also had its Mainside, the Naval Air Station, Corpus Christi. But unlike the red brick, prewar buildings of Pensacola, Corpus had all wooden structures, built in haste at the outbreak of World War II. He checked in and filled out forms, including a request for the type of aircraft he wanted to fly. He could request seaplane patrol bombers, twin-engine antisubmarine, or single engine. He put in his request for the latter. If he got it, he'd be assigned to either Kingsville or Beeville. Both bases were about fifty miles from Corpus, in the even hotter interior. The enlisted man who took his paperwork told him his assignment would have to wait until Monday. He checked into the BOQ, changed into a civilian coat and tie, and went to the officers' club. As he entered, he saw an acquaintance from Whiting Field.

He'd never flown with Jim Goodbody, but they'd drank together at Whiting's O' Club many times and Jim had lived in a snake ranch near his in Gulf Shores. Jim was a long-ball hitter with booze, and with the ladies. He was tall, blond, and handsome. Jim always had a smile on his face. He reminded Dario of his friend from San Francisco, Mat Haven, because of his outgoing personality which girls seemed to love. Like Mat, Jim made them laugh.

Happy hour was winding down, but Jim was already wound up. He spotted Dario as he was walking toward him. "D'Angelo, you asshole! Get your butt over here. Welcome to Co'pus, as these damned Texans call it. You just get in?"

Dario sat on a stool next to him. "Just this afternoon."

"What do ya want to drink?"

"Cuba Libra."

"Manuel, a Cubic for my friend, please." The Mexican bartender nodded an affirmative.

"Where're you going to train, Dario?"

"I don't know yet, won't know 'til Monday. I put in for Kingsville or Beeville. You here at Mainside?"

"Yep. Flying the old, leaky PBM flying boats. We don't do a touch-and-go, we do a splash-and-dash! I've been here almost a month. What're you doing tonight?"

"Nothing. I've got a room here at the Q, thought I'd have a few drinks, some dinner and hit the sack early. I've been driving for two days."

"Bullshit. Dario D'Angelo's not hitting the sack. You're comin' with me. I'm goin' to show you more horny pussy than they've got in solitary confinement at a women's prison. I'm telling you, D'Angelo, this place is nothing like that goddamn Pensacola. The girls here just love ensigns. Especially the L-B-F-Ms."

"What in the hell is a L-B-F-M?"

"Li'l brown fucking machines! Mexican broads. Chili peppers. The place is loaded with 'em. Man, do they love to dance, and can they move their asses. And they love to drink and make out. You just wait, you'll see."

Dario was ready to laugh off what Jim was saying as booze-induced over enthusiasm. He really was tired and he really wasn't interested in girls; only in one girl. He'd been thinking about Michelle since he left the lawyer's office in Mobile. The farther he drove away from her, the more he longed for her. He missed her. He missed her terribly. What seemed like a clean get away was becoming a sad ending. During the drive to Texas, he kept thrashing over their break up in his mind. *Perhaps I was too hasty in agreeing to the annulment. Perhaps I should have tried to talk her out of it. Perhaps . . . perhaps . . . perhaps I should try to find a bottle of slivovitz,* he finally told himself.

"I always liked you, Dario, especially after you were in the Madman Flight and showed up that jarhead, Hildripp, for the asshole he is."

"Thanks, Jim. It's great to see someone I know here."

"Manuel, two more Cubie's here, please. Come on, D'Angelo, let's drink up before happy hour's over and the price of drinks goes up to thirty-five cents."

* * *

By the time they'd eaten, and had a few more drinks, Dario agreed to go with Jim. He wanted to see something of Corpus with someone who knew the place. Jim drove his Chevrolet sedan with precision and good speed control, even though he was drunk. After twenty minutes of driving on country roads, with very little traffic, Jim drove up to the gate of a navy base. The guard at the gate saluted Jim's officer's sticker and waived them through.

"What's this place?" Dario asked.

"Cabaniss Field. It's got the wildest O' Club in all of Navydom. The Friday night dance goes on until nobody can dance anymore. They have two bands that rotate and the bar stays open as long as anyone can stand up to order. But the beauty is, the gate's wide open. They let unescorted ladies come through as long as they turn right and go to the O' Club. The single girls of Corpus wait all week for tonight. They'll be pouring in. Guys come up from Beeville and Kingsville just for this night. There'll be fucking going on in the parking lot and in the BOQ, which is just across the street."

Low and Slow

Dario could hear the Mambo music from the parking lot behind the club where Jim parked his car. They entered through a side door into the bar room. It was packed with people standing, drinking and smoking. They had to work their way through the crowd to get up to the bar. Dario recognized other faces from Basic, students who'd been ahead of him.

"Two Cuba Libras," Jim shouted to the barman, while leaning between two men sitting on bar stools.

"Seventy cents," the bartender called out as he put the drinks on the bar in front of him.

Jim paid, took his drink and handed one to Dario. "I've got to find my little chiquita. I'll be in the ballroom."

Dario saw someone get up and leave a stool, so he hurried over and sat on it. Once seated, he turned on the stool and faced out, observing the people in the lounge. All the men wore coats and ties, and the women wore fine dresses, or blouses and skirts. The dress code, at least, was to a high standard. Most of the men were his age; students like him. The girls were also young, but some seemed very young, eighteen at the most. Many girls seemed to be of Mexican heritage, but not all of them. He turned and faced an older man sitting next to him. "Hi. I just got to Corpus from Basic. Met a friend at Mainside who brought me here. I didn't even know about this base. What aircraft do they fly here?"

His barstool neighbor had both elbows on the bar with two drinks in front of him. He lifted his arms and turned to face his questioner. Dario guessed he was thirty-five or forty years old, from the grey in his full head of hair and the wrinkles on his face, which he turned toward him. He was no taller than Dario, but much heavier. His suit was blue striped seersucker and the knot of his rep tie was slightly undone. Dario looked into the face and saw dark-brown eyes. He also saw it wore a frown, and that hair protruded from his ear holes.

"Aircraft? Aircraft? We don't fly aircraft here, nothing that delicate. We fly dogs. Able Dogs. Best damn flying beast ever built! Just ask any marine who fought on the ground in Korea."

"Oh, you mean ADs, Skyraiders, the old prop attack planes they flew in Korea."

Dario had read about them in a Pre-Flight class. The designation stood for A=Attack, built by D=Douglas Aircraft. It was the first attack airplane built for the navy by that manufacturer. In the old military phonetic alphabet, A was Able and D was Dog. In the new NATO alphabet, which Dario had just learned, it was Alfa Delta. He had also learned that they were being replaced by new A4D jets.

"What do you mean, old? They only stopped making ADs last January, that was the AD-Seven, the seventh version of the brute. We're flying the fours here. The Skyraider's the best bomber ever built, whether you're dropping conventional bombs or nukeys. The students we train here become the best dive bombers in the world, put a five hundred pounder through a shithouse window." He turned back to his drinks, one of which he drained in one tilt.

"You mean they're still training in props? I thought the A4D was replacing them."

He found out that was the wrong thing to say. His neighbor spun on his stool, and shouted, "That fucking stovepipe, smelly piece of shit. Flying one of those things is like flying a hurricane lamp. They stink of kerosene. Give me the smell of one-forty-five octane any day. Besides, those stink pots can't carry shit and they can't stay on station. Nothing will ever replace the Skyraider." He turned back and began working on his second drink, then turned and faced Dario again. "Say, what's your name, you a student?"

"Yeah. It's D'Angelo, Dario. I just got here, hit the boat last week."

"D'Angelo! You're a *paisano!*" He stood up and extended his right hand. "Put it there, kid, I'm Marco Renetti. I'm the AD maintenance officer here."

"Are you a marine, sir?"

"Jesus Christ, D'Angelo, you trying to start a fight? Do I look like a fucking marine?"

"Well, no, sir. It's just that you mentioned marines in Korea."

"You don't have to be one to bomb the gooks for them. You're not a marine, are you?"

"No sir, an ensign. I was an AOC."

"Good, good. I know we got a few dumb dagos who eat up that Semper Fi shit, mostly Sicilians. I can see you're not a Sicilian. You're too white. What'd you hit the boat in?"

"SNJ."

"Good, great! You know what a tail wheel is. You going to fly ADs? It's the last combat plane made with a tail wheel."

"No, sir."

"Knock off the sir, shit. We're in the club."

"No, Marco. I put in my request for jets." He said it almost sheepishly.

"Change it! Fly ADs if you want to learn how to fly. Any asshole can fly one of those fucking zoomers. They don't even need rudder pedals. They don't have any torque. Just push the handle forward and point the pointy nose where you want to go. Wait until you throw the handle forward in a Skyraider, and almost three thousand horsepower whirl that fifteen-foot, four-bladed prop and you have to shove your right foot to the firewall to keep the torque from rolling you to the left. The only real flying's sitting behind a round engine, not over a sewer pipe burning coal oil."

While he talked, he didn't look Dario in the face. He was looking off into space, although it was short space to the mirror behind the bar. Dario thought he could see a tear in one eye. Marco suddenly turned and this time he *was* looking straight into Dario's eyes. "You any good with the stick, kid, or are you one of the students who just gets by?"

Dario hesitated before speaking, because he had to think about his answer before he gave it. He decided to not equivocate. He'd tell what he thought was the truth, as immodest as it might sound.

"Nobody's ever asked me that question, Marco. What can I say without bragging? I think I'm good. My father taught me how to handle women, music and fast cars. I learned to love them all, but now I've added airplanes. When I climb in a cockpit and get strapped in, I feel like the airplane's alive and I'm a part of it. I feel the same way when I'm with a girl, or I sit down at a piano or get into my car for a race. Then I use every sense in my body, every faculty to make my performance the best I can make it. I try to fly the same way. It seems to work." He looked at Renetti's face. It was expressionless. "You probably think I'm crazy."

Renetti put an arm out and rested his hand on Dario's shoulder. "Crazy! I feel the same way. I even talk to the fucking things." He sat back on his stool. "You've got to fly ADs, Dario. Wait 'til you play one. You'll make a concerto! And they're very much like a women because they'll hurt you unless you give them all your love and attention." Renetti swung his arm around, showing the people, the party, the activity going on in the club. "And, besides flying a real airplane, you get all this at Cabaniss. If your father taught you to love women, this is the place to practice your lessons."

"Yeah, it sure looks like this is the place," Dario responded.

"Your father sounds like quite a guy. What's he do?"

"He was the best goddamn foreign car mechanic in San Francisco, Marco. He had his own shop for a while, before he died. He didn't know anything about airplanes and neither did I, but if he'd lived, I know he'd be very proud to see me in a navy cockpit."

"Sound like your dad died young, like mine. Was it an accident?"

Dario hesitated before he replied. "Sort of. It was lung cancer. He went fast."

"Sorry, kid. It's tough when you lose your father. No matter whether they were saints or bastards, they never leave your thoughts."

Before he left the bar, he'd promised Renetti he would meet him Sunday morning to look at an AD. He went into the ballroom and found Jim sitting at a table on the edge of the dance floor with two girls. One was a little older, around twenty-eight, and the other looked to be in her very early twenties. Both girls were obviously Latin, and very attractive. They made room for him, and Jim made the introductions.

Low and Slow

"Jou Italiano, no?" the older girl named Alicia asked.

"Yes, I'm from San Francisco."

"Me, I'm from Puerrrto Rrrrico, from San Hwaun." In a few minutes he was on the dance floor with her, doing a bad but a vigorous job of dancing the Mambo.

"You come here every Friday night?" He almost yelled to make his voice heard over the blaring trumpets.

"Oh jes. I loaf it here. Much fun." He held her closely, swinging her around to the music. She was much shorter than even his average height, but her black hair was combed up like a beehive, giving her more stature. Her dark skin was accented by her orange lipstick and her low-cut, pearl-white satin dress. It had pom-poms on its knee-length hem, which made the bottom of her dress sway opposite to her hip movements.

"Jeem say you just got here. Jou like this place?"

"*Sí, me gusto mucho,*" he said in his best high school Spanish, squeezing her closer to him as he spoke.

"*¡Muy bueno, Chico!*" she screamed, throwing her head back and laughing. They returned to the table and ordered more drinks. The girls were drinking Brandy Alexanders while Dario and Jim stuck with rum and Cokes.

"You going to play the piano for us tonight?" Jim asked.

"Oooh, do you play? I love the piano," Jim's girl, Carmen said.

"Does he! We used to sit around the piano at the Whiting O' Club and throw song requests at him. Dario knows them all."

"I'm not up on Latin music, but I'll talk to the leader during their break. Maybe they can do something I know." The Mexican band leader was more than happy to let him sit-in with them; it was an officers' club and Dario was an officer. They did a standard song and he played blocked jazz chords to the band's Samba beat. When they finished, the leader made Dario take a bow and thanked him with an invitation to sit-in anytime. Alicia and Carmen were all over him when he sat down.

"*Fantastico!*" Alicia said, kissing him. He had no intention of sex that night; he missed Michelle and the thought of any woman but her was almost anathema to his libido. He'd come to Corpus feeling sorry about his loss, and resolved to avoid women and entanglements. But, as the dancing continued and the drinks flowed, he soon forgot his resolve and all the sadness. Jim left the room with his girl and was gone for about thirty minutes. Dario kept dancing with Alicia, who was looking better and better to him. He liked her good humor and vitality.

When Jim and Carmen came back to the table, he leaned over and spoke into Dario's ear, "Here, take my car keys. The parking lot's dark, they purposely turn the flood lights out. You can make out with Alicia in the back seat. I just took Carmen there." Dario took the keys from Jim's hand under the table.

The next time he and Alicia were dancing, he asked her if she wanted to go out for some fresh air. "Oh, jes. I'm very hot. It's time for some fresh air." She led him to the parking lot, knowing her way in the dark. When they got into the back seat of Jim's sedan, Dario began kissing her, but he soon just sat back and let her take over. She had her satin dress off in a second, and her panties and bra followed in quick succession, carefully laid over the front seat. Dario took off his jacket and unzipped his trousers. They kissed, he fondled her breasts for a minute, but Alicia was impatient. She sat on him and worked herself up-and-down, gritting her teeth and breathing through them, working herself to a climax. It was all over in what seemed to Dario like a few seconds.

"Jou got a cigarette?"

"No. I'm sorry. I don't smoke."

"Oh, that's OK. I got'a quit anywaze." She kissed him, moving her tongue around in his mouth. It was a very narrow, sharply-pointed and very long tongue. Dario bit on it gently. It was the first time he'd ever done foreplay *after* sex. She put her head against his. "Jesus, Dario. You getting me all hot again. I'm gonna want some more fresh air, right awayze."

They returned to Jim's rear seat again at three a.m., just before the dance ended.

Low and Slow

* * *

Carlo Renetti climbed up on the Skyraider's wing stub and pushed the actuator, which opened the bubble canopy. "Climb up," he beckoned to Dario. "Put your feet in those spring-loaded steps in the flaps."

The AD sat so high off the ground, the huge flaps had to be in the down position for access without a ladder. Dario climbed up and got into the cockpit while Renetti stood on the wing next to him. The first thing Dario noticed was the folded wings almost touching over his head, making a tepee silhouette. The second was, unlike the SNJ, he could see over the engine cowl. In fact, the bubble canopy of the single-seater gave him excellent forward and side vision. The smell of oil, high-octane gas, and electronics was even more pronounced than in the SNJs. The instrument panel was a maze of gauges, dials and armament switches.

He grabbed the stubby control stick and found a gun trigger and buttons. Renetti noticed him fingering them. "Four wing-mounted twenty-millimeter cannons. When you fire all four, the recoil slows you, like dropping the dive brakes. There's also buttons for rockets and bombs. This bird carries more ordnance than a World War II B-17. In Korea, one squadron even dropped a kitchen sink with a bomb in it."

Dario saw an enlisted man with a fire extinguisher standing to the side of the AD, a requirement when starting the engine of a navy aircraft.

"Set the throttle forward about an inch. Turn on the battery, there," Renetti pointed to the switch, "and hit the starter and primer buttons, there. Turn through eight prop blades and then switch on the mags. The bird's tied down, so don't worry about jumping chocks. I want you to hear how eighteen supercharged cylinders sound."

He followed the instructions. When he turned the magneto switch, there was a loud rumble, followed by a roar. His vision of Renetti and the enlisted man disappeared in a cloud of blue/white smoke, which soon dissipated in prop wash. The engine ticked over in a loud clackety, clackety that thrilled him. It was mechanical power, the internal combustion kind of power his mechanic father taught him to love. He let the engine run for several minutes. Renetti stayed on the wing, the prop wash making ripples in his uniform and blowing his hair astern. After a few minutes, Renetti reached in and pulled the mixture control to cut off. The exhaust noise stopped and the engine revolutions slowed, and valves, push rods and connecting rods clanged like a bucket of loose bolts until the engine came to a complete stop.

"Think you can play a concert with one of these?"

"I can't wait to unfold the wings and hit a crescendo."

Renetti put his hand on Dario's shoulder. *"Buono, paisano. Benvenuto!"*

Dario didn't tell Renetti he'd made up his mind the day before. He'd driven southwest Saturday afternoon, to look at Beeville and Kingsville. He took one look at the sagebrush and mesquite-surrounded bases and headed back to Corpus. He was a city boy and, although Corpus Christi wasn't much of a city, it was the closest thing there was in the area. He'd also learned from several students he'd talked to that, despite Renetti's enthusiasm, AD fleet squadrons would all be transitioning to the A4D jet in the very near future.

Most of all, he liked the action he'd seen at Cabaniss Friday night. *I've got to be honest with myself. The reason I joined this outfit was to get laid. Not to fly jets.*

* * *

The yeoman who gave him his orders to Kingsville Monday morning was surprised when Dario told him he wanted to change to Cabaniss Field. "But sir, nobody's *ever* done it that way. Students always want to change when they *don't* get what they asked for."

"I know, but I've decided I want to fly ADs."

The yeoman shook his head in wonderment. "You'll have to see

Commander Smart, the Admin officer. He's the only one who can change your orders."

When he was led into the commander's office, the first thing he noticed was the desk name plaque. CDR Richard R. Smart, USN, was carved into it. There was a snow covered, cone shaped mountain in the background which Dario didn't recognize. But it wasn't Fuji or Vesuvius, or even Etna. And, there were totem poles on each side of his name. He stood in front of the desk. Commander Smart was sitting behind the desk, looking down at typed papers. Dario could only see the top of his head, which was shiny skin beneath the few strands of side hair which had been carefully combed across the top.

"Have a seat," he said, without looking up. "I don't understand, D'Angelo. We gave you what you asked for, now you want to change. What happened?" Commander Smart sat back in his chair. He had a pleasant, plump face of swarthy complexion. Dario counted four rows of ribbons beneath his wings.

"I met Lieutenant Commander Renetti. He convinced me to . . . "

"Oh, hell. Say no more. If that AD fanatic got to you, you're brainwashed." He shuffled some papers on his desk. "The only problem is time. We're not starting any new classes at Cabaniss for a couple of weeks. I can't let you just sit around here. Would you be willing to take some leave to get Cabaniss?"

"Yes, sir. I'd like a few days at home."

"All right, then. Come in tomorrow morning and my yeoman will have your leave papers and your orders ready." Smart stood up and walked around his desk. "Where's home?"

"San Francisco, sir."

Smart sighed. "San Francisco. I love that town. I used to go to a bar called the Yankee Doodle, just across from Union Square."

"I know it well, sir. It's one of my favorites. Commander, what mountain is that in your name plaque?"

Smart looked at the mountain and sighed again. "Mount Rainier. My last duty was in carrier heavy-attack, flying AJ Savages. We were home-based at Whidbey Island, near Seattle. Local Indians carved these things out of cedar. God, I miss flying those heavies. The worst part of a naval career is flying a desk on shore duty, D'Angelo." Smart shook his hand. "Good luck. You keep listening to that nut Renetti and you can't go wrong. He was one of the best low-level attack pilots we had in Korea. He can put a rocket in your pocket. Saved many of our soldiers and marines by blasting away the enemy just a few yards in front of them. Got the Navy Cross for one attack. Bombed so low, he blew off bits of his own tail."

* * *

That evening, while drinking at the Mainside O' Club bar, he saw someone else he'd flown with in Basic Training walk into the club. It was Ensign Charlie Burner, a slow-speaking, slow-moving student from Missouri. His speech and manners had already earned him the nickname, "After Burner." Tall, slim, and gangly described him best.

He spied Dario's "come here" hand gesture, and complied. "Dario, when'd you get in?" Burner sat beside him and ordered a drink.

"Last Friday. How about you?"

"I've been here a week."

"What'd you get for duty?"

Burner looked at him for several seconds before answering. He spoke clearly and deliberately, with just a hint of a drawl. "I took ADs. Cabaniss is were the female action is. But I've got two weeks to kill. I'm taking leave, going back to Malvern to see my folks."

"Me too. I mean, I got ADs too, in two weeks. We'll probably get a class together. I'm going home to see my mother."

Burner's drink arrived, and he sucked ice cubes into his mouth and chewed them as he spoke. "You interested in moving into a snake ranch when you get back? I met a buddy from my ROTC class who's been here two months." Burner stopped talking and took several sips from his drink. "He's found an old house for rent." Again, sip, sip, sip. "It'll be four guys, twenty-five bucks a month each."

"Where is it?"

Low and Slow

Burner chewed more ice cubes before answering. "It's on the road between Mainside and Cabaniss. It's a big house, in a field all by itself, behind a Mexican dance hall called the Laraga. We can make all the goddamn noise we want to, have some wild parties."

"Include me in!" Dario shouted.

CHAPTER THIRTY-THREE

H E DROVE his MG to San Antonio the next day and got a hop on an air force cargo plane at Randolph Field. It was going to George Air Force Base, east of Los Angeles. He spent a night there, drinking in the officers' club, and flew to Travis Field, on the northern edge of San Francisco Bay, the next morning. He had to wear his uniform, but the space-available flights were free. He took a bus from Travis to downtown San Francisco, and a taxi to his mother's house. She opened the door within a minute of the first ring and saw him standing there, in his khaki uniform with the one gold stripe epaulets on his shoulders and a small suitcase in his hand.

"Dario!" There was alarm in her voice. "What are you doing home? Did you get fired from the navy?" She opened the door wide, and took his suitcase from his hand as he walked into the house.

"No, no, Mama. Everything's fine. I just got a few days of vacation between Florida and my new base in Texas. I start Advance Training next week. I'll be flying combat aircraft, soon."

The alarm was in her voice again. "Dario, I worry about you, gonna fly faster than I can hear, way up high in the sky."

Dario laughed. "Don't worry, Mama. I won't be flying faster than sound. The aircraft I got isn't a jet, and it flies low, and slow. Very low, and very slow, as a matter of fact. That's its mission. It sneaks up on the enemy."

"Ah, I see. You fly an airplane that's like a cat. Good, good. But what if the enemy has an airplane that's like a dog, a big dog?"

Dario just smiled and said nothing. He knew better than to get into an argument of analogies with his mother.

* * *

He spent several days fishing with Uncle Lezio during the day, and being with his family at night. On his second day on the boat, Dario stood next to his uncle, who was steering his double-ended boat under the Golden Gate Bridge, heading for Fisherman's wharf. Dario was staring off into the distance. He hadn't said much to Lezio, even when they were pulling in salmon after salmon on the lines.

"What's wrong, kid. You seem to be in the dumps. You got some problem you want to tell me about? Maybe I can help."

"Naw. I'm OK, Lez. Some girl's making me crazy, that's all. I left her, but I can't get her out of my mind. I'll get over it. It just takes time." He hadn't told anyone in his family about Michelle. This was the closest he got.

"She worth all the grief? Why'd you break up if she's got you so upset?"

"It was an impossible situation, Lez. I'll be OK. It just takes a little time."

"Look, *nipote*. I know better than anyone that you're a skirt chaser, just like your father was, just like I am. It's in the blood." Lezio instinctively made the Italian hand gesture to emphasize his remark by tapping his upturned wrist with the fingers of his other hand. "But don't get into trouble like your dad did, please. It would kill your mother."

D.E. " Butch" Bucciarelli

* * *

He didn't call Wanda, or even go to the Yankee Doodle or any jazz clubs because he was too sad; he missed Michelle. He knew he was still in love with her and probably would always be, just as Isabelle had predicted. He also knew that slivovitz would not replace his longing for her; nor grappa, nor another girl.

After three days, he'd had enough of San Francisco. Lezio drove him back to Travis where he stayed overnight at the BOQ, and got a flight to Randolph Field the following morning, landing there in the early evening. He drank three Cuba Libras at the O' Club and decided to put a few quarters in one of the slot machines. He'd never been a gambler, but he didn't mind giving a few dollars to the slots; they helped pay for the cheap drinks and food at the clubs. On his third pull he was rewarded with ten dollars worth of quarters. He'd put three dollars back in the machine when he was struck with an idea. He gathered up the quarters out of the tray, put them in his jacket pocket and went to a row of pay phones in the lobby. He put a quarter in one and dialed the operator.

"Please give me Mobile, Alabama information," he said when the operator answered.

Next, he gave the long distance operator the number the information operator had given him for Eighton, Donald S., and plugged the phone with the remaining quarters. When a man answered he almost hung up, but the three drinks gave him the courage to go ahead with his plan. "Donald?"

"Yes, who's this?" The voice was deep and precise, with a souther accent.

"It's Dario D'Angelo. I'd like to speak to Michelle, please."

There was a slight hesitation on the other end. "Just a moment."

He could hear Donald's muted voice talking to someone. Finally, he heard Michelle's soft, sweet, voice. "Hello, Dario. What is it you want?"

"I want you. I miss you something awful. I have to see you and I just know you feel the same way. If I'm right, make a sentence with a number in it."

His hand holding the telephone was shaking as he waited for Michelle's response. She was silent for only ten seconds, but it seemed like much more.

"Donald and I were married three days ago. The annulment was granted four days ago. You should receive your copy in one or two days, maybe three. Certainly not five."

His hand steadied as a great feeling of relief surged through him. Everything was going to be all right.

"Great job, Michelle, you're brilliant. I love you, I love you. Will he be leaving on a flight soon? Just make a sentence with 'yes' or 'no.' "

"Yes, it went through without any problems."

"Will he be leaving tomorrow?"

"No. We had a small ceremony."

"Will he be leaving the next day?"

"Yes. I'm glad it's over too."

"Can you meet me at the White House in Biloxi, the day after tomorrow?"

"Oh, yes!," She said it with exuberance. "I'm very happy, now!"

"I'm in San Antonio. I'll be at the hotel Thursday morning. I can't wait to hold you, to kiss you. I know what you'd say if you could."

"What?"

"I love you."

She paused for about five seconds, which, again, seemed much longer to Dario. "Yes, you're absolutely right," her voice was low, and serious, ending with a sigh. "It is going to turn out well."

"Goodbye, Michelle, my love. See you Thursday."

"Goodbye, Dario."

The constant ache in his stomach was gone. His future looked bright; he'd be with Michelle soon. He slept soundly that night, looking forward to his drive in the morning back along the Gulf, back to the magnolias and the gardenias.

He registered again as Ens. and Mrs. D'Angelo, and he was able to get the same room they had at the White House Hotel on their short honeymoon. It was on the third floor, with French doors and a balcony facing the Gulf. He was standing there, looking out to sea when he saw a new, bright red Triumph TR2, with its top down, pull into the parking lot. The driver's auburn hair shone in the morning sunshine. It was Michelle.

I'm not going to have a bottle of slivovitz hidden in a cupboard, Isabelle. I'm going to have the real thing.

He stood by the door as adrenaline rushed through his body. He swore he could smell gardenias a second before he heard her muted knock. He threw open the door. Michelle was standing there, smiling, showing her brilliant white teeth through an even more tanned skin than he remembered. Her freckles were darker too, retaining the contrast. She wore a green satin, low-cut dress and carried a small overnight bag. She looked more beautiful than he had ever seen her, even more beautiful than when she was covered with engine oil, that day on the beach when he knew he loved her. He reached out, grabbed her hand and pulled her in as he pushed the door shut behind her. He held her tightly in his arms as he kissed her, inhaling her scent. She bit his lower lip. "Ow," he cried, touching his lip and looking at the blood on his fingers as he held his hand out. "What'd you do that for?"

"Next time, don't take so long to call."

* * *

He kept running the end of his tongue over the swollen tissue of his lip during the drive back to Corpus, as a reminder of Michelle and her passion. He longed to be back in the hotel room, back in bed with her in the coolness of the hours before the sun rises. They'd spent most of their two days together in that bed, leaving the room only for rejuvenating walks on the beach and a few meals.

"I was so excited when I heard your voice. When I realized what you wanted me to do, it became a simple game to play. How did you think of telling me to use a number, Dario?"

"I saw it in a spy movie. It just came to me when I thought of calling you."

She was sitting up in bed next to him, naked. More time in the summer sun had darkened the color of the freckles on her breasts to the same reddish brown as her nipples. During their first sexual frenzy, she'd moved her body position constantly, until they'd performed sex in every manner Dario had taught her, as if to insure that such sex was still possible. He wanted to ask her if Donald only did it in the missionary position, but he didn't. He'd decided he wouldn't deride Donald, and the best way to avoid derision was to avoid the subject of him, her marriage to him and her new life.

He needn't have been so concerned; Michelle brought up the subject. "Donald is such a child. He thought I was attracted to you because of your MG, so he bought me the Triumph as a wedding present. Donald thinks if I loved you because of your MG, I would love him more because a Triumph costs more. It's the way his mind works. He doesn't have a clue of why I ran off with you."

What can you expect from a navigator? he thought. Then he remembered the song some F-86 fighter pilots were singing at the bar at George Air Force Base. *"Oh, there are no fighter pilots down in hell. It's all full of queers, navigators and bombardiers. Oh, there are no fighter pilots down in hell."*

"Did he ever ask you why you married me?"

"No, we almost never talk about you. You are definitely a non-subject. You don't exist. You never existed. I'm certain Donald chalks you up as the last fling of my youth, one I've outgrown." She leaned over and kissed him softly on his cheek. "I'll never outgrow you, Dario." Her voice had dropped in tempo, pitch and volume. "You unleash a madness in me I can only restrain for short periods. When will you meet me again?"

She'd answered his unasked question. This wasn't a one-time assignation, a get-it-out-of-my-system-once-and-for-all romp. Michelle also saw it as the start of a new relationship. They could enjoy each other's bodies—and love—without the burden and responsibility of marriage.

"I don't know?" he answered her. Maybe I can catch a cross-country hop some weekend, but how will I know if Donald's away? I can't keep calling you up and asking you about our annulment in code."

"Oh, I have it all figured out. I'll send you notes telling you when he's going to fly overseas and when you can phone me. Oh, Dario, I love the intrigue." She nuzzled her head next to his and kissed his ear. "And you started it with your phone call, you sly home-wrecker."

For a fleeting second he had a pang of remorse, but he quickly dismissed it. He didn't consider himself a home-wrecker. Donald would have his home with Michelle and the pomp of Montgomery society. All he wanted was the madness in her now and then, which he deserved, because he released the genie from the bottle on the hood of his MG, under stars falling on an Alabama cotton field.

They made love for the last time as the still hidden sun was nearing the eastern horizon and turning the bottoms of wispy, grey clouds hovering over it into gold. He wanted to stay longer and have breakfast together in the room again, but he'd stayed as long as he dared. He had to be at Cabaniss the following morning. He held her close, and he didn't know she was crying until he felt the wetness of the tears on her face when he kissed her cheeks in the dark. "What's wrong, Michelle? Why are you crying?"

"Oh Dario, I know I'm weird, but I love you more than I ever did. How can I be so mixed up? I still want you as my lover and I'm afraid I'll lose you. You're not jealous of Donald, are you, Dario?"

He rocked her gently. "Of course I am! But I accept what has to be. We did what we had to do. But, I love you, Michelle. And here's a corny line from a million movies. I'll always love you."

"Oh, Dario," she sobbed, I worry about you. Donald did tell me that if we hadn't split up, I'd probably be a widow before long. He said the navy's accident rate is ten times the air force's. Is that true, Dario. Is the flying you do so much more dangerous?"

"It's just air force propaganda, Michelle. But, in a way, he's right.

Low and Slow

Carrier flying is a lot more dangerous than sitting at a navigation table eating hot soup for lunch. And, thank God it is! I'd be bored silly doing that. You wouldn't want me to, would you?"

"No, no. I want you just the way you are. My Dario, landing his crippled airplane on the beach for me." She kissed him softly on his lip wound. "I know what you do is dangerous. You've already lost two friends and you're just in training. What's it going to be like when you live on a carrier?"

"Yeah, Joe Schade and Ralph Kramer. The good die first, Michelle, so I'll survive to be with you again." He laughed a sham laugh.

She squeezed her body tightly against his as if she was trying to weld it to him so they couldn't separate. Suddenly, she released him and turned over, putting her back to him. "I know you have to go, you can't be late," she said. "Come to me again, soon, my darling."

He took a deep breath just before he left, but in a few minutes his swollen lip was his only physical reminder of her.

CHAPTER THIRTY-FOUR

DARIO HELD his breath as the sailor in Cabaniss Security looked over his records, then sighed relief when he put a base sticker in the lower left corner of the MG's plastic windscreen. He silently thanked Captain Levin and his forgetful chief. The sticker would make his life a lot easier, especially since he was living in a snake ranch ten miles from the base. Snake ranches for flight students were unknown in the Corpus area. The BOQs were adequate, so a housing allowance wasn't given to bachelor students. But those who'd lived off base at Gulf Shores had been spoiled. They learned to appreciate the departure from military life when classes and flying were finished for the day. And, on weekends, the Laraga would be a party facility set in the privacy of a South Texas field, where all they'd disturb were a few coyotes, rattlesnakes and jackrabbits.

* * *

Not since playing in the VFW teen-age band had he done anything as boring as full-time instrument flying. He'd been anxious to fly the T-28 and feel its power and performance, which was much greater than the SNJ, but all his flights were from the back seat. His instructor was a pleasant enough lieutenant from Kentucky. He seldom said a word that didn't apply to instrument flying, and in his whining, hill-country accent, Dario came to loath his commands over the intercom. On each flight, the instructor would start and taxi the T-28 to the end of the runway and line it up with the centerline. Dario would then pull a fabric canopy over his head, which cut off his vision outside the cockpit. He would then add power slowly, watching the compass to keep the airplane going straight down the runway. He took off solely by looking at the instruments.

For two hours, more-or-less, he would fly the aircraft by looking only at instruments. Occasionally, he would get disoriented. His inner ear would send him false readings and he would think the airplane was spinning or diving. A quick peek under the fabric canopy, which never covered completely, gave him reference to the ground and dispelled the vertigo. It was all low frequency range and the sound of the Morse Code dah-dits and dit-dahs and the hillbilly voice of his instructor bored him more-and-more during the two-month syllabus. On the last instrument approach of the day, his instructor would say, "I've got it," take the controls and land the airplane. Dario could then "pop the hood." He finished the course on his thirty-second instrument flight, after almost 70 hours of flying "under the bag." Back in the ready room he was issued a standard instrument card. He was getting closer to being a real naval aviator; he now had a carrier qualification card and an instrument card.

The only break he got from the boredom of the instruments course was his cross-country. Every student was allowed to fly anywhere in the USA for a RO2N (remain over, two nights), weekend flight, providing he could find an instrument instructor who'd take him. Dario would have opted for a flight to Mobile to meet Michelle, but he received a note telling him Donald's unit was going through a training phase and he'd be home for some time. So, he decided to try for a flight to NAS Alameda to visit his mother and family.

Lieutenant Craig "Leaky" Potts was an instrument instructor, and a bachelor, unlike most of the other instructors. He often showed up at the Laraga at their after-happy hour parties and hit on any girls who came alone, or whose dates had passed out. He was almost always successful. Leaky was over six feet tall, with broad shoulders and a thin waist. He'd played football at Stanford where he'd been a favorite of the faculty, the alumni, and the coeds. Dario heard of his reputation as a good pilot, drinker and womanizer; all the traits that identified a good naval aviator. Dario had watched him work, and decided that what Leaky had that was so special was his innocent smile. He had a way of tossing his head back and smiling, which made him look about twelve years old, and sweet and innocent. Girls believed anything he told them.

"I saw your request on the bulletin board, Dario," Leaky told him in the instrument training unit's ready room. "You want to fly to Alameda for your cross-country."

"Yeah, I'd like to see my family and maybe hit the Alameda Friday night happy hour, if it's possible."

"Tell you what I'm going to do for you, Dario my lad. Forget Alameda happy hour. I'll take you on a little flight to open your eyes to the big time, make Cabaniss and Alameda happy hours look like a Girl Scout slumber party. We'll fly to North Island. It's time you discovered Coronado. And, I guarantee you'll make out."

"Where's Coronado?"

"Jesus Christ!" He mocked surprise by slapping his forehead with his hand. "Don't they teach you anything in Basic Training anymore? They sure don't wind up Dilberts like they did when I went through. It's across the bay from San Diego, just a few miles from the Mexican border, you provincial dolt."

"I would like to see my mother in San Francisco."

"Mother, mother? I'm talking getting laid! Mothers are there forever, getting laid on a cross-country is a fleeting thing."

"You think like my father."

"Why's that?"

"He told me a sexual opportunity missed is lost forever."

"Your Dad knows what he's talking about. You want to see him too, I guess?"

Low and Slow

"I'd like to, but he's dead. But he did teach me to appreciate girls, and I do. I've been doing pretty well here, you know. There are lots of girls at our snake ranch every weekend." He didn't want Leaky to think he had to fly to Coronado to get laid.

Leaky dismissed the statement with, "There are more available girls in Coronado than in Corpus and Pensacola put together. How about this? We takeoff at one minute after midnight Thursday night, but it's really Friday so Thursday doesn't count. We fly to El Paso, where we'll get fuel, then it's about two-and-a-half hours to North Island. We'll get some sleep in the BOQ, then hit happy hour and the Mexican Village."

"Where's that, in Mexico?"

"No, you neophyte hedonist! You mean you never heard of the Mexican Village, MexPac, the most important bar in all of naval aviationdom? It's in Coronado, just a few blocks out the North Island gate. By eight o'clock, the place will be full of single school teachers and telephone operators, plus WestPac widows."

"What's a WestPac widow?"

"Dario, your lack of education is seriously alarming me. A WestPac widow is the wife of a navy man who's deployed on a ship to the Western Pacific. As soon as they wave goodbye to their men, as the ship leaves the quay wall, they head for the Mexican Village. It's the action center of San Diego, and San Diego is filled with good-looking girls who couldn't wait to finish college and get out of Michigan and Nebraska and head for the beaches. Anyway, after a night of total and delicious debauchery, we'll awaken at a godly hour—say noon—and fly to Alameda. You can spend the night with your family while I'll try to be content with second best, San Francisco. We'll fly home Sunday. You can sit up front and fly while I sleep."

"How much do I have to pay you and will you take a check?"

"You just buy me a drink at the Village. And I'll take care of the paper work. You do have to fly the airplane on instruments, you know. These cross-country flights are not boondoggles. They're sanctioned by the Chief of Naval Air Training so students can learn to operate in the commercial airways over long distances. They are not to be used as personal transportation conveniences." They laughed in unison.

Dario flew by instruments to El Paso, but after takeoff from there, Leaky let him pop the hood and look out. Not that there was much to see on a clear August night over the Southwestern desert; a few lights of some small towns and the bright lights of Albuquerque and Phoenix. They landed at North Island just as the sky was brightening. It was the first time Dario had ever flown an airplane to get somewhere. Every flight he'd ever made had been a training flight that departed and returned to the same field. They got a ride to the BOQ, had breakfast, and Dario was asleep by nine. He was to meet Leaky at the officers' club at four.

Leaky was sitting at the bar of the O' Club, which was built between the beach and the runway. He was wearing a sport coat and tie, just like Dario. There were four officers standing around him, who were wearing dress khakis: a commander, two lieutenant commanders and a lieutenant. Dario was just a little intimidated by all the rank, but as Leaky saw him approach, he lit up his face with a smile which put him immediately at ease. "Here comes my student, Dario D'Angelo. I predict great things for him. Unlike the other students we get at Cabaniss, who move a record player and a set of encyclopedias into a BOQ room and call it home, D'Angelo and three others opened their own snake ranch and it rocks every weekend, girls everywhere. If he can accomplish that while in training, think of what blasphemies he'll commit when he gets to a squadron."

Dario blushed a little, but he felt complimented. He could tell Leaky had been to the bar for some time, so he ordered a Cuba Libra to catch up with him. Dario learned that Leaky's friends had been squadron mates of his in a jet squadron. The commander treated him like he was one of the boys, and so did the others. This was his first taste of the fleet navy, and he liked it. He wasn't being treated as a student, he was being treated as a naval aviator, even though he still had several months to go. And, he didn't see any marine uniforms at the bar.

Low and Slow

The Mexican Village was a lot smaller than he expected such a famous bar to be. There were small swinging doors at the front and a wishing well in the center of the barroom, with wooden booths lining the walls. Behind the bar was a painting of Mexicans in various native costumes, lined up and pointing to the one standing next to him. At the end of a chain was a pot-bellied peon with his hands and shoulders up in a shrugging motion, as an old man held a shotgun on him. Standing next to the old man was a beautiful Mexican maiden with a swollen belly. Speedy Gonzalez had done it again! As Leaky entered, two bartenders cried out a welcome. "Batten down the hatches, lock up the virgins, Leaky's in town."

"Hi Freddie, hi Stan," Leaky answered with a toss of his head. "Good to be back. I hear things have been slow around here. Rustle up a couple of stingers and let's get this show on the road. Leaky's the name, and fun's the game."

Things got hazy for Dario later, after some tacos and quite a few drinks. He met lots of girls and he and Leaky left the Mexican Village with two for a "Coronado pub crawl." They went to a place called the Island, and then the Manhattan Room. After that, they headed for Tijuana.

When they crossed the border, he told Sandy, the girl driving, it was the first time he'd ever been out of the USA. "Welcome to international travel, but don't judge the rest of the world by TJ or you might stay home for the rest of your life."

They went to a bar where two musicians played piano and conga drum, and sang in close harmony, in Spanish. Sandy seemed to have latched onto him, but Dario wasn't complaining. She was in her late twenties, pleasant and attractive. She told him she worked for the telephone company and she was very emphatic that she was not an operator; she was a supervisor. They danced and he got very close to her, kissing her on the neck and lips. He told himself to lighten up on the Mexican rum or he'd miss a chance with her, but himself seldom listened.

When they left the bar the sun was breaking, exactly as it had 24 hours before when he was landing at North Island. He fell asleep in

Sandy's car when he hit the seat. When he awakened, he was in a bed with her and the sun was bright in the sky.

"Where are we?" He nudged her sleeping body, gently.

"Chula Vista." Her voice was somewhat groggy.

"Oh Christ, we're still in Mexico! I've got to get to North Island."

Sandy laughed and turned over to face him. "Relax, we're in California. We're only thirty minutes from your base. I'm to get you there by eleven. Leaky's orders."

He picked up his watch from the night stand and looked at it. "It's nine now."

"Good, lots of time. There's a new toothbrush in the bathroom."

It took him a few foggy seconds to comprehend her meaning, but when he did he smiled and kissed her on her forehead, careful not to exhale toxic rum fumes.

"I'll go clean up. I don't imagine I was a very exciting date after we left Tijuana, but I'll try to make up for it."

* * *

Leaky was outside the BOQ waiting for him, already in his flight suit, when Sandy dropped him off. He looked like he'd just awakened from twelve hours of sleep, although Dario doubted if he got even the three hours or so he had. "Well, did I lie to you D'Angelo," he asked as they rode in a van to operations, his smile concealing the truth with his look of perpetual innocence.

"No. It was just as you promised, Leaky. In fact, you didn't do it justice. You didn't tell me about Tijuana. I'd never been out of the country before. To hell with Alameda. I'm going to try to get North Island for duty."

"Good, good. I knew you'd appreciate this place. Tijuana's just one of the added benefits of being stationed here. Christ, I can't wait to finish my goddamn Texas shore duty and get back to a squadron."

Leaky let him fly the T-28 from the front seat, visually. They flew up the coast at 500 feet, cutting inland on a northwest heading just past

Low and Slow

Los Angeles. They hit the shore again at Morro Bay, flew along Big Sur and over Monterey Bay, then cut across to San Jose and up the east side of the bay to Alameda. It was exhilarating for Dario to see places in his native state he'd only heard and read about.

* * *

"No, Mama, I haven't gotten a raise yet. I don't get a pay increase until I get promoted, and that won't be for six months."

She sat across from him at the kitchen table of her new house. The furniture was all white oak and flowery fabrics and the new stove and refrigerator were chrome and pastel colored enamel. Her hair was nicely groomed in a new style, short and fluffy. She wore a colorful blouse and slacks. Since his father died and she married Vito, she no longer wore only drab housecoats and she no longer wound waist length hair into a bun each morning. Dario was happy that she was becoming more American every time he visited her. Even her English was getting better, although she still spoke to him in Italian.

"You mean they pay you the same money now when you know how to drive the airplanes as they did when you couldn't drive them? That's crazy."

"Lots of things in the navy are crazy, Mama. They call it tradition."

"What happens to you when you finish learning to drive airplanes? Does the navy teach you how to drive ships?"

"No, Mama," he laughed. "The navy would teach me how to drive a ship much later in my career, if I stay in the navy. When I finish in a few months, I'll be assigned to a squadron, one that does bombing."

"Where?"

"I don't know. Could be the Atlantic or the Pacific? Maybe I'll be lucky and get Alameda, although if it's San Diego, I could still fly up and see you all the time."

"Do you have to pay for the gasoline when you come to see me?"

"No Mama, the navy never makes me pay for the gasoline. They pay for it."

She rocked her head slightly with a smug smile on her face. "Good, good." She slapped a hand on the table and stood up. "I get to work. We have ravioli tonight."

"Oh Mama, that's too much work, and I have to leave in the morning."

It took his mother two days to make ravioli. She made them stuffed with Swiss chard, veal, onions and calves brains. She ground the stuffing by hand in an antique contraption that clamped to the side of the kitchen table. Then she mixed the pasta dough by hand and rolled it into sheets. The procedure was very time, and labor, intensive.

"We have them tonight! I make ravioli by electric, now, Vito bought me all the machines. I make ravioli in an hour."

* * *

She proudly announced to his grandmother and grandfather, and the other family members who had come to see him (and for the ravioli), "Dario drove his own airplane home, for free! And, he will drive it back to Texas tomorrow. Just think, the navy actually pays him to come across the country to see his mama."

It would be a waste of time for Dario to explain to her about proficiency cross-country training, so he let it lie. But, as with most things, Mama's peasant understanding of a situation was usually closer to the truth than the official explanation.

After dinner he begged off a game of cards with Lezio and went to bed. He was very tired from the night in Tijuana, and the morning in Chula Vista. He was in bed and just about to turn off the light when there was a soft knock at the door. "Dario, it's Vito. Can you give me a minute?"

"Sure, Vito. Come on in." When Vito entered, Dario beckoned him to sit in the chair next to the bed. He sat up in bed, propping the pillows behind his back.

"Dario, I just wanted to tell you how proud we all are of what you have accomplished. To have one of our Italian boys as an officer in the navy, and flying one of their airplanes to visit us, makes us all realize how lucky we all are that our parents came to this wonderful country. In the 'old country,' only the nobility could do what you have done."

He deeply appreciated his stepfather's statement. He was humbly aware that, until him, no member of their families ever graduated from college, let alone got a military commission.

"You just wait and see, Vito. We'll have doctors and professors in our family before long. I'm the first to finish college, but only because I'm the oldest of the grandchildren. And Vito, I couldn't have done any of it without everyone helping me."

"Yes, I know, there are so many chances in this country. But, what you did, you did all by yourself. You'll always get what you want, Dario, because you've got drive and determination."

Of course, Vito had no idea of how much trouble he'd gotten into and how close he'd been to getting washed out of the program so many times. And getting what he wanted the night before was making it hard to stay awake, but he couldn't be rude to Vito. His stepfather had become very dear to him. He could never replace Babbo in a million years, but Dario had learned to respect him because his mother loved him, and because he made her happy, and because he'd become his friend.

"Thank you, Vito."

"Now Dario, I want to talk to you about your mother's finances."

Suddenly, Dario wondered if he'd been too quick to accept Vito's sincerity with his mother's money. After all, Vito was a shrewd banker, while his mother had no knowledge of finance. She only knew how to deposit money; she never drew any out.

"Not one penny of the money your mother received from your father's life insurance," Vito said, "and the money she got for the sale of his garage business and their house, was used to build this house or anything else she has. I used the money I got from the sale of my house, and what I had saved. I make a good salary, and I will continue to support your mother, as long as I live. Well, as you must know, it's every Italian's dream to own property. Beatrice has invested her money wisely. She now owns a small apartment house here in the city. She decided on the building herself, and I must tell you, Dario, she was a demanding negotiator. She got the property for much less than the asking price."

"That's my Mama," Dario replied. "Babbo always said she could buy a dollar bill for ninety-five cents."

Vito chuckled. He loved his wife, and understood her frugality. It also pleased him to see her spending his money on appliances and furnishings for their new home.

"You are the beneficiary of her property, Dario, not me. I insisted. That money came from your father and it should go to you, should your mother pass on."

Dario noticed that Vito used the conditional Italians always use regarding death, denying its inevitability. They begin their wills with: "If I should die . . . "

Vito got up and stood next to the bed, put one hand on Dario's shoulder and took his hand with his other. "You are now the heir of property, Dario, so take care of yourself with your flying. We worry about your safety."

"Me? Nothing's going to happen to me, Vito. I fly low, and slow."

* * *

Uncle Lezio was impressed with the cockpit of the T-28. He drove him to Alameda where Dario took him up on the wing to show him his "office."

"Look at all those dials and needles. You really know what they all are, Dario? Me, I'm lucky to read my compass and get my ship-to-shore radio to work." He was still shaking his head in wonder as they climbed down the flap steps to the tarmac. "When I was out in the Pacific, I used to watch our planes fly off carriers and shoot down the Kamikazes, right in front of our LST. We loved those guys, Dario, they saved our ass more than once. We always wondered how those pilots did it, day-after-day. I never dreamed my nephew would be one, someday."

When he introduced Leaky, Lezio took off his wool cap. Dario was afraid, for a second, that he was going to bow, but Leaky, with his usual smile, put Lezio right at ease with his friendly manner. "You got an outstanding nephew here, Mr. Cresci. Dario's doing just fine. He's going to make one helluva naval aviator. You'll be proud of him."

Lezio was wearing a plaid lumberjack coat. He put his cap on and nodded his head slowly, up-and-down. "Yes, thank you. But we're already proud of him, Lieutenant Potts. We've always been proud of Dario. He's always been good to his mother, his grandparents, and his aunts and uncles. Even if Dario should fail—which he won't—we'd still be proud of him, because he's a good boy. That's what's important to us."

Christ. Vito last night, now Lezio dripping maudlinisms all over me. Dario almost felt that he deserved them as he hugged his uncle goodbye.

CHAPTER THIRTY-FIVE

SATURDAY BECAME party day at the Laraga. Students drove up from Kingsville and Beeville for the Cabaniss Friday night, open-gate girl frenzy, and stayed for the weekend. Bill Metz, who'd finished instruments and was flying jets at Chase Field, was a regular couch or floor occupant. At first, the parties were spontaneous, starting with mild drinking in the afternoon, and ending with a few invited students and instructors with dates dropping by throughout the evening and into the early morning. Soon, the word got out, and they were inundated with single girls on the prowl, single flight students on the prowl, plus the regulars. No one was ever turned away; it was always open house at the Laraga. There were often over twenty cars parked in the field around the ramshackle house.

With relief from the requirement of studying for instrument flying, the Laraga occupants began to do more planning for their parties. They had a Sputnik costume party when the Russians made their spectacular shot. Flight suits, oxygen masks and flight helmets were modified in a myriad of ways to become space suits, and many of the girls had scooped the space scientists by calculating what space woman of the future would wear, which was very little. After Burner came up with an IFR (Instrument Flight Rules) punch. Fruit juices, vodka and rum went into a large ice chest, into which he threw dry ice. The heavier-than-air CO_2 fog created from the dry ice stayed above the liquid in the chest, and the potential drinker of the concoction had to fly his glass through the fog, in the blind, to fill it. There were a lot of crashes.

There were always a lot of bodies lying around on Sunday morning, so After Burner decided to have a milk-punch party on one occasion. Forsaking his cooler, he bought a new, green wheelbarrow and mixed his punch in it. He wheeled it up to a prostrate form and awakened him or her with a cup of his formula. Unfortunately, the latter contained a high percentage of rum, which didn't dissolve the wheelbarrow paint but lifted it from the metal in quarter-size, film-thin pieces. These were unnoticed by the half-awake partakers and ignored by them later when they had their second or third drink. By noon, everyone at the Laraga milk-punch party was oblivious to the green lipstick they were all wearing.

* * *

After Burner was the only Laraga resident in Dario's Skyraider flight, which was composed of six students and their instructor, Lieutenant Commander MacArthur. They'd picked the call sign, "Road Runner," for their flight. The other students were three married ensigns and a NAVCAD. Of the six, Dario was the only student who'd flown the SNJ. The others were concerned about flying a tail wheel aircraft after flying only the easier, nose wheeled T-34s and T-28s.

Dario continued to run into Renetti at the officers' club. He was almost as excited about Dario's forthcoming AD training as he was. "These students coming down the pipeline with only training wheel experience are having trouble keeping the Able Dog on the runway. It'll be a breeze for you, Dario. The Skyraider's easy compared to the Jay—you can see over the cowl when the tail's on the ground. Just remember, when you pour the coal to it, stick your right foot on the rudder, hard! Don't be tender with it. You can't bend it."

Renetti had the reputation of being a curmudgeon, but Dario always found him to be pleasant. He knew they identified with each other because they were the sons of Italian immigrants, promoted well beyond the wildest dreams of their fathers. As maintenance officer of the Skyraider unit, Renetti was responsible for the readiness and reliability of all its aircraft, and he once confided to Dario that keeping those Korean War relics together was quite a task. The age of the airplanes was telling in many ways, but not in the engines; there were seldom engine failures. Problems came mostly in the hydraulics and electrical systems.

During happy hour one Friday afternoon, the club's loudspeaker directed all students to leave the bar, walk to the end of the parking lot and watch a wheels up landing by a student whose landing gear would not come down. They were also informed they could take their drinks with them, "and one roady." By the time they got to the runway's perimeter, the first third of it had been sprayed with fire retardant foam. The wheel-less Skyraider made a normal approach, flaps down, and floated past the foam (the student forgot the airplane had less drag because of no wheels), and landed on the concrete runway beyond it. There was a loud scraping noise as the airplane slid to a stop. The fire trucks rushed to its side, but no smoke or flames erupted. The student pilot casually climbed out and was blasted with foam by the overcautious crash truck crew. He walked across the wing—looking like the Pillsbury Dough Boy—took off his helmet and stepped down. He then dropped to his knees, bent over and kissed the ground. The spectators, who had been silent through concern and awe, erupted simultaneously in one giant cheer, while waving what drinks remained in the air.

"I guess it's what they mean by 'Any landing you walk away from is a good landing,' " After Burner droned to Dario.

"Yes, it's a good landing, but not a great landing. Marco Renetti told me a great landing is when you can use the airplane again."

Low and Slow

* * *

Dario's first experience in the Skyraider was not a flight. His class had spent two days sitting in the cockpit, learning all the switches, radios, armament systems and flight instruments. Blindfolded, he could reach out and touch anything called out, and he could simulate any emergency procedure short of bailing out. He sat on a 90-pound parachute pack, which also held a life raft and emergency supplies. When the big day came when he would actually start his engine, everything went well. Each student was in radio contact with their instructor, who told them when to start their engines. Battery on, hold down the primer button and the starter button through two full rotations of the engine, and then switch on the magnetos. The rumble that ensued sounded like a freight train passing by. When the engine was running smoothly and hydraulic pressure was up, he executed his first—and very important—carrier aircraft procedure. He unfolded the wings. They came down slowly, and when they were both in place, he locked them.

For his first operation, Dario taxied onto the runway, lined up with the center line and slowly, but evenly, pushed in two-thirds of the engine's power, while also pushing in lots of right rudder as the speed increased, to keep the nose lined up with the white center line. The Skyraider accelerated with more force than he'd ever felt. The thrill of acceleration was pumping the adrenaline through him as he felt the tail wheel come off the ground and the fuselage come level with the runway. He desperately wanted to let it accelerate to 100 knots and pull back on the stick, but he didn't. When the tail wheel came up and the aircraft settled in level position, he cut the power to idle and controlled the airplane as it decelerated to taxi speed. Then he taxied off the runway so the student behind him could make the identical run. The rumor of a machine gunner at the end of the runway who was ordered to shoot down any student who became airborne on the high-speed taxi hop was discounted as instructor harassment.

Dario went to sleep that night in nervous, but exhilarated anticipation of the next day's flight, when he would push the throttle to the
full power mark and pull back on the joystick, with no concern about
a mystical runway gunner. After Burner was as excited as Dario, but he
looked forward to his first takeoff with more foresight. "Don't forget,
Dario. Once we get the hog off the ground, we have to bring it back."

Going to full-power was more of a thrill than he'd even imagined,
the power almost made tears flow from his eyes. He got airborne,
pulled up the wheels, and pulled back the throttle and prop to climbing power. He continued climbing and joined the formation led by
MacArthur, their instructor, who was orbiting at 4500 feet. Dario was
flying in the number three slot, and when they were all joined up and
in cruise formation, the realization of what he'd done and was doing
hit him. He looked at the other Skyraiders. They weren't painted
high-visibility, training yellow. They were painted low-visibility fleet
blue, for stealth. There were two things sticking out of each wing's
leading edge which weren't instrument probes. They were twenty-
millimeter cannons. There wasn't an instructor or an empty seat behind him. He was flying a single-seat, 2700-horsepower, combat airplane. He was excited, but he was also in awe of the beast. Unlike
yellow training airplanes, blue combat airplanes did not tolerate stupid mistakes.

They flew to an outlying strip at Aransas Pass, where a Runway
Duty Officer was waiting to talk them through their first touch-and-go
landings. Dario had no trouble getting his airplane to land three
points. It *was* easier than the SNJ because of the greater visibility, just
as Renetti had promised. As he added takeoff power while still rolling, he also heeded his advice and stuck his right foot hard against
the right rudder pedal, keeping the nose from going left. He had to
control the airplane's direction with the rudder, or the engine would
do it with torque and take him where he didn't want to go.

The RDO was very busy with some of the other students, telling
them to lower or raise their noses for a three-point landing, and when
to cut or add power. Dario had made four touch-and-goes and was

climbing for his fifth when he heard the RDO's voice suddenly scream-ing over the radio, "Cut your power 9-2. 9-2, cut your power, cut your power!" 9-2 was Ensign Gardenet, one of the married students in his flight. There was silence for a minute, then the RDO spoke in almost a normal voice. "We lost another one, Ken. It just exploded."

As Dario turned back toward the field, he saw the column of greasy black smoke arising from the edge of the runway and heard the ex-pected transmission from his instructor. "Road Runner flight, this is 3-3. Join up on me. We're returning to home plate." As Dario circled to join up, he could see the orange flames causing the black smoke. He couldn't take his eyes off the burning airplane, knowing that Gardenet's body was still in it, burning to a crisp. The remaining flight flew in silence until they got back to the field. Just before they flew over the field for the break, MacArthur radioed, "Keep calm, keep cool. Just land as you've been taught. I know you'll all be fine."

Renetti was standing by Dario's aircraft's wing as he stepped to the ground. "I watched you land, Dario. You were at a good three-point attitude, but you were too fast. You bounced. When your plane touches the ground, it should stay there."

He wanted to tell him that one of his flight mates just got killed at Aransas Pass, but Renetti read his mind before he could speak. "When someone around you buys the farm, concentrate on not buying it yourself, you understand? Don't ever let pity or regret get in the way of your survival. Make sure it's always the other guy, that it can't happen to you. As sorry as I am that we lost a student, at least his death should show the rest of you that you can't take this airplane for granted. Like I told you when I first met you, Dario, this bird is like a woman. You have to love it, be tender with it, but always, always, you have to control it or-it-will-hurt-you!"

"Yes, sir. And, thank you for your advice, sir. And I did remember to really abuse the right rudder pedal."

"Knock off the sir shit when we're alone, *paisano*."

D.E. " Butch" Bucciarelli

* * *

Ensign Gardenet, the student who was killed, lost directional control as he added power to takeoff on his fourth touch-and-go landing. Insufficient right rudder allowed the engine torque to pull the airplane to the left. Instead of pulling off power and aborting the takeoff, he tried to lift the airplane off the runway. It hadn't gained enough speed to fly, but just enough to lift the nose, which let the left wing dip, dig into the dirt next to the runway and cartwheel the airplane. It landed on its back and burst the fuel tank, which then exploded. Gardenet died from asphyxiation, as the flames surrounding his body consumed all available oxygen. His body was badly burned, requiring a sealed coffin funeral a week later at his home in Montana. There was a memorial service for him at the base chapel, but Dario didn't go. It wasn't disrespect, it just seemed meaningless to hear the prayer which ended, "Home is the sailor, home from the sea," and sing the "Lord protect the men that fly," hymn. They all knew what they were doing was dangerous, and that the danger would take its toll. That's why they got flight pay. Dario also believed what Renetti had told him. Plenty of right rudder was a lot better than prayers or hymns.

They flew their scheduled hop the next morning, after they'd reviewed procedures to avoid making Gardenet's mistake. Dario was determined to get his airplane slower on landing, to avoid any embarrassing bounces Renetti might see.

* * *

Michelle sent him a note saying Donald would be flying in Europe for the next month and she would try to be by her phone at six each evening. They'd agreed not to write each other newsy letters or telephone one another just to talk. Neither of them were interested in what the other was doing with their lives. The only purpose for their communications was assignation. He wanted to be with her, desperately, but there was no way he could drive to Mobile and return in a weekend. If he had car problems and missed a flight or class on Monday morning, he'd be in just the kind of trouble he was determined to avoid.

CHAPTER
THIRTY-SIX

CAPTAIN POPOVICH, the CO of Cabaniss Field, hammered on his glass with a spoon to get attention during one Friday's happy hour. Next to him stood a lieutenant colonel, recently promoted, whom all the students knew was his new executive officer because he'd been aboard the field for a week or so, and he stood out like a ruby in a pig's ass. Lieutenant Colonel John "Jack" Collins was the clone of Major Nug Hildripp from the neck down, resplendent in his tailored gabardine shirt and matching trousers, with four rows of World War II and Korean War ribbons on his chest, below his wings. Above the neck, he was much more handsome than Nug, with a full head of wavy black hair, with grey sideburns cut perfectly horizontal and at precisely the level of the center of his ears. He wore a black Ronald Coleman mustache, perfectly trimmed to points so sharp they looked as if they could penetrate skin. Beneath the perfect mustache were an upper and lower row of very large and very bright teeth, which were always exposed in a grin which could be taken as congenial—or sardonic. His nickname had preceded him and, although about to be introduced by the CO, he was already well known as "Smiling Jack."

When Dario first saw him being shown around the hangars, a chill went down his spine and he had an almost uncontrollable impulse to start polishing his shoes and belt buckle, and head for the barber shop.

He felt that, as sure as the sun would set, he'd be knocking on Smiling Jack's door frame one day.

"Gentlemen," the CO said, standing on a chair in the center of the barroom. "Standing next to me is my new executive officer, Lieutenant Colonel John Collins. Colonel Collins has been flying the Skyraider for as long as it's been in the fleet, so he brings with him years of operational and combat experience. As his first assignment, I'm going to ask him to make an announcement, which is a message we received this morning." The CO stepped down from his chair and was replaced by the XO, who received a moderate round of applause. Dario faked his.

"How do you do, gentlemen. I just want to tell you how happy I am to be working for Captain Popovich and to be on this base. The AD has a special place in my heart and it's a pleasure to see its heritage passed on to the next generation of aviators. But, that's not what I want to tell you about. I thank the CO for allowing me to bring you this message, because I have no concern with this one. I know it's *one* time the messenger will definitely *not* be shot!" There was slight laughter from the puzzled crowd.

"In order to compete with the air force, who seems to pin wings on its students shortly after they finish ground school, the navy will immediately begin designating aviators at the completion of the familiarization stage in combat aircraft."

Dario looked at After Burner, who shrugged his shoulders in wonderment in return.

"This means, when your flight completes the fam stage in the Skyraider—which is usually seven hops—you'll get your wings."

The bar exploded in a roar. It took a few seconds for it to sink into Dario's brain that his flight, the five students remaining, would get their wings after only three more hops. Students were yelling at the XO who had his hands extended, trying to quiet the crowd. "Let me continue, let me continue. Those of you who've already completed fam stage will get your wings on Monday. The CO's already contacted the Navy League, who supplies your first wings as gifts, and he's scheduled a designation ceremony at fifteen hundred in the hangar. I think you should know that Captain Popovich has seen to it that those eligible be designated without any of the usual red tape delay. Our yeomen are working now, and will work all weekend if necessary, to complete the required paperwork." There was another yell from the crowd, ending with applause directed toward the CO. "But, there's one caveat, gentlemen, just one. Don't think the training's going to be any easier because you're wearing wings. You're still students, and we still have Speedy Boards. The only difference is, if you screw up, you'll have holes in your shirt when we rip your wings off."

There was a loud moan, in unison, from the crowd. "What about NAVCADs?" someone yelled from the rear when the moan subsided.

"Thank you for asking. That's one of the best parts of this message. Let's face it, gentlemen, the only difference it will make to you officer students is you'll get to wear wings on your uniform, but you'll get the same pay. But all NAVCADs who have completed fam stage will be commissioned, as well as designated. Be ready to lend your extra gold bars to your NAVCAD mates, gentlemen, because we know the exchanges will be out of them by noon tomorrow. We've already told the club manager to order more beer and liquor, because they'll all be in here drinking with you next week.

"Now, that's enough official business. The skipper told me they found some overlooked profit money in the back of the club's safe, so the drinks are on the house for the next two hours. Drink up!"

About an hour later, Dario was standing with a group of students when Smiling Jack, who'd been mingling with the crowd, joined them. They all introduced themselves, shook hands with him and did a few minutes of small talk. A little later, as Dario was returning from the head, Smiling Jack intercepted him.

"Ensign D'Angelo, is it?" He leered, with his rows of teeth exposed.

Get ready. Shitty-little-job-officer on USS Alwaysatsea, here I come, Dario told himself as he grimaced a poor imitation of the XO's smile.

"Yes, sir." He spoke in a lower than his normal tone, trying to gain composure and not let his voice break.

Low and Slow

"Nug Hildripp is a very good friend of mine. He was just behind me in flight training, and we served in a wing together. I'm an above-board kind of guy, D'Angelo. I just want to let you know, I'd do anything for Nug. I talked to him on the phone the other day, he's out at El Toro in California. He told me what you told him before your road race, about staying on his ass. Well, I'm telling you, I'm going to be on your ass this time. You make just one little mistake . . . " He did the 180 degree waltz, spinning on his highly-polished Cordovan shoes and walking away, before Dario could reply, which was just as well. Smiling Jack had made his point and Dario had nothing to say. He trembled in silence.

* * *

The XO was right. Wearing wings on their uniforms made absolutely no difference, except to morale. They were still students, still mustered, inspected, tested and suspected. Dario's flying was becoming very demanding, but more-and-more exciting. Each flight was a new experience and he was eager to get in the cockpit every day, press the primer and starter buttons, and switch on the magnetos. The ensuing backfires, rumbles and coughs from the engine before it settled down to a smooth roar was a new kind of music to him.

* * *

A week after he had his wings, he heard through the scuttlebutt-rumor-channel that two instructors were flying to Pensacola for the weekend, leaving Friday afternoon and returning Sunday night. There were a few AD-4NAs in the Cabaniss inventory, night-attack versions of the standard AD-4s. The NA could mount a large radar pod on the right bomb rack, and there was a seat down in the fuselage with a small access door on the side for the radar operator. The radars were all removed, but the seats were still intact. If one of the cross-country airplanes was an NA, Dario could ride in the "hell hole."

He called Michelle at six that night. "Yes." Donald was gone. "Yes." If he got a hop, she'd pick him up at Mainside Pensacola's Sherman Field. "Yes." They could spend Friday and Saturday nights in Fort Walton Beach. And "Yes." She'd be sitting next to the phone at six every night until she heard from him again.

With the cart put before the horse, he approached one of the instructors and asked if he could ride in the hell hole.

"Sure, but I don't know if we'll get an NA. If we do, you're welcome to ride along."

Renetti was sitting at his usual spot at the officers' club bar that afternoon. Dario told him he wanted to hitch a ride to Pensacola. "To see an old girl friend."

"Why? I hear you Laraga boys have more snatch running around your snake ranch than you can handle. What's so special about this girl?"

He decided to be up front with his friend. "She's married to some air force asshole. He's going to be out of town, so it's the only time I can see her."

"Say no more. I'll schedule *two* NAs so you'll be sure to have a ride home if one of them has a maintenance problem."

"Thanks, Marco."

Dario was slowly learning the real way the navy worked, by the book; but, many things were accomplished by reading the book between the lines. Between the lines were friends, contacts and the swapping of favors. He knew he was fortunate to have Renetti as a friend.

* * *

She was there as promised, sitting in her Triumph with the top up and side curtains installed. He inhaled her the minute he closed the passenger door behind him, and kissed her as the bouquet of gardenia swirled through his brain and body.

"Michelle, Michelle," he murmured in her ear as he squeezed her breasts tightly against his chest.

She pulled away from him, suddenly. "Ow, something's sticking me."

"Oops, sorry. It's my wings."

The early October weather in western Florida was perfect; dry and warm during the day, and cool at night. For Dario, being with Michelle after months of separation was almost like finding her all over again. It was like the early days of their romance, before they became two impractical people facing the practicality of married life.

The only time Michelle mentioned Donald was while they were still in bed, just before they had to return to Pensacola for Dario's return flight. "Sweetheart," she began, "I've some good news. Donald is being assigned to a wing at Travis Air Force Base. That's near your home, San Francisco. He's going to be flying back and forth to Japan. You simply just *must* get assigned to the West Coast. You'd be close to me, we could see each other every time Donald goes away."

"I'm going to try for the West Coast, but there's a good chance I'll be sent east. The needs of the service, you know. Almost every graduating student requests California, and we hear those requests are ignored over at Mainside. We get what's next on the list when our number comes up. I won't know where I'm going until a week or two before I finish."

"And, when will that be?"

"Mid-December, if everything goes right."

"Maybe we could be together during the Christmas holidays, in your hometown. Just think, San Francisco. Oh, I'm so excited! You could take me to all the jazz places you've told me about. You could introduce me to your mother."

He put his left hand behind her head and held his face six inches from hers, looking straight into her beautiful, blue eyes. "Of course you can meet my mother. She doesn't know anything about you, so I'll just tell her you're some broad I picked up in a dive in the Barbary Coast. That's where the strip shows and B girls are."

"Oh, Dario." She kissed him and gently nibbled his lip. "You tease. What would you really tell her?"

"Well, I'd tell her you are my secret mistress for life. You're married to a wealthy man, and you force me to make love to you over-and-over again, every time we meet."

"What would your mother say to that fairy tale?"

"She'd probably tell me that since you're rich, you should pay me for it. My mother is very practical when it comes to money."

It was fun to tease, but he knew he could never introduce Michelle to Mama. Mama would know he was lying if he made up some story, and Mama would never tolerate the truth about their relationship.

* * *

There were two more fatalities from landing accidents in Skyraiders during the month of October, but none in the Road Runner flight. They went through a phase of instrument flying, making landing approaches and doing acrobatics on instruments. There was a fabric canopy to cut off vision from outside, but it was even less effective than the one in the T-28. It was easy to see outside, to get references. These were one-on-one flights. The instructor would fly a close formation on the student flying his AD "under the bag," to monitor his performance, and to keep him from hitting the ground, or another airborne aircraft. Like before, Dario found instrument flying boring, but he did what he had to do to pass the phase.

The flight's previous NAVCAD, Tommy Donigan, was now a marine second lieutenant. Dario, and the other ensigns in the flight, hadn't realized that he'd been intimidated by them because they were officers and college graduates. Donigan had resented the difference, but hid it with silence. He'd always been quiet and reserved but, once he got his commission, he had his hair shaved at the sides and buzz-cut on the top. With the haircut and the uniform with the gold bars, he at last felt equal, and his contempt surfaced.

Dario sat next to him at the bar one afternoon and was greeted with, "Hey there, if it isn't Ensign D'Angelo. You think you're pretty hot shit, don't you, living in a snake ranch and getting lots of pussy.

Low and Slow

Well, you may be 'hotel sierra' with the pussy, but I bet I can fly your ass off. Wait'll we start bombing and strafing. I'll beat your ass every time."

Luckily, Dario was sober. He looked at the cocky marine, who was two inches shorter and twenty pounds lighter, and just said, "Sure, Tommy. If you can shoot your cannons off as well as your mouth, you'll be the 'Deadeye Dick' of the flight." He left the bar, without having a drink.

CHAPTER THIRTY-SEVEN

"DEAREST DARIO," the letter from Michelle began. When he opened it and saw that it was a full-page letter, not the usual note she sent telling him when Donald would be away, his heart sank. He was panicked with fear that it was a "Goodbye, Dario," letter. It wasn't; but, it was bad news. Donald had gone through her oil company credit card bill and saw that she bought gasoline in Pensacola the weekend she spent with him in Fort Walton. Donald confronted her, accused her of being with him and in the resulting argument, and in anger, she admitted it. "I told him I just met you to talk, just as I met him when I was married to you. I told you understood when I met him, so he should understand why I met you. I denied sleeping with you, but he doesn't believe me. I told him believe me or don't. I couldn't care less.

"But the really bad news is, Donald is being vindictive. He's going to write to the navy and accuse you of adultery. He says it's against military law."

* * *

Dario received a message to report to the CO's office the following week. He polished his shoes, his belt buckle, and put on his

Low and Slow

T-shirt dickey. He didn't have time for a haircut, but he combed his hair to be as flat to his head as he could make it.

Captain Popovich was in his mid-forties. Tan, and muscular, he wore his light brown hair just a little longer than regulation, and his large mustache was also a statement of individuality. He'd been in the navy for twenty-four years, always flying light attack aircraft. He was a good commander for a training base, because he was patient, tolerant, and he believed that good pilots came from good training.

After knocking on the door and entering, Popovich, who was sitting behind his desk, told Dario to sit down. The office was almost a carbon copy of the many commanding officers' offices he been in. Standard navy furniture, stars and stripes on a pedestal in one corner, the navy flag in the opposite corner. Dario saw the name plaque with another mountain he didn't recognize. This one wasn't the usual snow covered, cone shaped, inactive volcano like Fuji, Vesuvius, Etna or Rainier. It was more of an unequal triangle.

Popovich held a letter in his hand and slightly shook it as he talked. "This letter was addressed to the Chief of Naval Air Training, who forwarded it to me for action. It's from an air force First Lieutenant Donald Eighton. He's accusing you of illicit sexual relations with his wife, namely adultery, several weeks ago. He's found some military law against it. I had legal look it up and it's there in the Uniform Code of Military Justice."

Dario smiled, trying to not look as concerned as he really was.

"Did you have sexual relations with this guy's wife, D'Angelo?"

"Yes, sir. She was my wife for a while. We had a annulment."

"Where did this affair take place? Not here on Cabaniss, I hope."

"No, sir. Not on any base. It was in a motel, in Fort Walton, in Florida."

"Fort Walton! How'd you get there?"

"I got a hop to Pensacola with Lieutenant Rawler, in the hell hole of an NA. She met me and we drove to Fort Walton."

"Did this air force lieutenant catch you in the sack with her?"

"No, sir. She wrote me about it. I sort of expected that his letter would be coming through channels."

"This one came from the top," he waved the letter in the air before him, "from Vice Admiral Jasper Bates himself. He sent it to me with a note telling me that you AOCs are getting into more trouble when you're on the ground than you are in the air. Says he's had to double his legal staff. I'm sure the admiral would have shit-canned this letter himself, but he's in a precarious position with inter-service rivalry, and all that. He passed it down to me with a good understanding of what I'd do." Popovich tilted his chair back, and shook his head. "What a crock of shit! If we start enforcing this regulation, we'd have some big morale problems!" He leaned forward and sat the letter on his desk. "You going to see this lady again, D'Angelo?"

Dario hesitated, he knew he should say, "No, sir," but he always thought about Lieutenant Lawrence's admonition about lying to a superior officer. "Yes, sir. I probably will. But I don't force myself on her. She wants to see me as much as I want to see her."

Popovich sat back in his chair again and smiled. "The lady in must be something special."

"She is, sir."

"Then why did you get an annulment?"

"It's a long story, Captain . . . "

"The good ones usually are."

" . . . but simply put, we're happier meeting occasionally than we could ever be married to each other."

Popovich laughed. "You're right. That *is* simply put. I wish I could put some situations I have that simply." He shook his head, as if to shake out the thoughts he was thinking. "Well, as far as I'm concerned, this is a private matter, not a navy matter. If I were Eighton, I'd find you and kick the shit out of you, not write a letter. He must be a wimp."

"I've never met him, sir."

"Just promise me one thing, D'Angelo."

"Yes, sir."

"When you get to a fleet squadron, don't make a cross-country flight to this guy's base to make out with his wife. That could really fuck up our relations with the junior service. Promise me you'll always do your illicit screwing on civilian territory."

"I promise, sir."

"OK. That's all I have."

Popovich stood up and Dario did the same. He was about to come to attention and do his about face exit when he said, "Captain, excuse me, but I'm curious. What's that mountain in your name plaque?"

Popovich reached across his desk and picked up the wooden plaque. "It's Diamond Head, in Hawaii. I once had shore duty there, at Barber's Point, on Oahu." He rubbed the mountain of golden wood and sighed. "It's a local wood, monkey pod. God, I had a great time out there." He looked into Dario's eyes. "Lots of bored air force wives at Hickam Air Force Base in Honolulu. Lots of secluded beaches, like the one where Burt Lancaster nailed Deborah Kerr in the movie, *From Here to Eternity*." He sighed again.

"I remember the scene. And thank you for understanding my situation, Captain."

"Yeah, I understand. I'll have my yeoman file this letter in his never-find-again file. He's good at that."

"Thanks," Dario said simply, turned slowly and walked from the office.

CHAPTER THIRTY-EIGHT

THERE WAS no sophisticated navigational equipment aboard the AD. A tray pulled out from below the instrument panel, just clearing the top of the joystick. It was a navigational plotter, amusingly called the Ouija Board. By using pencil marks to record the departure spot, the aircraft's flight path, and the carrier's predicted courses and speeds, the pilot could plot a direct interception course to return to the carrier after leaving his target.

They gave his flight a written test on the procedure, and Dario failed, as did Finegard, the remaining married student. Their initial pencil points had been a few degrees off, which acerbated the final result. It was the only test Dario had ever failed.

"You've got to go before the Speedy Board and ask them if you can retake the test, Dario," Mac Arthur, his instructor, told him. "If they let you, and you flunk it again, you'll be washed out."

He almost fainted. He couldn't believe he'd be dropped for such an insignificant failure. Lots of students failed plotting board problems and simply took the test over again, after sharpening their pencils. "What about Finegard, does he have to go before the board, too?"

"No. He's never had a down before."

"But sir, the down I got was a technical one. There was a midair and I saved my buddy, got him to bail out. The down wasn't because I couldn't fly."

"Sorry. It's out of my hands. We got word from the XO's office. You go before a Speedy Board tomorrow. I suggest you get a haircut and polish your shoes before you go in."

"Thanks, sir. Unfortunately, I know the drill."

He spent the rest of the day, and most of the night, in his room, working on plotting board problems. Smiling Jack was out to get him, but he still couldn't believe something so ridiculously simple could get him sent to a destroyer. He was a good student and a good pilot. His down was just a technicality, but he remembered the CO of Whiting Field's warning when he got his first nine driving demerits: "It's the technicalities that get us in the end."

"How're you doing, Dario? You need any help with the problems?" It was After Burner, who looked in on Dario after returning to the Laraga from a local bar-crawl, at 11 p.m.

"Thanks, but I know how to do 'em. I just have to be careful and not misplace my pencil dots."

"I was at Mainside tonight, ran into Leaky Potts at the bar. He gave me a message for you. I'm afraid it's not very good news."

"Just what I need."

"Smiling Jack's on the Speedy Board. Leaky says he's got a standard question he asks whenever a student's flunked navigation. Leaky had a student go before him several weeks ago."

"Lay it on me, Charlie. I'm ready for anything."

"He'll ask you if you're a good swimmer, and when you tell him you are, he'll ask you if you think you can swim around and find the carrier after you run out of gas, because you screwed up your navigation."

"What did Leaky say I should do, wear my Mae West to the Speedy Board?"

"Nope. He didn't say what you should do, just told me to tell you to be ready for Smiling Jack's question."

* * *

"We've reviewed your records, Ensign D'Angelo. This is your second appearance before a Student Pilot Disposition Board, which makes only one thing certain. This is your last appearance before one." The commander who spoke sat with three other officers and Smiling Jack behind a long table covered with green felt. "You're here because you failed a written examination. Do you have anything to say?"

He'd rehearsed all the things he might say, like the down he got for Brandon's midair was only given to him because of Hildripp's attempt to get him court-martialed. He could tell him the tolerances for the plotting board test were ludicrous, if he got within a few miles of the carrier in actuality, he'd find it. And what about his wingman or leader? There'd be two plotting board solutions to find the ship. But he said nothing because he knew the answers he'd get: "What about limited visibility, your wingman shot down, etcetera, etcetera, etcetera."

"Yes, sir. I should have been more precise with my plotting points. I know where I erred, and I've done dozens of problems and corrected my mistakes. If the board will allow me another chance to take the test, I know I will pass it. I sincerely want to complete the syllabus and join a fleet squadron."

"And if you don't pass it?"

"I know what the consequences will be, sir. I'll lose my wings, I'll lose my flight pay, and I'll probably be assigned to a destroyer."

"Not necessarily, D'Angelo." It was Smiling Jack who spoke. He was pounding the eraser end of a pencil on a yellow pad sitting on the table in front of him. "You may not be sent to sea duty. I hear there's an opening for officers' club manager at our base in Kodiak, Alaska. Your piano playing talents should be of real value there."

"Yes, sir." Dario lowered his head and looked at the reflection of his face in his shoe tip.

"Are you a good swimmer, D'Angelo?"

He raised his head and looked directly into Smiling Jack's teeth, which were fully exposed in glare-mode.

Low and Slow

Sure, colonel. You know I had to swim a mile with my clothes on to get through Pre-Flight, he wanted to say.

Instead, he said, simply, "No sir. Not that good."

"Oh, you know that one, do you? I should have known you would. It fits. I've reviewed your record too, D'Angelo, officially—and unofficially. It's the record of a wise-ass. I talked to Sergeant Major Pflueger at Mainside, Pensacola. He gave me a rundown. Your official record shows you barely made it through Pre-Flight. Caught out-of-uniform and out-of-bounds, you came within five disciplinary demerits of being washed out. Unofficially, there was constant disrespect to your noncommissioned officers, and a shirking of duty as the band manager. Once you got your commission, your record gets even worse. Officially, two Captain's Masts for speeding tickets, which resulted in the loss of your base driving privileges, which some how didn't transfer to Advance Training. Next, court-martial charges for disobeying orders, which were dropped, but you did get a down from the Speedy Board. Unofficially, illegal transmissions as The Road Runner, and involvement in an unauthorized flight with certain instructors, the infamous Madman Flight. Then, you land your SNJ on a beach in front of your girlfriend, disobeying your instructor's orders to land at Canal Field. Your next act was a quick marriage, followed by an even quicker annulment. When you got here to Cabaniss, the BOQ wasn't good enough for you. You have to live off base in the first student snake ranch this base has ever had. And, your most recent escapade was a charge by an air force officer that you committed adultery with his wife!"

Jesus! Did I do all that? Dario asked himself.

Smiling Jack's face became more-and-more flushed as the condemnations spewed from his normally grinning mouth. It was almost beet red by the time he finished. "I don't know how you got this far, D'Angelo, but as far as I'm concerned, you're not going any further . . . except to the far-off Arctic!"

The commander in charge spoke again. "Do you have anything further to say, D'Angelo?"

D.E. " Butch" Bucciarelli

I stole the bread because my ten children were starving. I plead temporary insanity and throw myself to the mercy of the court, he wanted to say.

"No, sir."

"You'll be advised of the decision of the board. You're dismissed." He then did the one military maneuver he'd perfected. He stood at attention, spun an about-face on one toe tip, and formally exited from the presence of senior officers.

* * *

"The Speedy Board's over, Dario. I've got some bad news, some good news, and some bad news for you," MacArthur told him later in the day. "Which do you want to hear first?"

"After Smiling Jack's performance, I'll bet the only good news you can give me is the navy's issuing me electric underwear. Is that it, sir?"

"No. The good news is you get to retake the test. First thing in the morning at the Nav Office."

Dario felt a tremendous relief. Since he was notified of the pending Speedy Board, he'd been unable to eat, sleep or think of anything but the failure he'd be to his family if he got washed out—and that he'd lose his MG. For the past 6 hours, he'd added Kodiak, Alaska to his distress.

"That's great, sir. That's wonderful. But, how can there be any bad news? Do I have to take it in the dark? Do I have to use a blunt crayon instead of a sharp pencil?"

"You're amazingly close, Dario. No, you take it in full light and with a sharp pencil, but the tolerances for error are cut in half. You can't be more than one pencil point off."

"Shit! Who thought of that? Smiling Jack?"

"Are you kidding? If he had his way you'd be on your way to Kodiak in your tropical khakis, without *any* underwear. You really did something to piss him off, Dario, he really wants you gone. Fortunately, most of the others on the board couldn't believe you could be as bad as he made out. I told them you are one good stick man, and I stuck my neck out. I said I know the mental attitude of my students and I guaranteed them you'll pass the exam. It would be a shame to lose you this close to the end just because of a stupid plotting board test. By the time you get to the fleet, the AD and the Ouija Board will be on their way to the junk heap, because the age of electronic miracles is near. But, Collins put up such a stink they made the odds tougher by cutting the tolerances, as a concession to him. You think you can hack it?"

"I'll do it, sir. If not for myself, for you, for standing up for me. I really appreciate what you did for me."

"I know you won't let me down. Oh, there's one more bad news."

"I have to clean Colonel Collins's toilet for the rest of my time at Cabaniss."

"No. Smiling Jack's orders. You have to report to the pass office with your car. They're scraping off your sticker. That shouldn't be any problem for you, though, you can ride in with Charlie Burner."

* * *

He took the test alone. The ground instructor, who administered it, corrected it immediately. "Four oh, D'Angelo. You hit every point, perfectly."

What Dario really heard was, *We, the members of the jury, find the defendant, Ensign Dario Enrico D'Angelo, USNR, completely innocent of mayhem, murder, rape, treason and failing a piddling little navigation examination.*

"Thank you, sir. What a relief. I tried to be as precise as I could, but I never dreamed I'd get them all, right on the nose."

"You did. Right on the button, every time. You must be the smartest ensign in the navy."

* * *

"Congratulations, Dario. I hear you've still got a chance for Mexican Village action. I don't know what happy hour's like in Kodiak, but I'll bet those Eskimos and grizzly bears are no substitute for telephone girls."

"Thanks, Leaky. Shit, what a close call. Thank God I cooled the test, I never want to go through that again. I'll bet they don't even have telephones in Kodiak, let alone telephone girls."

"Did you know the lieutenant who administered the test, Dan Miller?"

"No. I've seen him around, but I never had him for ground school."

"He put in a request for an AD for a cross-country this weekend. What, with the push to get students out before Christmas, planes have been in short supply, lots of weekend maintenance to keep them up. Guess who guaranteed him he'd have an aircraft for his RON, *if* you passed your test?"

The smartest ensign in the navy suddenly realized he wasn't. "Marco Renetti."

Leaky nodded his head in agreement. "You just about did it on your own, Dario, your answers were close to tolerances. But just to be sure, what with the bullshit curve the board threw you to appease that asshole, you were right on, every time. Count your blessings. You've got friends."

He *was* privileged to have friends like Renetti and Leaky, and he was learning how friends could help him. Unfortunately, Hildripp had Smiling Jack as a friend. That thought never left him.

CHAPTER
THIRTY-NINE

THEY BEGAN dive bombing in early November, dropping small, cast-iron bombs loaded with a shotgun shell charge for marking the hit. Although tiny, they fell with the same trajectory as the real iron bombs in the navy's arsenal. The Skyraider was an accurate dive bomber because of its barn door dive brakes, which opened from both sides and the bottom, slowing the diving speed dramatically. This allowed more time to get the bombsight pip on the target and release the bomb in time to pull out above 1500 feet. The bombing range was on South Padre Island, an uninhabited barrier Island that ran from Corpus Christi to Mexico. The instructor orbited outside the target at 1500 feet and it was an automatic down to fly below him. Target fixation was the killer he was guarding against. Students were supposed to hit the target with a bomb; not with their airplanes.

The next phase of training was the one Dario enjoyed most. Although he'd anticipated it for weeks, he was, nevertheless, happily surprised by the sensation when he squeezed the trigger on his joystick and his cannons spit out shells that ripped up the floating flare the instructor had dropped. They were twenty miles out in the Gulf of Mexico.

Looking at the blue wing instead of a yellow one was still a thrill, but when he strafed for the first time, and the recoil slowed the aircraft so suddenly he pitched forward against his shoulder straps, he really understood what a potent weapon of war he was commanding. It was death and destruction spitting out of those sticks in the wings. All his training, so far, was to enable him to maneuver through any kind of air, navigate over any terrain or water, just to get this gun platform to the target and wreak havoc on the enemy. For the first time since his carrier landings, he yelled into the cockpit at the top of his lungs when he first fired. He didn't yell intelligible words. It was an attack scream coming from a rogue male!

He didn't know why he was so accurate with his guns, but he seemed to be able to anticipate where the shells would hit when he squeezed the trigger. He set up a beat for his bursts, and counted, like in music, as he fired. He gave the song a lilting rhythm. He was so accurate that on his third pass he shattered the floating flare, sinking it.

"OK, 3-6, that was either luck or you've got the range. Try to hit just to the side of the flare. I've only got one left," MacArthur transmitted.

"Aye, aye, sir," Dario answered. "Which side?"

Donigan made the next pass, after the replacement flare was dropped. His pattern hit all around the flare but didn't hit it, although it was evident he was trying to.

"Ease off, 3-8. Make a good, tight pattern *next* to the flare. Just because D'Angelo sank one, you don't have to prove you're better by spraying the ocean, trying to sink another."

On subsequent strafing flights, MacArthur had Dario and Donigan follow one or the other, fostering their competition. He also carried six flares, instead of two. Dario consistently sank more flares than Donigan.

* * *

"Road Runner leader, this is Road Runner 3-1. My engine is running rough and my cylinder head temperatures are high." Dario heard Donigan's transmission when the flight was eighteen miles offshore, heading out for their strafing practice.

Low and Slow

"What are your intentions, 3-1," MacArthur responded.

"Request permission to fly direct to the beach and return to home plate."

"Permission granted. 4-8, you're his wingman. You go with him. Both of you empty your guns in a clear area before you go feet-dry."

"Aye, aye, sir," Dario replied from 4-8. For some easily understandable reason, their shipmates at the base didn't want students landing with loaded cannons pointing at them. Although, as his wingman, there was nothing Dario could do for Donigan if his engine quit, he could at least climb to altitude and reach someone by radio who would summon Search and Rescue. Then he would remain on station to vector the rescuers to the downed pilot.

He joined up on Donigan as he took the most direct heading to dry land, which was South Padre Island. Dario noticed that Donigan was flying at normal cruise speed, so his rough runner wasn't affecting its performance. They were flying at 2500 feet, but ten miles from the beach Donigan started to descend. Dario assumed they were going low so they could empty their guns into the water, but Donigan hadn't said anything about arming and firing. "What are your intentions now, 3-1?" Dario radioed, still on their assigned tactical frequency. Donigan spun his head around and looked at him, then held up one finger, then five. Dario switched to channel 15, a channel for air force towers. As the closest tower, Harlingen, was more than fifty miles away, nobody should hear their transmissions. Students often used this ruse when they wanted to communicate with each other without an instructor, or a navy tower, hearing them. "I'm up on button fifteen, Tommy. What're you doing?"

"Let's go coyote hunting. Any asshole can hit a flare. Let's see how you are on real targets."

Dario knew immediately what Donigan was talking about. They'd all heard rumors about instructors who "modified" the rules and took their flights strafing along South Padre Island, shooting up anything that made a target. The lower island was uninhabited, with just one paved road running its length. Whether there really were coyotes to shoot, he didn't know. To Dario, it was just one of the many tales of flight training folklore that survived from one class to another, year after year. He made an immediate decision; he wasn't going to participate in a shoot-up of the island—he was still having nightmares about Kodiak. He armed his guns and fired short bursts into the sea, until they were empty. He jotted the time on his knee pad. 1547.

Donigan saw the tracers arcing ahead, looked over at Dario and radioed, "Chickenshit."

Dario held up his middle finger for Donigan to see, *not* signaling channel one. Although he'd decided not to join him, he would stay with him until they returned to Cabaniss. He could have climbed, reached MacArthur by radio on the tactical frequency and reported Donigan, but he wouldn't turn in a fellow officer. Even though what he was doing was against regulations, Donigan was only going to do what others had probably done before him. Dario would have loved to join him and shoot imagined coyotes, but he didn't, because he'd already used up his nine lives of violations and he wanted to finish and get to Coronado and telephone girls; and Alameda, and Michelle. Donigan could have his fun now; his would come later.

He pushed his transmit button and said, "Happy hunting, Tommy. I'll orbit above you while you get your guns off."

When they crossed the beach, Donigan dove for the ground. Dario flew a weaving pattern above him, keeping him directly below. He saw the abandoned car just off the road about the same time Donigan did, and saw him change his heading and fly down the road toward it. Donigan's first burst was very accurate. Dario could see sparks and dust fly as his shells hit the rusty sedan. (Their shells didn't have the explosive charges they would use in combat, but they still left a big impression on anything they hit). Donigan pulled up sharply, made a turn to the left and flew down the road in the opposite direction for about a mile. Then he turned 180 degrees, flew very low along the road and made another pass at the car.

"Take that, you dirty Commie bastard," Donigan screamed over the radio as he fired. Dario could detect something eerie, almost unnatural in his voice. It was a scream of madness. He'd heard the same sound in Hildripp's airborne voice. Donigan was out of control.

Donigan made three more firing passes at the car, then continued up the road, very low. There was a metal road sign alongside the road and Donigan fired on it, walking shells up the road. Donigan screamed pure joy over the radio as the sign was disintegrating into small pieces. He continued firing at the sign until he was almost on it, getting too close, and too low. Dario could see he was fixed on the target and not watching his altitude. Then Dario saw sparks fly as his prop tips hit the pavement of the road, repeatedly. Donigan immediately pulled his Skyraider up steeply, straining for altitude.

"Now I really have a rough runner, Dario. My engine's tearing itself to pieces," he shouted over the radio.

"Shut it down, Tommy, shut it down," Dario answered. He knew a damaged prop could vibrate the engine with such forces it would tear itself free from the aircraft. He'd felt the effect begin just before the prop shaft broke in his SNJ. Without the weight of the engine, the aircraft would tumble out of control, and Donigan didn't have anywhere near the altitude he needed to bail out. "Drop your gear and land dead stick on the road, Tommy, you're all set up. The road is clear."

Donigan didn't follow this advice. Instead, he turned 90 degrees toward the Gulf and landed wheels-up in the desert, cutting a swath through sand and sagebrush, but stopping right-side-up. There was no smoke or fire. Dario dropped his flaps and slowed his aircraft as he flew over him, low. The only damage he could see was the prop blades bent back.

"Dario, do you read me? I'm OK," Donigan transmitted, still sitting in his aircraft.

"Affirmative, read you loud and clear. You'd better turn off your battery, Tommy, there might be electrical shorts and fuel leaks. I'm going to climb and make a Mayday call. We should have a helicopter here before dark."

"Listen, Dario, listen, we've got to get this straight. Here's the story.

My engine was running rough, and finally quit when we reached the beach. I tried to glide to the road but couldn't make it, had to put it in the sand. The props all bent up, they'll never know it hit the road. You'll cover for me, won't you Dario? You'll go along with my story."

Dario didn't answer him. He put in climb power and switched to guard frequency. While he climbed, he composed in his mind the Mayday alarm he would broadcast.

* * *

After Brandon's and Joe Schade's midair, and his lost prop, this was the third accident report Dario had to write. In it, he simply told the complete truth, even the part about considering climbing and reporting Donigan's actions to MacArthur, but not doing so. He also admitted that he didn't try to dissuade Donigan, but in fact wished him, "Happy hunting."

When he told Donigan that he hadn't lied for him, the marine almost went berserk. "You prick, you promised me you'd cover for me."

"That's bullshit! I didn't even answer your transmission." They were in the hangar, outside the ready room the day after the crash. "You're the one who fucked up. Why should I put my ass on the line for you?"

"Because I'm a fellow officer, that's why. We're supposed to have a code of silence. You're not supposed to rat on me."

Dario didn't want to argue with Donigan, because there was nothing to argue about. The deed was done, his report was already turned in. He should have walked away from him like he did that day in the officers' club, but he was too angry to be rational. He pointed a finger at Donigan's chest and said, "Listen, Tommy. If you hadn't crashed, I never would have reported you. You're going to lose your wings, and maybe your commission. I don't want that to happen to me. I'm an officer, and even though my office is lower than whale shit on the ocean floor, I'm beginning to take it seriously. I'm not going to lie to my superior officers, because there's no room in the navy for liars."

"Fuck you, D'Angelo, you chickenshit flag waver." Donigan turned and stormed away, then turned back, and in a voice much more composed and calculating, yelled, "We'll see who loses their commission, asshole."

CHAPTER FORTY

❝THE XO wants to see you in his office at fourteen-thirty," MacArthur told him as he entered the ready room the following morning. "I won't bother to remind you to polish your shoes and get a haircut before you go. You're an expert at it."

Dario also bought a new long-sleeve shirt and tie at the uniform shop, just for the occasion. He wouldn't need his dickey. When the yeoman told him to go in, "The colonel is expecting you," he knocked on the closed door and heard the colonel call, "Enter and close the door behind you." He did, walked to the front of his desk and stood at attention. Smiling Jack had a name plaque on his desk with wings on it, but no mountain. Only the marine corps emblem with its "Semper Fi" motto.

"At ease. Pull up a chair and sit down." As soon as he was seated, he handed Dario several sheets of paper covered with handwriting. "Read this."

It was written by Donigan. In it, he refuted his earlier report. He admitted he lied to Lieutenant Commander MacArthur about his rough runner, fired on the abandoned car and a sign, and flat-hatted so low his propeller cut into the road and caused his engine to fail. He didn't land wheels-down on the road because he hoped to hide his actions with a crash landing. He'd read Ensign D'Angelo's report, and decided to tell the truth.

"Ensign D'Angelo lied in his report. He joined me in my strafing runs, shot up the automobile and the sign, and did everything I did except hit the road and lose his engine. He begged me not to tell, begged me to lie for him, which I did in my first report. Now, I feel I must tell my superior officers the truth since I am now an officer and there's no room in the corps for liars."

"The son of a bitch! He even stole my lines!" Dario said it aloud, unintentionally. He looked at Smiling Jack. He wasn't smiling.

"Confess, D'Angelo. I'll give you one more chance to write a truthful account of your actions. It might go easier with you at your court-martial." His words hit Dario hard. It was dawning on him that he was in deep trouble, even by his standard.

"No, sir, colonel. I've told the truth. There's not a word I want to change. I had a confrontation with Lieutenant Donigan yesterday. He was angry with me for not lying on his behalf. I told him I couldn't, that it was too serious a matter. He told me, 'We'll see who loses his commission.' " He held Donigan's report up and shook it slightly. "This report is his lying attempt to implicate me, it's his revenge, because I didn't lie for him. You've got to believe me!"

Smiling Jack leaned back in his chair, looking up at the ceiling. "You've been in trouble from the day you got in the navy, mister. You've disobeyed orders and gotten away with it, but I think your sordid past has finally caught up with you. Why should I believe you?" He spoke very slowly and deliberately.

"Because it's the truth, sir. I told the truth, all of it. My recruiting lieutenant gave me advice before I got in the navy, and I've always followed it. I never lie to superior officer. I thought about joining him, colonel, I really did, because I love to strafe. It has a rhythm to it, and a power which fascinates me. But I decided it wasn't worth losing everything I've worked for." He suddenly realized he was rambling, wasting his feelings on a hard-ass marine. He hesitated, and then spoke much more slowly. "I know I can be faulted for not trying to radio our instructor, and I'll admit, if Donigan hadn't crashed, I wouldn't have informed on him. But when I wrote my report, I told the whole truth. I didn't leave anything out."

Smiling Jack sat forward in his chair and leaned his elbows on his desk. "There's something you don't know, something we just found out. We're not talking about out-of-bounds, and speeding tickets, D'Angelo. We're not talking about screwing another man's wife. We're talking about willfully lying to your superior officers, disobeying standing orders, destroying government property . . . and manslaughter!" Smiling Jack's face broke out into a smile that made all the others Dario had seen on his face look like a yawn.

"Manslaughter!"

"You heard me. There was a Mexican Wetback in the abandoned truck, evidently sleeping out of the sun. You two made dog food out of him. That's navy property down there, so it's a federal crime. They're starting the Article Thirty-Two investigation over at Mainside, even as we speak." He leaned back in his chair and put his hands behind his head. "I'll admit I wanted you washed out, there's no room for a wise-ass like you in a navy cockpit. But now it seems we're not only going to wash you out of flight training, we're going to wash you out of society. You'll get twenty years in Portsmouth Naval Prison." He sat forward and put his arms on his desk. "Want to confess now? It might get you out with only fifteen years—with good behavior." He laughed, a loud, guttural laugh.

The shock of what Smiling Jack said not only scared Dario, it also infuriated him, and the laugh was just too much for him to take. He jumped up from his chair and shouted, "I'm innocent, and my father didn't raise me to belly-up and let some jarheads like you and Donigan frame me. You goddamn marines have been on my ass from the first day I joined this man's navy, and I'm sick and tired of it. Fuck Donigan and his lies, and fuck you, colonel."

Smiling Jack jumped up, completely caught off balance by Dario's outburst. He pointed a trembling finger at Dario and he had trouble getting his words out. "I'll . . . I'll add gross insubordination to your other charges, D'Angelo!"

Dario had calmed down. Telling Smiling Jack to fuck himself had relaxed him. He lowered his voice and said, slowly, "Big deal. What will

I get? Twenty years and thirty days? You shot your big gun with the manslaughter charge, colonel. Don't try to scare me with a pee-shooter."

"You're restricted to the BOQ, D'Angelo." Then Smiling Jack took several deep breaths and sat down, composing himself. "You'll have orders to Mainside in the morning, wise-ass, assigning you to Special Services until your court-martial. Donigan's over there now. He's permanent Barracks Duty Officer. You're dismissed, unless you want to confess."

Dario didn't come to attention. He turned and walked casually out of the office. He left the door open.

* * *

Dario called Lieutenant Fox at Whiting Field. "You in hot water again, D'Angelo?" Fox laughed. "You'd be a dream client in civilian life, if you had any money."

"Foxy, this isn't fun and games. I'm in big trouble, Foxy, and the funny thing is, this time I didn't do it. This time I'm really innocent!" He told Fox the whole story, then asked, "What's an Article Thirty-Two investigation?"

"It's the thirty-second article in the Uniform Code of Military Justice. It's like a grand jury. They have to convene a board to look at the evidence. If they think it's sufficient, that a felony's been committed, they'll recommend a court-martial. It's a very solemn business, Dario."

It was the first time Dario had ever heard Fox talk in a serious tone. It got to him. "I'm really scared, Foxy. I'm really scared this time. I need help. Can you get down here and defend me?"

"It's your word against the other pilot's, Dario. Too bad there weren't other witnesses, seems the only one at the scene of the crime got killed. You've got to get that marine to change his story, tell the truth. Otherwise, sounds like only a miracle can save you."

Dario was unaware that he was biting on a fingernail, and moving his head from side-to-side. He was still having trouble believing what was happening to him.

"That bastard won't tell the truth, Foxy. He knows he's going down, and he wants to take me with him."

There was a pause while only static came over the line. "When they charge you, I'll see if I can get temporary orders as your defense, but I can't promise anything. I would like to represent you, though. It should be an interesting case. But then, all your troubles are interesting."

"Come on, Foxy, you're supposed to be concerned about the truth, you're supposed to want to defend me because I'm innocent."

"Yes, there's that too." He laughed again and told Dario to keep him posted.

* * *

Renetti came to his BOQ room that evening, with a bottle of scotch. "Here, the condemned man can still have a drink. Booze will help ease the anxiety." He spoke with laughter in his voice. Dario didn't think it was very funny.

"I'm innocent until proved guilty, remember. That's every American's right—even Italian Americans."

"Calm down, kid. I believed your statement and I knew Donigan's first one was all bullshit. To think I couldn't tell the difference from a prop that hit concrete and one that hit sand! What a jerk. Thank God you didn't try to cover for him, you'd really be in deep-shit if you had."

"What do you think I'm in now, deep-clover? I'm grounded, I'm restricted to the base, I'm going to be court-martialed, lose my wings, my commission, my car, and my family will disown me. And that's just for starters. Then I'll spend twenty years in prison making license plates, and something tells me there aren't any Cuba Libras or pussy in Portsmouth. I call that damn deep-shit, Marco. Over my head deep-shit, and I *ain't* got a snorkel!" Dario sat down on the edge of the bunk. "I'm really scared." His voice was lower, sincere. "Smiling Jack is after my ass, and I don't know how to cover it. I want to fight back, but I don't know how."

Low and Slow

He drained his drink and Renetti poured another and laughed again. To Dario's ears, the laugh was just like Fox's over the phone.

"You're the second guy in two hours who's laughed at my little problem, Marco. What am I missing? Where's the humor? What's so damned funny?"

"You. I told you, I believe you and there are others who do, too. You've got more friends than you know you have, kid. Relax. The truth will win out."

"Oh, that's something to live by." There was mockery in his voice. "God, I wish I'd said that. 'The truth will win out.'"

Renetti stood up and said, "I've got to go. Want me to leave the bottle?"

"No, thanks anyway. My stomach's churning, but booze isn't helping." Dario looked up at Marco, right in his face. "Marco . . . there's something else."

Renetti sat down in the room's one chair again. "What is it?"

"Remember when I first met you, I told you my father died of lung cancer."

"Yeah. What about it?"

"Well, that wasn't quite the whole story. He did have lung cancer, and it would have killed him, but they found it because a jealous husband shot him in the chest. That's what really killed him, Marco. Bullets. Babbo was a woman chaser. He cheated on my mother all the time. When he got his own garage, he took care of several society ladies' sports cars, took them for two hour test drives in the afternoon. He was driving a new Jaguar back for a tune up when the husband stepped into the driveway and pumped two bullets in him, then shot himself in the head."

He wiped his brow with the back of his hand, then rubbed the back of his head. "My mother was devastated by the scandal, Marco. She's recently remarried and she's living a happy, normal life at last. If I go to prison, my whole family will be crushed, but my mother will take it the hardest. It will kill her. I just can't let that happen to her,

Marco. But what can I do? How can I get that bastard off my ass? Should I confess to something I didn't do, to get a lighter sentence?"

Marco stood up. "No! Don't you even think of it. I believe you, Dario. You keep the faith, kid, just keep the faith."

* * *

Three days after Dario was on temporary duty at Mainside, he got a call from Captain Popovich's yeoman, telling him to come to the captain's office the following morning at 0900. He had to take a bus to the gate, drive to Cabaniss and park outside the gate, and wait for the bus that took him to the Administration Building. He was very sad when he entered the base, realizing that he would never fly the Skyraider again—or anything else.

He hadn't eaten much, nor slept much, since the ordeal began, and he looked haggard and disheveled when he entered the CO's outer office. He knew it, but he really didn't care. He didn't even comb his hair, or wipe his shoes on the back of his pant legs.

Marco Renetti and Ken MacArthur were there, each carrying a briefcase. When they entered the inner office, the CO was sitting behind his desk, with Smiling Jack seated at his right.

"Take come chairs and sit down, gentlemen," the CO instructed. Renetti and MacArthur took two chairs and placed them in front of the desk. Dario took one and sat behind them.

"Thank you for seeing us, skipper," Renetti said. "Kenny and I think we can save everybody a lot of time and trouble by clearing up D'Angelo's problem. We asked you to have him here, also, so he can fill in any blanks we have."

"Jack's the one who's on top of this case," Popovich said. "Whatever you have, tell it to him."

Smiling Jack raised a hand and pointed a finger at Renetti. "Before you say anything, Marco, let me fill you in on the latest development." A self-satisfied smile spread across his face, exposing two-thirds of his teeth. "Seems we have a witness to the shoot-up of the abandoned car after all. The Border Patrol caught an illegal trying to get back *into* Mexico. He was almost in shock. When they questioned him, he told them he didn't mind being chased by dogs or men in jeeps, but when the government starts shooting at him with airplanes, he's staying in Mexico." Smiling Jack tapped a folder sitting on the corner of the CO's desk. "Here's a copy of the interrogation. In it, the Mexican tells how he was out of the car and behind a mesquite tree taking a dump. He saw the two airplanes zoom down and shoot at the car, where his companion was sleeping. He laid low until the airplanes left, then went to the car, saw what was left of his friend and started running back to the border. His statement's here, as well as its translation. He clearly says there were two airplanes shooting. His statement supports Donigan's, and contradicts D'Angelo's. Two to one. Proves he's a liar, wouldn't you say?" He looked directly at Dario as he spoke to Renetti.

"Can I look at the Mexican's statement, Jack?" Renetti asked.

"Of course, Marco. Help yourself."

He tossed the folder across the desk. Renetti picked it up and opened it, turning pages until he stopped at one and began reading. "While I read this, Ken, why don't you tell them what you found out."

"Sure. Well, skipper, I took an AD and flew down to Harlingen Air Force Base two days ago. I told them about the incident and asked them if I could talk to the tower operator who was on duty when it occurred. I wanted to know if he'd heard anything from Donigan's and D'Angelo's transmissions that day. The operator was very helpful. As usual, the air force got the jump on us with funding. They've got a recorder running whenever the tower's open. It's some new kind that records on a plastic tape. They made a transcript for me of all the transmissions received between the time Donigan and D'Angelo left my flight, and the time D'Angelo made his Mayday call. Parts of Donigan's, 'Let's go coyote hunting-any asshole can hit a flare-let's see how you are on real targets,' was caught on the tape, although it's badly garbled. But at exactly fifteen-forty eight, they caught a loud and clear, 'Chickenshit.' "

"What's that supposed to mean?" Smiling Jack asked.

"It means D'Angelo was telling the truth. He said Donigan called him a chickenshit because he emptied his guns. He wrote the time down, fifteen-forty seven. At that time, by my calculations, they were still at least ten minutes from the beach."

"What made you note the time, D'Angelo?" the CO asked him.

"I don't know, sir. It's just a habit. I always write times on my knee pad. Time I takeoff, time I land, time we arm our guns."

"That's no proof!" Smiling Jack said, loudly to MacArthur. "He could have written down that time later. His guns were empty, but not at fifteen-forty seven. They were empty when he ran out of cannon shells after shooting up the car and the sign! And just who-in-the-hell authorized your flight to Harlingen, MacArthur?"

"I did." It was Renetti who spoke. He looked directly at Smiling Jack, his finger at the middle of the page he was reading, to keep his place. "Ken flew a test hop for me in a plane that just came out of its scheduled maintenance check."

Smiling Jack stood up, shouting, "Goddamn it, I'm in charge of this investigation. You had no right to let him fly there. He had no authorization to land at an air force base and ask questions." He turned and faced Popovich. "What do you say about it, captain?"

Popovich had been leaning back in his chair. He leaned forward, put his elbows on his desk, turned his head and looked directly at Smiling Jack. "I say sit down and listen, Jack. We've all made unauthorized pasture stops. I want to hear what else these two have to say." He turned to MacArthur. "Did they get anything else on the recording?"

"No sir, just some more garbled, broken noise. Of course, after D'Angelo emptied his guns, they dropped down to a very low altitude. Much too low to be received at Harlingen."

"Yeah. Six inches below ground level in one case," Smiling Jack injected.

"Jack. Be quiet and listen, please," Popovich told him.

Dario was almost dumbfounded by what he was hearing. His head moved from officer to officer as each spoke. It was like watching a

Low and Slow

tennis doubles match. Through it all, however, he felt good about what he was hearing. And it seemed to him that Smiling Jack looked worried; like the marine corps had found out his father and mother were legally married

Renetti closed the Border Patrol file. "I speak and read Spanish pretty well, skipper. Took it in school. It was easy for me to pick up, from speaking Italian as a kid. This statement's translation is ambiguous. In English, the Mexican says he saw two airplanes 'firing,' but in Spanish, he says that there were two airplanes 'attacking' the car. D'Angelo admits he flew low over Donigan and watched him shoot up the sign and the car. And, the Mexican says he pushed his face into the sand every time he heard the guns shoot. It would be easy for him to be confused, to think that both aircraft were firing. This statement is worthless."

"That's for the Article Thirty-Two board to decide," Smiling Jack shouted.

"Goddamn it Jack," Popovich yelled, "stop being so damned negative. If D'Angelo's innocent, it's our duty—and it ought to be our pleasure—to clear him."

Smiling Jack jumped up again. "But I'm in charge of this investigation. You put me in charge, skipper. How can you condone these guys going behind my back?" He pointed at Renetti again, who wore a smug grin on his face. "You're way out of line, Renetti. I'm going to have your ass for letting MacArthur fly to Harlingen."

"Give a shit, Jack. But, wait 'till you hear what's coming next. I'm going to ruin your whole day, Jack." Renetti picked up his briefcase and opened it. He took out a folder and laid it on the desk, next to the Border Patrol file. He tapped it with a knuckle as he spoke. "Here's a report from the armorer. I sent him down with my crew when they recovered Donigan's airplane. He inspected the shot up road sign and the car. All the twenty-millimeter ammo in the training command is painted with color codes, for the fighter jocks at Beeville and Kingsville. It's how they know which student pilot is hitting the towed banner in air-to-air gunnery. We don't do air-to-air, so our students' shells are a random mix. The armorer checked the barrels of the wreck, and the barrels of D'Angelo's AD. There's always a little paint residue in the barrels after firing. Donigan had brown and red. D'Angelo had green and yellow. The armorer found lots of brown and red paint on the road up to the sign, on the sign, and on the car. There were no green or yellow hits—anywhere."

"And I'm prepared to testify that D'Angelo's one of the best shooters I've ever trained," MacArthur added. "And Lieutenant Snider, who flew a check hop with my flight two days before the incident, is ready to back me up. We'll both testify that if D'Angelo had fired on the car, it would be *full* of yellow and green holes."

Dario wanted to stand up and shout! This was the miracle Foxy told him he needed. He felt good, he was going to beat the rap again! He looked at Smiling Jack. His face was white. He started to speak, but nothing came out of his mouth. He just sat still in his chair, and kept quiet.

It was Popovich who broke the hush that lingered for a full minute after MacArthur's statement. He spoke softly. "I'm taking over this investigation as of now. Marco, Ken, you've done a fine job. I'll get your information over to the admiral immediately." He then turned his head and spoke to Smiling Jack. "It's our job to send the fleet the best nugget attack pilots in the world, Jack, and we do. But we don't send them robots, automatons. We send them men who are independent, reasoning individuals who will obey orders and bore into a target, no matter what's thrown at them, and destroy it. They obey the orders because they have faith in the leaders who gave them the orders, Jack. It seems to me that you've brought a personal predisposition into this matter. That's something a leader must never, never do. I've lost faith in you." Popovich then turned his head and spoke to Dario. "D'Angelo."

Dario stood up and stood at attention. "Yes, sir."

"You go back to your assignment at Mainside. I can't speak for the admiral, but I have a pretty good feeling the charges will be dropped.

You should be back in a cockpit in no time at all. Thank you for your cooperation. You're excused."

"Thank you, sir." He did his turn and marched from the room correctly, but without his feet even touching the floor.

* * *

Word came after lunch that he was relived as Special Services Camping Equipment Issuing Officer, and was to return to Cabaniss and meet with his instructor. He checked out of the Mainside BOQ, took the bus to the gate again, and walked to his MG. He drove to Cabaniss and pulled into the small parking lot next to the gate, only to be hailed by the guard on duty. "Ensign D'Angelo?"

"Yes, I'm Ensign D'Angelo."

"CO's orders, sir. I'm to put a base sticker on your car."

Astounded, as he had been since leaving Popovich's office that morning, he asked, "What's the date today, sentry?"

"Why, it's December the third, sir."

"You sure? You sure it's not Christmas?"

The sentry just shook his head, "No sir. I'm sure it's the third. I get Christmas off this year."

After his sticker was in place, he drove to the hangar. He greeted MacArthur when he entered the ready room with, "Merry Christmas, sir."

"What're you talking about?"

"Just kidding. It just seems like Christmas because I've gotten the best present I'll ever get in my life. My freedom."

"Well, you deserve it. You got snake bit, through no fault of your own. And you'll love this. Scuttlebutt has it that right after our meeting, the CO fired Colonel Collins, doesn't want him on his base anymore. He's packing up now. The admiral made him the Community Relations Officer over at Kingsville."

"Yahoo," Dario yelled. "There must be a God!"

"Yeah, and for you his name's Renetti. He's bent over backwards for you, Dario. I hope you appreciate it."

"I . . . I do, sir. But what can I do to show him how much I appreciate it, other than thanking him?"

"You've got a lot of flying to make up to finish by the fourteenth, when we shut down for Christmas. Your next three hops are rocket firing. Put them right on the target. That'll give Marco more pleasure than all the thanks and handshakes you could manage."

* * *

There was an impromptu party at the officers' club that evening. Lieutenant Commanders Renetti and MacArthur, Lieutenants Miller, Snider and Potts, and Ensigns D'Angelo, Burner and the others from his flight were present. After many drinks had been drunk, Dario caught Renetti alone, as he was returning from the head.

"*Mille grazie, Comandante Paisano.*" It was very difficult for him to speak with the lump he had in his throat. "I could get down on my knees and kiss your feet, Marco, but I know you wouldn't like it. I just want you to know, you've shown me there *is* a code of silence amongst naval officers. It's a silence of trust, of belief."

"Knock off the maudlin shit. Have you called your mother with the good news?"

"No. She doesn't know anything about what happened and long distance phone calls scare her. They're usually bad news, and they cost a lot of money."

"Call her anyway, just to say hello. It'll make *you* feel better. And Dario, speaking of your mother. Don't you ever worry about how she'd feel if you get caught in bed with that married woman you're screwing? After what you told me about your father, seems like you're following in his footsteps. Maybe he taught you too well."

Low and Slow

Just before midnight, a very drunk Ensign D'Angelo got a very sleepy Lieutenant (junior grade) Fox out of his bed in Pensacola, which was in the Central Time Zone, the same as Corpus. "Foxy, guess what? I beat the rap, Foxy. I'm just like Big Al in the movie, Foxy, 'Thirty arrests, no convictions,' Foxy. I'm back on flight status, I'm going to catch up with my flight, and I've even got a base sticker, Foxy. And the best part, the best part is, Lieutenant Colonel Smiling Jack Jerkoff will be shining his big white teeth before the Ladies' Bible Club of Bumfuck, Texas this Sunday, while I'm shooting off rockets."

"What are you talking about, Dario?"

"Just like you said, Foxy. I needed a miracle. Well, I got one. I got an Italian miracle. They're the best kind, Foxy."

Next, he called his mother. "Hello, Mama. I just called to tell you hello, Mama. Everything's fine, Mama."

"Dario. Why are you calling? Something must be wrong. You sound just like your father, when he was in the grappa. And this call is costing you a lot of money."

"It doesn't matter, Mama. I can afford it Mama. I get flight pay. I'm going to keep getting flight pay! Everything's wonderful, Mama. And, Mama. I don't drink grappa. I drink rum!"

"Go to bed, Dario. It's ten o'clock."

"Yes, Mama," he said obediently, looking at both hands of the clock on the wall touch the 12.

CHAPTER FORTY-ONE

GRADUATING STUDENTS ahead of The Road Runner Flight had been getting orders to Fleet Air Support Squadrons in either Jacksonville or Norfolk, where the assignees would linger, flying various airplanes towing targets, delivering mail to carriers and flying test hops until an East Coast attack squadron needed a replacement or a new Forrestal-class carrier came on line needing a new air group. Dario felt his chances of living the good, wild life in Coronado seemed very remote.

He mentioned his concern about orders to Cora Lou, a local girl he dated now and then. With the casualness of one who's been asked the time of day, she told him, "Oh, that's easy. My hairdresser's husband is the yeoman at Mainside who passes out the orders. She tells me about it all the time. I had a boyfriend last year, a NAVCAD, who wanted to know where he was going. I got Laura to find out from her husband, and told him. Since it was Quonset Point in Rhode Island, he bought a sedan instead of a convertible when he graduated."

"Do you think he can get me what I want?"

"I don't know, but Laura told me he'll do anything for Wild Turkey bourbon."

Armed with two bottles of the expensive whiskey, Cora Lou had her hair done the next day. When the other students in Road Runner

Low and Slow

Flight received orders to a FASRON in Key West the following week, there were no orders for Dario. The Cabaniss yeoman told them he would get on the phone to Mainside and try to find out what was wrong, but Dario told him he was in no hurry. The yeoman looked at him askance, being used to ensigns screaming for their orders.

They finally arrived during the last week of his training. He was assigned to an AD carrier squadron, shore based at NAS North Island, Coronado, California. Just what he wanted. He rushed to the officers' club where he found Renetti sitting at the bar. He told him about his good fortune and how he had assisted it, and drank to Cora Lou, Laura, Laura's husband, Wild Turkey whiskey, and the navy's way of getting things done. "Up your ass Sergeant Pflueger, wherever you are," he said, holding his Cuba Libra toward the sky. "You're not the only one who can massage the system."

* * *

The next afternoon, while nursing a hangover, Dario flew his last training flight. It was scheduled to be a 3.5 hour radar avoidance flight at 500 feet, up and around San Antonio, then south, down the center of Texas to make a mock low-level attack on a bridge over the Rio Grande River. He flew with a make-up group, a new instructor and three students he'd never flown with before. When he saw the bridge, after almost 3 hours of flying, he was tired, he had a headache and his mouth was dry; he'd finished off his canteen of water an hour before. He hadn't eaten any breakfast or lunch, and his empty stomach was burning with acid.

Each student made an independent attack on the bridge. When Dario's turn came, he went to full power and made his run-in very low and did a mock over-the-shoulder bombing maneuver by pulling his AD up into a loop with a force that tripled the weight of his body. If he had a bomb, it would be released in the early stage of the loop, soar up high and lob over and down to the target, giving him time to complete the loop and roll out near the ground to, hopefully, escape the bomb's atomic blast. He felt dizzy at the top of the loop. The G forces and his hangover did not mix well.

After each individual run, the student joined up on the orbiting instructor. When all four were in formation on him, they headed home to Cabaniss, one hundred and twenty miles to the north. Dario looked to his left and saw the sun, a dull orange glowing ball, low in the west. It would be almost dark when they got back to their base. They flew up South Padre Island, along the familiar coast and over the spot where Donigan had crashed landed his AD. Dario was glad to fly past it and know he was finished with the area and its bad memories.

They were about forty miles south of Cabaniss when the instructor radioed the flight. "I've just called the tower. A front moved through and dropped the dew point temperature so they've got a layer of fog. Cabaniss is below minimums so we're going to Mainside where they've got a ground controlled approach. You've all made practice GCAs, now you're going to make a real one. We'll only have about thirty minutes of fuel remaining, so make your approach a good one."

The flight orbited a radio beacon five miles south of Mainside, still flying formation on the instructor. Three aircraft were ahead of Dario and the instructor would make his approach after him. After ten minutes of orbiting while aircraft who had arrived ahead of them made approaches, the last plane in the formation broke-off, was picked up by radar and began his descent to the glide slope. Dario and the others continued circling, waiting their turn. Dario felt as if they were taking forever, but he knew the procedure was a slow, and precise one. As he flew his position next to the instructor, he glanced at his fuel gauge and saw it was below a quarter-of-a-tank. It was eery; he'd never seen the needle that low. When the student before him finally broke-off, Dario became very tense. He was next, and the prospect of flying through the cloud layer suddenly frightened him.

When his turn finally came, Dario followed the approach controller's instructions, flew his AD to a 90-degree angle from his final approach heading, and dropped his gear. There was still some light, although the sun had dropped below the horizon. He was turned to the final heading and switched his radio frequency. He heard the final GCA controller's voice, speaking in a low monotone which didn't sound completely human.

"Navy 5-7, this is your final controller. Make no further acknowledgments of my transmissions. You are one mile from glide slope, four miles from touch-down. Continue on your present heading and altitude. You will intercept the glide slope from below. Present weather is above minimums, ceiling three hundred feet, visibility three-quarters-mile. Pilots report top of overcast is 900 feet."

Dario tensed up even more. The weather was only a little above minimum visibility. His adrenaline pump went to maximum. He was glad he didn't have to talk, because his tongue was stuck to the roof of his mouth. His hands were wet with sweat inside his leather flying gloves and his right leg was shaking slightly as it pushed the rudder pedal to keep the airplane on its heading. His stomach felt like it had a small fire in it.

"5-7, you are approaching glide slope."

Dario dropped his flaps, slowing his AD to 90 knots airspeed.

"Begin your rate-of-descent," the controller continued. "In the event of communication failure or missed approach, climb straight ahead to two thousand feet and contact Corpus Approach Control."

Dario reduced power, held his speed at 90 knots, and let the airplane begin to descend. His eyes constantly scanned the flight instruments. He needed them to keep from getting too slow and stalling, and to keep on heading and on the correct rate-of-descent to the end of the runway. He looked out over the cowl and tried to see the runway ahead. He saw only a slight horizon, the contrast between the twilight of the sky and the darkness of the top of the foggy cloud cover.

"5-7, you are slightly left of course, make a slight correction to the right. You are dropping below glide slope. Decrease your rate of descent."

This surprised him. Just looking out had made him wander.

He added a little power and made a slight right turn. Then he entered the fog. He looked at a wing and saw a halo from the wingtip light reflecting on the moisture. He looked over the cowl again, hoping he would see runway lights. He saw only black. Suddenly, he felt as if he were making a hard turn to the left and was in a spinning dive. He was dizzy and his head began throbbing with an ache just above his forehead. He actually shook it, trying to make it feel right. He turned the aircraft right, pulled up the nose slightly and added a little power.

"5-7. You are drifting off course to the right. You are going above glide slope. Make the necessary corrections."

Dario began to panic. He was disoriented, and he couldn't peek under a fabric hood to make it right this time.

"5-7. You are off course, you are above glide slope." The monotone showed just a hint of alarm. "5-7, wave off. Wave off. Execute missed approach. Contact approach control."

When he looked back at his instruments, the compass was swinging through twenty-degrees off the correct heading and his altitude was much too high. And, his airplane was slow—near a stall. He jammed in power, raised his gear and flaps, and swung back on course. In a few seconds he was above the fog again, and he looked up and saw bright stars above him. He looked below and it was all black. There wasn't even a twilight horizon, now.

He switched his radio frequency and called Corpus Approach Control. The controller answered immediately, then asked, "Navy 5-7, what is your fuel state?"

"Fifteen minutes," Dario answered, but he knew he was being optimistic. He did not look at his fuel gauge.

When he transmitted, he thought his own voice in his headset, built into the crash helmet, sounded strange. He couldn't believe the situation he was in. It was almost like a dream—a bad dream. He was above an overcast without enough fuel to fly inland to a clear field. He knew he had only two options: He could fly out over the Gulf and bail out. If successful, he would spend a cold, wet night, floating around in his rubber dinghy. They wouldn't find him until daylight. Then there'd be an accident report, and the humiliation of being washed out on his last training flight. The other option was to make another GCA approach. But if he failed again, he knew he wouldn't have enough fuel to climb to bail out altitude. He would crash in the fog, in the dark, and die. He really had no decision to make. Option one was out. He'd rather die than look bad.

Corpus Approach Control gave him radar vectors and once again brought him back to the final GCA controller. He went through his check list, made certain that his gear, flaps and power were correct, and started down the glide slope. The wing lights glowed when he got into the fog, and again, he felt as if he were diving and in a turn, but this time he did not look out of his cockpit. This time he fought off the turning, diving sensation, and concentrated on his instruments. His sweaty hands and feet were shaking, but he held his throbbing head still and kept up the scan of his instruments with his eyes: Attitude, altitude, heading, airspeed. He sweat, he shook, and he ached, but he rejected the false signals his inner ear was sending his reflexes. He kept the needles where they were supposed to be. The monotonous drone of the final controller was his only comfort. "You are on course. You are on glide slope. Continue your present rate of descent. You are one mile from touch down. Check gear down and locked."

He did. They were.

The ground was less than 500 feet below him, under the fog. It was coming up fast and he almost panicked again and pushed the throttle to full power to get away from it. But he kept his head in the cockpit and held what he had, although it took every bit of concentration and will power he could muster. He watched the altimeter creeping down to 200 feet, the minimum altitude to which he could descend in the fog. His right hand on the control stick and his left on the throttle were squeezing them so hard, the picture of Brandon, frozen at his controls flashed through his mind. Dario didn't know what he would do next as he saw the altimeter needle on the 200 mark.

Then the zombie voice said, "You are at minimums. You should have the runway lights in sight. Take over visually and land your aircraft."

Dario looked up over the cowl and saw rows of high intensity lights leading to the runway threshold lights. They looked like his mother's arms, outstretched. He flew over them, cut power, and landed. The adrenaline began to filter from his bloodstream. He began to relax. He had made it. He was on the ground.

He had avoided looking at his fuel gauge on the approach, but he looked at it when he taxied off the runway. The needle was on empty.

They don't give an accurate reading on the ground with the tail low, he remembered.

The ground controller radioed taxi instructions to the transient tie-down area. A crewman was waiting there with glowing light wands to guide him to his parking spot next to the other four ADs from his flight. Dario folded the wings before taxiing close to his instructor's parked aircraft. He turned off the radios and put his hand on the fuel mixture handle to pull it to cut off, but before he did, the engine quit firing. It made a few noisy, dying revolutions, and stopped. His hand shook, and the acid in his stomach felt like it was burning through the lining. He pulled the handle back. A glance at the clock in the instrument panel told him he'd been airborne for 4.5 hours. He wrote the time on his knee pad. He switched off lights, battery, and the magnetos and sat still as a crewman climbed up on the wing stub and unfastened his seat belt, shoulder harness and parachute. The crewman had to help him climb out of the cockpit and down the steps in the wing flap.

* * *

The instructor debriefed the flight on the bus ride back to Cabaniss He only talked about the radar avoidance and bombing runs, critiqu ing each student's performance. All were satisfactory. All had flowr their last training flight. Nothing was said about Dario's missed approach.

I made it again! I'm a lucky son-of-a bitch, he complimented himself.

He slid down in the bench seat, rested his aching head against the bus window, and slept for the remainder of the ride. When he awoke, his head was throbbing so hard he thought it was going to explode until he realized that someone was pounding on the outside of the window it was leaning against. He sat up and looked out into the darkness. He could barely make out a face. It was Marco Renetti, gesturing for him to come out.

"I want to talk to you, hotshot," Renetti told him as he stepped off the bus. "Let's go to my office."

Dario followed him to the maintenance hangar. He knew he was going to get a balling out, but he didn't care. He'd made it, he didn't get a down, he was through with training.

Renetti's office was dark, but he switched on all the lights as soon as he entered. The small office was cluttered with dozens of thick manuals and small aircraft parts in open boxes on tables along the walls. Large plexiglass sheets hung above them with aircraft numbers and their status written in various colors of grease pencils.

Renetti walked behind his desk and pointed to a chair in front of t. "Sit down," he ordered. Dario sat. Renetti remained standing behind his desk. He was steaming. His face was red and Dario thought he hair sticking out of his ears seemed longer than usual. He pointed a finger at Dario and yelled, "How much fuel does an AD's tank hold?"

"Three hundred and sixty gallons," Dario answered, immediately.

"Very good, very good." Renetti spoke in a condescending tone. And how much fuel did Mainside just put in your AD's tank?"

"I don't know? I guess I was a little low."

"A little low! It took three hundred and seventy gallons because hose self-sealing tanks stretch with age. You were absolutely empty! 'ou're lucky you made it to the tie-down area."

"Yeah. I know it was empty, ran out in my spot. I, I guess I was a little .ucky."

Renetti looked up at the ceiling and held up the palms of his hands in supplication. " 'A little lucky,' he says. A little lucky." He looked down and stared at Dario, looking him right in his eyes. "It was dumb luck! You count on luck in this business, my fine Italian friend, and your family will soon be listening to a bugle and twenty-one rifle shots. And your mama will get a nice, new folded flag to remember you by."

And she'll be arguing that it wasn't my fault after she reads my emergency sheet, Dario laughed to himself.

"What in the fuck happened to you up there? Why'd you blow your first approach?" Renetti eased himself into his swivel chair and leaned back in it.

"I got vertigo. I didn't realize it, but when I was in the soup, it felt like I was diving and I panicked . . . wanted to climb, get away from the ground. I was scared, scared shitless, Marco. When I got back on top, I realized I'd had vertigo. I got it again on my second approach, but I fought it, believed my instruments. I made a good approach and got the airplane back in one piece—and me too. The instructor didn't say a word about it in his debrief."

"Hell no! He wants to forget it too, because he fucked up. He's new, but he should have checked the weather earlier. There was a student recall two hours before he finally got the word. You students should have been on the deck long before the fog came in."

"Nobody's perfect," Dario laughed. He could be magnanimous. He was still feeling euphoric about cheating death.

That really angered Renetti. He stood up again and yelled. "You cocky little shit! It's been easy for you, hasn't it? You fly, shoot and bomb better than most Dilberts as long as you're flying by your twenty fifteen eyeballs. But when it comes to flying on the gauges, you're just a punk amateur. You know why you got vertigo?"

"Sure. I was tired. It was a long hop."

"Bullshit! You were hung-over! I know you stayed at the club long after I left last night. Listen, Dario. There are a lot of old sayings in

his man's navy, and one of them is, 'You can't hoot with the owls and
fly with the eagles.' "

"OK, Marco, OK. I fucked up. But believe me, I was scared up
here, scared in an airplane for the first time in my life. It wasn't the
fear of dying. I was more afraid of looking stupid. I'll admit I didn't
take instruments seriously because it was boring. I realize now that it's
like practicing scales and arpeggios on the piano. Boring, but important. When I get to my squadron, I'm going to fly on the dials all the
time—and I'm not going to peek under the hood."

"You'd better, if you want to stay alive. Coronado gets pea soup that
makes this shit look like a light mist."

Dario laughed again, hoping Renetti was through with the lecture. "You've made your point, Marco, and I appreciate your concern.
Since I got in the navy I've constantly been chewed out in senior
officers' offices. This is the first time it's been for my own good."

Renetti walked around to the side of his desk and sat on its corner, close to Dario. He lowered his voice and spoke in his normal
manner. "Yeah. And I know it's none of my business, but maybe you
should take a long look at your lifestyle. Sometimes you get vertigo on
the ground, kid."

Dario hadn't been looking at Renetti. He was staring at the front
of his desk. He wanted to change the subject, so he said, "Marco, how
come you don't have a name plaque with a mountain in it?"

Marco stood up. "Who needs that 'I was there' bullshit?" He walked
to the door and put his hand up to the light switch. "Come on, get out
of that stinky flight suit and I'll take you to the club for just one night
cap."

"I'm through flying for a month. I'm checking out tomorrow."

"Two, then."

"Make it three. I'm really hurting, Marco."

CHAPTER
FORTY-TWO

AFTER CHECKING out of Cabaniss the following day, he returned to the Laraga and began packing. He would spend the Christmas season with his family in San Francisco—and hopefully, a few days with Michelle if Donald had been transferred to Travis. He didn't have to report to North Island until mid-January. It was dark by the time he put his few belonging in his MG's trunk, behind the seats and on the passenger's seat. It would take him three long days to drive to the coast. He was anxious to get going, to leave Texas and flight training behind him, forever.

He had the MG's hood up and was checking the oil, straining to see the mark on the dipstick in the beam of his flashlight, when two large hands wrapped around his neck from behind. He tried to yell out, "Herbie" but a sound never passed his choked wind pipe. Instinctively, he started his own hands toward those of his attacker's, but his hand-to-hand training eclipsed his instincts. He raised his right foot and brought his heel down hard, scraping it along the shin of his opponent and smashing it into his ankle. He heard, "Ow," and the hands came off his throat. He spun around, crouching, with his hands forward, fingers held tightly together and supported by his thumb. In the darkness, he couldn't identify the face of his attacker. But he knew it wasn't Herbie. The man was at least six feet tall.

Low and Slow

Dario shot his hand for the other man's throat. It was easily knocked aside by a hand that had also been trained. Then, a fist slammed into the right side of Dario's lower jaw. He fell back and his flailing arm dislodged the rod that held up the MG's hood. It fell on him. On his back, spread across the MG's fender and engine with the hood over his face, his attacker punched him in the stomach twice. Then again. Then again. Dario slumped to the ground, scraped his face on the underside of the hood, and vomited.

His attacker pulled up his hair, forcing his head back. The man bent over and spoke directly into his face, and Dario heard a heavy southern accent. He recognized the voice.

"I'm not going to kill you this time, you little dago bastard, but if you mess with my wife again, I surely will. I tried to get you court-martialed, but your chickenshit navy won't even answer my letter. I was told I was wasting my time writing it, that you navy fly-boys always cover each others' asses. So I decided to take matters in my own hands. Michelle is my wife now, and you better keep away from her. You hear!"

Dario puked again, although little came up.

"You stay away from her, wop boy, if you know what's good for you."

Shit, what corny lines. He must watch only low budget movies, Dario thought, as he listened to footsteps fading away. He heard a car start and drive off; then he passed out.

Burner found him an hour later, lying in his vomit. He carried him into the house, put him on his bed and washed him off. He shook Dario slightly until he awoke.

"You want me to take you to sick bay, Dario?"

"No, no," he mumbled. "I'm OK, just got the shit beat out of me, that's all. I don't want any record of it. Too embarrassing."

"Who did it? Some marine? Smiling Jack?"

Dario tried a slight laugh, but it hurt so much he cut it short. "No, the marine corps is innocent, this time. My ex-wife's husband, an air force weeny. I . . . I've been with her. He found out."

"Dario, you crazy, horny little bastard! You really fit the old saying,

'God gave naval aviators big dicks and big brains, but not enough blood to work them both at the same time.' "

"Yeah. I've been fitting a lot of old sayings lately."

Burner chuckled. "Now you've got the corps *and* the air force pissed off at you. All you've got left to go to war with is the army!"

"How about the coast guard?" Dario couldn't help laughing as he spoke, although it hurt.

"Naw, they don't count. They're only a military service in wartime," Burner countered.

CHAPTER FORTY-THREE

THE ASPIRINS Dario kept popping in his mouth as he drove only took the sharp edge off the numbing the pain in his rib cage and the cut inside his mouth where Donald's fist had landed. There was a slight mist when he left at first light the following morning. He drove all day, not even stopping for lunch. He made it to El Paso about midnight, and got a room in a cheap, roadside motel. He let the soothing hot water from the shower run over his body until it began to run cold. His bruises were already turning from purple to mustard brown.

The next morning the weather was crystal clear and the cobalt blue sky was a vivid contrast to the golden sand of the New Mexico desert. But it was cold; very, very cold. Dario was surprised. He thought all deserts were hot. He wore his leather flight jacket, his silk scarf and his flying gloves, but he was still freezing in the open car. In desperation, he stopped and put his flight suit on over his pants and shirt and wore his flight helmet and goggles. This gave his head, which was in the airstream, some protection from the icy air.

Several hours later, as he was cruising along the highway at 60 mph in the bright afternoon sunshine, he began to smell wood smoke. He paid no attention to it at first but as it became more pronounced, he began to wonder why there was wood smoke in the desert. He couldn't see any fires. There was no forest.

D.E. " Butch" Bucciarelli

He came up behind a slow moving truck, slowed to 30 and saw smoke come up between his legs. He looked down and saw flames around his feet. He pulled onto the shoulder of the road, pulled on the emergency brake and jumped out of the car. The flames were now burning fiercely, the floor mat was on fire. He pulled it out and threw it away from the car. The plywood floor board was also burning around a hole in its center, about six inches in diameter. He grabbed a handful of sand and threw it on the flames then he opened his trunk and took his survival knife from his Mae West and used it to cut out the smoldering wood around the hole. When it stopped smoking, he got down and peered under the car. The cause of the fire was easy to identify. The exhaust pipe from the engine had broken just before the muffler, which then hung down slightly and deflected the hot exhaust gas up against the floorboard. Normally, Dario would have heard the roar of the escaping exhaust but because he was wearing his helmet, which had ear pads to keep out noise so radio transmissions could be heard, he'd heard nothing.

He went to the burning floor mat and stomped out the flames. The excitement had exhausted him and made his body hurt again, so he sat on a rock and rested. As he sat there in the bright sunlight and chilled air of the high New Mexico desert, he rested his elbows on his knees, put his head in his hands, and reflected. *What am I doing here? I'm freezing. My body aches. My jaw hurts, and my mouth feels like I ate a martini glass. Three days ago I had the world by the short hairs and now I'm sitting on a rock in a desert, feeling sorry for myself. I almost busted my ass in fog. I got beaten up by a jealous husband. My car almost caught on fire. Maybe Marco was right about the ground vertigo?*

After a few more minutes of reflection, he said the words aloud: "Babbo. You're why I don't have a windshield. You're why I ache. Maybe you did teach me too well?"

He drove slowly to the next town to have his pipe welded, enjoying the warmth from the noxious exhaust fumes coming through the ole in the floorboard. A car came up behind his slow-moving MG and honked. Dario adjusted his mirror and looked in it.

"I'd better start paying more attention to my six o'clock position! he told himself.

* * *

We're having ravioli with Gorganzola sauce tonight," his mother announced after she'd hugged and kissed him in welcome. "And Dario. A letter came for you yesterday. It's not from the navy, it's from the air force."

She took if from the top of the refrigerator and handed it to him. He recognized Michelle's handwriting on the envelope. He'd given her his mother's address. The postmark was Travis Air Force Base. He said nothing to his mother, although he knew she was so curious she'd read the postmark.

He waited until he was alone in his room to open it. "Darling Dario, I'm settled at Travis and Donald is off to Japan until Christmas Eve. I have a room for us at the Mark Hopkins. I'll be there on the twentieth, registered under *our* name. I'll leave a note for you. I'm so excited. I can't wait to see you and *your* San Francisco, and meet your mother. All my love," she'd signed it with just her initial.

* * *

"I'm Ensign D'Angelo. Has my wife checked in yet?"

The reception clerk at the Mark Hopkins looked in a register, and then turned and took a small envelope from a cubbyhole. He handed it to Dario, saying, "Mrs. D'Angelo checked in an hour ago, sir. She left this for you."

Dario opened it. "It's noon. I'm in room 1507. Hurry!" There was her usual "M."

* * *

He stood before the door and stared at the polished brass numbers. He imagined he could smell her gardenia fragrance. Every fiber in his body told him to knock on the door, take her in his arms when it opened and spend the next two days making love to her. He loved her, he would always love her. She was a very special part of his life at a very special time of his life. He almost raised his fist to knock, hesitated, then he turned and walked slowly to the elevator as if in a trance, barely overcoming the vertigo of passion by reading his instruments of reason. He pushed the elevator's down button and saw the inverted triangle light up.

The slight change of the G force in the descending elevator caused his stomach to send a hunger signal to his brain. He remembered the two-day old ravioli in his mother's new refrigerator and his mouth watered.

Babbo refused to eat them as leftovers, he recalled, *said they got soggy. He was wrong, I think they're better. The pasta's absorbed the sauce.*

THE END

In the sequel, *FLIGHT SONG*, the second book of the D'Angelo trilogy, Dario discovers new challenges on the West Coast, on an aircraft carrier, and in the Far East. He also confronts some of the old ones.

Made in the USA
Lexington, KY
15 November 2011